IF I SHOULD DIE

The Fellowship Dystopia, Book Two

LYNETTE M. BURROWS

ROCKET DOG
PUBLISHING

Published by: Rocket Dog Publishing, Mission, KS 66202 U.S.A.

https://lynettemburrows.com

Cover by MiblArt.com

Library of Congress Control Number: 2022908382

ISBN: 978-1-7325822-8-6 (ebk)

ISBN: 978-1-7325822-9-3 (pbk)

ISBN: 978-1-7325822-7-9 (hbk)

Chapter One
____

Miranda Clarke guided her yacht, *Lady Angelfish*, alias *Serenity*, down the Illinois River, desperate to deliver the package on time. A snafu at the locks outside of Chicago had cost them hours. Though she itched to open the throttle, she steered the yacht toward the Mississippi River as slowly as a late fall vacationer. Unlike a vacationer, she piloted the *Lady* through the predawn hours. The calm Illinois River made their travel less dangerous, but boating in the dark made her and everyone on board a target.

Frogs croaked from the shore. Owls hooted from bare tree branches. Wispy patches of fog blanketed the river and shoreline, and stars filled the heavens above. Nights on the river were her favorite. It was so peaceful she could almost let herself believe that the fighting was over, the rebels had won, democracy ruled again, and there was a lasting peace.

The fog grew denser and rose from the river—a column reaching to the sky? *Smoke.* Her throat tightened. She grabbed the mike. "Beryl, wake up."

"I see it. Wanda's securing the package. I'm coming on deck." A moment later the forward hatch opened and her aunt, Beryl Mitchell, climbed up onto the deck. She closed the hatch and came to the upper cockpit, drew both her pistols, and watched the eastern shore.

Miranda said nothing. She didn't have to. Beryl had been her savior, her mentor, her training sergeant, and for the past three years, her first mate. They could finish one another's sentences.

"Kill the lights," Beryl said.

Miranda hesitated. It was against safety regulations, but if the smoke was what she feared… She tightened her grip on the wheel and killed the lights. Stole glances at the shoreline and kept *Lady* in the river's channel.

The frogs stopped croaking. The owls stopped hooting. Between tree trunks, light flickered.

The light grew brighter, and over the *Lady's* purring motors, the snap and crackle of fire filled the air.

The trees thinned, and a clearing came into view. In the middle, flames licked the walls of a wooden structure, danced along its roof. Gray smoke rose above the building, caught the breeze, and drifted downriver.

Crack! What remained of the roof fell, and the walls collapsed.

The collapse revealed a ten-foot burning cross.

Behind the cross stood another smoldering structure—a barn, probably.

"Do you think anyone survived?" Miranda wanted to believe everyone had escaped.

"You know that's not the Klan's way," Beryl said. "If someone tried to escape, one of the Klansmen shot them—or worse."

Miranda released a shaky sigh. Guided the *Lady* past the scene, and a scent similar to a smoky campfire sharp with the acrid smell of smoldering plastic and rubber stung her nose.

"How many times do you have to see this?" Beryl's tone was harsh, but she didn't stop scanning the shore.

Miranda didn't answer. They had seen it more times than she wished. She loathed the Fellowship almost as much as Beryl did. *But I can't believe all Fellowship members know their tithes fund the Ku Klux Klan. That the Klan and Fellowship plan to kill all non-white, non-Fellowship people.*

She didn't try convincing Beryl that the Fellowship had good people and bad, that peace was possible anymore. If she had been imprisoned and tortured in Redemption for ten years, like Beryl had, she might believe nothing and no one in the Fellowship was good either.

But people needed them, were counting on them. So they lived a lie and flew the Fellowship flag that flapped on her beautiful yacht's staff pole. *The lie we live probably wears on Beryl too. Keeps the memories, the pain, too fresh.*

Beryl silently kept watch for another couple of miles downriver, then holstered her pistols and went below.

Miranda's chief engineer and cook, Wanda Terry, relieved her for breakfast and a nap. They didn't discuss the Klan. Wanda had seen far too much of them in her life.

Six hours later, Miranda relieved Beryl and took the pilot's seat again. As the *Lady's* captain and most experienced pilot, it was her responsibility to navigate through the confluence to the Mississippi River.

Almost as devoid of barge traffic as the Illinois River, the wide Mississippi flowed much faster. Nearly leafless trees lined its shores, sometimes in thick groves, other times only rarely.

The navigation system beeped. Miranda cupped her hand over the bill of her cap and scanned the eastern shore for Smitty's flags. They should have been easily seen. But no flags peeked through the bare branches. Her heart lurched, and she gripped the throttle with a sweaty hand. Double-checked the navigation charts and her instruments. Hoped the river's shimmering reflections of the unseasonably warm October sun had fooled her. She couldn't bear finding one more place burned to the ground.

The marina's floating dock and gas station came into view. High above Smitty's dock, the Fellowship flag, a white cross embedded on a red winged-shield, flew above the stars and stripes. Below those two flew a yellow Illinois state pennant. Signaled the all clear. Relief weakened Miranda's grip on the wheel.

She bowed her head briefly, then keyed her radio mike. "We are approaching Smitty's. ETA, two minutes."

"Aye, Captain," Beryl said. "I'll stow the package."

"On deck." Two levels below, Wanda crossed the main deck. She wore a Fellowship-approved gray servant's dress and a matching kerchief over her gloriously thick, kinky hair. Ebony skin radiant in the sun, she stood ready at the starboard gunwale.

In public, they all had to pretend to be someone else. Beryl played the Fellowship member and rich, widowed owner of the boat. The dreadful Fellowship-designated role of the servant fell to Wanda, a role no one ever questioned because of her race.

Playing the part of a hired boat captain, Miranda eased the vessel along the dock parallel to the shore and shut down the engine.

Wanda leaped down onto the dock and secured the boat.

Opening the helm's hidden compartment, Miranda couldn't—wouldn't touch the pistol inside. She would fire the gun to protect the others, but she would never again shoot another person, not even one of the Fellowship's cruel Second Sphere agents.

Between them and shore, tarp-covered, winter-ready pleasure boats filled the slips of the fishbone-like piers. Three connected buildings on the banks made one extra-long boat barn: Smitty's, a be-all-things marina.

Wanda grabbed the rail and leaped up on deck. Deployed the gangplank.

Strutting out of the portside salon doors, Beryl wore a sailor blouse and dotted white-on-red, split-skirt culottes. Her silvery hair, trimmed in this year's popular pixie cut, completed her faux rich tourist costume. Without a word or a backward glance, she disembarked, sauntered down the pier, and disappeared behind the buildings.

Water slapped against the dock. The breeze died, and in the cloudless blue sky, the sun's heat grew warmer.

On guard, Miranda stayed at the helm. Smitty's was rebel-friendly but served all watercraft, regardless of the boat owner's status in the Fellowship.

During the first six months after the rebels blew up Hogg Island, Miranda had nursed her aunt back to health, supported them with odd jobs, and rebuilt the thirty-six-foot wooden yacht that became the *Lady*. Eventually, she had engines built that looked normal but gave the boat wings if one had to evade pursuit by the Second Sphere. Constructed hidden secret compartments throughout the boat. And chose luxurious furnishings and finishing touches to distract and to classify the *Lady* as a pleasure boat. A pleasure boat welcomed at marinas all along the inland waterways.

Beryl paraded back toward the boat, whistling their all-clear song, "Blessed Assurance." She strolled imperiously up the gangway and demanded, "Fetch my pocketbook."

Playing the dutiful servant, Wanda hurried up to the walkway and into the salon.

With two fingers, Miranda picked up the pistol, placed it in her pocket. She straightened, smoothed her impractical white dress with its large faux-wood buttons down the front and descended to the main deck. Stood at ease to convince any unseen watchers that Beryl was the boss.

Pocketbook in hand, Wanda returned. Offered it to Beryl with her eyes downcast like a proper Fellowship servant.

"Savannah will have our burgers and fries ready for us," Beryl said under her breath. She grabbed the large pocketbook and announced, "You may take an hour's shore leave." She disembarked again, followed by Miranda, and finally by Wanda.

From the pier, Beryl sashayed into Smitty's.

Miranda paused, scanned for unfriendlies. A brand new '65 wine-red Thunderbird and an eight-year-old brown '56 Ford Crestliner offered the only obstacles in the otherwise vacant parking lot. She signaled go.

Wanda servant-shuffled to the side door, the "non-Fellowship" door. The door designated for non-white people.

The door Miranda didn't even notice for most of her life, her life as one of the elite. Remembering her ignorance, her face heated.

Wanda reached for the door handle and stiffened.

Warning tingles shot down Miranda's spine. She reached for the pistol.

Without looking at Miranda, Wanda gave a slight shake of her head. She snatched a sign from the door. Ripped it in two and threw it to the ground. Chin up and shoulders squared, she entered the building.

With pretended indifference, Miranda moved closer to the sign Wanda had destroyed. Glanced at it. The still-recognizable swastika-like symbol of the Ku Klux Klan fired run-and-hide messages through her. Her muscles tensed, but she didn't run or hide. She scanned the parking lot and beyond.

With no one, especially no men in white hooded robes, in sight, Miranda's heart rate slowed. She needed to warn Smitty and get her crew out of here as quickly as possible.

She moved to the front of the building. Scanned the parking lot one last time and entered Smitty's through the front door. A sign proclaimed it the door for Fellowship Members Only.

The first of Smitty's buildings held souvenirs and trinkets for tourists and tantalizing aromas of grilled burgers and French fries. But no one—white or black—was in sight.

The back of Miranda's neck grew warm. She licked her lips and fired glances, searching for someone, anyone.

Three steps down into the next building, a new model speedboat sat on a display ramp to the right of the steps. Its sign boasted of its twin engines and speed and a $1,999 price tag. *Sheesh. Only half the price of a house.* A price someone like Wanda could never afford.

Miranda hadn't understood that until after she'd escaped her parents and Beryl helped her escape Redemption.

She shook off the memories and headed down Smitty's main aisle. Passed more speedboats, and canoes, and shiny aluminum flatboats. And no customers. Her palms grew damp. Was it normal for a Tuesday afternoon at the end of the boating season or a sign the KKK would strike soon?

Three more steps down, she entered the grocery and drugstore area and strolled to the luncheonette on the inland side of the building.

In front of the hot-pink Formica counter, six pink pedestal tables stood on alternate rows of black and white checkerboard tiles. A jukebox blasted Frank Sinatra's latest jazzy hit, "Jesus is a Rock."

She glanced around again. *Where is everyone?* She hurried past the tables, slipped through the "Staff Only" door into the storage area.

Perpendicular to the main aisle stood metal shelving units laden with gallon-sized canned foods. At an unmarked door between the row of canned vegetables and the row of canned fruits, she knocked the first five beats of "Amazing Grace."

"Silverthorn." Miranda used her code name in a low voice and entered Smitty's hidden dining room. Warm, humid air, thick with aromas of fried foods, greeted her. Her mouth watered.

Secreted between the public dining room and the non-Fellowship dining room, this was a safe space for rebels. Two round hot-pink tables crowded the middle of the room.

Wanda moved away from the wall on Miranda's right. Slipped her pistol back into her deeper-than-regulation pocket.

To her left, Beryl uncocked her pistols. "It's about time. I'm starved." She re-holstered her guns.

"Did Wanda tell you?" Miranda asked her aunt.

"I'll answer even though you didn't ask me." Wanda settled at the first table. "I told her we should carry on like normal." She jutted her chin forward. "I told Savannah too. She knew, of course. She and Smitty are protecting themselves, but they won't hide. And neither will I."

Her gaze on Wanda, Miranda gave her friend an apologetic smile. "You're right. On all counts. Old habits are hard to break, but I will. I promise."

"I know," Wanda said. "We're both learning." Her broad smile forgave all.

Miranda pulled out a chair and settled into place. "There's no one in the store. Not even Smitty. Is that because of the Klan?"

"Tourist season's over," Beryl said. "Smitty probably saw it was you and went back to his end-of-season ritual counting thingamabobs."

The waitress came into the room carrying a tray of drinks. A messy bun of red hair tucked in a hairnet, Savannah, Smitty's grown daughter, placed glasses of cola on ice in front of each of them.

"This came for you." Savanah handed Miranda an envelope.

"Mail? For me?" They rarely had their mail catch up to them until they had stopped for the winter. "Thanks." She waited for Savanah to leave the room before she glanced at the envelope. The familiar handwriting sparked a sharp gasp.

Irene. The last time Miranda had seen her sister was when she'd forced Irene, at gunpoint, to choose sides. Irene had joined their parents. Miranda had banished them all. She had heard they wound up in Buenos Aires.

A year later, Ethan told Miranda of her father's death and her mother's disappearance. She had heard nothing from Irene in the following three years. Not even six months ago when Irene had returned to the States with her so-called miracle-working husband.

"Whose letter reached you here?" Beryl set her half-empty glass down with a thud. The ice clinked.

The truth will trigger her paranoia. "It's personal." Miranda couldn't decide if she'd ever read it. She folded the envelope and tucked it into her pocket.

Beryl gave a sly, knowing grin. "A love letter?"

Ignoring her aunt, Miranda sipped her soda. The bubbly cola burned her dry throat.

Savannah returned holding a plate filled with hot matchstick French fries and a juicy hamburger in each hand and one balanced on her left forearm.

"Almost mooing for you. Catsup on the side." She set Beryl's plate down. Took the plate on her forearm and placed it in front of Wanda. "Medium-well, no pink in the juice. Lettuce and tomato on the side." The last plate was Miranda's. "Well-done with pickles and grilled onions."

"Thanks, Savannah." Miranda picked up her burger with two hands. Mashed the fresh-made bun down so it would fit in her mouth. Hot, meaty flavors mixed with sharp dill and sweet onions filled her mouth. She closed her eyes and pretended to swoon.

Savannah laughed. "You're welcome, Silverthorn." She didn't know their real names. Safer that way. She hurried back to the kitchen.

"What, my cookin' isn't good enough?" Wanda's tone held a teasing note.

"I hired you to be my engineer, but I keep you on for your cooking. Your stews and fried catfish are beyond compare." Miranda tried to keep a straight face. "But I gotta say no one's burgers compare to Savannah's."

"Huh."

"Me." Beryl popped a trio of French fries into her mouth. "I'd eat one of your steaks any day of the week." She swallowed. "If we could afford them any day of the week."

"Mmm." Wanda mumbled around a mouthful of burger. She nodded, wiped a dribble of beef juice from the corner of her mouth.

The room lights went out, warned them to be quiet. Someone was at the in-store lunch counter.

Although they expected a contact, Miranda's muscles notched tight.

The three of them exchanged wary glances and put their food down.

Beryl wiped her mouth and tossed her napkin onto the table. Drew her pistols, crossed the room, and flattened against the wall next to the door.

Head down but watching the door, Wanda reached into her pocket.

Miranda swallowed her disapproval. They both knew how she felt about guns. With the potential of the KKK appearing, they both rightfully ignored her.

Five knocks at the door had the rhythm of "Amazing Grace." Miranda signaled Beryl to put away her guns.

The door opened. The room lights came back on.

Nick Rosenthal stepped into the dining area. His green eyes scanned the room, brightened and lingered on Miranda.

"Well, if it isn't Nightshade." Beryl slid her pistols into her deep pockets and winked at Miranda. "Better than a letter, huh?"

Miranda's cheeks heated. She'd met Nick the day she had joined the rebels, the Soldiers of the American Bill of Rights. He'd trained her.

"Good to see you, Foxglove, Silverthorn, and—?"

"You can call me Zinnia."

"Zinnia. A beautiful name for a beautiful woman."

Wanda's smile hovered between skepticism and pure suspicion.

He faced Miranda. "You're looking good, Silverthorn. The sun and water still agree with you."

She wished she could say the same about Nick. The scar from his cheek to his chin had faded to a pale pink but puffy purplish circles under his eyes and the extra sharp angle of his square jaw spoke of his true state. The underfed look worried her.

His glances darted around the room as if he expected danger from every corner. *What happened to him?* In the aftermath of the Hogg Island bombing and Beryl's terrible injuries, he'd been calm seas for her. He'd stayed with her. Made sure Beryl—made sure they *both*—got what they needed. Held her on the nights she needed strength and hope and… more. But that was long ago.

"How long has it been?" She pinched her lips closed too late.

"Almost a year." Regret colored his tone.

Beryl picked up her plate, gestured at the chair she'd vacated. "Sit."

"Good to see you too," Nick said with a laugh and sat. "How have you been?"

"Keeping busy." She popped the last bite of her burger into her mouth.

"Good." His gaze slid to Miranda.

She leaned toward him, but the look in his eyes stopped her.

"You two know each other?" Wanda tossed a back-and-forth glance between them.

"You could say that."

Tension radiated from him, sent ice through Miranda's veins, twisted her gut, and froze her heart. She had to know. "You've never taken delivery of a package before."

"It's on route to my next mission." His weary, resigned tone turned the river of ice in her veins to deep arctic frozen. She hid her trembling hands and kept smiling.

Beryl tapped Wanda on the shoulder. "Come on, Zinnia. Let's help Savannah." She jerked her head toward the sizzling meats and clinking water glasses in the kitchen.

Wanda's generous lips spread into a suggestive smile. "Yeah. We'll help Savannah."

With a click and whir, the jukebox started playing "Moon River."

Miranda smiled at Nick, who smiled at her. She twisted her hands in her lap.

"The package is still aboard." She scooted her chair back. "I'll take you to it." Placed a hand on the table preparing to stand.

"In a minute." Nick placed a warm hand over her cooler one.

She sat iceberg still. "Something *is* wrong."

"No. But we need to talk." His smile reached his eyes, but the trench furrowed between his brows spoke of a Grand Canyon of concern. "Things are about to get hot for SABR. It might be a long time before I can see you again."

Longer than a year? The Soldiers for America's Bill of Rights have already asked so much of him. Of us. "SABR always wants to keep things hot, don't they?" She tried to keep her tone light.

A grim grin flitted across his face. "You know I can't say more."

How long and how dangerous is this mission? Or is he trying to warn me about some other danger? "Does it have something to do with the Ku Klux Klan?"

"Why? Are they threatening you?" He half rose from his chair.

"They posted a sign on the non-Fellowship door here."

He threw a glance around the room. "Smitty is taking precautions?"

"He told Wanda and Beryl they were."

"Good." He eased back into his chair. "Look, I can't stay long. I took this mission because I wanted to—to see you, to—talk." He hesitated, licked his lips. "I've been thinking about you…and me… and—" He reached into his pocket and pulled out a folded piece of paper. No, not paper. A glossy page from a magazine.

The paper crinkled when she unfolded it. A soft gasp escaped her. A charming yellow Cape Cod house with a red tin roof surrounded by a colorful flower garden and a white picket fence filled the page. Overcome by a dreadful déjà vu, she gulped. "That's —um—beautiful." A partial caption identified the picture as a real estate ad. She gulped again. "Are you thinking about buying a house?"

"It's a dream," he said, his voice wistful. "Someday, after the fighting is over, I'd like to live in a place like that. Wouldn't you?"

How do I answer? Her chest ached for a romance-novel ending. "I dream of peace," she began. "Of being able to—" Her throat closed against the wish. Until there was peace, real, forever peace, his till-death fight against the Fellowship would make a happily-ever-after unlikely. After a moment, she tapped the picture. "Dreams like this don't come true for people like us."

He leaned forward. Wrapped her hand in his. "I'm only asking that we hold on to a shared dream for now. Can you do that?"

She wanted to, for Nick. But she knew how precarious his life was. Both their lives were.

"If we don't look forward to a beautiful future, what are we fighting for?"

Beautiful future? "Will anything beautiful survive the fight?" She clamped her mouth shut. *Shouldn't have said that.*

"The country's fractured, but there's still beauty. If you look, it's everywhere." He cupped her cheek in his warm hand. "Especially here. Now."

She took his hand from her cheek. Traced the star-like, puckered scar on the back of his hand with her finger. Gazed up at him. "You know what I want?" She didn't wait for an answer. "To hear you play the Music Hall again. When was the last time you played your violin?"

He gently freed his hands, stuffed them into his pockets. "Violin playing isn't much use to SABR"—his shoulder jerked in a brief shrug—"to a rebel."

She refolded the picture and held it out to him.

"Why don't you keep it for a while?" His half-smile and the hope in his eyes melted her.

She slipped the picture into her pocket. A corner of her sister's envelope poked her.

The room lights blinked off again.

Adrenaline flooded Miranda's heart, lungs, and muscles and melted the ice inside her. She slid to the edge of her chair.

The lights came on again, and Savannah appeared in the kitchen doorway. "Sorry to intrude." She crossed to the table, offered Miranda a sealed envelope. "Special delivery for you."

A second letter? "For me?" Now *her* paranoia flared. *Must shove off —now. And skip Smitty's all next season.*

The name on the return address was unknown to her, but its first letter was the stylized, hand-drawn saber representing the rebels, the Soldiers of the American Bill of Rights. She glanced at Nick, left the table.

Inside the envelope, on a dirt-smeared, half sheet of paper, the coded message read: "Level 4, Missouri #49, upriver. 10-21, 5:00pm. Hawthorn." She swallowed. Her guts twisted into double and triple knots.

"Hawthorn," her baby brother David, was in danger, level four out of five danger. *Missouri River mile marker forty-nine? By five tomorrow? Have to hurry.* She crossed back to Nick. "New mission." Her voice cracked. She cleared her throat. "We need to launch, and you and the package need to get clear before the KKK returns."

His disappointed smile morphed into a resolute one. "Right." He led her into the storeroom, cracked the "Staff Only" door open, and peered out. "Clear. I'll follow."

Moments later, she boarded the *Lady.*

Visible through the windows, Wanda sat in the salon at the lower helm. Gave Miranda a nod and kept scanning the pier and water.

Beryl stood at the upper helm scanning the shore, gun hand concealed under the counter. She exchanged a glance with Miranda, went to the forward hatch, and climbed below.

Miranda settled on the starboard bench, leaned against the bulkhead. The shadow of the upper deck fell across her face.

Too many heartbeats later, Nick appeared at the gangway. "Permission to board?"

"Permission granted." She rapped on the bulkhead. Beryl brought the package to Nick.

At the upper helm, Miranda watched Nick and the package, a slender Chinese-American man in borrowed paint-splattered coveralls and a straw hat, disembark. In moments, they stepped off the pier and disappeared behind Smitty's.

She took a shaky breath, refocused. "Prepare to launch."

"Bowline clear." Wanda trotted to the aft line and cleared it too.

Miranda waited for Wanda to stow the gangplank, then pointed the boat downriver.

Chapter Two

Irene Earnshaw took another nibble of her caramel cream. Sweet and light, it was the perfect finish to a perfect meal. She sat at a splendid U-shaped table arrangement for eighty, covered with fine white linen tablecloths and adorned with tabletop candelabras and golden baskets of orange, red, and yellow flowers. Dressed in her new pink, long-sleeved evening dress, her appearance was acceptable at this State Dinner. But as the guest of honor at the White House, she was cheap taffeta in a sea of shimmering silk.

From under her lashes, she stole a look at President Joseph P. Kennedy, Jr., seated beside her. He leaned left, spoke to the vice president's wife. The table chatter of the Meritorious Fellowship members around the tables obscured his words.

Cabinet members, senators, representatives, military leaders, and their wives were all here to honor the newly ordained Prophet, her miracle-working husband, Felix.

In his regal black robes trimmed in red, Felix sat on a diagonal across from her between the president's elegant wife and the speaker's wife. They laughed politely at something he said.

"Lady Irene? Lady Earnshaw?" A male voice pierced the wall of sound.

Startled, she glanced up to see who spoke.

"Excuse me, Lady Earnshaw. Will you be staying for the entertainment this evening?" He sat on the inside corner of the U. Peered at her with intense green eyes set in a square face. Longish, light brown hair swept back from his forehead.

Oh, no. Smiling her Good Fellowship Wife smile, she hesitated. Feared she'd say the wrong thing. She wished she'd paid attention when Mama was the First Apostle's Lady. *But by then I was married and the mother of a five-year-old.* "Of course, I'm staying. And you?"

"I am. Perhaps you'll indulge me in a bit of conversation during the intermission. I could use your help with a special project." Young with thin lips and a big chin, gleaming teeth filled his smile.

"A special project?" He was a doctor—Doctor Gallaway, if she remembered correctly. *Don't ask if the project is on the list of activities appropriate for the Prophet's Lady. Most likely it's on the longer list of should nots.*

A bell rang. One of the head butlers held the First Lady's chair. She rose.

"May I help you, madam?"

Startled again, Irene acknowledged the butler behind her. She turned back to the doctor and smiled sweetly. "I'd love to hear about your project. Later?"

He dipped his head. "After cigars and brandy."

At the butler's direction, Irene joined the president's wife.

"Ladies," the First Lady said, "please join us in the Blue Room for after-dinner coffee."

Chair legs scraped across wood floors and husbands held chairs for their wives, who then gathered behind Irene.

Mrs. Kennedy, who insisted Irene call her Victoria, took Irene's hand and guided the finely dressed ladies into the Blue Room.

Royal blue wallpaper and drapes and chairs with matching cushions lined the room. A silver coffee service sat on a marble-topped table in the center of the oval parlor. Servers in splendid, white cutaway tuxedos attended the coffee service or offered trays of assorted nuts, dinner mints, and other candies. The scents of coffee and perfumes mingled pleasantly.

At the coffee table, Irene requested and received ice water. The etched crystal bowl of the stemware bore the presidential shield.

"That's part of President Garner's crystal service," Victoria said.

Irene reverently cupped the ice-cold crystal bowl in both gloved hands. After President-Elect Franklin D. Roosevelt's assassination, President Garner's executive order created the Fellowship Council to guide the president's cabinet. The Prophet's Lady must not drop this valuable heirloom.

Victoria crossed the room to a small group of chatty women. "Ladies, let me introduce our guest of honor's wife, Lady Irene Earnshaw."

"This is the Second Lady, Pat Nixon. And the wife of the speaker of the house, Harriet McCormack."

"Nice to meet you," Irene murmured to each of them. She never dreamed she'd be surrounded by so many powerful people. *Mama always favored Miranda. If only Mama had lived to see me now.* Prickles of guilt made her smile waver and tightened her neck. She banished the sinful thought and restored her smile.

Victoria took her arm. "We mustn't monopolize all of Lady Irene's time. There are many others who wish to meet her. If there's time, we'll be back."

Victoria guided her to another cluster and introduced her to the wives of the secretaries of agriculture, interior, and labor.

"How are your children adapting to life in the District?" Barbara, the secretary of agriculture's wife, asked.

"My daughters are doing well, thank you."

"How old are they?"

"Sandra is seven but thinks she's older. And we think Annabelle is ten this year."

Barbara blinked at her. "Excuse me?"

"She's adopted," Irene explained. "An orphan." She tried to block the horrific images and smells of the plague of hemorrhagic dengue fever that killed thousands in Buenos Aires two years ago.

"Oh," said another of the wives. "She's the Prophet's first healing, isn't she?"

The other wives murmured appreciation but exchanged arch looks.

They disapprove of my miracle child? Irene's jaw tensed behind her Good Fellowship wife persona.

Victoria smoothly excused the two of them and led Irene through the crowd.

"Lovely to see you again, Irene," gushed a short, elderly woman in a sequined pink satin formal with a black mink collar.

Irene bent forward to hear her gravelly voice better. "Do I know you?"

The woman's bright brown eyes twinkled. "I used to bribe her with my icebox cookies years ago," she said in a confidential tone to the First Lady, then looked up at Irene.

Mama's friend. Irene's stomach dropped. The three miracles Felix had performed had gained so much publicity the Fellowship Council couldn't deny Felix was the next Prophet. But they'd strongly suggested she and Felix pretend Irene's parents and their fall from Grace didn't exist.

She assumed the warm smile of her Good Fellowship Wife persona and extended a gloved hand. "Mrs. Wynter. I'm sorry. I remember you now—and the cookies."

"It's all right, dear." Mrs. Wynter took Irene's hand in both her thin frail hands. "They weren't very good."

Victoria joined their laughter with a light laugh. "I'll let you two reminisce." She stepped away, and a couple of women swooped in to speak with her.

"I hope my teasing didn't embarrass you."

"Not at all," Irene lied. She forced back memories of how the Fellowship had abandoned her parents. Mrs. Wynter had nothing to do with that.

"I stole you away to convince you to come visit me."

"I would love to—" Irene paused before saying *but*, tried to think of a polite way to put Mrs. Wynter off.

The old woman's face crinkled. "Excellent." She handed Irene a silver calling card. "My address. Thursday, time's on the card. There are—things—we need to discuss." Moving spryly for an old woman, she vanished into the crowd before Irene could reply.

Irene tapped her right thumbnail on her teeth and studied the card. *It's not like my social calendar is full. The girls will be in school. Maybe a quiet visit and gentle reminder…* She folded the card, tucked it discreetly into her bra.

The peals of the silver handbell rose above the women's voices.

Victoria joined her. They followed the butler through a cross hall, past gleaming marble columns into the East Room where the men also gathered.

The size of the rectangular East Room, the yards of crimson silk draperies, red marble accents, and massive crystal chandeliers evenly spaced down the center of the ceiling stole Irene's breath.

Voices rose, and spouses shuffled about, sought one another, and took their assigned seats. The president sat in the front row. Irene sat to his right again and Felix to his left. Victoria sat on Felix's left. Twenty members of the United States Air Force Strings, wearing their dress blues, marched in and took their places in the seats near the State Grand Piano. The Steinway itself would have filled Irene's Buenos Aires living room wall-to-wall.

The conductor waved his wand, and the lyrical "Tchaikovsky's Waltz" from *Serenade for Strings* filled the air.

They played a varied program for an hour. After a rousing rendition of "God Bless America," they broke for intermission.

Dignitaries milled about, congratulated her, and murmured other appreciations. She smiled and nodded until her cheeks hurt.

"Lady Earnshaw?"

She forced another smile and turned.

Dr. Gallaway towered above her, taller than he'd appeared at the table. "May I steal you away to a quiet corner?"

He offered her his arm and escorted her to the back of the room.

She welcomed the slightly cooler air. Sank onto one of the red velvet benches that lined the wall.

"I apologize for intruding during this celebration, but I could not reach you at home."

Irene cocked her head. "You couldn't?" *How could that be?* The Fellowship appointed-housekeeper did the chores, and the girls spent their day at school. A nanny helped the girls after school. And Felix's duties as the Prophet kept him all hours of the day and night. *I'm the least busy person in the house.*

"Your phone number is unlisted. And the secretary at the Fellowship Center was—shall we say—protective?"

The secretary at the Center? "Were you trying to reach the Prophet?"

"Not at all." He leaned close. His clean, citrus-scented aftershave pleased her. "Projects like the Center for the Advancement of Inborn Character have always been the Prophet's, or First Apostle's Lady's —your mother, for example."

Irene drew in a sharp breath, too uncomfortable to glance around.

"Did I say something wrong?"

She struggled to smile. "What happened to my parents was…

is…" She raised her eyes to his. "Something I'd prefer not to discuss."

"Apologies." He gestured at the vacant space between them and the other attendees. "No one overheard. But we'll discuss the details of my project in a more private place."

"Apology accepted." Smiled a Good Fellowship wife's smile. "You said this was a project for the Prophet's Lady. The Center for the—? I'm sorry, I didn't catch the name."

"The Center for the Advancement of Inborn Character or CAIC." He spelled out the acronym, then pronounced the word *cay-ache*.

"I've never heard of that before."

"It's a private project."

Irene pulled back a bit and fingered her clip-on pearl earring. "Private? Is it dangerous?"

His smile widened. "Not to you, Lady Earnshaw. Never to you."

"Well, I am intrigued," she said. "Go on."

The overhead lights flickered. The muted murmurs grew louder. Shoes clacked and chairs scraped and screeched across the floor.

"My card," he said. "Call me at your convenience tomorrow. We'll set up a private meeting and talk more."

His pale-yellow business card bore his name, Louis Gallaway, MD, PhD, Director of CAIC printed in the center and a post office box address in the lower left corner with a long-distance phone number across the bottom. She looked up and glimpsed Dr. Gallaway before he vanished into the crowd of guests returning to their seats.

The fullness of her heart threatened to burst through her ribs. She pressed the business card to her chest. The honor that God bestowed upon her and her husband meant she needed to be more than cheap taffeta and simulated pearls. And this special project could be the answer to her prayers.

Chapter Three

Annabelle Earnshaw sat in her pink bedroom on the frilly pink bed her adoptive family liked. She hated it. And she didn't know why. Mother and Papa treated her well. She even liked having a sister. Maybe it's because she didn't remember her before-life. Didn't remember what she liked or who she was. No memory of her real mother or father. No memory of a sister or brother. Nothing.

Her chest hurt like it needed to be bigger. Her stomach burned, and her hands knotted and unknotted. Something inside her needed —something. Worse than ever before. Restless, she crossed her pink carpet to the eighty-gallon desert aquarium in the corner. "Hello, Javier."

Her bearded dragon tilted his head and fixed an eye on her. She stooped and grabbed the dollar bag of live crickets and a lidless Tupperware sandwich box from the terrarium's bottom shelf.

Javier alerted, took a jerky sidestep. His mouth opened, and his tongue tasted the air.

Annabelle placed the empty Tupperware box in the tank.

Javier pranced in place.

She poured a dozen or two crickets into the box. They chirped and chirped, not knowing their fate. She sprinkled calcium dust over them.

Javier skittered into the box and snapped up two crickets, one, two. Three, four, five.

She snatched a tiny cricket out of the box before Javier grabbed it. Pinched the insect until its head popped off. The ache inside dimmed.

After the fifth beheaded cricket, the pain dulled to ignorable. She watched Javier eat. "*Ambos vivimos en jaulas antinaturales.*" Surveyed her pink frilly bedroom. "We are in unnatural cages, aren't we, *Ché*?" Mother had sent her to her room until supper.

She plopped into her purple beanbag chair.

It wasn't fair. That girl had deserved a bloody nose. An accent doesn't make me dumb. And I'm not Mexican. Why did she say that? She knows I'm the miracle girl. Annabelle put her elbows on her knees and her chin on her fists.

Mother had said the principal's telephone call scared her. *Was she afraid I died again? Wouldn't Papa just make me alive again?*

Her head pounded. Her throat tightened, and her mouth grew desert-sand dry. *Is this fear?*

She leaped off the chair and went to the oversized closet stuffed with the smelly girly dresses that Mother loved. Mother said little girls should smell sweet like flowers. *Ugh.*

She ducked under the clothes. At the very back of the closet, stacks of boxes held a billion different dolls. Mother said little girls loved dolls. But Annabelle didn't. At least not those dolls.

She crawled closer to the stack. Sat cross-legged and dug through the boxes. Set aside the Sweetie Pie baby doll and the Nancy Lee doll, the Dutch boy and girl, the doll that wet her pants, and the doll that cried real tears. At the bottom of the pile sat a bright blue shoebox with the word Keds scrawled in yellow letters outlined in red. She pulled the shoebox onto her lap. Lifted the lid.

Inside lay Dolly, her loops of brown yarn hair mashed flat on her head. Her embroidered eyes, nose, and smile were thin and frayed. Dolly's grimy blue blouse still had all its buttons, and only a few of the shiny beads on her full denim skirt were missing. But the arms and legs made from old gaucho pants had shiny spots.

Mother said she'd sanitized and kept Dolly to help Annabelle remember her real mother. It didn't help. *Besides, whoever the woman in the hut was, she wasn't my mother either.*

Annabelle ran her fingers through the soft, scratchy yarn loops of Dolly's hair. The tightness inside eased. She hugged Dolly tight. Slowly, the hurt vanished. *Curious.*

Chapter Four

Miranda leaned against *Lady's* teak helm beside the pilot's wheel. The boat bobbed gently at the edge of the Mississippi behind a half-dozen trees rooted in a tiny island of mud. Visible above the trees, the sunset painted the clouds with flames of red and gold. Red sky—sailor's warning? She hoped not.

"Dinner's ready," Beryl called from the starboard salon doors.

"Not hungry."

Late-fall crickets sang on shore, but puffs of icy wind billowed Miranda's windbreaker around her life vest, sent a ripple of chills across her skin.

To the southwest, a giant dome of light arched above St. Louis. And tomorrow, instead of slipping past that Fellowship stronghold, she would navigate against the current, up the Missouri, right through the middle of the enemy's territory.

Beryl climbed up to the bridge. Leaned against the helm's safety railing opposite Miranda. "Worried?"

"We've passed through more dangerous places without a problem." *But this time it's for David.* Not to mention, she also had to figure out how to respond to Irene.

Beryl crossed her arms over her chest and gave Miranda the worried-aunt look. "Something's going on. Did Nick say something that upset you?"

"No." She didn't have the energy to explain. Not even to Beryl.

"I don't believe you, but—" She shrugged. "It's your business. I'll tell Wanda to keep your dinner warm." She grabbed the rail and climbed down to the main deck.

"Beryl?"

"Yeah?" She lifted her face toward Miranda. The ship's deck lights turned it into a pale oval hovering between the bridge's deck and the brass railing.

"Do you ever think about what you'll do—after?" Miranda waved her hand in the air.

"After—we beat the Fellowship?"

"Yeah. Will you—get a house—a job, maybe live with Uncle Ethan again?"

Beryl rubbed her mouth. "That's a big question. What happened? Did Nick propose?"

Miranda choked back a laugh. *Close, but—* "No. Nick did not propose. I'm just thinking aloud. Would you? Live with Uncle Ethan again?"

"I haven't thought about it. Too much can happen between now and then."

Yeah. The breeze slithered frosty fingers under Miranda's life vest and shirt. She shivered.

Beryl kept her face turned up toward Miranda. "Sure you don't want to talk?"

Watching the sunset fade, she said, "I'll be down in a few."

"Aye, aye, Captain." Beryl disappeared into the salon.

Miranda pulled Irene's letter out of her pocket again. Squinted to read by the helm lights.

BY THE TIME this reaches you, if it reaches you, Felix will be the new Prophet of the Fellowship. I don't like what you did to us, but if you had not sent us away, who knows what would have happened? You were part of God's plan.

While I may never be strong enough to forgive you, I am strong enough to try. Let's talk.

TALK. Miranda folded the paper, jammed it deep in her pocket. *To my sister, wife of the Prophet.* She rubbed her pounding forehead. *It could be a trap.* In her mind's eye, the windows of the little cottage glowed with warm light. *What if it's sincere? If there were peace, I could tell Nick how much I long for us to have a happily ever after in that cottage.*

"Captain?" Wanda shouted from the salon doors. "Dinner's going to dry out in the oven. Want me to bring it to you? Or I could make you a sandwich."

Miranda wriggled the tension out of her neck and shoulders. "Coming." She glanced up at the indigo sky, found the first star—and wished.

————

TIRED AND CRANKY, Miranda had started her second shift less than an hour ago. Sweat trickled under her life vest, made her back itch. The wind shifted again, chilled the sweaty areas. Storm clouds that had hovered on the horizon all day raced and scuttled across the sky, now blotted out by the westering sun.

She slowed the boat and switched on her running lights. Pointed the spotlight's beam at the swirling brown water in front of the bow. Kept centered between the channel markers they passed and avoided the submerged rocks, mud bars, and dead trees typical of the Missouri River.

At least all the sunny-day boaters had gone ashore. She had the river to herself.

The next channel marker reflected a bit of the boat's running lights. She spotlighted it. Above the green channel marker, a white sign read 35.

She aimed the light in front of the bow again and grabbed the VHF radio's mike. "Ladies, we just passed mile marker thirty-five. We're clear of St. Charles."

"Read you five-by-five," Wanda said. "Decks are clear."

Even on their private channel, they used code. Safer that way. The inland rivers had thousands listening to river chatter.

Miranda dreamed of the day this ruse wouldn't be necessary. *If Irene's letter held even a glimmer of peace— Focus—fourteen more miles to David. Irene must wait.*

Be-boop. Be-boop. Miranda jerked, hyper-alert. The two-toned alert from the VHF radio never meant good news.

"This is the U.S. Coast Guard. *Serenity*, heave to. Over."

Crap. She tightened her grip on the wheel. An over-the-shoulder glance took in the running lights outline of a USCG cutter two to three cable lengths behind them. *Lousy timing.* She wished she could warn David. Their thirty-minute ETA just became an hour or more.

Miranda dialed the proper channel on the radio and seized the mike. "U.S. Coast Guard, this is *Serenity*. Please state your intentions."

"This is the Coast Guard. *Serenity*, we're requesting permission to board for a safety inspection."

When the Guard asked for permission, they were being polite. Ignoring or refusing their request only led to trouble. If she'd been on the ocean, *Lady* could outrun the cutter. But on the Big Muddy Missouri? Trapped between a storm and the Coast Guard?

Miranda switched to her private channel. "Wanda? Did you hear?"

"Aye, Captain. We're shipshape. Over and out."

Shipshape meant all the trappings to show they were upstanding Fellowship members were on display. As long as their false identities were also shipshape, they'd be okay.

Three clicks of the dial, and Miranda switched back to the Coast Guard's channel. "This is *Serenity*. We'll comply with the heave to and grant you permission to board. Over and out."

She guided the yacht out of the main water traffic lanes, dropped the bow anchors, and cut the engine. Turned and waited for Beryl to finish her climb to the bridge deck.

Beryl settled onto the bridge's port settee at the mahogany table. She faced the stern, draped one arm across the back of the settee, rested her legs across the rest of the seat.

A throaty growl of thunder came from upriver. Miranda swiped one damp hand down her skirt-imitating culottes, then the other. Wished she could predict how fast the storm would come. Maybe foul weather will make the Guard cut the inspection short.

Wanda arrived on the bridge deck as well. Her brown skin gleamed under the lights. She took a scarf out of her pocket, captured the cloud of tight black curls on her head, and tied it down. Stood at parade rest against the bulkhead.

Overhead, the flags flapped and snapped in the wind.

"Relax, Miranda." Beryl drawled with her fake southern accent. "I'll have them eating out of my hand."

Astern, a dinghy full of guardsmen launched from Coast Guard vessel.

The knots in Miranda's stomach torqued tighter. She shot a ferocious glare at her aunt's lounging form. The Coast Guard had the right to inspect whatever they wanted, as long as they wanted. Anything beyond a routine inspection, and they would find the weapons and maps hidden in *Lady's* secret compartments. And if they found those—she and the crew wouldn't face simple brainwashing in Redemption, the Fellowship's prison. *No, they will torture us for information about Safe Harbor, then put us in front of a firing squad.*

Beryl tapped the underside of the table where a rifle sat in a quick-release hide. "I've got everything covered."

Miranda glowered at her aunt. *No shooting. Not on my boat. Not while David needs us.*

On the main deck, she scanned the port and starboard lockers and the door to the captain's stateroom. Wanda had battened everything down for the storm. *Sorry.* Miranda unlocked them all.

She crossed the main deck, unlatched the oak transom doors, and descended to the swim platform. The river smell of mud and fish grew stronger. On the starboard side, *Lady's* dinghy creaked in the wind, swinging on the crane.

Waves broke against the platform, splashed her with cold water. She ignored the chill that raced along her skin and assumed her old mask, the smiling-daughter-of-the-counselor one.

The Coast Guard's two-stroke motor whined, loud and menacing, bounced their dinghy across the waves, five lengths and closing. *Three—no, four. Four guardsmen? Not good.* A rush of adrenaline warmed her ears.

The guardsmen approached portside. Shut off their engine.

Miranda caught their bowline, secured the little boat to *Lady's* cleat.

"Welcome aboard, gentlemen." She didn't feel it, but her voice sounded steady.

A man wearing a U.S. Coast Guard windbreaker stepped out of his boat onto the platform.

A second guardsman came aboard. "Thank you," he said in a

professional tone. "I'm Chief Petty Officer Yarborough. Please have all crew and passengers on deck."

"Yoo-hoo," Beryl called from the upper deck railing in a bright, jaunty voice. "We're already up here, officers."

He nodded and climbed up to the main deck. The third man boarded and followed CPO Yarborough.

The fourth man stood.

Miranda's stomach dropped. She swore under her breath.

The fourth man's shoulder patch held a white cross bisecting a long, red oval. White wings hovered on either side of the top third of the oval—Second Sphere—a Fellowship enforcer.

She braced herself. Watched his awkward balancing act and wondered what she would do if he capsized the USCG boat.

Arms out like an acrobat, he made it safely onto the swim platform.

The urge to offer him her wrists for handcuffs nearly overwhelmed Miranda. Somehow, she kept her arms at her sides. Kept her smiling mask on.

He hurried up the ladder to the main deck and stood beside the chief petty officer.

Throat dry, muscles tense, Miranda followed him. *If he's not going to arrest us, why is an SS agent here?*

CPO Yarborough unfolded a sheet of paper with a snap. "Says here a Mr. Walter Wilkins is the registered owner of this boat. Where is he?"

Miranda tried not to gasp for breath, ignored her speeding pulse, and began their planned script. "Mr. Wilkins—" She dropped her chin, stared at her deck shoes for a second before she looked up again.

He glanced from Miranda to the bridge deck. "The owner is on board, isn't he?"

Beryl leaned across the brass rail and gave a sad laugh. "No, sir, he isn't. God rest his soul. My husband left me this gorgeous yacht when he passed on." She nodded at Miranda. "Andy is my captain."

The Second Sphere agent fixed a gaze on Wanda.

Arms at her sides, Wanda didn't react. This was her first USCG inspection, but not her first encounter with the Second Sphere.

The agent turned a handsome smile on Miranda, then focused on Beryl. "You mean you two ladies are traveling alone?"

Miranda bit the inside of her cheek. *He's ignoring Wanda, because he's going to arrest her or because of her skin color?*

Beryl gave the agent a scolding smile. "It wouldn't be proper for a widow lady to travel with a male crew, now would it?"

"Of course not, Mrs. Wilkins." He lifted his Coast Guard cap. "Sorry for your loss."

"Thank you, sir, but Mr. Wilkins has been at his rest for a while now."

"Next time you're at your home port—Miami, is it?"

"Perhaps you have the wrong boat? Fort Lauderdale is our home port."

"Oh, yes, that is what it says here. Next time you are in Fort Lauderdale, get your registration updated. But a fine woman like you should stay home and marry again."

"You wouldn't be available, would you?"

Miranda swallowed a laugh. She could've sworn her aunt even batted her lashes.

"Um." He cleared his throat. "No, Mrs. Wilkins." Held up his left hand, pointed at the silver band on his third finger. Cleared his throat again. "Seaman Walker will be available to answer your questions while the rest of us complete your inspection."

Seaman Walker stepped smartly forward, saluted the agent, then faced Miranda. His smooth, ruddy cheeks marked him as young, probably a trainee. *Was he watching them because he was a trainee or at the orders of the Second Sphere agent?*

Yarborough and the Second Sphere agent went down the three steps onto the white-oak and Brazilian-redwood pinstriped floor of the captain's quarters. The third guardsman climbed up onto the bridge.

He paused and studied Wanda. "Are you as well fed as you look?" He punched her just below her life vest—in the gut.

Wanda gasped soundlessly, doubled over.

Miranda froze. Her blood roared. She choked back her indignant shout and only kept her hands from knotting into fists because she grabbed the safety rail behind her so tight the skin of her knuckles hurt. Their survival, Wanda's survival, depended upon her calm silence.

He continued upward to the helm.

Wanda straightened, eyes downcast. Tears dripped off her

cheeks. Her chest rose and fell smooth and regular, as if she timed each breath purposely.

Miranda climbed to the upper deck and stood at the brass railing beside Beryl. *Why did he do that? No guardsman has ever behaved that way.*

"You may take a seat, ladies, if that's more comfortable," Seaman Walker said, joining them.

"Thank you, I believe I will." Beryl strolled to the port settee and sat.

The navigation lights flicked off and on. The blat of the boat's horn sounded. *Standard safety checks.*

Beryl draped her right arm over the back of the wooden settee again. Her smile couldn't have been more congenial.

Opposite Beryl, Miranda settled onto the cool, smooth wood slats of the starboard settee. They'd already stowed the canopy and the seat cushions to prepare for the storm.

"Any questions, ladies?" Seaman Walker asked.

"No, sir. Just wondering how long this'll take," Miranda said. *David's waiting.* "I'd like to get to our night's destination and get moored before the storm hits."

Seaman Walker flashed a smile he probably intended to be reassuring. "Maybe another thirty minutes, Miss. Good idea to get moored before the storm."

He ran an appreciative hand over the table's glossy mahogany. "Nice ship you have here."

"Thank you," Beryl said. "We think so."

The ship's luxury encouraged folk to overlook the extra depth of certain hanging lockers, shower stalls, and *Lady's* other secret compartments.

Miranda listened for the officers in her cabin, but rushing wind filled her ears.

She stole a glance at her wristwatch and fretted.

Hang on, David—

The wind grew colder, stronger.

The sky darkened. Lightning strobed behind the clouds overhead. Thunder rolled. It didn't seem to hurry the guardsmen.

The man on the bridge scurried across the walkway to the foredeck and back and forth, checking signal flares, life jackets, and hatches.

A USCG inspection doesn't take this long. It has to be the Second Sphere agent. What is he up to? Does he suspect us? Is he planting evidence against us? Making an extra thorough search?

If he finds one of the secret panels, he'll arrest us—or shoot us. David will never know why I didn't come.

Chapter Five

Irene climbed the yellow-gold carpeted stairs to the brownstone's second floor. The heaviness in her chest made the climb harder.

From the leafy-green sofa to the pink-and-gold-rhododendron chintz chairs and the pecan side tables, the living room sparkled and held a hint of sweetness in the air. A vase of fresh-cut golden mums stood on the oval coffee table.

She rubbed her temples. Waiting for the girls or Felix or some Fellowship meet-and-greet wasn't enough. Back home in Buenos Aires, she did all the childcare and cooking and cleaning. And she did all of Felix's correspondence. She crossed the room and leaned against the doorway to Felix's study.

The most masculine room in the house, it stood as long as the living room but only half as wide. A stately white-brick fireplace and built-in bookcases filled the spaces between the symmetrical windows on the far wall. Leather wingback-chairs graced each side of the braided rug on the dark oak floor in front of the fireplace.

Opposite the fireplace sat Felix's plain wooden desk. Her husband, the miracle-working Prophet, refused to give it up, and she couldn't deny him.

A messy pile of unanswered mail covered the desktop. Fellowship secretaries answered most of his mail, but there were still many letters he needed to answer himself. He was so busy praying over the sick that the mail languished on his desk.

That's it. I will help him with the mail. The heaviness in her chest lifted. A sign it was the right thing to do.

She lowered herself onto the seat cushion on his wooden roll-around chair. Ran her hand across the desk, tried to feel some part of Felix in this inanimate object. She shook her head. *What foolishness.* Slid his brass letter opener into the corner of the first envelope.

An hour later, she'd completed two dozen replies. She reached for the next envelope and frowned. *Pink stationery?* Picked up the envelope. Whiffed a familiar floral scent. *Jasmine? Pink perfumed stationery.* She eyed the loops and swirls of the handwriting. *Perhaps written by a wife or daughter on behalf of a father or husband.*

———

DEAR PROPHET EARNSHAW,

My heart aches to see you tirelessly work, saving the sick and dying. And you do it all alone. Your wife seems a brave and a reserved woman. I am not reserved, my dear Felix. However long you work, I will stand beside you because I know the time in our bed will be ours alone.

———

IRENE'S MOUTH DROPPED OPEN. Her hands shook. *OUR bed?* She huffed. Scrutinized the remaining pile of envelopes suspiciously. No more pink ones. She rifled through the stack, pulled out the hand-written ones.

One by one, she read six more letters where young women professed their carnal love for her husband. Rooted to her seat, her blood burned. *How dare they?*

She inhaled a controlled breath, released it for a count of three. They'd been in the states for six long months. *Felix doesn't hide things from me. Maybe he's just received them. But he's been the Prophet for six months. Surely these aren't the first he's received. Why hasn't he told me about these harlots?*

A tiny shiver ran through her core. She glanced down at her matronly form stuffed in a prim, navy-blue dress with brass buttons. Told herself that the *Prophet* wouldn't be tempted. Her *husband* wouldn't be tempted. *Felix* wouldn't be tempted.

Downstairs, the back door thudded open and running footsteps clattered across the kitchen tiles. Sandra's loud laughter echoed up the stairwell.

Irene stacked the correspondence neatly, front and center of the desk—minus seven letters. She dashed up to her third-floor bedroom. Hid the seven letters and the list in the drawer with her unmentionables, then rushed downstairs to greet her daughters.

Three hours later, Irene tried to listen to the girls' chatter at the dinner table, but she couldn't stop staring at Felix's empty seat.

She had delayed dinner for two hours. Then Felix had called to say he'd be late tonight. They should eat without him. *Again.*

The meatloaf turned flavorless in her mouth. *Is he with one of those harlots?* The lump of meat scraped against her throat. She decided she wasn't hungry after all.

"Mommy, why do some people want to hurt us?"

Jerked back to the table and her daughters' conversation, Irene held her fork in mid-air and focused on Sandra, who couldn't possibly know about the harlots.

"Why did they try to bomb the school?" Her daughter's nose wrinkled. *Right.* They had dismissed school an hour early because the apostates had planted a pipe bomb nearby.

Irene put down her fork. "Darling, I don't know. I think when Adam and Eve sinned in the Garden of Eden, it allowed some people to be born evil. They can't help but think and do evil things."

"Oh." Sandra tilted her head. "Was I born evil?"

"Of course not, darling." Irene rose from her seat and rushed to give Sandra a hug. "You were born into the Fellowship. Your daddy is the Prophet. You can't be evil." *And neither can he.*

"But—" Sandra stared at and stirred her mashed potatoes and gravy into an unappealing, brown goo. "Sometimes I do bad things."

Irene stroked her silky curls. "That's temptation, sweetheart. The devil will tempt you all your life. But you will always return to the Lord's light." *The harlots are the devil.*

"Really?"

"Cross my heart." She drew her finger across her chest.

"Good." Sandra grinned at Annabelle across the table. "Now you can't call me evil anymore."

Annabelle scowled at her but said nothing.

I should scold her for name-calling. Irene studied Annabelle's face. *No, now is not the right time.* "You've been awfully quiet this evening. Are you all right?"

"Yes, I am fine." She tilted her head, eyed the ceiling or beyond. "Mother, do you think some people are born extra good?"

"Of course I do. Your father was born extra good." *Too good a man to fall to temptation.*

"I know Father and the Fellowship Councilors are born extra good. I mean, could a girl like *me* be born extra good?"

Irene reached across the table and placed her cool hand on Annabelle's warm one. "You are an extra special girl, Annabelle. A miracle girl who was born *extra* good."

Annabelle forked a bite of meatloaf. "This is the very best meatloaf on the planet."

The abrupt change in topic startled Irene. But Annabelle was like that. Wise and curious beyond her years one minute and child-like the next. *Just like a preteen girl. Yes, I think we must have underestimated her age.*

"Mommy?"

"Yes, Sandra?"

"When will Daddy come home?"

"I don't know, darling. He's the Prophet now, and that is a very big job."

Sandra sighed. "Does he have to cure everybody?"

"If God wills it," Annabelle said.

"Even the pretty ladies?"

The catch in Irene's throat nearly made her choke on her mashed potatoes. She swallowed, took a hasty drink of sweet tea, and cleared her throat. "What makes you ask that, Sandra?"

"Daddy seemed so sad."

"When was this?"

"When he was in his office."

In the Fellowship Center? When—a few days ago—weeks ago? Irene let it pass. "What made him sad?"

"A pretty lady talked to him, then left. She made him so sad."

Irene ignored the painful twist of her heart. "She did?"

"Daddy said she needed his help, but he didn't know if he had the strength to help her. Does curing people hurt Daddy?"

Irene could barely breathe. *Was this woman one? A harlot?*

"It doesn't, does it, Mother?"

Annabelle's pleading tone brought Irene back to the here and now. "No, darling. It doesn't hurt Daddy at all."

"But he was sad."

"I'm sure he was." Irene struggled to stay focused on her daughters. "He, um, cares a lot—about *all* Fellowship members. And sometimes people who need help won't let him help." At that moment, it all came clear. *He'd tried to help that woman understand that a good Fellowship member wouldn't behave like a harlot.* Irene could breathe again. *If she won't accept guidance from Felix, perhaps she will from another woman. A woman like me.* "Um, girls, it's my job to help Daddy when he's sad." She leaned forward and in a conspiratorial whisper said, "If you see him being sad, you come tell me. And I'll help him not be sad."

"Okay." Annabelle said.

Sandra crossed her heart. "I will."

"One more thing," Irene said. "Don't let Daddy know that we're helping him. He'll, um, he'll pretend that he's okay, and we won't know when he's sad. Keep it extra secret, and you'll earn an extra dollar every month."

Two pairs of eyes lit up. The girls exchanged glances.

She gave her daughters a this-will-be-fun smile. "It'll be our secret." The pain in Irene's heart lifted. It was a sign.

Chapter Six

B lack thunderclouds and sheets of rain blanked out the world beyond *Lady Angelfish*, then a burst of lightning cracked. The world went white. In a blink, the light went out, and the void returned. With a practiced two-and-a-half step timed with the rock and sway of the boat, Beryl stayed upright and followed Miranda out onto the deck.

"You will get yourself captured or killed," Beryl shouted over the torrent of rain drumming on the deck.

"I can't leave him out there." Miranda's shout cut through the wind that whistled around *Lady's* cabin.

A gust blew the rain slicker's hood off Beryl's head. She was drenched in seconds. The wind blew and glued a wisp of hair to her face. "I'll go. No sense in risking more lives than necessary."

"He's my brother."

Beryl pressed her lips together. "He hasn't signaled. Maybe he's late."

"Or injured, in danger, or captured. Or—his batteries died while waiting for us."

It's not like her to insist on going without a signal— "Maybe he's hunkered down until the storm passes."

Miranda looked up from the swim platform to Beryl. "I'm going. You can come or not."

Beryl didn't want to be suspicious, but Miranda was keeping

something from her. Still—*I left my daughter once. I won't leave you, Miranda. You want your brother? We'll get your brother—or die trying.* She gripped the rain-slicked safety rails and descended the three steps to the swim platform. Waves broke over the platform. Flooded her already wet deck shoes.

Miranda untethered the dinghy from the edge of *Lady*. The little boat swung in the wind, held only by the crane. She punched the crane's control and lowered the dinghy into the choppy water.

Beryl grabbed the closest edge, the boat's gunwale, pulled it close to the platform.

Miranda climbed in and struggled against the wind to detach the boat from the crane's lifting harness.

"It'd be safer to swim or walk across." Beryl side-eyed the shore less than fifteen feet away. Unable to see what waited there. "Or anchor closer—"

"I will not risk taking *Lady* closer to an unknown shore. You and I could swim the Missouri's strong current. David could too. But what about his refugee? What if there's more than one? What if there are children?"

Beryl screwed her mouth to the side, acknowledged Miranda's point.

Miranda released the lifting harness, then grabbed the swim platform cleat, and held the dinghy in place.

Beryl climbed aboard.

The wind buffeted them, and the little boat bounced unnaturally. Thunder rumbled long and loud. And the rain drilled them and sizzled on the gurgling river water. Beryl's smile faded, and she tightened her grip on the gunwales to a stranglehold.

Miranda didn't give her a second glance and guided the boat toward shore. The trolling motor fought the chop and worked its way across the water.

Beryl ignored the bile that burned her throat. She had never grown to love life on the boat, not the way Miranda did. But she tolerated it for Miranda.

Three feet from shore, Beryl took her pistol out of her holster. Held it shoulder high. Hopped into knee-deep water. Gasped. Chill bumps raced along her skin. Determined, she sucked in air and pulled the dinghy behind her. In three strides, the waves lapped her ankles. She gave the boat a mighty tug and beached it. Hand up to

Miranda for "stay put." Pistol safety off, trigger finger alongside the trigger guard, she stepped further inland—barrel first.

The low visibility set her teeth on edge. Shadows of scraggly vegetation and trees swayed in the wind. No way to tell if a shadow was a shooter or Miranda's brother and his refugee. Only point in her favor, they couldn't see any better than she could.

None of the shadows shot back. She waved Miranda forward.

Miranda, no drier than Beryl, halted an arm's length to the left. Held her flashlight out and flashed the signal. No flash of light answered. No sounds above the hiss of rain and wind. Miranda turned thirty degrees, flashed the light again.

Swish. Beryl whirled toward the sound. A shadow figure hurtled toward them. She raised her pistol. Hesitated.

The man barreled into them, knocked them to the soggy ground.

She grappled with him, rolled him over. Sat astride him, her knees on his arms. Pistol barrel pressed to the skin under his chin.

The beam of Miranda's flashlight lit his face. "David."

Damn. "I could have shot you." *Should have.*

Why the hell didn't I shoot him? Because I recognized him? But I didn't. A lifetime ago, she would have shot him. A lifetime ago, it didn't matter if she killed the wrong person. A lifetime ago, she hadn't killed her own daughter.

I cannot hesitate ever again. Not if I want to stay alive—want Miranda to stay alive.

"Turn that off," David said in a harsh whisper. "Now."

Miranda killed the light.

"They followed us," he whispered.

"Here?" Miranda asked.

"Maybe."

"Who?" Chilly mud oozed in Beryl's sleeves, pant legs, and shoes.

"Second Sphere."

"Where?" Beryl scanned the area. A filmy, misty gray curtain covered the shoreline and woods. No matter how many times she blinked, no matter how hard she stared, she couldn't see more.

"I don't know," David whispered above the constant patter of the rain. "We lost them in Terre Haute. They found us again near Bowling Green. I think we lost them, but I don't know, so I didn't signal—why'd you come ashore?"

"You think I'd leave you in danger?"

"Shut up, both of you." Beryl strained to hear or see something, anything. The harsh drone of rain made a wall of sound. Bushes and trees thrashed in a world of gray and black and kept their secrets.

"When did you last see your tail?"

"Two hours before we got here. Before the rain started."

"Maybe they got lost. Or they left, went somewhere dry."

"Maybe we test out your theory." Beryl placed one foot on the ground, the other knee still buried in the mud at David's side.

"Do you want to get shot?" he asked incredulously.

No shot came.

She stood. No shot. No movement.

Took soft, careful steps to the tree line. Twenty feet west. Then returned.

"We're safe for now," she said. "But we'd best get on the damn boat and get out of here."

"Where's your refugee?" Miranda asked.

"Hiding. I'll get her."

Beryl grabbed his arm. "Can you whistle?"

He faced her. "Yeah."

"When you return, use a call and response." She whistled softly. Two high notes and one low.

David echoed her.

"No response—run."

"Right." He started inland.

"And David?"

He turned to her.

"Use it or die. I will shoot to kill."

He saluted and disappeared into a clump of bushes.

The rain washed away the squish of his footsteps, and the wind stirred the bushes. Impossible to track his movements. Or anyone else's. Her shoulders twitched. She swiveled, swept the shadows with her pistols again.

Miranda rose to her knees.

"Stay down." Beryl returned her focus to the bushes.

"But—"

"It's my job to protect you. Do as I say."

"Not your job anymore." Miranda stood.

If it isn't, what am I doing here? A flush warmed Beryl. She bit back heated words. And wondered why she did. *I can't be so grateful Miranda saved me from drowning, helped me heal—that I turn into—wait. Has she been* trying *to make me softer?* The squish of footsteps sounded. *David and his refugee?* She whirled that direction, barrel aimed, trigger finger ready.

A whistle. Two high notes and one low.

Beryl turned her gun and attention to protect David and his refugee. She whistled the response.

He came forward. A small person covered in an oversized slicker followed him. "Hurry," he said. "It's imperative she gets to Monkshood as soon as possible."

The name set off a dull ache in Beryl's middle. "I'll stand watch. You three get in the boat." She hadn't seen her husband, leader of SABR, in more than a year. Far less time than when she'd been a prisoner in Redemption, but somehow now she could only recall his voice, not his face.

"Beryl." Miranda's soft voice cut through the fog.

Beryl hurried to the boat and, with Miranda's help, shoved it into the water.

She glared at the shadows on shore, each of them lumps of menace. The irrational part of Beryl wanted to shoot every lump. Blamed her milquetoast response on two years of honoring Miranda's nonviolence policy.

The current, the wind, and the waves made the trip back to *Lady* rougher and longer. Throat tight, anger and determination burned instead of bile. Beryl glowered through the rain. David brought trouble with him. One suspicious move and, refugee or brother, she'd shoot first.

Miranda signaled Wanda with the flashlight, then maneuvered the little boat to the swim platform.

Beryl hopped out first. Tied the little boat's bow rope to the platform. Stood guard while David and the refugee boarded *Lady.*

Chapter Seven

Miranda slid open the salon door. A powerful gust drove biting rain in with her.

Wanda leaped off the adjacent captain's chair at the lower helm.

"Whoa! Shut the door, Captain!" Beryl shouted from her green velvet chair near the electric heater.

"Sorry." *Why isn't everyone in their berths?* Miranda slid the door closed and latched it. She wanted to search the salon without having to explain her suspicions.

Wanda shivered and swiped rainwater off her arms. Grabbed the yellow slicker that hung on the back of the chair. "Guess it's my turn."

"Stay put. No sense in standing out in that mess. Can't see beyond the bow light."

"I don't mind, Captain."

"No need. I dropped anchor. Wait until the storm dies down."

David and Leslie, a slight strawberry blonde girl, sat on the built-in leather bench that wrapped around the salon's gleaming Brazilian rosewood table. He scooted around the table, stood, and wrapped Miranda in a desperate hug.

She laughed. "Stop. Let me take off my rain slicker. I'm dripping wet."

"I don't care," David mumbled into her shoulder.

She hugged him tighter. The awkward silence in the salon penetrated her awareness. She stepped back and peered up at him. He had cleaned up and combed his ginger-colored hair. His borrowed jeans and blue plaid shirt deepened the blue of his gray-blue eyes. They weren't the clothes the son of the First Apostle would wear, but the clothes of refugees and rebels. Freshly shaved, his once pleasantly filled-out face had new lines and edges since she'd last seen him.

"It's good to see you." Her voice shook a little.

"I'm glad to see you too." His once-youthful voice, face, and eyes were heavy with the price of this rebellion. The Fellowship, the violence—its shadow—took a heavy toll on everyone. Now it lived in her little brother's eyes.

Her throat tightened, and a soul-deep wish for peace shot through her.

Leslie watched them from behind her bowl of stew. She also had an intense expression and haunted eyes. Hers were pale blue. She brushed a stray wisp of her strawberry blonde hair back and tucked it into her loose ponytail. "Thank you for rescuing us, Miss Silverthorn." Her accent was Virginian, maybe West Virginian.

The way the ill-fitting, green gingham dress she'd borrowed from the refugee locker hung off her shoulders made her look even smaller, younger. She could pass for a teenager. But tension radiated from her.

Miranda was familiar with that kind of tension. Violence made everyone guarded. Especially refugees. No one was safe until they got to international waters. Even there, no refugee ever completely shed their wariness.

"Don't stand there dripping," Beryl said. "Get dry and grab a bowl of stew for yourself."

Now Miranda recognized the aroma that made her stomach grumble, Wanda's New Brunswick stew. She was exhausted, too exhausted to even think of lifting a spoon.

"I warmed some leftovers," Wanda explained. "They hadn't eaten all day."

"So you arranged this slumber party?" Miranda said.

"No, ma'am. I just warmed up the stew for your guests."

Miranda gave Wanda a startled look. *Is she acting the servant?*

Wanda didn't meet Miranda's look but stared at her hands resting on her knees.

She is, and there's only one reason she'd do that. One of their "guests" had said something. Had put Wanda "in her place." Her *servant* place. Miranda took a deep breath, ready to tell her "guests" how rude they were, but Wanda made a tiny gesture with her hands. Waved her off.

Miranda set her jaw. *I can tell my passengers off, my* brother *off, if I want to.*

Wanda folded her hands together. A sign she didn't want a scene.

Miranda forced herself to relax. "I'll go stow my slicker," she said and went down the central passageway, to the lockers beyond the galley. The berths for the crew and refugees were forward. *I could search the berths while they're in the salon.*

A long roll of thunder sent vibrations through the boat. The wind howled. And the deck pitched to port. Miranda adjusted her stance automatically. *No, David or Beryl would come looking for me.* She hung her slicker in the locker, then went to the galley stove.

A steaming kettle sat on the back burner. *Bless you, Wanda. I'll find a way to let them know you that you are much more than a servant here.*

She let a tea bag steep until the water reached a deep brown color and an earthy aroma wafted from the mug. The warmth of the mug thawed her frozen fingers.

When she returned to the salon, rain and wind still lashed at the windows.

David and Leslie barely looked up from their nearly empty bowls of stew. Spoons clanked and scraped the sides of the bowls in accompaniment to the rain battering the windows.

Another gust rocked the boat. David and Leslie grabbed their bowls. No stew ended up on the floor.

Miranda pulled out the bench opposite Leslie and her brother and sat. "We're headed northwest, as you requested. Where are we going and why?"

The boat creaked and rocked in the storm.

"Leslie and I must meet Monkshood at a farmhouse outside a river town called Waverly at ten tomorrow night."

Miranda shot a glance at Beryl, who didn't react to her

husband's code name. *Okay.* For David's and Leslie's benefit, Miranda deliberately faced Wanda. "Can we make that?"

"I checked the charts," Wanda said. "It's about mile marker two-nine-three. A car would get them there faster."

Leslie glanced at Wanda, then back at Miranda. "She can read charts? Calculate distances?"

"Of course. Wanda is my chief engineer. She's very good at her job. And she is right. It would be faster by car." *But David knows that.* Miranda cocked her head and studied David. "Why didn't you take a car?"

"I had to see you, talk to you. I could have sent a message—"

"Why didn't you?" Beryl's smile softened her question.

Lightning flashed, and the crash of thunder overrode speech.

David pushed his over-long bangs away from his forehead. "I know how headstrong my sister is. A message from someone she doesn't know would've bounced off her hard head." He scooped another bite of stew into his mouth, chewed, and swallowed. "A message delivered personally from her little brother might get through." His sidelong glance at Miranda radiated affection.

She gave him a wry, you're-not-wrong grin.

"Besides, we really needed the help. Between roadblocks and Second Sphere agents on the ground, we wouldn't have made it."

Beryl, arms crossed over her chest, gave him the evil eye. "What were you thinking? Asking for us? Risking exposing us and the whole Safe Harbor system?"

"Look, I didn't signal for a pickup. I thought you'd wait until after the storm—until I could be certain they didn't follow us here. She—" He tilted his head toward Miranda. "Didn't wait." He glanced at the rain-sheeted windows. "Guess that's a good thing. This storm isn't going away as quickly as I'd hoped. And I've got to get Leslie upriver—" His spoon scraped across the sides and bottom of the bowl. He took a last bite of stew. Pushed the bowl away and locked eyes with Miranda. "Can we talk alone?"

Miranda glared over the rim of her teacup in case he was going to spout some racist crap. "David, I keep no secrets on my ship. I trust my *entire* crew with my life."

"It's not that I don't trust you all." He included everyone with a glance. "It's just that one slip and—"

"And who do you think we would slip that information to?" Wanda sounded more like herself.

He grimaced. "Sorry. Guess I've spent a few too many months in dangerous company."

Miranda covered her heartache with another sip of hot tea.

"Can you get us there or not?"

On the open ocean, Lady *could do that easily.*

Lightning strobed. The boat rocked back and forth as if to say, "I'm ready, let's go."

Fighting the Missouri's current filled with what's bound to be lots of rain-driven debris? Miranda questioned Wanda with a raised eyebrow.

"Against current and with the condition of this river, we have a high risk of fouled propellers or hull damage." Wanda's expression reflected her disapproval.

Miranda set her cup on the table, looked at Beryl. "Do we have enough gas to make it there?" With *Lady's* extra gas tank, she could run full speed for four days. But their last gas stop had been two days ago.

"Depends on the current, the weather, and whether *Lady* hiccoughs."

"Hiccoughs?" David asked.

"Lots of things can and do go wrong with a boat every day," Beryl said. "Especially on the river. Engines overheat. Any part you name can and will break at the most inopportune time."

"I've always thought of boats as sturdy workhorses. Didn't know they were so fragile."

A blast of rain-filled wind rattled the starboard windows. The boat rocked.

Miranda's mug slid across the table. She caught it. Waited until the wind died down, asked Beryl, "Is there a safe marina en route where we can stop for gas?"

"We'd have to stop at Tucker's Landing." She fixed Leslie and David with her stare. "They're old friends, but smack dab in no-man's-land. We'll have to put on the Widow Wilkins and her female crew show." At Leslie's and David's blank stares, she added, "Fake Fellowship personas."

"Will getting gas take long?" Leslie startled Miranda.

"If we're the only or first boat needing fuel—about twenty minutes."

David rubbed his freshly shaved chin. "I thought you had a national network of marinas and things that boaters need."

Miranda shrugged. "The Missouri River isn't on our usual run."

He drew back. "No matter how I try to protect you, I end up bringing more danger."

She gave him an are-you-serious look. "You don't have to protect me, little brother. I've been running Safe Harbor for two years. I can take care of myself."

"When the Angels of Death hunt you, you can't be careful enough."

"What?" Miranda asked, stunned. *If any Azrael had survived the explosion, we'd have known. Besides, they aged so quickly, even if some had survived, they would all be dead by now.* She glanced at Beryl, whose skepticism was clear.

"You knew that they'd target you," David said. "You almost destroyed the Fellowship."

"But you're saying the *Azrael* are hunting us."

He nodded vigorously. "Yes, they are—ask Leslie."

Her spoon clinked in her empty bowl. She pushed it aside. "I overheard some Fellowship bigwigs talking."

"*You*—overhead?" Miranda couldn't keep the disbelief from her voice.

Leslie folded her arms across her chest. "Yes I did."

Miranda pierced Leslie with a look. "How?"

"I worked for a scientist working on a top-secret Fellowship project."

Miranda leaned forward, elbows on the table, hands folded together. "Let me get this straight—a Fellowship scientist working on a secret project allowed a rebel to work with him? And you—what—became his confidant?"

"I didn't tell them I was a rebel." Her tone reflected how dumb that would be.

"Who did they think you were?" Beryl asked.

"Their nanny."

"Hired help hear lots of things," Wanda said. "We're invisible." She gathered the dirty dishes and disappeared into the galley.

Water gurgled in the galley. Dishes clattered in the metal sink. She'd become a refugee when her employer had ratted her out.

Beryl brushed the green velvet-arm of the chair, studied the patterns her fingers made. "And you heard them talk about the long-dead Azrael?"

"Not dead ones." Leslie rolled her eyes in that long-suffering-teenager way. "I know what I heard."

"We destroyed the Azrael," Beryl said in a flat tone.

Miranda shot her aunt a concerned look.

"Tell them how you got there and why," David said.

Wanda came out of the galley, sat at the lower helm again.

Leslie hesitated, her lips pressed tight. After a long moment, she drew in a deep breath. "My parents and oldest brother were Taken. Ian and I hid with our younger brothers in the Blue Ridge Mountains. I—got hurt—and while Ian tried to get a doctor, the Cleaners found us. My younger brothers and I were their prisoners." She swallowed more than once. "The rebels saved us and took us to Miss Gert—"

"Gert?" Beryl sat straighter. "Gert Howerton?"

"Yes. Did you know her?"

A distant look came over Beryl. "A lifetime ago."

Leslie waited.

The boat rocked and creaked and groaned.

Beryl said nothing more.

"Anyway," Leslie continued, "after that, the rebels asked us to help them from time to time. That's when I met you." She nodded at Miranda.

Miranda blinked and searched her memory. She offered Leslie an apologetic smile. "I'm sorry, I don't remember."

"That's okay. You were new, and Nick whisked you out of there pretty quick."

Ghosts flitted through Miranda's mind's eye. Manny… Hector… Both two years dead. A soul-heavy ache sank from her throat to the pit of her being. She forced herself to remember when Hector had introduced her to Nick. "Lynchburg. The church?"

"Yeah."

Wanda gave a soft, amused *ha*. "So whisking someone off into this life is something all rebels do."

Miranda gave Wanda a wry grin and head tilt of agreement.

"You were saying…" prompted Beryl.

Leslie crossed her arms over her chest. "Ian and I were told we were too young to fight the Angels of Death. We figured the adults could go after the Azrael, we wanted the *murderers* who sent the Azrael to our home." Her voice shook. She took two ragged breaths, then continued.

"We worked our way across to Pennsylvania. We'd take any available job until we gained a reputation for being hard workers and could get a job with a city official or a Fellowship deacon. One official would recommend us to one in the next town."

"No one questioned why you were moving on?" Beryl shifted her weight. The armchair squeaked.

Miranda glanced outside. Couldn't see anything beyond the glow of the stern light. Though the boat didn't pitch as much as before. And instead of sheets of water, the pit-a-pat of rain on the windows let droplets run down the glass. *The storm will be over soon.*

"We told them we were working our way north to join our older brother Harry."

"Your older brother? The one that was Taken?" *That had to have been difficult.* Miranda pressed her lips tight.

Leslie nodded.

"No one asked to get references from your hometown?" Beryl wasn't buying her story.

"When they did, we'd explain that we didn't work jobs before our parents died in a car accident. That Harry Junior took the job in Maine because there weren't jobs in our home town. And Harry didn't make enough money to pay for bus tickets for both of us to Maine. They'd feel sorry for us and offer us a job."

She stared out the window with such intensity, Miranda glanced out again. The view hadn't changed.

"We got a lead that took us to back west, to Springfield, Missouri. Ian worked at a dime store near the biggest Fellowship church. I applied for a position as a nanny and got the job."

There's more to that story than she's sharing. "How long did you work that job?"

"Six months."

"And while you worked there you overhead something and

assumed it was about Azrael who'd survived our attack?" Miranda couldn't stop glancing at Beryl, who had an unnerving half-smile on her face.

"I woke in the middle of the night. I heard voices coming from the heating vent. So I got down on the floor and put my ear up to the vent.

"The husband and wife were arguing about—something. The husband said they had to get rid of it. It was classified."

Wanda gave her a side-eye. "Classified—like documents?"

Leslie tensed, raised her shoulders and tightened her arms against her chest. After a moment, she released a big breath and relaxed a little. "Their voices weren't clear. Then the husband said, "we don't want the Angels of Death after you and me the way they hunt those two women.""

Leslie locked eyes with Miranda. "That's got to be you and her." She lifted her chin, pointed it at Beryl.

"So your news is that the Fellowship is hunting us, planning to kill us?" Miranda took a sip of her now-lukewarm, almost bitter tea. She couldn't believe they'd risk their lives for old news.

"They said the Azrael hunt you."

"The Fellowship has wanted me and Beryl dead for more than two years." She raised a quizzical eyebrow at David. "You think there's some new urgency?"

He fixed her with a disbelieving stare. "The Azrael make it urgent, don't you think?"

"David, this makes no sense. Why now and not before?"

"Maybe it took time to grow new Azrael."

Miranda shook her head. His words stirred a flurry of old fears, anger, and regrets that clouded her already fatigue-fuzzed thoughts. How could she believe more Azrael were being created?

"No maybe about it." Beryl leaned back into the armchair, made it screech. "We destroyed the lab, the records, and the whole damn island. There are no more Azrael."

"And what else do you think a Fellowship bigwig means when he says 'Angels of Death'?"

Beryl gave a who-knows shrug.

"You can stop worrying," Miranda said. "A couple of hours before we got to the rendezvous point, the U.S. Coast Guard stopped us for an inspection. If the SS officer on that team had recognized us, he would have arrested or killed us."

"He didn't have to arrest you. All he has to do is report your location to the Az—"

Beryl snorted. "I'm pretty sure reports don't reach hell."

David's face reddened. He rose to his feet. "You aren't taking this seriously?"

Miranda made calming, sit-down motions with her hands. "We are listening. But what you're saying is hard to believe."

"Your lives are in danger—"

"Our lives are always in danger." Beryl gave him a deadly sweet smile.

Miranda's head pounded. She rubbed the back of her neck. Didn't know what to believe. *Can't think. I need some sleep.* "Our lives have been in danger for the past two years. We take precautions. That's the reason we hired Wanda. The reason we have multiple identities. The reason someone is always on duty."

Wanda stood. "Guess that's the captain's way of reminding me that the storm's dying. I should get out on deck." She picked up the yellow rain slicker hung on the back of the captain's chair and shrugged it on. "See y'all in the morning." She slid open the door to the walkway. Cool, wet air roared in, but no rain. The dual latch clicked and shut off the wind.

"You're an easy-to-find target on this boat," David said.

"So you came here?"

"Yes, I—"

Miranda's mouth twitched into a smirk.

"Dang it, Miranda. Quit messing with me."

She stretched out her legs. "What would you have me do, David?"

"Come with me. Ethan will have a place for you to stay."

"You want me to live like Ethan? Afraid, never daring to stay in one place for long?"

"Is it that different from what you do now? This rebellion can't last forever. I want you to survive long enough to see peace."

"From your mouth to God's ear, let there be peace," Miranda said. She used to pray for peace. She didn't pray anymore. "*Serenity* is my home. And as long as there is a rebellion, my place is here. Helping everyone I can."

"You've helped hundreds, maybe thousands. You've earned a rest. At least until they find the last of the Azrael."

Beryl planted her elbows on the arms of the chair, knotted her hands together, and propped her chin on her hands. "Why are you so certain the Azrael are still out there?" She spoke in a low, almost pitying tone.

David's face reddened again. "Why are you so certain they aren't?"

Beryl wore a million-mile stare. "If you'd seen the island blasted to smithereens—almost died in that blast—you wouldn't have any doubts either."

Miranda motioned for both of them to stop. "It's been an exhausting day—for all of us. And tomorrow's going to be a challenge. Let's get some sleep while we can. We'll talk more tomorrow."

David looked surprised. "You're still going to take us to Waverly?"

"Of course," Miranda answered. "Transportation of refugees is what we do."

"What if *you* are a refugee?"

"We're all refugees," Beryl answered for her. "But not from the Azrael. They are dead. Wiped out. Gone—sent to the depths of hell."

Miranda stepped between them, glared a stop-now warning at each of them. "Enough. David, we have a job to do. If you can't accept that, then we can drop you off at the next marina."

He faced her, shock written on his face. "Then I guess we'll be getting off at the next marina."

His choice cut deep. She hoped it didn't show. "Get some sleep. See how you feel in the morning."

He opened his mouth. Studied his feet. When he met her eyes again, he had a mask-like face. "Where do you want me to sleep?"

"Here." Beryl reached under the table, lowered it to bench height, and clicked latches to secure it. "The bench cushions fold out to make a mattress. Pillow and blankets are in the locker under the seat. You—" She nodded at Leslie. "Come with me." She went up the passageway to the forward crew's quarters.

Leslie shot David a sad smile. "Goodnight."

"I—" David said, but Beryl shut the door behind them. He sighed. "Thank her for coming for us—for everything, would you?"

"I'll tell her." Miranda wanted to say, "Come south with us. Get some sun. Some rest." Instead, she said, "Get as much sleep as you can. Tomorrow's ride will be rough. The Missouri is full of snags normally, and after this storm it's bound to be worse. We'll launch at dawn."

Chapter Eight

After Irene read the girls a short Bible story and tucked them in with goodnight kisses, she stopped in her bedroom on her way downstairs. Took the letters and the list of harlots out of her unmentionable drawer.

At the telephone table, she cross-referenced names and return addresses and found a phone number for each name. Grabbed the receiver. Finger poised above the dial, she hesitated.

She wanted to scold and shame them, but the Prophet's Lady should rise above sinners. A letter would be more discreet.

After a quick visit to Felix's office, she returned to the table.

On a blank piece of stationery, she wrote:

———

DEAR MISS OBERLY,

Received your letter of October 12, 1964, and the Spirit moved us to respond. Understanding that even the most devoted Christian sometimes succumbs to temptation, we forgive you…

———

FINISHED WRITING, she stared at the two stacks of envelopes. Picked up the pink envelope stack and marched into Felix's office. Placed them on top of the neat pile of finished correspondence. Hurried back to the kitchen before she could change her mind.

Clutching the six letters she'd written, Irene strode down the sidewalk. The crisp night air swished dry leaves around her feet. Streetlights provided yellow pools of light all the way to the mail collection box on the corner.

She yanked the mailbox's letter door open. It squealed. A quick glance around confirmed no one watched, and she dropped the envelopes inside, let the door bang shut. Overhead, the clouds parted and a crescent moon smiled down on her. Warmth spread from her chest to her fingertips. She thanked the Lord for the sign and returned home.

Seated in the rose chintz chair in the living room again, she darned one of Sandra's dark-blue knee-high socks. She didn't care if she shouldn't do the mending. Or the correspondence. Being a supportive helpmate to... *Oh dear. What if a harlot tells Felix about receiving the letter?*

For the next hour, she stewed over whether she should tell him.

———

A QUIET CREAK floated up the stairs. *The front door. Felix.* Irene's fingers fumbled. The sewing needle pierced the waistline of Annabelle's pink dress and Irene's index finger. "Ow." She jerked her left hand out from beneath the skirt and peered at the bead of blood on her injured finger. One-handed, she freed her handkerchief from her pocket and staunched the blood.

Footsteps crossed the tile foyer floor downstairs, paused at the coat closet, then came up the staircase.

Bleeding stopped, she jammed her handkerchief into her pocket.

Felix entered the living room. His suit coat hung open, the knot of his blue tie undone, and the top collar button of his white shirt unbuttoned. "Hello, darling," He came to her chair, bent and swept a dry kiss across her forehead. "I'm sorry I'm so late tonight. Unfortunately, there was a terrorist attack." He sank onto the leaf-green sofa, draped his arms over the back on each side.

Her stomach twisted. She dropped her sewing onto the coffee table, faced him. "Where?"

"A power station on the west side. I went to the site to offer prayers."

I shouldn't have doubted him. "How many dead and injured?"

He snorted. "None. It was a false report."

The doubt and knots inside Irene returned. *Who would give the Prophet incorrect information? Why? Or—is this an—untruth?* "Then what kept you so long?"

"I went back to the church to finish up a couple of things. A young woman suffering with severe anxiety over the terrorist attacks came to me. She was in so much pain I couldn't leave until I'd done all I could."

A shiver stirred in her belly. *A young woman?* Outside, she remained calm. "I'm sure you did your best, dear."

He sighed. "I tried." Rubbed his face. "All I want is to crawl into bed and sleep, but I have a few more things I must do tonight."

A difficult discussion was in their future, but she wasn't up for it tonight. "Do you need something to eat?"

His weary smile didn't reach his eyes. "No, thanks. George got some carryout sandwiches for us." George was his secretary. Her real name was Georgia.

Lots of practice kept her expression unchanged. "A little chamomile tea is what you need. Wait here."

Returning to the living room with a cup of steaming hot tea laced with sugar, she discovered Felix had left the room. The door to his office stood open, and the lights were on. She lifted her chin and took his tea to him.

Seated at his desk, Felix looked up from the messy stack of indecent letters. The lines of his face etched deeper than a few minutes ago. "It was nice of you to do my correspondence for me." He tapped the pink perfumed envelope. "I'm sorry you had to find and read these."

"Do you get that many every day?" She needed to know.

"At least." He leaned back. His chair gave a faint groan. "Sometimes more."

Sparks flashed at the edges of her vision, and her chest burned. "Many from the same women?"

"I suppose so," he said. "I don't keep track, and I don't answer these."

"Oh?" Her tone had more fire than she'd intended.

He shot her a concerned look. "Of course I don't." Came to her and wrapped her in an embrace. "Our lives have changed a lot in the past year, but my love and faithfulness to you will never change."

His spicy scent and the warmth of his arms relaxed her. "I love you too," she murmured.

He beamed at her. "I depend on that. And here, let me show you what I think of these letters." He released her and returned to his desk, dropped the letters into the wire trashcan.

The weight of those letters slid off Irene's shoulders.

"Now." He strode back to her, wrapped an arm around her waist. "I'm exhausted. Let's go to bed."

"But your tea—the things you needed to get done—?"

"You finished my correspondence, thank you. The rest can wait."

She gave him a peck on the cheek. "You go on up. I'll rinse out this cup."

"Don't be long."

"I won't."

They parted at the foot of the stairs.

After tidying the kitchen, Irene went up to the living room level, noticed they'd left the light on in his office. She reached around the door to the light switch, and her gaze fell on the trashcan. Twisting her hands together, she glanced upstairs, then back at the trash. Crossed over to the wire basket. *It's not that I don't trust him...* Counted five letters. Dug around for the sixth letter, the pink one. It wasn't on the desk either. The sparks in her vision exploded white-hot.

Soft footsteps padded across the ceiling. *Felix may be the Prophet, but he's still human. A human tormented by evil temptresses. A human I love and will grow old with.* A human and a Prophet that she would protect.

She twisted her hands again. *I must trust that the Lord has set me on the correct path. But I need information.*

Her driver, Paul, could ask questions and make connections she couldn't. The burning in her chest eased. A sign that the Lord approved of her plan.

With the right information, she could determine her best course of action.

She flipped the light switch off.

Chapter Nine

The aroma of warm pancakes and syrup and the rumble of her stomach woke Miranda before her sleep shift had finished, and it had been shorter than usual. She'd gotten up after the salon had emptied. Searched it. Found nothing. If she was up now, she needed coffee. But the tiny galley already held two people. David stood at the stove flipping pancakes.

"Morning, Captain." Wanda offered her an earthy-brown ceramic mug. "Beryl's piloting. David's cooking. Mind if I go forward?"

Miranda took the mug. Lifted it and inhaled the fragrance of fresh coffee. "Go ahead." *Someone should get some extra sleep.* She sat at the lower helm, set her mug down. Watching the last of the fog roll off the river, she ran her hands under the helm. *Nothing.* She didn't understand it. *That Second Sphere agent had to have been here for a reason.*

"Peace offering," David said behind her.

She gulped back her startled shout, faced him. "You and I are not at war."

He stood, braced in the hatch to the galley against the motion of the boat. Held a plate with a lopsided tower of pancakes. "Still, I'm sorry. Guess my rebel-spy manners aren't guest manners."

Her smile broadened at the size of the stack. "That could feed an army."

"Not after I get my serving." His mouth twisted, rueful and hopeful at the same time.

"The crew of the *Lady*—of *Serenity*—doesn't hold to Fellowship standards of manners. Apology accepted."

He gave the salon an appreciative glance. "You've really turned this ship into a home."

Looking around the salon at the warm furnishing, all touches she'd given it, Miranda's throat thickened. Realized of all the SABR rebels in the country, she and her crew were the only ones with a sanctuary like this. "It *is* home. Always will be."

David raised the plate of pancakes. "Should I take some up to Beryl?"

"She's already had breakfast and will eat again in a couple of hours when I relieve her." Miranda peered down the passageway behind him. "Where's Leslie?"

"Coming," a lilting voice called. Typical landlubber, Leslie lurched down the passageway toward the galley. Her strawberry blonde ponytail bounced behind her. And somehow the borrowed gingham dress fit better today.

Soon, all three of them sat at the table and dug into breakfast.

When they'd had their fill, Miranda stacked the dirty dishes.

"I'll take care of those," Leslie said and took the dishes. Duct tape made an extra seam down the back of her dress.

"I need to say something." David said once Leslie had slid the galley hatch door closed. "Try not to get mad and just listen. Can you do that?"

Miranda folded her arms on the tabletop, leaned forward. "Say what you must, but I won't change my mind."

"Even if you don't believe that the Azrael are being grown again—think about what Leslie told us. There are Fellowship labs hidden in former mines hundreds of feet beneath the surface. That alone is cause for alarm. The Fellowship is up to something. If they're not growing an army of assassins, maybe they're making munitions, or a poisonous gas, or prisons for folk like us."

"And that's what you should focus on when you talk to Monkshood."

He tilted his head, studied her.

The thrum of *Lady's* engines and the slap of water on her hull filled the silence between them. Miranda scanned the salon casually, searching for anything that looked out of place.

"You still don't see that you and Beryl should take precautions?" His voice held disbelief and a tinge of anger.

She forced herself to quit searching. Focused on David. "They aren't doing that just for Beryl and me."

"No. They're doing it for you and your refugees."

Did he mean…? The idea of an underground Redemption made her ribs refuse to move for a breath. She swallowed. Wiped her sweaty palms on her culottes. "All right. You're right. Monkshood needs to know this. We'll make sure you and Leslie get to that meeting." She leaned forward. "But this doesn't mean that my mission has changed. It means Safe Harbor is more important than ever."

David set his mouth, then nodded. "Get us to Waverly. Maybe Monkshood will convince you that this means you have a new mission."

She almost laughed. *We'll see who out-stubborns who.*

Chapter Ten

Irene walked up the concrete steps to the front door of the brownstone. *No.* She forced herself to think—*home.* She'd finished her morning obligation: breakfast and a speech at the Ladies' Rotary Club. Now she had the rest of the day to herself.

She shrugged off her coat, hung it in the foyer closet. Her shoes clacked against the foyer's green and white tiles. She took in the patterned green wallpaper above the white wainscoting. *Nice, but plain. A splash of pink and yellow would help.*

A glance at the round entryway table centered beneath a candle-lantern-style chandelier revealed today's flowers were spidery white mums and dark green eucalyptus in a tall vase.

She wandered into the kitchen. *Spotless, as always. And I didn't have to work to make it that way.* A note on the Frigidaire listed tonight's supper menu and how to warm it. She stared at the note, and her chest emptied as if it had become a massive cavern of loss. *No. I will not cave like this.* She whirled and strode up to the living room.

Went to the sofa, sat. Then stood. Walked over to the fireplace, but didn't want to watch the fire alone. And the starburst clock on the wall said it was hours until the girls would be home.

She needed meaningful work. *The mail should be here. I'll work on Felix's correspondence and organize his files until the girls come home from school.*

At the door to Felix's study, she stopped, stunned. Her heart drummed a not-right, not-right tempo. Across the room, Felix's desk had an uncharacteristically clean, uncluttered desktop. *This isn't a holiday. There should be a dozen envelopes or more.* She checked his desk drawers. No letters there either. *Perhaps a breeze knocked them to the floor.* She peered under his desk. Something glinted on the dark oak floor.

She kneeled and groped under the desk. Grabbed the small and round and hard object. In her palm sat a small, perfectly round gold earring. She froze, barely able to comprehend what she held. *An earring?* She never wore jewelry other than her wedding ring. And the girls wore none. Ugly suspicions entered her thoughts. She huffed out one breath after another. But her rigid muscles wouldn't allow for a deeper breath. She squeezed her eyes shut, prayed that the Lord would remove her suspicions and give her a plausible explanation.

Felix never gave in to temptation before. *There is no reason to believe he's sinned.* Her knees ached. She struggled to stand on numb feet. *One of those harlots had to have been here, in his study. Shamelessly throwing herself at the Prophet. When? This morning? Why? Why would she come here?*

A twitchy edginess washed over Irene. *What if the harlot believes the lies about my parents? What if she means to ruin Felix? What if she planted that earring to cause a scandal?*

I must protect the Prophet. Protect Felix and the girls.

Her blood roared. Her legs carried her out of the study and up the stairs. Straight to the walnut waterfall dresser in her bedroom. She yanked open her drawer of unmentionables. Pushed aside her white panties and pulled out the list. Glared at the women's names and addresses. Should she send an agent to these women? *That would mean telling the agent. No, I must take care of this myself. In fact, I'll speak to the pink envelope lady now. Before dinner. Before Felix comes home.*

She trotted upstairs to the playroom. Scrawled a note for the nanny on the chalkboard. *On an errand. Back before dinner.*

Hurried out the door and to the car, powered by righteous anger. She drove herself out of her neighborhood, away from the Fellowship's high and mighty, to East 16th Street. The address belonged to a five-story brick apartment building. Behind the building, off an alley, the residents' parking held one vehicle: a familiar-looking teal and white sedan. A Bel Aire she'd seen in the Fellowship Center parking lot. *Does the strumpet work there? No—else she'd be there now.*

Irene parked and stepped outside. The chilly breeze peppered her with gooseflesh. She'd forgotten her coat. No matter. The long-sleeved, navy-blue wool dress she wore and her anger would keep her warm enough. She gripped the top button, pulled the Peter Pan collar close, and followed the sidewalk around to the front.

A cluster of brass mailboxes filled the wall to the left of the entry. Small, yellowed slips of paper labeled each box with a name. Bryant, the pink envelope woman, lived in apartment 2 C.

Irene hurried inside. Found the door marked 2 C. Rapped three times. Authoritative raps. Raps that demand an answer.

The door opened, revealed a middle-aged woman with dark hair and curves emphasized by a white button-down blouse and a black pencil skirt.

"Miss Bryant? Do you know who I am?"

Miss Bryant kept her composure. "Of course I do, Lady Earnshaw. To what do I owe this unexpected pleasure?"

"Unless you stop now, your sins will be unredeemable. If you never contact the Prophet personally again, we will forgive you."

Miss Bryant laughed. "I'll bet the Prophet doesn't know you're here." She made a shooing motion with her hands. "Go home. The Prophet is for the people of the Fellowship, and I am one of those people. Go home before you embarrass yourself even more." She pushed the door as if to close it.

Irene's vision narrowed. She stomped her foot in the door's path. Stopped it. *This conversation isn't over until I say it's over.*

The woman locked eyes with Irene.

What a stubborn and shameless sinner! "Harlot, you will honor the sanctity of my marriage to the Prophet, or you will feel the Lord's wrath in this lifetime." Irene whirled and strode down the hall. Her shoes clacked against the black and white tile.

Back inside her car, she didn't bother turning on the heat. Righteous anger kept her warm.

Chapter Eleven

Beryl muttered, "Damn you, David. We've evaded the Second Sphere for two years. If they find us because of you…" She steered *Lady* around trash in the muddy water, washed into the river by last night's storm. A green bottle bobbed past on the portside, and a newspaper page flapped in the rapid current to starboard. Avoiding trash meant she couldn't watch the shore as closely as she needed.

She glanced at the shore again, scanned for things that didn't belong. People that didn't belong. People hunting other people.

Thunk. The boat pitched hard to port. Adrenaline sent her pulse rocketing and heated her ears and neck. She lurched to counter the tilt. The boat righted itself and kept moving. *Damn it.* Already going slower than planned, Beryl lowered the boat's speed again.

"Know what we hit?" Miranda's voice came over the radio.

"Didn't see it," Beryl said.

"I'll check the bilge for a leak."

All we need right now is a leak to make us sitting ducks.

Wobble-wobble, thunk-thunk, wobble-thunk, screech.

Damn. She shut off the engines.

"That's the prop!" Wanda's bare feet slapped across the deck.

Beryl grabbed the pistol from the helm's hidden compartment and hurried after her.

Wanda paused on the swim platform, bent and peered into the muddy water. "Can't see a thing. I'm going in."

Before Beryl could say anything, Wanda jumped in feet first. Her yellow sleep shirt billowed around her.

Wanda bobbed to the surface. "Whoa! That's cold." She took a deep breath and disappeared beneath the surface again.

Three steps down to the swim platform, and Beryl peered into the muddy-brown water streaming past.

Wanda resurfaced. Gasped. Reached for the platform.

Beryl offered her a hand. "How bad?"

Wanda gripped the edge of the platform. "A rope has fouled both props."

"No leak," Miranda said, climbing out of the hatch to the engines and bilge. "What did you say about the prop?" She came to the transom, dripping bilge water from her clothes.

Wanda wiped water from her eyes and shivered. "Props caught a rope. Wound it tight. Give me a knife. I'll have to cut it free. Let me catch my breath, and I'll clear it."

Beryl pulled her combat knife from its sheath. Handed it to Wanda. "It sounded awful. How badly are the props damaged?"

"No damage I can see. When I've finished, we'll start her in idle, then increase speed five knots at a time. If she holds—we're good until I can get her to dry dock."

Beryl grimaced. Nothing she could do about it but wait. And she hated waiting.

A noise from the cabin drew her attention. David and the girl stood in the door to the salon. David frowned but said nothing. Leslie twisted a strand of hair that had escaped her ponytail.

"Don't worry." Miranda moved toward them, herded them back into the salon. "Just a snag. We'll be underway in a few minutes."

Even after they tested the motor and props, Beryl kept the boat at seven knots. Kept the boat in the travel lane. Cruised west-north-west up the Missouri.

The slap of water on rocks made a percussion counterpoint to the burble of the thankfully undamaged props.

Behind the trees to port, a car zoomed up a county road that twisted away from the river. Beryl kept her eyes on the water.

She spotted mile marker seventy-one. *Damn. Good thing David's meet isn't until nine o'clock tonight. It'll take us that long to get there.*

They would reach the staunch Fellowship town of Jefferson City about noon. Not the greatest timing. One more challenge this trip entailed.

Birds chirped. A soft, warm breeze caressed her skin and carried the fresh scent of damp earth. One could almost imagine the Fellowship didn't exist. *And that would get one killed.*

"Good morning," an unfamiliar female voice said.

Beryl spared a quick glance behind her.

The girl refugee, Leslie, stood on the main deck, set a bundle of wet clothes on the starboard locker.

Beryl focused on the water but couldn't ignore how her muscles tightened and her internal alarms pinged. Couldn't keep from asking, "Like to live dangerously?"

"Wanda said it was safe to come out now. It is, isn't it? I need to hang some wet things on the line."

"Be quick about it." Beryl guided the boat deeper into the travel channel. "We'll pass another Fellowship town in a few minutes."

"I'll hurry." The girl clambered up onto the locker.

The squeal of the retractable clothesline sounded. Soon, clothes snapped and popped in the breeze, and the girl's footsteps retreated into the salon.

That was okay with Beryl. She wasn't much of a conversationalist. In fact, she wasn't much of a people person. Ten years in Redemption's isolation cells had seen to that.

Flap-flap. She glanced over her shoulder. Two pairs of blue jeans, two shirts, and two jackets fluttered in the breeze. *His and hers?*

The boat pitched gently. She snapped her attention back to the water lane.

Honk-honk. Honk-honk-honk. A flock of geese flew over. Headed south.

We should be cruising south on the Mississippi. On our way to our winter hideaway, on Isla Mujeres's carefree beaches.

Instead, she piloted *Lady* against the current in the wrong direction. She couldn't fault Miranda for helping her brother. Beryl rubbed the back of her neck and maintained her course. The miles passed slow and steady.

A noisy groan came from behind her. She snorted, amused. Miranda's morning routine never varied.

"G'morning," Miranda called.

"Good morning."

"Ready for lunch?"

"Not hungry."

"You say that every day." Miranda's voice moved closer. "Any problems?"

"Other than trash and bumps and rock jetties in muddy water?" Beryl quirked her mouth. "Nah. No problems."

"Good." Miranda stepped into view on the starboard side. She wore what she called her captain's hat, a tan, red, and blue Chicago Cubs ball cap. A grateful refugee had gifted it to her. "Sure is a beautiful day."

"Yup."

"Eleven bells. Time for your break."

"Keep on visiting with your brother. I can wait until we get to Tucker's Landing."

"Nope. We agreed. Breaks every four hours keep us fresh, especially in waters with hazards."

Beryl bit back a retort about the earlier incident. Instead, she said, "The Missouri sure has those." She one-handed the wheel and stepped back, allowed Miranda to take over. "We're past mile marker one-two-zero. Tucker's is at one-seven-zero. The chart's pretty accurate on the winged jetties. But besides the floating trash, I've seen three sunken buoys—the Coast Guard forgot this section of the river."

"Got it," Miranda said. "Get below before David eats all of Wanda's hash."

She didn't say David was the last person she wanted to see. Didn't want to endure his arguments that the Azrael had somehow survived. She crossed to the hatch access for her bunk.

The clothes on the line made a sharp snap. She couldn't help but look. A familiar shape caught her eye. *Is that—a doll—a rag doll?* Her mouth went dry. *I must be seeing things—all that talk made me crazy.* Closed her eyes. Cleared her thoughts and—a second look showed only the jeans. But she couldn't turn away. She had to know.

Down three steps to the storage locker, then two to the main deck. The clothes on the line flapped again. Gave her another glimpse. *I'm not crazy.* A rag doll danced in the breeze. She froze. Her heart twisted.

Not just any rag doll. Anna's rag doll.

Same brown yarn hair. Same embroidered face. Dress made from an old sweater and a worn cotton apron.

It's a hallucination. Has to be. But something inside caught, not quite open and not quite shut. She couldn't move. Couldn't take a deep breath. Couldn't tear her eyes off that doll. Numbness spread from the center of her chest to her fingers and toes.

Old memories played grainy and halting: two-year-old Anna squealed and hugged the new doll. Seven-year-old Anna held the bloody puppy. Eleven-year-old Anna in the barn, blood-splattered and grinning amid the screams of the piglet.

Twelve carbon copies of Anna in a pool of blood.

Memories that shouldn't have escaped the deepest recesses of her mind looped over and over.

A warm hand touched her arm. "Beryl?"

The doll, hung by the shoulders of its dress on the clothesline, filled her sight. Her mind. Her heart. Her soul.

Far away, Wanda's familiar voice asked, "Are you okay?"

I killed my Anna—murdered all the Annas.

"Beryl?" Wanda's voice held an urgency.

The doll's legs moved in the breeze as if she marched. Each step trampled and paralyzed and numbed another of Beryl's muscles.

"What happened?" Miranda's voice sounded distant.

"I don't know. I found her like this."

The doll's black embroidered eyes indicted Beryl.

"Could it be sun stroke?"

"Doesn't seem that hot. Dehydration maybe?"

"I'm going to see if I can get her inside."

Gentle hands guided her. The doll vanished from Beryl's sight, but not before the judgment in those embroidered eyes dropped Beryl into a vast, lightless cave.

Chapter Twelve

Her driver opened the car door, and Irene stepped out onto the concrete apron in front of the seven-story, white-marble columned Fellowship Center on the banks of the Potomac. She'd been here a million times as a young girl and thought little of it, but now that Felix was the Prophet, the sight put a smile on her face every time.

She avoided the tourists who filled the doorway and streamed out onto the portico almost to the far corner of the building. Across the lobby, a glass balustrade protected the guard's desk and elevators behind it. She crossed to the glass gate in the balustrade and pushed the button that buzzed the guard's desk. He looked up, nodded, and the doors in front of her swung open.

She walked past the chattering tourists gathered around the larger-than-life painting of the Prophet Josiah's visitation by Gabriel and past the murmuring throngs gathered around the extra-large photograph of the Prophet Josiah and President John Nance Garner at the assassinated Franklin D. Roosevelt's bedside. Aromas of floor wax and multiple floral perfumes gave the place a sickly-sweet smell.

"Good morning, Lady Earnshaw," the guard greeted her. "I see that you're meeting with a Dr. Gallaway this morning." He turned the guest book toward her and offered her a pen.

"Good morning, Stephen. Yes, I am." She signed the book with a flourish and thanked the Lord that she didn't have to wear one of those gaudy ID badges on a lanyard. "Is he here?"

"He is. He's in classroom ten. Would you like an escort?"

Irene stifled a smug smile. "I know the way. Thank you." She strode past him and pushed the elevator call button.

Room ten was a tiered lecture theater. She entered at the top tier. Absent the perfumes, the air here smelled piney clean.

Standing beside a film projector halfway down the tiers, Dr. Gallaway greeted her with that charming crooked smile of his. He wore a snazzy brown and yellow plaid sports jacket over a yellow button-down shirt and brown slacks. Trotted up the aisle to shake her hand. "Thank you for coming."

"My pleasure. Our conversation the other night intrigued me. I can't wait to see your presentation."

His smile widened. "Then let's get right to it, shall we?" He led her down the aisle, past the projector.

Film snaked from a large, eight-millimeter reel on the top backside, through the machine, and to an empty reel on the bottom front.

She took a seat one row below the projector. The coolness of the wooden seat penetrated her lightweight yellow sweater and A-line dress.

Dr. Gallaway dimmed the lights, and the projected hummed.

The screen in front of the wall she faced erupted into a bright white. The film jumped a bit, and blue letters in an arc above a silhouette of a crawling baby appeared on the screen. It read "The Center for the Advancement of Inborn Character."

"Do you worry," the narrator began, "that the United States will fall behind the Federation of Germany because of unfit and diseased inborn characteristics?

"The Federation of Germany has improved the characteristics of its citizens by eighty-percent after winning the War for Europe. While here, in America, our Eugenics Records Department shows only a ten-percent shift toward a more eugenic population."

A colorful map of Western Europe appeared on the screen. The Federation of Germany stretched from the British Isles to the whole of Western Europe and most of Eastern Europe. In all the major cities, and most of the minor ones, splashes of blue meant there was complete genetic control in those locations.

"Do you worry," the narrator continued, "that controlling the breeding of the weak and sick is only addressing part of the problem?"

On the screen, the logo faded and revealed the words Virginia State Colony for the Unfit. The camera's focus moved off the sign to reveal three stately red-brick buildings with columned porticos. Entering the building, the camera revealed the lunatics inside. Dressed in dingy shifts, they screamed, and fought restraints, and foamed at the mouth.

Irene averted her gaze and twisted her wedding band around and around her finger. *Some things are just too horrible to watch.*

"Worry no longer. We, at the Center for the Advancement of Inborn Character, are dedicated to breeding stronger, smarter Americans." The male narrator spoke clearly, confidently. "We can and will build better Americans."

Irene gave the screen a side glance. A pristine laboratory came into view. It was an older laboratory with wooden tables and chairs and antique microscopes. She settled into a more comfortable viewing position.

The camera zoomed in on two gentlemen in white coats seated behind a counter. "In 1952, Doctors Aaron Locke and Louis Gallaway worked diligently to unlock the secret to better babies." Images of the two men raced around the lab while a time and date stamp ran forward. "In 1954, they successfully produced perfect newborn mice." The camera zoomed in for a close-up on a cage on the table in front of the grinning doctors. Inside the cage, a white mouse lay beside a dozen pink wriggling baby mice.

The scene cut to a delivery room. Bach's Unaccompanied Cello Suite No. 1 played in the background. The two doctors stood by, watching a young woman in labor. When the baby was born, the two doctors clapped one another on their backs. The narrator continued, "They developed a method of fertilization that produced girl children of perfect appearance and intelligence." Dr. Gallaway, the younger of the two doctors, took the baby in his arms and left the room.

The image faded into an aerial view of a building with a gaping hole at one end and rubble strewn all around it. A long shot revealed an entire island with every building in a similar shape.

Irene stifled her gasp of recognition and pressed her hand to her mouth. Felix, Sandra, her parents, and she had been on that island.

She heard the explosions but never saw the damage. Her face warmed and tingled. Her breath hitched in her throat.

"Rebels destroyed Dr. Locke's laboratory before he could perfect his technique."

Not just rebels. My sister. The surge of heat from deep inside chased the room's chill from Irene's skin. She clenched her jaw and slowed her breathing.

"Fortunately for the people of the United States," the narrator continued, "Dr. Gallaway survived that attack and redoubled his efforts to take Dr. Locke's methods of parthenogenesis to the next level."

The camera cut to a view of two babies in diapers sitting side by side on an exam table. One baby had an armband labeled A, the other armband read CIAC.

"Dr. Gallaway did better than succeed," the narrator said.

On the screen, a younger Dr. Gallaway examined both girls. Recorded the numbers on a standing chalkboard behind the exam table. The girl with CIAC band consistently had higher scores.

Irene suppressed a prideful smile. Both her girls had scores as high as the CIAC girl's scores. *Well, Sandra scored one percent lower, but that was statistically insignificant.*

The camera cutaway again, revealed two dozen ten-year-old girls standing at attention in a grassy area. The background music, "Onward Christian Soldiers," swelled.

An off-camera voice shouted, "One hundred jumping jacks." As if they were soldiers, the girls responded, performing synchronized jumping jacks. A montage of camera views followed the girls through a variety of exercises, then showed them at a shooting range and using a knife. The last image showed a girl dressed in black sneak behind a young woman and cut her throat.

Bile burned the back of Irene's throat. She closed her eyes and fought for control of her churning stomach.

"Dr. Gallaway discovered a more efficient womb," the narrator said in his soothing tone.

She reopened her eyes. On the screen, a red, uterine-like sac with a fetus morphed into the same type of sac holding a ten-year-old child. The sac pulsed and writhed, then split, and the child spilled out onto a gurney with sides.

"Today, the Center for the Advancement of Inborn Character is in the top ten research centers in the world. It has the potential to gather and store material from the world's best donors and produce perfect offspring at a rate that will completely replace the unfit population within ten years. Just think, by 1975 you could live in the perfect Fellowship world. But not without more funds and more protection from the rebels. We need help.

"Will you invest in a better America?" The image of the logo with the center's name reappeared, accompanied by the "Star-Spangled Banner" sung by Elvis Presley and the Blackwood Brothers Quartet. Then, white letters spelled Kodak on a black screen, followed by the number 10, then 9, 8, 7.

Dr. Gallaway turned off the projector's light. "What this film doesn't say is that, just as Dr. Locke did, we've created these girls to be Azrael for the Fellowship. For the right price, we will also grow citizens, but creating every newborn citizen will come later. Right now, the Fellowship has a rebel crisis that we can solve with these girls."

Irene sat back in her seat. Tried to process all he'd shown her. "You want me to what—sponsor—the CIAC, the Azrael?" *Me, responsible for the defeat of the rebels?* The idea filled her with the breathlessness of an adrenaline rush that warmed the back of her ears.

He crossed the aisle, squatted to eye level with her, and broke into his crooked smile. "You lend us your name, your support, and you can take part as much or as little as you wish."

I'll be in the history books, not just because I'm the Prophet's Lady, but because of this. It took effort to control her growing excitement. "I need to see for myself."

Chapter Thirteen

Miranda kept both hands on the pilot's wheel and cast a glance over her shoulder. *What's going on with Beryl?*

Wanda took Beryl's arm and guided her into the salon.

Did she see something astern?

Miranda glanced over her shoulder again. *Lady's* engines babbled in the water. And the jeans on the clothesline fluttered in the breeze.

To port, beyond the riverbank, a set of railroad tracks cut through vacant fields with yellowing crops. Trees crowned with a smattering of fading orange and gold and rust-colored leaves lined the starboard shores. The air smelled of damp earth, fish, and diesel fuel. Nothing alarming or suspicious.

The boat bounced against the river's current-driven waves. Miranda adjusted her course to the center of the travel lane but couldn't keep her mind on the river. *Beryl was fine one minute and not the next. What the hell is going on?*

"Captain?" Wanda stood half in, half out of the salon doors and peered up at Miranda. "Did she say anything to you?"

"She reported river conditions, handed over the conn, then climbed down to the main deck. Took sixty seconds, tops. What happened?"

"I don't know. She isn't talking. Only moves when I move her.

Maybe she needs to eat. I'll give her some soup and fresh bread. Oh, I know, I have some cookies…"

The clothes and a rag doll on the clothesline flapped and popped in the wind. Miranda glanced back at them. Refocused on the water. But the question of what happened to Beryl kept circling around in Miranda's thoughts. *Is Beryl sick? What illness would—*

Miranda's throat tightened. *A stroke?* The doctors who put Beryl back together after the explosion had said she had an eighty percent chance of a stroke during the first year. The chances went down after that. *It's been more than two…*

Static erupted from the radio.

"Captain? Wanda here. Beryl let us put her to bed and she shut her eyes, but she still hasn't said a word. I think she needs a hospital."

A deep, breath-robbing ache filled Miranda. "A hospital?" She chewed her lower lip and studied the charts. The closest hospital was an hour away in Jefferson City. Crawling with Fellowship offices, the capital of Missouri was the most dangerous place they could land. *Not an option.*

In an ocean of the enemy… "Tucker's is the only rebel-friendly place I know between here and Kansas City. It's four hours away, and the closest rebel-friendly hospital is near Columbia, another fifteen miles inland from Tucker's. Can Beryl wait that long?"

"I don't know, Captain. That's a long time."

Miranda keyed the mike again. "Is Beryl having trouble breathing?"

"Not that I can tell."

She searched two-year-old memories for the other warning symptoms. "Any slurred speech? One-sided weakness? Fever? Is her heart racing?"

"Slow down, Captain. No weakness. But the other stuff—let me check."

Miranda jerked the wheel starboard and narrowly avoided a "bump" in the water. *Crap. The propellers can't take another hit. If we're dead in the water, Beryl might be dead too. Focus.* She swept her gaze across the water, alert for more hazards.

Two or three minutes later, the radio *shush-shushed.*

"No fever, Cap. Pulse feels strong and normal. She doesn't react to anything I say or do." The radio buzzed. "Not even when I slapped her."

The pit of Miranda's stomach dropped. "You actually slapped her? She didn't stop you?"

"That's a negative. She didn't lift a finger." Even over the radio, Wanda sounded sheepish and scared.

"You stay with her. Watch her. If she—" Miranda pressed her lips tight against the words *gets worse*. "If anything changes, let me know. I'm opening the throttle. Tell David—"

"Don't worry about us," David said through the radio. "We'll find a ride out of this Tucker's place."

"Thanks." She pushed the throttle forward. They sped through the water, past random shanties and fishing shacks. A flatboat on the starboard side held a figure wearing a large-brimmed straw hat and hunched over a fishing pole. She eased the throttle back. If she scuttled a fisherman's boat with *Lady's* wake, they'd get attention they didn't need.

Miranda murmured a brief prayer that she'd get Beryl to help in time.

Chapter Fourteen

The twelve-paneled oak door of the Spring Valley mansion had a brass lion's-head door knocker centered on it. Irene lifted the ring, clacked it three times.

The door swung open noiselessly, revealed the same butler in his black suit and white gloves that she remembered from years ago. "Good afternoon."

"Good afternoon, Jeeves," Irene said, a fallback to her childhood. "Remember me?" His name wasn't Jeeves, but she'd read a book with a butler named Jeeves and had insisted on calling him that. It stuck.

"Of course I remember you, Lady Earnshaw." His formal manner didn't change, but the corners of his mouth twitched. "Mrs. Wynter is expecting you."

Irene followed Jeeves down the lengthy blue-and-white tiled entryway, past the curved staircase. She loved the arched doorways and the library paneling. He stood in the archway to the living room and announced her. In the elegant white-on-white room, the deep sapphire-blue, camel-back sofa drew her eye just as it had when she was a little girl. The intense wall of heat that dampened her skin? *Don't remember that. Ugh.*

On the sofa, in a powder-blue, lace-over-satin dress, Mrs. Wynter sat near the roaring fireplace. She held out a hand; her lace sleeve belled. "Come, darling. I'm afraid I partied too long the other day, and these old bones insist I sit for a few days." Her gravelly voice had a breathy, tired quality.

Irene crossed the room, kissed the old woman's hand. "Thank you for inviting me." Gave the room a fond, nostalgic once-over. "I'd almost forgotten how much I loved the elegance of this place." *The heat, not so much. At least it'll be a good excuse to make my visit brief.*

"Sit and visit with me." Mrs. Wynter gestured at the upholstered, bent-wood armchair on the other side of the coffee table.

"Thank you, I will," Irene murmured and settled into the chair. So near the fireplace, perspiration dampened Irene's skin.

"There's tea and icebox cookies on the table, if you like." She waved a hand at the silver service sitting on the coffee table.

The room held a hint of the aroma of rose-scented tea. Mrs. Wynter's favorite. Six round icebox cookies lay on a fine china plate with sapphire-blue cornflowers on it. Irene glanced down at her figure. Resolved to avoid the cookies and anything hot to drink in this room. "Thank you, but I couldn't. I've just finished a big lunch." She'd started reading Dr. Gallaway's notes at lunch and had barely touched her food.

Mrs. Wynter folded her crepe-paper hands in her lap and sat back. "It's been what—ten or fifteen years since your last visit?"

"Probably." *More than twenty.*

"Frankly, darling, you could have bowled me over when I heard your husband had performed a miracle. And now he's the Prophet and you're Lady Earnshaw…" She shook her head. Her silvery pin curls jiggled. "My, my…seems like just yesterday you were scampering around here in your play dresses and begging for another cookie."

"It was a lot longer than yesterday to me," Irene said, smiling to take any edge off her words.

The old woman's shrewd, pale-blue eyes pierced her. "Buenos Aires is a delightful place to visit, though I expect it's not so delightful to live there. But I'm too tired for all the social folderol today. Let's skip forward to the reason you're here." She leaned forward, picked up a silver handbell that sat on the rectangular coffee table before her.

The silvery ring hadn't stopped before her butler appeared in the doorway.

"Bring that thing—"

He crossed to her, handed her a manila folder.

She took it and dismissed him with a flick of her wrist. "Now, I know you are wondering what all this is about. But first, I have a story to tell you."

"A story?" *Please let it be short so I can get out of this heat.* She drew her handkerchief out of her purse. Pretended to wipe her nose so she could swipe the beads of sweat gathered on her upper lip.

"A long time ago, before the agnostics, before the Council, even before the first Prophet, Mr. Wynter was the front man for a young preacher. The preacher had received a mandate from God that he should go unto all the United States and warn the people."

"You're talking about the Prophet Samuel?" Irene asked in a hushed tone. She'd never known Mr. Wynter had worked for the first Prophet.

"He wasn't the Prophet then. He was a young man, a holy man, and had a gifted tongue. When he spoke, you couldn't help but listen and know his words were God's words." She fell silent and stared off into the distance.

"And Mr. Wynter was his front man?" Irene prompted. "What does a front man do?"

Mrs. Wynter startled and blinked and gave a throaty *ah.* "Forgive me, my mind wanders sometimes." She twisted the plain gold band on her left hand. "Mr. Wynter booked the tent revivals for Samuel, always at least two cities ahead of him. That's how I met him, back when we lived near Cincinnati. He wanted to use Papa's farmland for the revival.

"We'd heard of Samuel, of course, but Papa feared the crowds would trample his crops and frighten the livestock. Well, Mr. Wynter invited us into town to have dinner at his expense. We ate at Lydia's, the best restaurant in town, and had a fine meal. Mr. Wynter could quote the Good Book better than our own preacher, and he told us about Samuel. He told us how his Follow Team would clean up after the Revival. So Papa agreed."

She lifted her face to stare at the portrait hanging above the fireplace. "I thought Mr. Wynter a fine figure of a man. A God-fearing man, and I envied his life of travel. I was sixteen, and I hadn't been farther than downtown Cincinnati. I yearned to learn about the world. I asked him about the places he'd been. His stories enthralled me. Well, I guess he saw something in me that night 'cause four weeks later when Samuel and his team pitched the tent in Papa's field, Mr. Wynter came back. He stayed the whole two weeks of the Revival and sat in the front row, next to me, every night. And after the service, we'd discuss the Word and how to serve the Lord."

As sweet as Mrs. Wynter's story was, her quavering voice droned on and on. And in that overheated room, Irene couldn't help it. Her eyes drifted closed, and her head dropped.

"And before the tent came down, he asked Papa for my hand in marriage." Mrs. Wynter gave a wheezy laugh.

Irene sat straighter and stifled a yawn.

"Papa refused until Mr. Wynter offered him a hundred dollars and said that if he didn't make me happy, Papa could use that money to send Mr. Wynter to jail. That did it. Samuel married us the next night." She stared at her wedding ring.

Irene eyed the icebox cookies, licked her lips, and refocused on Mrs. Wynter.

"Papa didn't have to worry. Mr. Wynter was good to me, and I was very happy. We traveled across the country and prepared the way for Samuel. Then Samuel called Mr. Wynter long-distance. Said the angel Gabriel had visited him—" She smiled a broad smile full of crowded, age-yellowed teeth. "He needed Mr. Wynter and me to be with him. We left that very night."

"We became the Prophet's family—took proper care of him, made certain he ate and slept. Mr. Wynter helped manage the Prophet's affairs. He was there at the first Council meeting. And— when the evil began."

Irene leaned forward. "The evil?"

"Some folk took issue with the Council's rule-making."

Irene drew in a sharp breath, exhaled. "Uncle Ethan and Aunt Beryl."

"Yes. They were the ones inside the Prophet's closest circle. But there were others too. More and more of those folk tried to hurt the Prophet, and me and Mr. Wynter too."

Irene's mouth dropped into an *O.*

"Well, Mr. Wynter vowed he'd protect us. So he created a small private group of protectors. And they kept us safe. They still watch over me." Her eyes locked on Irene's. "The evil is still out there, dear. And that's why I brought you here."

Irene's pulse doubled. "You think Felix and I—and my daughters—are in danger?" She swallowed, tried to digest that idea. "But Felix—the Prophet—has bodyguards. Do my daughters and I need bodyguards?"

"That's for the Fellowship Council to decide, dear. What you need is information."

"About?"

Her eyes narrowed, and a sly expression flickered across her face. "Let's just say that a wise woman always has more information than she needs. After your years in Buenos Aires, you don't have a network here, do you?"

"I—" *I can't tell her about Paul.* She let her shoulders droop a smidge. "I guess I don't."

"I didn't think so. It has taken me a lifetime to build one." That sly expression returned and stayed. "Your mother and I were dear friends. We both knew the value of information and we agreed on how to get it. I miss her. If a lack of information destroyed her daughter, the Lady of the Fellowship—well—I can't allow that to happen."

"Mrs. Wynter, please, just tell me what it is you think I should do."

"Take this folder." She put it on the coffee table and pushed it toward Irene.

A brass fastener at the top of the file held thirty pages in place. Bold blue letters on the first page read "Property of the Lady of the Fellowship." On a diagonal in the bottom center, red letters declared "Eyes Only." She glanced up at Mrs. Wynter.

The old woman leaned forward, waved an impatient hand. "Go ahead. Open it. It's for your eyes only," she declared.

A familiar face stared up from the first page. Irene tensed. "My driver? Paul? Is spying on me?"

Mrs. Wynter laughed. "Not on you. For you. He's the head of your network. My gift to you."

Irene glanced from the page to Mrs. Wynter's yellowed smile. "I don't understand."

"Drivers are invisible to most people. They hear and see all kinds of interesting things. And Paul is one of the best. Not only will he fill you in on things your guests talk about, he is an exceptionally skilled driver, bodyguard, and has connections everywhere. All you have to do is ask."

No wonder he agreed to get my letter to Miranda. Irene thumbed through the two dozen images and information sheets of men and women. She closed the folder, put a hand on top of it. "I don't know what to say." She wanted to say, "Do I really need this?" But insulting Mrs. Wynter wasn't smart. "Except, thank you. I appreciate your wisdom and your gift."

Mrs. Wynter's cackle turned into a hacking, coughing fit. She waved her hand at the tea service.

Irene poured tea from the silver teapot into a china cup decorated with blue cornflowers. Handed the cup to the old woman.

Mrs. Wynter sipped until the coughing subsided. Gave Irene an approving look. "You've already mastered the diplomatic answer, dear." She rang the handbell again. And when her butler appeared, she said, "I am tired. Please call for Lady Earnshaw's car."

In the limo, Irene studied her driver as if he were a strange species.

Chapter Fifteen

Annabelle Earnshaw sat cross-legged on her frilly pink bed. She bent over her navy-blue leather diary and wrote: "I was born in Buenos Aires." But she didn't know that for sure.

Mother had given her the diary for her adoption day celebration a couple of weeks ago. Annabelle didn't know what it was for. Today she knew.

She caressed the thick book that lay on the bed beside her. The glossy photographic image on the cover of Orianna Pascal's biography of the first Prophet, *Crying in the Wilderness*, was an overhead shot of a young man preaching in a revival tent. The congregation paid more attention to a drunk falling off a bench than to the poor preacher.

"I will write of the miracles and life of my very own adoptive father, Felix. Mine will be a much better book because of my miracle." She wrote cursive letters with a blue fountain pen as neatly as she could.

Blood oozed from my hot skin whenever anything touched it.

Mother said that the dengue fever stole her memories.

An invisible monster shot needles through my eyes into my brain. I figured my brain bled too. I lay down on the dirt floor next to one of the dead bodies. And I died. But then I heard a kind voice, and a gentle hand touched my forehead.

She was proud to be Father's first miracle. *God had an unfinished plan for me. Someday He'll reveal his plan, and I'll do something really special.*

Her bedroom door banged open. Sandra, her seven-year-old sister, bounced into the room. "Annabelle, Annabelle—play with me."

Annabelle locked her diary. "You're supposed to knock before you come in."

"Oops. Sorry." Sandra ran out of the room, slammed the door behind her, and immediately knocked—hard and loud. Over and over and over.

Annabelle slipped her diary under her mattress. Covered her ears. Hoped Sandra would go away. Knew she wouldn't. "Come in, Sandra."

Sandra skipped into the room. "Come on. Let's play with the puppets."

Boring. "How about let's play hide-and-seek?"

"It's too close to bedtime. Linda says we have to play inside games."

Annabelle didn't like their nanny, Linda. She much preferred their life in Buenos Aires when Mother made their lunch and read them stories. "We can play inside hide-and-seek," she told Sandra.

"Really?"

"Of course, but you must find the best hiding spot. And be crazy quiet, so Linda doesn't know. Oh, and stay in your hiding spot almost forever 'cause this house is humongous and it will take the seeker an eternity to search."

"Okay."

"Good. I'll be It. I'll close my eyes and count to ten. You hide. Bet I'll find you."

"No, you won't."

Annabelle put her hands over her eyes. "One—two—"

Sandra's feet thudded across the floor and down the hall.

"Three—four." Annabelle peeked between her fingers. Her door stood open. A thrill vibrated in her chest. "Five, six, seven-eight-nine-ten." She uncovered her eyes and hurried across the room. Peered down the beige hall without even stepping on the thick green carpet and called, "Ready or not, here I come!" She grinned,

then eased the door shut. She had at least a half hour of uninterrupted time. *Sandra is so easy.*

Chapter Sixteen

Miranda guided the boat around the next bend. Tucker's floating gas station came into view; two eight-by-twenty-foot wood platforms atop flotation barrels bobbed gently on the river. A small, pay-here shed sat on the closest dock. The fuel pump sat on the downriver dock. The shed's window awning was closed, and no flags waved from their poles high above the platforms. Miranda's chest hollowed. Tucker's always had the U.S. and the Missouri flag flying. *There's no smoke….* She clutched the pilot's wheel tighter. *They're okay. They have to be okay.*

She eased *Lady* close to the dock. A faint acrid odor tainted the air. An oily sheen arched out from the dock's bumpers. Her stomach tightened. *Why aren't the booms and absorbent floats out to contain and clean the spill? The Tuckers would've— Something must have happened. They wouldn't ignore a spill.*

Switching the engines to idle, she scanned the steep riverbank that led up to Tucker's picnic table area. Beyond the empty picnic tables stood the short end of the store, a rectangular metal building the size of a football field and painted a soft yellow. The store sold groceries, camping, hunting, and fishing supplies, plus whatever else caught Tucker's fancy.

Only the rutted and pitted corner of the gravel parking lot was visible. The front door of the store faced the parking lot.

It's the end of the season. That's why no one is in sight. But the burn in her chest grew more uncomfortable. *Can't bypass Tucker's. We've got to get Beryl to the hospital.*

She grabbed the mike. "Something's not right. I'm going ashore to check things out."

"Need me at the helm?" Wanda asked over the radio.

"Any change in Beryl's condition?"

"No."

"Then stay there." Miranda stared at the compartment that hid the helm pistol. Beryl would want her to take it, but she couldn't. She dropped anchor, then hopped over the gunwale and onto the deck. Strode across the six-inch gap between the platforms to the pay-here shed.

Before she reached the shed, she noticed the window awning was down but not latched closed. *Not a good sign.* She licked her lips and scanned the shore again. Scanned the river. *No Second Sphere or KKK members visible.* She blew out a long, slow breath and slid along the side of the shed, turned the corner. The entry door stood open. A rush of blood emptied her chest and filled her ears.

She eased forward and peered inside. With the window awning closed, there was no light and only unrecognizable lumps. She ran her hand along the smooth, painted inside wall. No light switch. *I'll have to raise the awning for light.* One foot into the shed, her toe nudged something on the floor. Something soft. She lifted her foot to step over it. Nudged it again.

"Uhhh."

"Who's there?" she gasped. Made it to and raised the window awning, whirled.

Tucker's teenaged son lay on the floor in a pool of blood.

"Glenn?" She knelt at his side. "Oh, my God. Who did this? Where are you hurt? Where are your parents? Your brother?" She shook her head. He wasn't in any condition to answer. "I'm sorry. Can you talk?"

He didn't react. His face was so pale he was almost gray.

She placed two fingers on the cool skin of his neck. Gently pressed in a second and third place before she found his weak, barely there pulse.

Desperate, she glanced around the shack. The cash register that had been on the window ledge lay on its side on the floor. The round bar stool lay against the wall, kept from falling by the empty shelves on the short wall. *Where's the first aid kit?* "Wanda? Do you hear me? Wanda? Bring the first aid kit!"

His eyes flickered open. "Mm—da."

"Yes, it's me. Hang on, we'll get you some help."

His lips moved, and unintelligible, barely audible sounds came out.

She leaned down, took his face in her hands, patted his cheek. "Glenn? What did you say?" Positioned her ear inches from his mouth.

"Second Sphere." He took a rattly breath. "Shots in store." He didn't take a breath for long seconds. "Mom, Pop…" He sighed and closed his eyes.

"Wanda, the first aid kit." She sat straighter, yelled louder. "Wanda?"

He took another rattly breath.

"Where are you?" Wanda called.

"In the pay-shack."

His head moved slightly to his right.

Miranda leaned close again. "Glenn? Are you trying to say something?"

He was so very still. And it had been a long time since his last breath.

She put her fingers to his neck again, but she knew. She dropped her head, sank back onto her heels, and wrapped her arms around herself.

"Here it is," Wanda said. "Oh." She hugged the first aid kit. "I didn't understand you. And Beryl was still—and… I am so…"

"He was going to graduate from high school in the spring." Miranda's voice shook. She cleared her throat and looked up at Wanda. "He said he heard shots in the store. We have—I have to go up there. Find his parents…"

Wanda glanced over her shoulder, toward shore. "Did he say who did this?"

"Second Sphere."

Wanda darted glances over her shoulders, toward shore. "Do you think they're still here?"

"I doubt it. The *Lady* is quiet, but she isn't silent. They would have heard her. Heard me." The heaviness in Miranda's chest made it impossible for her to stand. Holding onto the window shelf, she pulled herself up. Something cold and wet brushed her knees. She ran her fingers across her right knee. It was gelatinous, sticky. *Blood. Glenn's blood.*

She took a deep breath, raised her gaze to the building on shore, and fought the tightness in her throat and chest. "Come on." She stepped over Glenn's body and pushed past Wanda.

"Where are we going?"

"You're going to get Beryl ready to disembark. I'm going to find Glenn's parents. If there's danger, I'll—scream or something."

"You can't go up there alone. There could be an agent or a booby-trap."

Miranda quirked her mouth. Wanda wasn't wrong. "I'll ask David to come with me. Leslie can help you."

Miranda boarded the *Lady*, offered Wanda a hand. When Wanda was aboard, she said, "I can't put David's mission at risk. I am the captain. I'm giving you an order. Help Beryl. I'll make sure it's safe, then we'll get her to the hospital."

Wanda raised her chin, crossed her arms over her chest, and glared. "I don't like it, but I'll do it." She stood there a moment longer, then entered the salon.

Miranda climbed back up to the helm, opened the secret compartment again. Stared at the gun. Stared at the store. Closed the compartment. She reached for the ignition, intending to shut down the engines. Hesitated. *If there is an agent up there, we'll have to get out of here quick. Better I draw the agent out while the* Lady *is running and raring to go.* She flipped the rocker switch for the horn on-off twice. *Blatt! Blatt!*

"Why did you do that?" Beryl asked.

Breathless, Miranda whirled.

Hands clamped over her ears, Beryl focused on the clothesline on the main deck.

Wanda stood on the portside of Beryl with her hands held in a mid-air, hands-off gesture.

Beryl walked to the end of the clothesline, faced the rag doll hanging there.

"Beryl?" Miranda called. "Are you all right? What happened?"

Beryl's shoulders raised in a visible deep breath. She snatched the doll off the clothesline and marched into the salon.

Wanda, then Miranda, dashed after her.

Beryl grabbed Leslie by the collar, dragged her out from behind the table. Shook the doll in her face. "Where did you get this?"

"It was—Alexander's. I told you. I was his nanny." Leslie wriggled under Beryl's grip. She tried to grab the doll, but Beryl jerked it away.

"Why did Alexander have it?"

Miranda touched Beryl's shoulder. Under her hand, Beryl's muscles bunched. "You were catatonic. Maybe you should take it—"

Beryl whipped around. Snarled at Miranda. "Wasn't catatonic. Had to think. Done thinking." She turned her glare back on Leslie. "Why did Alexander have it?"

"I don't know."

"What do you know?"

"Dr. Russell threw a fit about it the day before I left."

"Who is Dr. Russell?"

"Alex's father."

"And?"

"I worked for him. He was a research scientist."

"A research—you worked for a *Fellowship* scientist?"

Leslie's gaze darted from Beryl to David and back. "Yes. He worked on a top-secret Fellowship project."

Cold disbelief filled Miranda. She stared at David. *Did you bring a Fellowship member aboard?*

"Why would a Fellowship scientist hire you?"

"They needed a nanny." She hesitated.

Beryl released her with a shove. "Tell me when, where, how long —*everything.*"

She stumbled backward, steadied herself against the table. "Why? What's it mean to you?"

Beryl glowered and took a step toward her.

Miranda tensed, ready. Though she didn't know who she'd protect from whom.

"My references were excellent. I thought the Russells knew something about who killed Harry and my parents. They didn't know who I was. No one did."

She worked undercover? For SABR. Miranda shot a glance at Beryl, then back to Leslie.

"Get to the point."

"Dr. Russell demanded that Betty Jean, Mrs. Russell, get rid of the doll. He said it linked them with you-know-who. That's what he said, *you-know-who*. Betty Jean took the doll away. Alex cried inconsolably for hours. Later that night, she gave it to me. Made me promise to hide it from Dr. Russell. I figured you-know-who had to mean the Azrael, so the next day I took the doll and ran."

Beryl's stillness sent Miranda's pulse thundering.

Beryl ran a glance around the room. "Any of you see this before?"

"Uh-huh."

"No."

"Nope."

She focused on the doll. Stroked its loops of brown yarn hair.

"Beryl?" Miranda had seen that despair on Beryl's face only once before, toward the end of the battle at Quantico. "What does it mean?"

"It's identical to the one I made—" Her lips moved soundlessly. She swallowed, then blurted, "For my daughter, Anna."

"Oh." Miranda's chest tightened. She reached for the doll. "Let me take it."

Beryl raised her head, shook Miranda's touch off. "No." She glanced down at the doll. "This is proof." She stood toe-to-toe with Miranda. "Don't you see? The Azrael are back. Ethan needs to know. Now. We have to stop them before..."

Miranda couldn't speak. She wanted to say, "Yes, of course, I'll be there with you Beryl." *But—another battle? More killing—I can't. Not that.*

"Now wait just a doggone minute," Wanda said. "How did she" —Wanda pointed her chin at Leslie—"get a doll that she"—her chin swung to Beryl—"made? And you—you have a daughter? How did I not know this? All this after, we thought you were dying—" She bounced a glare between Beryl and Miranda. "What the hell is going on?"

Beryl focused her gaze a million miles beyond the river outside the window. "My daughter was—one of the first Azrael."

Wanda gaped at her. "Your daughter was an Azrael?" Her nostrils flared, and her chin quivered.

"Anna had something—bad—inside her. Evil people influenced her. I couldn't—save her." Beryl set her jaw and turned a hard look on Wanda. "They mutilated her corpse. Copied her somehow. They were growing thousands of—copies—murderous abominations." She drew a breath. "I thought I stopped the bastards."

Beryl's pain-filled voice opened a door to Miranda's memory. The blood and death and pain she'd barred from her thoughts hit her like a shard from a storm-shattered window. Reopened old wounds.

"We"—Beryl tipped her head toward Miranda—"destroyed everything. Their barracks, the labs, and those damn dolls. There shouldn't be any—anywhere. This doll means—" She locked eyes with Miranda. "Am I hijacking this boat?"

Miranda turned away. Gripped the cool, smooth granite countertop of the lower helm. "We need to think this through." Focused on the brass compass and the orange binder of navigation charts. "The boat may not be your fastest option. We've just passed mile marker one hundred seventy. And Waverly's at two hundred, um —" She thumbed through the charts.

"Two-nine-three," Wanda said. She remembered things like that.

"Four and a half hours by boat—three if I open her up and we miss all the hazards." Miranda applied her scaled ruler to the map. "Eighty-nine dry miles. Two, maybe two and a half hours by car."

Beryl nodded. "I'll find a car." She shot a look at Leslie and David. "Get your things. We leave in five." She strode down the passageway toward the crew's cabin.

"Wait," Miranda said. "I found Glenn wounded—dying—in the pay-shack."

"What?" Beryl drew her pistols and whirled to face shore.

"Stop. There are no hostiles anywhere close."

Beryl cocked her head at Miranda. "How do you know that?" She twisted her lips in a grimace, nodded her head. "The horns."

"Yeah. But we have to go search the store." Miranda spoke in a rush to keep Beryl from asking more questions. "Before he died, Glenn said there had been shots in the store. He said Second Sphere did this. We have to look for his family."

Holstering her weapons, Beryl said, "All right, I'll look for them while David and Leslie get supplies, but in five minutes I'm leaving for Waverly." She positioned the boarding ramp, strode down it to the dock.

Miranda closed her eyes and decided. "I'm going with you," she called. "To search the store and to Waverly."

"But—" Wanda said. "What about the boat?"

Miranda scanned the salon of her beloved yacht. Throat tight, she gave Wanda a strained smile. "I'll sign her over to you, if you want her."

"If I want—" Wanda caressed the varnished mahogany tabletop. "Oh, boy—do I want." She glanced around the cabin with eyes that shimmered. "I want her so much." She caught a ragged breath. "But the first time I run into a Fellowship member, he'll claim I stole this gorgeous boat. Don't matter what papers I have or don't have. They won't believe me. And they won't send me to one of them Redemption places." She blinked, and faced Miranda. "Guess I'm riding with y'all."

Miranda nodded. "Better hustle. When Beryl says five minutes, she means five."

"We need supplies," Wanda said. "More than we have onboard."

"Then you can go shopping while I help search."

Wanda blinked at her, looked up at the embankment at Tucker's. "Right."

Chapter Seventeen

eryl took the wooden steps up the steep riverbank two at a time. She didn't like this. Even if the SS were long gone, the Tuckers would never have let their son die alone on the dock. *They are gone, or dead.*

A faint odor reached her. *Not gas. More like something rotten.* The hairs on the back of her neck stood.

Hand up, halt. Miranda and the others stopped behind her. No one made a sound.

Beryl signaled Miranda and the others to wait. Pointed at Miranda. Gave her the sign to keep your eyes open.

Miranda signaled she would go with.

Beryl shook her head, gave her an emphatic halt sign.

After a nod of agreement from Miranda, Beryl crept to the corner of the building. Peered around to the front.

The two Shell Oil gas pumps in front of the store were vacant. A lone, beat-up old pickup truck sat in the parking lot. More rust than green paint, it wore a thick coat of dust.

Somewhere in the distance, a train rumbled. Its horn blasted. Her taut muscles tightened another notch.

She eased around the corner, hugged the wall of the building. The stench grew more powerful the closer she got to the store's display window. Long-buried memories bumped against the mental barrier she'd constructed. She pushed them away and focused on the job at hand.

Only shards remained of the display window. Broken inward. *Vandals?* She drew her pistol and listened. Blood rushed in her ears.

Birds chirped. Insects buzzed.

She ducked below the window and scurried to the front door.

Tucker's front door stood ajar. Its glass broken. An "Off Season— If You're Honest Come On In" sign hung from one chain. The sun streamed through the door and window. Beyond the reach of the sun, nothing but ever darker shadows. A faint motor noise came from within. The rank odor definitely came from inside. The stench meant the attack happened days ago.

She slipped through the door. Glass crunched beneath her shoes. The overwhelming stink of rot forced her to breathe through her mouth. Dark shadows shrouded the farthest reaches of the store. Dark enough someone could hide there. Her already jazzed blood warmed her neck. Her muscles tensed, ready to spring. *Too quiet. The stench was too great. No one alive is in there.* A quick scan reinforced that idea.

The register lay open and upside down on the floor. Any money it may have held was long gone. Dried blood sprayed across the glassless display case and the floor. Drawn in the blood—an oval with wings—the Fellowship symbol.

A rush of heat swept through her. In a perverse way, it pleased her. *I am still me. Still filled with hatred for the Fellowship.*

Somewhere in the recesses of the store, a machine whirred and whined like it was dying.

She pulled the two-cell flashlight from her belt. A nearby shelving unit leaned like a domino about to topple. Shattered and smashed merchandise littered the shelves and floor. *Damn. The bastards looted the place too. Doesn't look like there's enough left to supply us.*

She stepped over debris, made her way to the north wall. Worked her way back. Stepped over and around shattered tourist trinkets. Cereal crunched underfoot. She avoided the aisle where shattered jelly jars filled the floor.

Past the front door, she reached the reeking freezer and refrigerator cases. One of them whined, though no cool air came from it.

After a brief glance at the contents of that freezer, she avoided looking at the others.

She passed a pile of flashlights on the floor, paused, and backtracked to it. Most of them had broken, but two of them worked. She stuck them in her belt.

In the hunting section of the store, jagged pieces of fishing poles, empty tackle boxes, and range bags and empty ammo boxes covered the floor.

She stepped on something that rolled. Regained her balance and swept her flash across the floor. Whoever had taken the weapons and bullets had been in a hurry. Cartridges and brass ammo lay between glass shards, wood splinters, and odd bits of merchandise. The rifle racks set into the wall behind the counter were empty. So were the low shelves below the racks labeled ammunition.

She reached the south wall without finding a body. Darted back outside. Sucked in air that held more earthy odors than rotten ones.

Trotted back to where she'd left Miranda and the others.

Miranda raised a questioning eyebrow.

"Fellowship raid."

"Oh, no. Glenn was right." Miranda glanced at the store. "The Tuckers?"

"No sign of them."

"Maybe they got away?" Leslie said.

"Hope—" Beryl said. *What am I doing?* She shook her head. "No, they didn't. No bodies, but there's the blood in the front—"

Wanda glanced at Miranda. "Should we go back to the boat?"

"No," Beryl said. "The place is a mess, but we need whatever useable supplies we can find."

David sighed. "I'm sorry about your friends." Heaved another heavy breath. "Do you really think it's worth taking time to search for supplies?"

Beryl didn't answer. Handed him a flashlight. "You'll need this." She turned back toward the store, stopped, and faced the others again. "If you have a handkerchief or something to tie over your mouth and nose, do it."

They looked at each other. Shook their heads. None of them had anything.

"We'll search for ten minutes. If I whistle once, find a place to hide. Two long whistles, pack up, we're leaving."

"Breathe through your mouth," she warned and led them inside.

The others made noises of distaste and coughed. She glared at them, and the noise stopped.

She pointed her flashlight at an overhead sign with arrows pointing to camping, hunting, fishing, and the other sections. "David and Leslie, look for rucksacks for each of us—sleeping bags, lightweight pup tents, blankets—anything to keep us warm and dry. Wanda, pick up any dry goods or canned food, cookware, matches, and Sterno cans if you can find them. Miranda and I will salvage what we can from the hunting goods area."

They picked their way across the floor, littered with broken bottles and dented cans, toward their assigned areas.

Beryl led Miranda to the hardware section first. They found a pair of heavy-duty pliers and a hammer among the debris on the floor. She motioned for Miranda to help her, and they righted the overturned shelving unit that blocked the main aisle of the hunting section. Snatched up the hunting knife and sheath they uncovered.

"Be careful where you step," Beryl said, then led the way to the hunting aisles. She bent and carefully picked through the debris. Gathered a fistful of bullets of assorted sizes. She pulled off her shirt, tied it into a sack, and dumped the bullets into it. "Go get one of the range bags," she told Miranda. "Near the back wall."

"Will do," Miranda whispered in a voice blunted like she had a cold. She disappeared behind a still-standing metal shelving unit.

Beryl had dumped another two fistfuls of ammo into her shirt before Miranda returned with a cloth range bag.

"Should we sort it?" she whispered.

Beryl gave her a what-are-you-doing glare. "Load your magazines, dump the rest in the bag." She didn't whisper. "Pick up any ammo you see. We'll find a use for it."

Miranda's cheeks pinked. "Right." She helped shake the ammo out of Beryl's shirt. The brass clinked and tumbled into the bag.

"Miranda?" Beryl stared pointedly at Miranda's waistline, unadorned with a holster and pistol. "Where's your gun?"

Miranda glanced at her waist. She'd meant to get it. "You know I haven't touched it since—"

"We're going through the heart of Fellowship country. You're going to have to carry."

"I—"

"Carry or go back to the boat."

Miranda sighed. "I'll run down to the *Lady* and get it. Back in a sec." She hurried toward the door.

Chapter Eighteen

On the bank above the river, the breeze tossed Miranda's hair across her eyes. The air held loamy scents from the surrounding forest and the electricity of a coming storm, but the sky was clear. Miranda hurried down the embankment and stepped onto the gently rocking dock. Her insides roiled. The idea of picking up her Browning Hi Power pistol again made the knot at the base of her throat dryer, thicker.

What am I doing? Am I really going to leave the Lady? *You said you'd never pick up a gun again. But I owe Beryl.* She set a mental barrier against her doubts, but her footsteps slowed. *I'm not looking to fight. I'm going to protect her.* She took another two and a half steps. *Semantics.* Her feet wouldn't move.

I want a chance at a happily ever after. She pulled the magazine ad from her pocket. Gazed at the charming yellow Cape Cod house with a red tin roof and a white picket fence. Living with Nick in a house would be like living in a romance novel. *But—*

The Fellowship won't let us live in peace. She glanced at the pay-here shed, then up at Tucker's store. *Not even if we lived like obedient Fellowship members—and neither of us would be happy doing that.* She put the picture back in her pocket. Squared her shoulders and hurried aboard the *Lady.*

Went straight to her the antique dresser in her cabin. Pulled open the bottom drawer. Nestled in an old, hooded sweatshirt sat a holster and a cigar box. Deep breath. She picked up the holster. Shaped to make a smooth draw, the leather had kept its stiffness. She placed it on top of the dresser. Two handed, she removed the cigar box from the drawer and put it next to her holster. The deck lurched. The box and holster slid. She grabbed them, placed them on the bed where they wouldn't slide.

Her heart beat in her throat. Hard. She opened the box. Inside, a red rag swaddled her gun.

The sweet smell of tobacco plants surrounded her. Her blood and breath rushed. The rustle of the leaves…the man with the gun…his expression when she shot him…

Waves of nausea sent heat to her face. She leaned forward, pressed her forehead to the ground—no, the cool wood floor of the boat. Her boat. *Lady Angelfish.* Her heart rate slowed, so did her breathing. She opened one eye, peered at the wood floor, touched it. *Real. It's real.* She rocked back on her heels.

The boat bumped the dock, hard. She stood, took a seaman's stance, and stared at the box still open. Still sitting on her bed. The red cloth still wrapped around the pistol.

Beryl has defended me and this boat and our passengers for two years. But more fighting will not get Nick and me together. I owe her. Without peace, it doesn't have to be one or the other. I can carry a gun long enough to get Beryl to Monkshood. Be gone two, three days at most.

Curtain-filtered sunlight streamed through the windows of the captain's cabin. The boat creaked, the only sound other than the slap of water against her hull.

The Lady *will wait for me, but who or what else will be waiting when I return?* Miranda had searched most of the boat and found nothing left by the Second Sphere agent. He had to have boarded during the inspection for a reason. The only place that was never unoccupied, that she never searched, was the salon. *It'll only take a minute. If there's nothing there, then I'll know I was wrong. And the* Lady *will be safe, will wait for me.*

She hurried into the salon, searched the storage lockers under the benches. Found nothing under the table or in the seat cushions. She ran a hand around all three doorframes. The sliding window's frame. Got on her knees and visually inspected under the helm. *Nothing.* She sighed. *Guess I can't put off leaving any longer. Beryl's waiting.* She reached for the light switch and froze.

The box for the light switch stood out from the wall. Its wires ran in a metal conduit painted the same color as the walls. If she wanted to hide something in plain sight, something so familiar... She followed the conduit with her eyes up to the ceiling, across the ceiling, then came back to the light switch. She bent, peered underneath the box. There it was, an oblong object about the size of a matchbox. Attached to the bottom of the light switch box, it had two wires coming out of it, running up and along the conduit. A chill swept through her. *It has to be a listening device or a homing beacon. Why didn't I think to check the light switches before?*

She darted down the passageway, checked each of the light switch boxes on the *Lady.* Every one of the light switches had one.

They heard everything.

They know where we are.

Her pulse drowned out the sounds of the boat creaking and waves slapping the boat's hull. She ran to the deck, scanned for them. *They could have been listening from miles behind us. Ready to grab us. That fisherman—what if he wasn't really fishing? But why not nab us then? Why wait?*

Only one reason she could imagine. *They plan to grab us during the meet with Monkshood.*

I have to stop them. How? Take them on a wild goose chase? Up the river to Kansas City or down river to St. Louis? Either would be suicide.

I have to fool them into thinking we've gone somewhere else or died or something. Lead them away or what? The boat couldn't drive itself...

She stiffened, relented, let the idea play out. It was a terrible idea. But if the boat wrecked, the Fellowship might assume they'd all drowned. She caressed the beautiful mahogany of the table. An ache welled deep in her chest. It had been a fantasy that she could dock *Lady* here, go to the meeting with Monkshood, and return to her. She couldn't come back until she'd tried to talk Monkshood into making peace. If wrecking the boat gave her enough time to do that... At least the *Lady* would perform one last service for the rebels.

Miranda retrieved her gun from her cabin. Cinched the holster tight around her waist. The weight of it and the gun weren't half as heavy as her feet, her heart, her soul.

In the salon, she stomped on the floor as if the five of them had returned to the boat. "I know, David. But you saw the store," she said aloud in as natural a voice as she could muster. "We have to pull back. You'll have to reschedule. Monkshood will understand." She stomped around and muttered, played the part of her crew, her brother, and her refugee. Went to the lower helm. Switched on all the safety lights, even the flashers. And finally started the motor.

On the dock, she paused. The tightness in her chest and throat kicked up another notch. It hurt to breathe. She scanned the graceful lines of *Lady's* bow, skimmed the familiar helm, and her sturdy stern, committed them to memory. It had taken months to earn the money to buy her, longer to restore the derelict that became the *Lady Angelfish*. Two years to develop Safe Harbor.

The Lady *is home. How can I destroy her?*

Safe Harbor is bigger than one boat. It was as if Beryl whispered in her ear. *Investing emotion in a place or thing will get you killed.*

Miranda struggled to make her fingers loosen the ropes from the dock's cleats. Shoved the yacht off into the current. *You were a great boat, a great home.*

The boat bobbed and swayed until the main current caught her. Carried her around the bend and out of sight.

She'll crash. Scatter wreckage in the current. Should delay and confuse pursuit for a day or two. Miranda swallowed the lump in her throat.

She turned her back to the water. *I'll help get Leslie and the doll to Ethan.*

She knew better than to plan further ahead than that.

Chapter Nineteen

Miranda forced herself to climb the steep wooden steps toward Tucker's. Part of her screamed, "Save *Lady*." She refused to look back.

Beryl startled her at the top of the embankment. "You deliberately set *Lady* adrift?"

"Yeah." Miranda couldn't help it, glanced back at the river.

The choppy, muddy water flowed past unchanged, unfeeling, unaware she'd just sent her life away.

Crack! She flinched. Her heart jammed into her throat. Her ribs ached. "The agent that boarded us set us up." She stared down river. Filled Beryl in. "I turned on all her lights to warn other boaters."

"We need to get out of here." Beryl whirled and strode toward the parking lot.

Miranda ignored the ache inside and followed her aunt.

They rounded the building.

David and Wanda bent under the open hood of the truck. Leslie sat in the driver's seat.

"Now," Wanda shouted.

Beryl bellowed, "Wanda—"

The truck's engine stuttered again and again. The third time, it roared. David pounded Wanda on the back. Wanda grinned and lowered the hood.

They took back roads past crop-shorn fields, acres of bare trees, scattered farmhouses, and tiny towns. David, Wanda, and Miranda rode in the truck bed, squeezed between five rucksacks and bags of supplies and ammo.

She tucked her icy hands beneath her. The grit in her eyes and the taste of dust distracted her. The rattle and rumble of truck gave her a headache and an excuse not to tell Wanda what she'd done.

An abrupt turn threw Miranda against the side of the truck.

They bounced down a jaw-jolting gravel road. Every bump aggravated Miranda's headache. She clenched her teeth and blamed Beryl.

The road curved and paralleled the route they'd just abandoned. Miranda's eyes widened at the long line of idling vehicles stretched toward the river. At the head of the line, police lights flashed.

A roadblock.

The ice inside her vanished. Nausea roiled, burned.

The route they followed curved away from the roadblock. Gravel dust rolled after them.

They stopped in a short drive that ended in a wooden fence. The stink of farm animals filled the air. Droppings marked the patch-work of grass and weeds on the other side of the fence.

The truck doors whomped open.

"Did you see the roadblock?" Leslie said. "We have to find another bridge."

Wanda hopped over the edge of the truck bed, landed on the gravel with a crunch. "Where's the next one?"

"Don't know." Beryl spread the state map over the hood. "Normally, I'd say we go for it—shoot it out. But we need to get these two to Monkshood."

"Something to be grateful for, I guess," Miranda muttered.

"What did you say?" Beryl asked.

"Never mind."

Beryl studied the state map.

The truck's cooling engine popped and pinged.

"Where are we?" Miranda touched a corner of the map. Jerked her hand away from the burning metal.

The Missouri's blue line meandered across the map in a mostly western direction.

"About a mile north of Booneville." Beryl tapped the map. "Just outside of Franklin."

Glasgow was the next city with a bridge.

"Guess we're going to Glasgow then."

"Isn't there another place we can cross?" Leslie said, her voice high-pitched and tight.

One look at Leslie's drawn face, and feathery tendrils spidered across Miranda's shoulders. "Do you know something we don't?"

"Bad things happened in Glasgow." She wriggled her shoulders. "Sorry, I'm being silly." Her unconvincing smile trembled. "It was in Virginia—hundreds of miles away, but I'd rather not enter it or any of its namesakes—ever again."

"We should turn around," Wanda said. "Take *Lady* to Waverly."

"Can't." Cold sharper than a knife, more painful than ice, spread through Miranda. She couldn't focus on the map. Wouldn't look at Wanda. "Glasgow's small enough they might not—"

"I know I said *Lady* would take longer," Wanda said. "But we could avoid roadblocks. And I don't think—"

"*Lady* is—" Her admission clotted in her throat.

"The *Lady* was compromised," Beryl said. "We destroyed her."

She's protecting me again. The clot thinned.

"What?"

"Compromised how?"

"You can't be serious."

"*I* destroyed her," Miranda said, her voice calmer than her heart. "I discovered the Second Sphere bugged her. Bugged us. Beryl saw me set her adrift. The Second Sphere and Coast Guard will investigate the wreck—we need to use that time and get as far from them as possible."

"You're saying they knew we were at that marina—they know where we're headed?" David scanned the surrounding horizons. "They know we're meeting Monkshood." He drilled Miranda with a glare.

Her stomach knotted. "You haven't told us, so they don't know the exact location."

"You should have told me. We could have—I have to warn him."

"How?" Beryl's arm swept the empty fields around them.

"We could have called from the store."

"No, we couldn't. They cut the phone lines. And if we used *Lady's* radio or destroyed the bugs so we could use the radio, guess who would've been up our asses?"

"We're wasting time," Miranda said between clenched teeth. She didn't say, "You're wasting time I bought you by destroying my home." She forced her jaw to relax. *They didn't make me do it.* "We have to assume roadblocks are everywhere. How do we get past them?"

"They don't know what we're driving. But they know there are four women and a man. Let's change that." Wanda moved toward the back of the truck. "How far to the bridge?"

"Twenty to thirty minutes to Glasgow." Beryl folded the map, followed her. "A roadblock could triple that time."

"It won't be comfortable, but we need camouflage." Wanda pulled a tarp out of the truck bed. "If some of us hide under the tarp, then there's only two or three people in this truck."

We're still identifiable. "They know who we are," Miranda said. "What Beryl and I look like. But camouflage is the right idea. Wanda and I will take the next leg. Beryl—ride in the back with David and Leslie."

Wanda locked on Miranda, pursed her lips. "I see. Give them what they expect."

Hands on her hips, Beryl set her jaw. "No."

Of course Beryl objects. "They're not looking for a farmer's wife and her help," Miranda said as calmly as she could.

Like a soldier relaxing from attention into at ease, Beryl shifted her stance. "True. But it'll be me and Wanda up front."

"You have a great rich widow act, but you won't convince anyone you're a farmer's wife. You need to help David and Leslie escape—get to Monkshood."

Beryl rubbed her chin. "You're willing to shoot your way through the roadblock?"

"If we have to." *Don't plan to.* "I need your shirt, David."

David took off his sweatshirt, then his green plaid flannel shirt.

She slipped on the shirt along with David's scent. Rifled through her rucksack and found her cap. Eyed her reflection in the truck's side mirror. *This has to work.* "We'll follow the route you found, Beryl. You're right. They won't expect us from the north."

Beryl, David, and Leslie crawled under the tarp. Knotted the corners near the cab so they could untie the tarp themselves.

Wanda drove down the rutted gravel road. Focused and not talking.

The rattle and squeak filled the cab again. But Wanda's silence was louder.

The sun bore through the windshield. Perspiration dampened her skin, her clothes. Miranda rolled her window down. The cab filled with dust.

Wanda didn't react. That worried Miranda even more. She tried to read Wanda's mood.

Without changing her clothes, Wanda looked like a completely different woman. She slouched behind the wheel and wore an expression that somehow looked tired and small. Deep brown eyes darted from the road ahead to Miranda and back again.

"Something wrong?" she asked.

"No. You're doing great. Don't know how, but you look like the help."

Wanda stared out the windshield. "I've played this damn role my whole damn life."

Miranda's stomach dipped. She looked away, out at the barren fields waiting for winter. She hadn't asked Wanda if she wanted to do this. Hadn't thought about how it would make Wanda feel. She put her hand on Wanda's arm. "I'm sorry…"

Wanda didn't take her eyes from the road. "Why didn't you tell me? About *Lady*?"

"It"—Miranda licked her lips—"hurts too much."

Wanda met her eyes. Gave a sharp nod. Focused on the road again.

They turned onto a paved, two-lane road. Traveled north. Fences and fields and trees passed like images in a flip-book.

About fifteen miles out from Glasgow, Wanda said, "I've got a bad feeling about this. Maybe it's different with a white person in the front seat, but every time the police stop a black person, they search the vehicle *and* the clothing of someone like me."

"They do?" Miranda asked.

Wanda nodded.

Miranda tried to think of similar situations with her family. Couldn't. "I'm making assumptions again. I'm sorry. I had no idea. But this means we have to come up with another plan, fast." She checked their route again. "Maybe we can use the river. Pull over. We need to talk to the others."

Wanda gave her a side-eye, stopped the truck. "Better plan?"

"I hope so. Help me undo the tarp." She got out of the truck. "Come up for some air," she said and, with Wanda's help, lifted the tarp.

Beryl and the other two popped up, noisily inhaled fresh air. "Not to be ungrateful," Beryl said, "but why are we stopping? Another roadblock?"

"Wanda says she always gets stopped and searched. And I've been thinking, we'll never outrun the police in this truck, much less the Second Sphere. If we have to stop at a roadblock—they'll find you and our supplies."

Beryl pulled one of her pistols out of her holster. Held it pointed to the sky. "Isn't that why we have guns?"

Throat tight, Miranda glared. "A shoot-out with the Second Sphere will kill us all."

"What's your plan?" Beryl smiled as if she indulged a child.

"You three cross the river. It's only a few hundred feet wide here. Find a boat if you can. Swim if you have to." She spread the map on the tarp in front of Beryl. Drew a finger along the railroad tracks that ran along the north side of Route 240. "The tracks parallel the highway bridge and for about a quarter mile beyond the river, then they separate. We'll meet you on the south side of the tracks, a quarter mile beyond the turn."

Beryl looked up at the cloudless blue sky. "Air's warm enough. Water'll be cold." She eyed Leslie. "Are you a solid swimmer?"

She grimaced. "I can swim. Don't know how solid."

"We've crossed a few rivers," David said. "She's a solid swimmer."

"Good." Beryl gave Miranda a slight nod. "Meet you on the other side."

Wanda traced an unnamed road with her finger. She double-tapped the map. "There's probably a dock—"

Beryl put her hand on Wanda's. "Best that neither of us knows the other's plan."

"Good luck." Wanda folded the map and climbed into the driver's seat.

"When I knock on the window, exit on the passenger's side."

"Right." Beryl climbed under the tarp.

"Don't get caught with the supplies and ammo," Beryl said.

Miranda swallowed. *Pretty sure we will be.* "Don't worry, we won't get caught."

"If you're caught—we need that ammo. If we have to fight the Azrael…"

"We'll be fine. I'll hide the supplies." *No idea how.* Held her hand up to stop Beryl's next question. "Better you don't know."

Beryl quirked her mouth. "One more thing."

"Yeah?"

"We'll wait fifteen extra minutes, then we move on."

"Understood. If we don't make it by then, we'll meet you in Waverly."

A few minutes later, she and Wanda watched the others grab their rucksacks and disappear into the trees.

"They'll make it," Miranda said, more for herself than for Wanda.

They drove on in silence.

"I won't surrender." Wanda kept her eyes on the road and hands on the steering wheel, but she tightened her grip on the wheel.

"Don't worry. We're going to sail through without a problem."

"How do we hide the ammo?"

"I don't know." Memories of Redemption flared. *If we're caught, there'll be no re-education. We'll face a firing squad.* Miranda's muscles bunched. "We won't surrender. No matter what."

She chewed her lower lip, tasted copper. No matter what she told Beryl, she wouldn't shoot it out with the police.

Wanda stopped the car at an intersection.

Miranda couldn't help it. She looked left, then right. A sign blocked her view of the highway. "Manure for sale. Open seven a.m. to five p.m." A red arrow pointed right.

She glanced at her watch. As long as it didn't take more than ten or fifteen minutes… "I have an idea. Turn right."

Chapter Twenty

The spring-like temperature and the blue sky unmarred by clouds raised Irene's spirits. She missed Buenos Aires, but the District's air smelled fresher, greener. And the shopping… Being the Prophet's Lady was growing on her.

She swung her daughters' arms back and forth, back and forth. Each girl carried a Garfinkel's bag with new saddle shoes in her free hand. Annabelle scowled. Sandra kept up a nonstop cheerful chatter.

A perfect day, despite Annabelle's dislike of shopping.

Half a block down, a neon sign shaped like an ice cream cone hung above a small shop. She grinned. She knew how to turn Annabelle's scowl into a happy daughter expression. "Girls, want some ice cream?"

Annabelle's scowl lightened. "Can we have whatever we want?"

Irene winked at her. "Banana splits coming up." Annabelle first tasted that sweet confection a few months ago. Now she couldn't get enough of it.

The little shop teemed with happy, chattering people. They buzzed back and forth in front of the display case. Exclaimed "oh" and "ah" at the dozens of choices. Ordered ice cream cookies, ice cream cones, and scoops with berries or nuts or sprinkles.

With three fresh-made banana splits in hand, she settled the three of them at a round, pink table with heart-shaped, wire-backed chairs. Took a bite of cold, creamy strawberry ice cream. Annabelle attacked her banana split in an orderly way. Precisely, one bite from the chocolate, next the strawberry, and then the vanilla. Sandra dug into a pile of whipped cream and chocolate-sauce-covered banana. Spoon over-filled, she jammed it into her mouth, left a whipped cream mustache behind.

Annabelle giggled. Just like a normal girl.

Irene put a hand to her chest to keep her expanding heart from exploding.

A brilliant flash of light blinded her. Spots danced in her vision. *Boom!*

The front window shattered.

A blow knocked the wind out of her. Rocked her chair back.

The table wobbled. Pebbles of glass rained on them.

Air whooshed out of the room.

For a split-second, time stopped.

Her ears popped.

Screams and shouts roared.

She gasped, sucked in air. *What's happening?*

Noise hammered her ears. Her heart slammed against her ribs.

Sandra screamed and screamed and flailed her arms.

Irene leaped to Sandra's side. Blood oozed from minor cuts, but there were no big bleeders or obvious broken bones. Irene wrapped her arms around her daughter, murmured soothing sounds. Reached for Annabelle. Nearly fainted. *Annabelle?*

Inexplicably, Annabelle stood near the shattered front window. Head tilted, she stared down at an overturned table and a bloodied woman who lay on the ground.

The woman's open eyes didn't blink. Irene's throat went dry. *She's dead.* "Annabelle. Come to Mother."

Annabelle shrugged and walked toward the glassless window.

"No, Annabelle. Come back here. *Now.*"

"Is your little girl hurt?" a young woman shouted above the screams and moans around them.

Irene flinched. "What? My little girl." She bounced a look from Annabelle to Sandra. "No. My girls are okay." She focused on the speaker. "What happened?"

"I don't know." The young woman wore an apron with the store logo on it.

"A car exploded," Annabelle said in a matter-of-fact tone.

Irene gawked at Annabelle.

Her daughter's cheeks were flushed, and her eyes glinted.

"A car? Exploded?" the clerk repeated. "Do you think it's a rebel attack?"

Irene's heart galloped. "Annabelle." She held a trembling hand out for her daughter. "Please, get away from the window." Her voice squeaked through her tight throat.

"Why? It's already broken."

Irene picked up the still-sobbing Sandra and charged after Annabelle. Glass crunched underfoot.

Down the street, billowing black smoke blotted out any recognizable landmarks.

She seized Annabelle's hand and retreated to the back of the store.

Crouched behind the display cases, the sweet aroma of chocolate and the coppery odor of blood made Irene nauseated. Every nerve in her body fired signals of hot and cold and run and hide. Her entire body trembled.

She hugged both her girls tight so they couldn't see the blood and debris splattered across the shop. Survivors gathered around them. Most of them wept.

The air thickened and grayed. Acrid rubber burned Irene's eyes and throat.

Annabelle pinched her nose.

Sandra's hands covered her face. *Cough-cough.*

Around them, people hacked and coughed and gasped for air.

"Girls, cover your nose and mouth with your handkerchiefs." She drew out her own. The faint scent of lilacs didn't have a chance against the nasty, stinging stench of burning rubber.

Sirens wailed and whooped and drew close. A man wearing a bloody sweater peered out the front door. "Help!" He shouted and waved. "We need help."

We need to get out of here. Irene stood. "Come, girls. We're going home."

A hand gripped her upper arm. "You can't leave."

She whirled on the older woman. "My driver is waiting."

"You're a witness to a crime. The police will want to talk to you."

She shrugged off the woman's touch. "We saw nothing.

Annabelle, take my hand." Irene took both her daughters' hands and led the girls around the debris to the store's useless front door.

A uniformed police officer met her there. "Step back inside, please."

"My driver is waiting."

"We've cordoned off the area. He'll wait."

She drew herself up. "Do you know who I am?"

"I'm sorry, Lady Earnshaw. We'll get you out of here as soon as possible."

Down the street, the smoke had thinned, grayed. Firefighters aimed hoses at blackened cars. Her knees jellied. *I can't stay here. Can't let the girls be here. They'll let me leave if Felix tells them to let me go home.*

The officer picked up a chair, set it upright. "Sit down. I'll have a someone check you, your daughter, and her friend out."

"I need to call my husband, the Prophet."

Chapter Twenty-One

Lightheaded, Irene blinked and blinked. But everything and everyone in the ruined ice cream shop remained fuzzy and out-of-focus. She cradled Sandra in her lap. She couldn't keep Annabelle from gawking, but Irene kept her other arm wrapped firmly around Annabelle's shoulders.

The crunch of glass underfoot came from a distance. A fuzzy form stepped in front of her. "Irene?"

Her vision sharpened. "Felix!" She wanted to fall into his arms, but they weren't alone.

"How badly are you and the girls injured?"

"Minor cuts. We're okay."

Like a magnet, the white tarp that covered the dead woman drew her gaze. The puddle of blood beside her belonged to a teenager. Firefighters had carried the boy out on a stretcher.

Felix brushed his warm, dry lips across her cheek.

She ran a hand through her hair. Glass pellets fell to her shoulders. "What happened?"

He put a hand on both her shoulders. Peered at her. "A car bomb went off."

"I know that. I mean—how? How did this happen this close to us?" She clutched his sleeves. Tried to stop coughing. Tried to control her ragged breathing.

"They're agnostics—terrorists. That's what they do."

"They could have killed Sandra or Annabelle or—all of us." She suppressed a shudder.

"Our police and security do their best, but they cannot predict what the rebels will do next." He looked pointedly at the dazed and bloodied people milling around them. "Let's get you home. After all this—excitement—you three need to rest." He scooped Sandra into his arms.

Sandra stirred, gazed up at her father, wrapped her arms around his neck and closed her eyes again.

Rest? Who can rest after this? "What time is it?" Irene asked. *Cough. Cough.*

"Five forty-five."

Her chest ached. *We've only been here an hour and fifteen minutes? But the explosion happened—lifetimes ago.* Closed her eyes. *We're alive. That's what counts.*

The stench of blood and smoke and burning rubber had lessened, but Irene couldn't stop coughing. It tore at her throat less than before.

"I'll help you, Mother." Annabelle wrapped her hands around Irene's upper arm.

Irene forced a stiff smile. "Thank you, darling. I'm all right." She stood. "See? Let's go."

They picked their way around a bloody yellow jacket laid across the face and torso of a man.

Outside, dozens of emergency vehicle lights strobed. Dirt and glass and bits of bricks and wood littered the sidewalk and street.

A tall, clean-shaven man in a charcoal gray suit followed them.

"Who's that?" she whispered to Felix.

Felix didn't even glance behind them. "My bodyguard. You and the girls each will have one from now on too."

Irene's chest tightened. "We won't ever be safe again, will we?"

"A precaution," Felix said. "No cause for alarm."

No cause— Irene bit the inside of her cheek. Tasted blood. Willed her thumping heart to slow.

They rounded a corner. The smell of burning rubber lessened. The debris disappeared. People walked the streets blissfully unaware of the recent explosion. And traffic roared past.

They stopped at a forest-green limousine. A uniformed driver opened the passenger door.

Felix gestured for her to get in. She did. Annabelle followed. Then Felix. The chauffeur handed Sandra to him once he'd gotten seated.

"How many people died, Father?" Annabelle asked.

Irene put a hand to her chest. *Poor Annabelle. She has experienced so much pain and loss in her life.*

"No need to worry yourself about that." Felix's voice held a note of tension.

Irene's stomach rolled and knotted. "She needs to know. How many?" *Knowing the facts might help her.*

"It's too soon to know for certain."

She buried her fists in her skirt. "You couldn't protect us from the terrorists. Don't protect us from information. How many?"

Felix eyed her. "Eleven dead, forty injured. Seventeen seriously." His tone was quiet, measured, not nearly horrified enough.

His words sent a chill through her. *They could have killed our girls.* She focused on the warm, soft leather of the car seat. Tucked her hands close to her sides for warmth.

She turned her attention to the scene outside the car. Peaceful brownstones. The car pulled up in front of the brownstone that was the Prophet's residence. She caught her breath. A pair of armed Second Sphere agents stood on the stoop, guarding their front door.

Irene couldn't look at Felix. "Tell me you're doing more than assigning bodyguards to us and our home."

"Please, Irene. Everything *will* be all right." He handed Sandra to the chauffeur.

"Don't. Tell. Me. That. It's not all right. Nothing is all right."

He stiffened. Climbed out of the car. "Annabelle. Go inside."

Annabelle bounced a glance between him and Irene, then exited the car.

"Make sure they stay upstairs," Felix instructed the chauffeur. Waited for them to close the door behind them.

He turned back to the car, bent, and whispered, "I know you were frightened. But you must calm down." Held out his hand for Irene. "Trust me, we will beat these terrorists."

Irene took a deep breath. Put on her dutiful-wife persona. Placed her icy hand in his sweaty one. Stood beside him. "You'll beat them?" she said in a sweet tone. "How?"

He glanced around him, over his shoulder, and over the car.

"Our Second Sphere agents have infiltrated a rebel cell. They'll work their way into the upper levels. Once they do, we will take down the terrorists."

She almost blurted out that the Second Sphere should take lessons from Mrs. Wynter. But Mrs. Wynter kept her teams private. *I will too. And I will make certain the rebels never come near my family again.*

Chapter Twenty-Two

Miranda wrinkled her brow and avoided breathing through her nose. *What was I thinking?* Even bagged. Even with the bags in the truck bed. Even with the windows closed tight. The day-old cow manure had an overpowering stench. *This has got to be the worst idea I've ever had.*

Wanda drove one-handed. She covered her mouth and pinched her nostrils shut with the other hand. Shot Miranda another you-did-this-to-me side-eye.

Slowing down for the city of Glasgow's slower speed limit only made it worse. They followed the ten-vehicle morning-rush-hour traffic down the business route.

Downtown sported a bank, a barber, and a dress shop. The filling station's red neon Open sign glowed. A gravel parking lot gave them a glimpse of the river and of the railroad bridge up ahead.

"This'll work," Miranda whispered without looking at Wanda. She bounced her knees double time.

The road curved. Tall, dirty-white grain elevators blocked their view of the river. Past the second set of elevators, traffic in front of them came to a full stop.

Less than half a mile ahead, the railroad bridge soared over the road. Under the bridge, four patrol cars with strobing rooftop lights blocked traffic. A black sedan with the red Fellowship symbol blazoned on the front door sat in a gravel lot between the last grain elevator and the bridge.

Miranda pressed her back into the seat. Swiped her damp palms down the thighs of her pant legs. She glanced at Wanda, who kept her eyes on the road.

In front of them, a teal and white sedan waited behind a woody station wagon that waited behind a white panel truck.

Police officers sauntered toward a vehicle in front of the white truck.

The gag-worthy stench of manure grew thicker inside the cab.

They crept forward one car's length.

Four police officers descended on the panel truck ahead of them.

One officer escorted the driver to the gravel lot in front of the Second Sphere car.

The driver took his ball cap off, put it on, took it off again. Rolled it in his hands. Three officers opened the truck's front and back doors. They searched tool boxes and looked under tarps. Searched the cab and used mirrors on poles to search the underside of the vehicle.

"I've got something," an officer shouted. He raised his arm above the passenger side door.

A Second Sphere agent stepped out of his car and marched over to the officer.

After a moment, he lowered his head and marched toward the driver.

The driver shouted, spun, and ran toward the river.

The Second Sphere agent pulled his pistol, aimed. *Bang!*

The man fell face forward into the gravel.

Miranda gulped back a yelp. Choked on the nose-burning odor of manure. Tried to steady her breathing. Tried not to look at Wanda. Tried not to look desperate.

An officer parked the panel truck under the bridge near two other civilian vehicles.

Another officer waved the woody station wagon forward, and the next inspection began.

Thirty minutes later, the woody safely crossed the bridge. The sedan got a pass too.

They were next. Miranda's throat turned to sandpaper. Her neck muscles bunched.

The patrolmen closed in on their truck. Stopped. Backed up.

After a whispered conversation, three of them returned to their vehicles. The gray-haired officer adjusted his cap, then clumped toward Wanda's side of the truck.

He wrinkled his nose and squinted past Wanda. "We're looking for a team of dangerous criminals," he said, his voice tight and nasal. "A man and several"—*cough-cough*—"women." *Cough-cough-cough.* "Seen anyone?"

Miranda leaned forward, peered around Wanda. "No, sir." Her voice strong, confident.

"Maybe your colored girl saw someone?"

Wanda sat stiff and statue-still and stared straight ahead.

Forcing a smile, wishing she could apologize to Wanda for what she had to do, Miranda said, "You may answer the officer, Wanda."

Wanda turned her lowered her head toward the officer. "No sir. I —ain't—seen no dangerous women." She looked down at her lap but hung on to the steering wheel as tightly as if she were drowning.

Cough-gag-swallow. His eyes watered. "That's some fresh manure you're carrying. Got anything else in there?"

"You can smell what we got." Miranda tried to speak without breathing in. She stifled a cough. "Dig around in it if you don't believe me."

"I believe you," the officer said. "Move along." He hustled away from the truck and waved them forward.

Wanda put the truck in gear and drove slowly away.

It worked. Miranda sagged into the seat.

A quarter mile down the road, the railroad trestle curved away from the road. They turned onto a dirt track that followed the raised railroad tracks.

"That is some fresh manure you're carrying," Wanda said in a near-perfect imitation of the patrolman's nasal tone. "Never seen a man move so fast as when you said he could dig around in the shit." She snickered. *Cough.*

Miranda laughed. *Choke. Cough.* A giggle-cough fit of hysteria took over.

Wanda pounded the steering wheel with one hand and laugh-coughed.

Miranda couldn't catch her breath. Each time she tried, the foul air triggered more coughing and more laughter.

"Stop. Stop!" She coughed some more.

"I can't." Wanda's laugh ended in a spasm of coughing.

"Back up." *Cough-cough-cough.* "Just passed—where we meet— the others."

Wanda backed the truck up. Switched off the engine.

Miranda sobered. The morning sun peeked over the treetops, cast deep shadows on this side of the wooden railway bridge. *No sign of Beryl and the others.*

"Shouldn't they be here?" Wanda asked.

"They're not late." *Yet.*

Miranda checked her watch again. *Beryl is more than capable, but anything that can go wrong— Can't just sit and wait.* "Might as well unload those bags."

"Are you serious?"

"Did you think we'd make the others ride on top of it?"

Miranda opened the tailgate. "We'll toss them under the trestle."

She climbed into the truck bed, strained to lift a bag. Couldn't hoist it high enough to get it over the side.

Wanda struggled with a bag too.

Without a word, Wanda released her bag and grabbed the free corners of Miranda's bag. They tossed it over the side.

After they heaved the tenth bag over the side, Miranda coughed and blew out a tired wheeze. "Gotta stop for a minute." She perched on the side of the truck bed. "How much do you figure those bags weigh?"

Wanda shrugged, sat on the opposite side. "At least ninety, maybe a hundred pounds."

"Feels like a ton." Miranda scanned up and down the tracks over and over.

Finally, Beryl, David, and Leslie came into view.

Miranda stood and waved. "You made it."

"Now they show," Wanda said. "When we're almost done."

Beryl stopped before they crossed beneath the railroad. So did David and Leslie. They exchanged grimaces.

"Why do you and the truck smell like shit?" Beryl asked in a nasal voice.

Miranda grinned. "Hey, Wanda. When did we stop smelling it?"

"Did we get used to it?"

"How can you get used to that?" Leslie pinched her nose, turned her head away.

"Is that *really real* shit?" David covered his nose and mouth.

"Day-old cow manure."

"What the hell?"

"Don't knock it," Miranda said. "Got us through the roadblock."

"Well, don't let us stop you from unloading it," Beryl said and gestured for the others to step back.

Miranda stood. "Help us unload, so we can get going."

Beryl, David, and Leslie exchanged glances.

They grumbled the entire ten sweaty minutes until Miranda and Wanda tossed the last bag over the side.

Miranda trudged to the front of the truck, opened the passenger door. Did a double take.

"Oh, no, you don't," Beryl said from behind the steering wheel. "You two reek."

"If we stink, so do you."

"Not like you do," Beryl said. "Ride in the back."

"We don't stink as bad as the tarp."

Outvoted, Miranda and Wanda rode in the back.

Chapter Twenty-Three

Beryl crouched behind a stack of dusty suitcases in the loft of an old barn outside of Waverly. The rot of a small, dead creature fouled the air up here. Reminded her of her cell in the bowels of Redemption. Of ten years of torture. She curled and uncurled her toes.

Behind her, silhouetted by the barely open hay door, Wanda kept watch on the fields.

"Movement," Wanda said in her husky whisper.

Hot electricity zipped through Beryl.

"Five. Split. Four west. One East."

Beryl flattened against the floor and inched toward the edge. The pickup, a charcoal gray shape, faced the carriage doors. She couldn't see Leslie, who sat in the driver's seat.

David's shadow-shape darted out from behind the pair of barrels positioned at the truck's ten o'clock to the barn's east window. "Confirm one."

Beryl eased away from the loft's edge. Returned to her hiding place. Cocked her pistol and steadied her aim on the top suitcase.

"West. Split," Miranda whispered, barely audible from her position at the back door. "Three north."

One of the barn's main doors creaked opened. A male silhouette slid inside. The door closed.

David spotlighted him with his flashlight.

The man stopped, arms outstretched, fingers splayed. The hood of his sweatshirt hung over his eyes. *No way to recognize him.* "Wolfsbane isn't about a wolf." His unfamiliar baritone held an edge.

Beryl aimed at his center mass. "And Monkshood isn't about a monk's hood, yet they are the same." She projected a calm, confident tone. Inside, her adrenaline-spiked nerves and muscles hummed.

"They are. I'm going to bring him in. All right?"

"Do it," she said.

The man took three steps backward. Rapped on the door three times, then two-one-two. The door opened again, and two more men entered.

One of them came forward. "David?"

Ethan. Beryl's heart lurched. She hadn't seen her husband for two years. Not since the night he'd visited her on the boat. Told her the remaining Azrael would all die of that old-age disease. She uncocked her pistol. "Clear." She closed her eyes.

"I'm here," David said. Footsteps shuffled across the concrete floor. The scratch of a match sounded extraordinarily loud.

She waited for the hiss of the lantern and a glow beyond her eyelids. Peered down. The lantern on the floor threw a circle of light. As instructed, David stood behind the barrels. Ethan and his men stood near the door. One positioned on Ethan's left. The other guarded the door.

She gave Wanda the signal meaning "cover me."

Wanda moved to a position behind a stack of old tractor tires at the loft's front edge.

Beryl holstered her weapon and descended to the barn floor. Pulled her pistol and held it at her side.

"Your message said you had urgent information," Ethan said.

The lantern radiated heat and the acrid odor of kerosene.

She took her position at nine o'clock to David's twelve. A stack of apple crates filled with junk stood within diving distance.

Ethan had changed his appearance again. His shoulder-length salt-and-pepper hair and a bushy, unkept jet-black beard had completely transformed him. *Not your best look.*

"Beryl. It's been a while." His flat tone made it impossible to gauge his emotions. "Let's get to the point quickly. Meeting here is risky—for all of us."

She didn't recognize either of the men in his security detail. "The information is—sensitive."

A wry smile flitted across Ethan's face. "I trust these men with my life. What's so important?"

"You can come out now."

Leslie came out of the truck, one arm behind her. She strode toward Ethan. "I owe you a huge thank you—"

Ethan's bodyguard darted forward, placed himself between Ethan and Leslie.

Beryl aimed her pistol at the man's knee. When he fell, she'd have a clear kill shot on the other one.

Ethan put a hand on his man's shoulder. Sent the man back to the shadows with a jerk of his head. He faced Leslie. "Hello, young lady." Shook her hand. "I don't know you, do I?"

"No, sir." Leslie said. "After my parents were Taken, my brothers and I hid in the mountains. I got hurt, and the Cleaners caught us, me and my younger brothers. Your men rescued us—" She sounded genuinely grateful. Looked at him as if he were a hero.

He stared blankly at her.

Beryl's chest tightened. *A lie?*

"From an abandoned church near Ambrose—"

"Right. Ambrose, Virginia. I remember. Underwood's crew." His expression warmed.

Okay. Not a lie. Beryl toggled the safety and holstered her pistol.

"Gertrude agreed to care for four orphans, three boys and a girl. You're the girl?"

Gert? Beryl's chest ached, not as sharply as before, but the ragged hole Gert's absence left remained. *Leslie was one of Gert's kids?*

"Yes, sir. Gert was the best—" Leslie's voice grew strained. She cleared her throat.

"I'm sorry for your loss," Ethan said. "You have information for me?"

"It's about this." She held the rag doll by the neck. Its legs swayed.

He sucked in a breath, took half a step back. "What is this?"

"It's an Azrael's doll. I found it."

"You found it?"

"It belonged to the son of a research scientist."

"Who? I need a name."

"Dr. Russell."

Ethan's men ran to the windows, guns drawn, scanned outside.

They recognize the name. Consider it dangerous. More of Leslie's story confirmed.

"You stole from Russell and came to me?" Ethan's voice held incredulity tinged with anger.

"I'm not an idiot. I pretended Alex had lost it in the park. Even helped look for it. After a few days, I got a telegram that said my older brother was dying. They granted me leave."

"And you concluded that this child's toy is what—an Azrael's doll?" Ethan's voice was low and tight. He glared at Beryl, then Leslie. "Who put you up to this?"

"Put me up to what?" Leslie asked. "I came to warn you."

"Goodbye." He spun and headed for the door.

Beryl's ears grew hot and her palms damp. "What if they are growing Azrael again, Ethan?"

He whirled to face her. "How can you believe that? You were there—We destroyed their place at Quantico, the lab and the whole Frankenstein island."

Memory transported her—she stood in the blood of a dozen little girls who looked exactly like her daughter. She dug her fingernails into her palms, drove the memory away. "Yes. We destroyed all that. Think Ethan. Where else would she get that doll?"

"She could have made it, stole it, bought it—I don't care. We destroyed the lab. If any Azrael survived, they would have died of that old-age disease by now."

"The doll is real. She knows things she shouldn't have been able to learn. Someone must have gotten away—"

"I saw them," Leslie said in a firm voice. "I saw the little girls, the Azrael."

Beryl's stomach tightened. *I knew she wasn't telling me everything.*

Ethan scoffed. "You saw little girls—probably the daughters of unsuspecting Fellowship members. But they aren't the same," he said. "They aren't the abominations that—"

"They were identical—like twins, but there were at least a dozen of them. I saw one of them kill…a woman…" Her voice drifted off, soft and quivery.

Beryl went cold. The Fellowship had destroyed her daughter. She wouldn't—couldn't—allow them to continue.

Ethan regarded Leslie for a long thirty seconds. "How?" His question hung in the air.

Leslie closed her eyes, took a couple of shaky breaths, then said, "With knives."

"Not what I meant. How did you see this murder?"

"Alex's nursery was in an office near their lab."

"Go on," David said. "They need to hear it all."

She gave him a wan smile. "Alex was fussy. So I broke the rules, took him into the hall for a walk." She wrapped her arms around herself. Shivered. "It's weird to be in a cave that huge—"

"A cave?" Beryl exclaimed. Ethan echoed her.

She gave them a bewildered look. "Yes, I mentioned that before, didn't I?"

"No," Miranda and Wanda chorused from their positions, guarding the backup exit.

"The lab is in Springfield, in this gigantic warehouse inside a cave. Actually, it's a former mine. Spooky. No sunlight. Huge rock pillars everywhere…"

"We get the picture," Beryl said. "You took Alex for a walk and…?"

"Right." Leslie licked her lips. "It's big enough it has its own park with potted evergreen trees and stuff. A bunch of girls stood on the other side of the park. I thought they were Brownies or Girl Scouts." She took a deep breath. "The woman started screaming when the girl stabbed her. Killed her. Then a loud voice said, 'And thou shalt not allow any creature, man, or woman, to harm thee. His will has been done.'" Leslie's voice shook. "I recognized the voice—it was Betty Jean—Mrs. Russell."

Ethan stiffened. "Dr. Russell is the Fellowship's number one psychiatrist. His wife is a psychiatric nurse." He locked a glare on Leslie. "Why should we trust you?"

Leslie put her hands on her hips. The limp doll dangled from her right fist. "You of all people should know I would never work for the Fellowship. Ever."

"Ethan," David said, "she fought hard alongside me to bring this information to you."

"I believe her," Wanda said.

"Why?" Beryl asked.

Wanda tilted her head, regarded Leslie. "Knowing who to trust —that's how I survived."

Beryl nodded. "What if our intelligence was flawed two years ago?" she asked Ethan, cold, hard. "If we missed one lab—we could have missed more than one."

Ethan scrunched his face. Studied each of them. "Obviously you all believe what's—impossible for me to believe. Why tell me?"

Beryl glowered at him. "SABR needs to help find and wipe out all the labs—completely this time." Clenched her jaw until it ached.

Ethan scratched his chin through his beard. The *scratch-scratch* pierced the tense silence. Finally, he shook his head. "Sorry, I can't believe it. If the Fellowship had Azrael all this time, people would have been Taken all along." He moved toward the door.

"Wait." Miranda stepped into the light, toward Ethan. "I have an idea." She gave Beryl a brief glance. "You know my brother-in-law, Felix, is the Prophet now. He has never been a leader. Did nothing unless my sister, Irene, told him to. We can talk to Irene—"

"Miranda—" David whispered.

"Talk? To the Prophet's wife?" Ethan's tone held a warning.

Miranda ignored it. "We can avoid more bloodshed and deaths. She'll agree to a temporary truce."

"They murdered a woman, and you want a truce?" Leslie's voice rose in pitch.

Ethan purpled. "A truce? Seriously?"

David cleared his throat. "You should have spoken to me about this first," he muttered.

"Have you forgotten what Redemption's like?" Ethan asked.

"Colored folk don't get prison." Wanda's voice trembled.

"We can't fix the dead," Miranda said, "but we can stop the bloodshed and deaths. Irene agreed to a truce, to peace talks."

"The sister you exiled will grant a truce?" Beryl's jaw twitched. *Miranda needs some sense shaken into her.*

"It doesn't matter," Ethan said. "I'm not putting a single life in danger based on the hope of a truce."

"This is our chance for peace," Miranda said. "We've got to try."

"Not when trying is dying." His fists knotted.

"I didn't say it'd be easy—"

"Dying is easy," Ethan bellowed.

"No one has to die." Miranda's cheeks held two bright spots.

"Whoa, whoa." Wanda moved into the light, held her hands up in a stop gesture. "Are you people even on the same side?"

"If he'd just listen, we can work through this," Miranda said through her teeth.

Beryl huffed out a breath. "Enough. While you and" —she pointed at Miranda, then Ethan—"you are negotiating, they are growing an army of Azrael." She stared at Miranda. "You didn't see the lab on the island. They cut cells from—a woman—grew babies in vats. Turn them into killers." She'd never forget the bloody knives in ten-year-old hands… She faced Ethan. "You know what I've said is true."

Ethan shook his head in disbelief. "The doll isn't proof. I can't spend SABR resources on maybes. We have a plan—we have to focus on that." He started toward the door again. "It's not safe to stay here. This meeting is over."

An idea popped into Beryl's head. "What if I—if we—did some recon?" *Someone has to do it. Might as well be me.*

Ethan stopped, gave her a "what-now" glare over his shoulder.

"If I see Azrael with my own eyes, would you take my word for it?"

Ethan canted his head and considered her. "If they exist, spying on them could get you killed."

"If the—abominations—are being created again, they'll kill us all."

His stare didn't waiver. "Let me talk to my lieutenants." He and his three men disappeared into the shadows.

Beryl strained to listen. Their unintelligible whispers verged on the edge of understanding.

Ethan came back. Stood before Beryl. "If you can find the Azrael, if they exist, we will help destroy them. But we have four conditions."

"Only four?" Beryl muttered.

"What was that?"

She gave him a tight smile. "Nothing. Go on."

"I'm sorry. We need more than your word—more than a doll— we'll need photographs."

"Photographs? Where am I going to get a camera?"

His eyes met hers. "You'll have to be careful, very careful."

His soft tone reminded her of other times, gentler times. The weight of a lost lifetime tore through her, ripped away scabs she'd thought healed. She bore the pain for a half-second, then hardened herself. "And the other rules?"

"You'll take one of my lieutenants with you."

Beryl eyed the men at the edge of the lantern's ring of light. "Which one?"

"Karl Irvine."

A man stepped forward. Put his hood down. He had an eager-to-please smile, thick, wavy brown hair, and baby cheeks with a barely there five o'clock shadow.

"I don't have time to train your soldiers, Ethan." Beryl pinched her lips closed, too late to keep the words in.

"Karl's earned my respect. He deserves yours too." Ethan's familiar, measured tones warned that if he lost his temper, she'd lose her only opportunity.

A steel band tightened around her chest. *If I didn't need your damn army* — "I'll give him a chance to earn mine," she said. "Next?"

"If you haven't found proof in one week, seven days from today exactly, we"—he waved his hand at all of them—"won't speak of Azrael ever again."

Hands on her hips, she glared at him. "One week isn't long enough to search multiple locations."

He nodded. "I thought you'd say that. Okay. Two weeks. Fourteen days. Not one minute longer. No photographic proof, and the hunt and all talk of this is over. Agreed?"

She worked her tongue against the back of her teeth. She'd never lied to him before. "Agreed."

Chapter Twenty-Four

Miranda's turn at the steering wheel took them to the outskirts of Springfield, Missouri. She followed Leslie's direction and turned off the business route. Drove between sheer rock walls that closed in a steep, two-lane road down to Springfield Underground. On her right, the rock wall gradually fell away. Three pairs of railroad tracks came out from behind a small grove of trees, paralleled the road.

At the bottom of the quarry, the first and second spurs of the railroad entered the rock wall through two different extra-tall garage doors. A sign with a huge red arrow labeled "Underground Storage" pointed to a smaller door.

The truck bumped over the third spur, hard. *Don't do this, don't do this* ran in circles in her brain. Her chest tingled.

"A working quarry." Beryl stared out the passenger window she sat next to. "No one would look here for a secret lab."

Miranda glanced at Leslie, who sat next to her. Leslie nodded, and Miranda drove through the regular-sized garage door. Ironworks gates pushed up against the walls held a sign that read, "Open Mon-Fri. 6 a.m.-6 p.m." Putty-colored rock walls surrounded them. The cool, dry air held a dirty mineral odor.

High overhead, a triple strand of fluorescent lights brightened the road. The putter of the truck's engine bounced off the walls. The eerie sound raised the hairs on the back of Miranda's neck.

At a four-way stop, the road opened up to generous two lanes and brightened under more fluorescent lights. Miranda stopped the truck. Her hands ached from gripping the steering wheel so tight.

At each corner of the intersection, massive rock pillars rose from the floor to the rock ceiling nineteen feet above them.

An eight-foot-tall sign up on the right held a dozen arrows, each painted different colors, each pointing different directions with a range of numbers on each arrow. Below it a speed limit sign read 5 mph. *Holy crap. Seven hours won't be enough time.*

Beneath the arrows, a wire rack held maps.

Beryl hopped out, got a handful.

"You sure you know how to get there?" Miranda asked Leslie.

"I remember," Leslie said. "Follow the main road."

Miranda eased the truck across the railroad track, followed the main road.

Every fifty feet, another pair of pillars stood on opposite sides of the road. The bottom three feet of each pillar was squared-off and smooth and painted. Numbered signs marked each warehouse dock recessed in the space between the pillars.

An open garage door gave a glimpse of dozens of Ford sedans in rows that vanished from sight.

Miranda slowed and gawked. "That warehouse is huge." She eyed the road ahead of her, fearing that the sign claiming this was the biggest underground storage in the world was true. "Are all of the warehouses that big?"

"According to this they are," Beryl said, "or bigger."

Most spaces between pillars were closed off, with walls of painted concrete blocks. Big red letters declared those spaces For Lease or Rent.

"How big is this place?" Miranda asked.

Wanda leaned through the slider. "The pamphlet says there's more than seven miles of road. Doesn't give a total space measurement."

"That's a heck of a lot of space," David said. "I'm glad Leslie knows her way around down here. Even with this map, I'm lost already."

Miranda glanced at the review mirror. David and Wanda studied the pamphlet. Karl's head was back as if he studied the ceiling.

"The main road circles the whole place." Beryl leaned forward to study the map spread out on the dashboard, with several serpentine side roads and lots of dead-end roads in every direction. "At least it's color-coded."

Beep-beep-beep. Startled, Miranda scanned the road ahead and behind her, searching for a vehicle backing up but only found an empty road. "Where is it?"

"Sound carries down here," Leslie said. "It's probably from a room down the road we just crossed."

"Where's the red section?" Beryl asked.

"There isn't one."

Beryl turned a glare on Leslie. "You said the lab had a red door."

"Secret labs don't get on maps." Leslie faced Miranda. "I'll tell you when to turn."

At the next intersection, orange pillar bases signaled a new section.

"Keep going," Leslie said. "Turn right at the next intersection. The light blue section."

The rock walls closed in on them. And the light grew dim. Negotiating the narrower road with only a single row of fluorescent lights sent Miranda's heart into overdrive. Her hands grew icy and damp.

"After the next pillar on the right, you'll see a red door in a white corrugated-metal wall," Leslie said. "That's the lab. Don't stop. The window in the door is a one-way-mirror. They can see you, you can't see them."

Beryl knocked on the back window, pointed to her eyes, then pointed two fingers to the right wall in a scanning motion.

Visible in the rearview mirror, Wanda, David, and Karl gave thumbs up signs.

Miranda stuck to the five-mile-per-hour speed-limit.

Eight metal steps with red safety rails led up to the red door in the white metal wall. That was it. No other windows. No other doors. No docks. And no signs.

And someone is on the other side of that door, watching. Prickles skittered down Miranda's back.

After the next intersection, Miranda parked in the deep shadows of an empty dock. She left the truck idling. *Beryl's going to want to barge in through the door. There's got to be a better way.*

"How did you get in?" Beryl asked. "Does everyone have a key or is there a signal?"

"When I came with the Russells, they just held up their security badges."

"Security badges." Beryl's mouth twisted in a lopsided frown.

"Where are the loading docks?" Miranda asked.

"I don't know," Leslie said.

"There's got to be loading docks, don't you think?" Miranda aimed her question at Beryl.

"Right. And at least one other exit in case of fire."

"Dr. Russell spoke of going to the docks to see if some supplies came in," Leslie said. "But I never saw it."

"How big is the lab?" Wanda asked through the slider. "How many people work there?"

"Big enough to have a park," Leslie said, exasperation coloring her voice. "And big enough to drive a golf cart down the hallways."

Beryl rubbed her mouth and chin. "Get us out of here, Miranda."

She was happy to oblige.

A mile down the road, she stopped at a small city park. Unoccupied swings swayed and creaked. Dry leaves swirled at the base of an unused slide.

They sat at a picnic table despite the chilly breeze. Ate the donuts and orange juice Wanda had found at Tucker's.

"Did you see the power cables going into that place?" David wiped powdered sugar from his mouth. "And the ventilation shafts? The lab must be huge."

Wanda put her purple jelly dripping donut down on a paper plate. "With all the cloak-and-dagger, one entrance, an unmarked door with a one-way mirror, security's going to be a nightmare. Heck, they probably watched us drive past. We'll never get in."

"There's always a way," Karl said. "No security system is fool-proof." He folded his arms on the tabletop and leaned forward. "The loading dock is our way in. We find it. Wait for a big delivery. While they're busy moving stuff, we sneak in."

"Were you seeing the same setup I was?" David asked. "Someone will notice us."

"No, they won't. Not if we stay overnight. There are plenty of dark, unoccupied docks to hide in, watch from. They will never know we're there." Karl sat back with a pleased expression on his face.

Wanda rested her elbows on the table, her chin on her folded hands. "I'm going to guess they don't keep the lights on all night."

The idea of staying in the cave overnight sent gooseflesh down Miranda's chilled arms.

Leslie finger-painted in the sprinkles that had fallen onto her plate.

David pinched his lips.

No one spoke.

The swings gave a louder-than-usual creak. Miranda jumped.

"It might work," Beryl said. "We'll need a camera, of course. Some flashlights. Black spray paint to block security cameras—"

"I hate to be the dissenting voice," David interrupted. "But if the lab is half as big as we think it is—" He held up three fingers, pointed to the first one. "One, how many days will it take to search it? Two, how do we map the lab in case we need to return? And three—how do we get out?"

"How to get out is the first thing we need to figure." Wanda made a deliberate, comical grimace. "Staying overnight scares me. But"—she squared her shoulders—"I'm in if everyone else is."

Beryl rubbed her forehead. "We need a breadcrumb trail that no one else can see, erase, or alter."

David picked at a loose splinter on the tabletop with his penknife. "Chalk won't work."

"They'll notice paint," Karl said, tapped the side of his paper cup.

Miranda couldn't believe it. They want to do this.

"In my drama class...." Leslie said in a quiet voice. Her eyes misted. "We used a luminous paint on the edge of the stage so we wouldn't fall off in the dark."

"Don't you need black lights to see that?" Karl asked.

"They pointed hooded black lights at the paint line."

Beryl looked cautiously optimistic. "Where do we get luminous paint and hand-held, battery-powered black lights?"

"Our hardware store had the paint." Leslie gestured toward town. "Springfield's much bigger than my hometown. One of their hardware stores probably carries both."

"So what?" Wanda asked. "So we find a camera, some lights, and some paint. We still don't have a plan to get out."

"We wait till morning," Karl said. "Workers will come in, and delivery trucks will go out. They won't notice one more truck leaving."

"Right," Beryl said in a droll tone. "One problem you all have overlooked."

Karl shot her a puzzled look. "What?"

"I saw several alarm systems." Beryl spread the map on the wooden table. The wind picked up the paper and made it pop.

Four hands anchored the corners, and they huddled over the map. Beryl circled the location of the red door. It sat in the middle of a bunch of grayed-out spots. Beryl argued those were the vacant rooms. David thought they should search one of the occupied warehouse spaces on the road behind the red door road first.

The last bite of Miranda's cinnamon-covered donut tasted like sand.

Beryl snapped a finger against the map. "Each of us will carry one of these maps and mark our progress on it. An X means you ruled out that location, and a question mark means it needs a second look. Remember," she continued, "we're looking for trucks delivering medical supplies, laboratory equipment, things like that."

"The Russells brought treats to the nursery," Leslie said. "There has to be an automat or a cafeteria in there."

"So large shipments of food, medical supplies, lab equipment, and what else?" Wanda asked. "School supplies? Clothing for growing girls? Rag dolls?

"Watch the power cables and ventilation shafts overhead too," David said. "The lab needs lots of power. That means larger-than or more-than-normal cables and ventilation."

"If one of us finds the lab," Karl said, "how do we signal each other?"

"Radios probably don't work down there," Wanda said.

"Probably not," Beryl said. "We'll meet back at the truck every hour."

Miranda ignored the roller-coaster-riding donuts in her belly. *If they can do it, so can I.* "Let's go shopping."

Chapter Twenty-Five

The limousine windows magnified the heat of the Kansas City sun and raised beads of perspiration on Irene's upper lip. She blotted it with her lace handkerchief.

Next to her, Sandra squirmed and fanned her skirt up and down. She exposed an indecent amount of leg above her knees. Irene gently lowered Sandra's toasty hands.

Across from them, Annabelle rolled her eyes at her younger sister's antics.

Sandra wriggled. Her bare legs made the leather squeak.

The limo crossed the Missouri River, then turned east again. The vehicle trundled down a narrow two-lane road between limestone bluffs on their left and the river on their right.

"Look girls," she said. "Inside that bluff is where we're going." She pointed out the north window at the sheer rock bluff. Crystals within the limestone glinted in the sun. *Pretty, but inside we'll be beneath tons of rock and dirt.* This time it wasn't the sun that increased her perspiration.

They passed asphalt and concrete drives that led to garage doors set into the limestone. Then came a stretch of uninterrupted rock walls until they reached and turned onto another concrete drive with a taller-than-usual garage door.

Twenty-five feet in front of the closed garage door, the limo stopped alongside a post with a covered keypad. The driver punched keys that emitted musical tones, and the garage door raised.

The limo inched forward. Sunlight that spilled into the entrance dimmed, then vanished. Chill bumps ran down Irene's arms.

Strips of artificial lights strung down the center of the ceiling provided sufficient but lackluster light.

Annabelle rolled down her window, peered at the rough rock walls painted a brilliant white. Cool, dry air rolled into the limo.

Irene's nose twitched at the mineral scent, and her stomach twisted.

They rode down a two-way concrete drive. The limo stopped at a railroad-crossing sign.

"Look, Mommy." Sandra's face reflected her wonderment. "A railroad train comes in here."

"It's so they can bring in and carry out supplies," Annabelle said. "If you'd studied, you'd know that." Annabelle always prepared for the trips they took. "The train tracks run along the front here with spurs that reach further back."

The limo bumped over the tracks and drove deeper into the cave. The walls opened up. On each side of the road, passenger cars and vans were parked nose-in between massive rock pillars. The pillar-lined road stretched ahead of them until it vanished.

They passed an area between pillars with a two-story wall that looked like an office building. Irene couldn't fathom who would want to work down here.

A roaring, whirring sound filled the air.

"What is that?" Sandra asked.

"Fans," Annabelle said in a superior voice. "Huge fans pull fresh air through the cave."

Irene worried her lower lip. Dr. Gallaway's presentation had been impressive and a bit frightening. She prayed he would keep his promise and today's tour would be appropriate for the girls.

"Look, Mommy. Four pillars with colored stripes at the bottom mean there's a cross street." Sandra pointed at a pillar.

"The color helps with one's orientation," Annabelle said. "You should have read your homework."

They turned again. Fans roared, drove air deeper into the cave.

The limo bounced and swayed down a darker, narrower roadway. Irene's chest tightened. She suppressed a shudder. *Mustn't upset the girls.*

They turned between a pair of pillars and pulled to a stop alongside a post with a covered keypad.

"There's no train tracks here," Sandra said. "Why is there a gate for a stupid garage door?"

The driver punched five keys. A whir sounded, and the gate raised.

They drove forward. The garage door clanked and rattled and rolled up. Blinding light spilled out.

They entered an area with dozens of private coupes and sedans parked between pillars. Chains clanked behind them. The garage door lowered.

On their left, a half-dozen DayGlo green golf carts filled a parking area. The limo driver parked, then opened the door for Irene and the girls.

Sandra raced to one of the golf carts. "These are like the ones Papa uses. I want to drive." Her voice echoed in the rocky chamber. She squealed. "Did you hear that?" Her voice echoed again. Giggles burst from her, echoed, and she erupted. Her laughter came back at them from every direction.

"Awesome." Annabelle glowered at her sister.

Irene refrained from giggling at the two of them. "Yes, Sandra. We hear it. No, you may not drive. Now please settle down and behave like the young lady I know you are." She reached for the sweaters she'd brought, then changed her mind. *It's warmer in here than I expected.*

"The ceiling is nineteen feet high," Annabelle said. "I didn't think it would echo."

"It's cray-zee!" Sandra shouted and laughed.

"It's science." Annabelle's tone had a pinch of smugness.

The limo driver seated them in a golf cart. Walls of shiny white tile filled the space between the pillars on their left. But on their right, parallel parking places ended in a steep ramp to a ground level four feet higher than the main road. Dim light from the road only reached as far as the third pillar. The pitch black beyond gave Irene the willies.

"Are we going to see all of the mine?" Sandra asked.

"Of course not," Annabelle said. "This mine covers thousands of acres. There are ten thousand pillars. Each of which is twenty-five feet in circumference and forty feet apart. There's more than twenty miles of paved road and five and a half miles of train track. And the temperature is sixty-two degrees all year long."

Annabelle's brain worked like a Multivac computer. Whatever she read, she could recite later.

Sandra frowned. "Do all the people down here work for you, Mommy?"

Irene suppressed a smile. "No one down here works for me. The people in the lab work for all the Fellowship members, darling. We'll be meeting Dr. Gallaway in a few minutes. Listen carefully. One day, you girls may supervise a project like this."

"I'll be a good boss, Mommy." Sandra flashed a gape-toothed smile.

A grin escaped Irene. *Thank goodness it isn't a sin to favor your natural child.*

The driver parked in a nose-in space.

They entered through double glass doors set in a wall of frosted glass framed by white tiles.

Inside, pristine chrome and turquoise armchairs created conversation areas in the lobby. A thick, brown rug lay between each set of chairs, covering most of a polished concrete floor. A fresh pine scent wafted in the air. If one ignored the rock walls at each end of the room, one wouldn't know they were underground. Irene embraced the illusion.

Dr. Louis Gallaway's shoes clacked down the hallway. He came into the lobby, toward Irene with his hand outstretched. Flashed his perfect white teeth. "Irene, welcome." He took her hand in a cool but firm grip.

"Thank you for offering us this tour." She placed a hand on Sandra's shoulder. "This is my daughter Sandra."

Sandra held out her hand. "How do you do, Dr. Gallaway?"

The doctor solemnly shook her hand. "I am well and charmed to meet you."

"And this," Irene turned to include her adopted daughter, but she wasn't there. *Annabelle? Where are you?* Her stomach hollowed. She whirled, searched. *Ah, there.*

Annabelle stood a few feet away.

The tension in Irene's body released, left her shaky.

Annabelle had her back to them, faced the front wall.

Dozens of plants hung on this side of the frosted glass. Round topiaries, spiky ferns, and cascades of variegated philodendron made a pleasing geometric presentation.

"Mother?" Annabelle asked, her head cocked to one side. "How do they not die in here?"

"The lights above them are growing lights," Dr. Gallaway said. "They mimic the sun."

"Annabelle, please come here and greet Dr. Gallaway properly."

Annabelle straightened, then complied. She looked Dr. Gallaway straight in the face, offered her hand.

The doctor's mouth dropped open. He pulled his hand back.

Before Irene could react, he recovered and shook Annabelle's hand. "Very nice to meet you." He glanced at Irene. "I can't help but notice—"

Irene clenched her teeth behind her courteous smile. *No matter Annabelle's birth country, her miracle rebirth makes her Fellowship. Makes her family.* "Annabelle's my adopted daughter." She kept her tone cool and distant.

Dr. Gallaway's smile widened. "I meant no offense." He turned back to Annabelle. "My apologies for my surprise, young lady. I think you will—all of you—will understand soon. But first, let me show you our facilities and explain our work. Follow me." He whirled on his heel.

Irene's need for Dr. Gallaway's army to defeat the rebels warred with her instinct to show him her back. She ran her tongue over her teeth. *We've come all this way. We should probably at least complete the tour.* She took each of her daughter's hands and followed him through a door into a wide hallway.

Normal-sized walls punctuated with wooden doors lined both sides of the hall. After every fourth door, a large pipe rose from the floor to the ceiling. Peering overhead through the bank of overhead fluorescents, Irene discovered a network of pipes overhead held by steel trusses bolted into the natural rock ceiling.

"The builders just finished this front area—our offices. We haven't spent a lot of time in them yet. We use them to type reports or make phone calls or have private meetings." He turned a corner and entered an open area with DayGlo yellow golf carts.

"Oh," Sandra began.

Irene squeezed her hand, and Sandra quieted.

"Lady Earnshaw, would you like to sit in the front?"

"Thank you. I'll sit in the back with Annabelle. Sandra may take that seat."

They climbed in the golf cart, and Dr. Gallaway drove along one end of the building. Tiles filled the spaces between pillars on one side.

On their left, the asphalt sloped up again. This time, the raised level was brightly lit and filled with a running track and exercise equipment. Dr. Gallaway called it the Obstacles Course.

They drove straight into a light-filled warehouse lined with heavily laden shelves.

"This is Central Supply," the doctor said over the hum of the golf cart's engine. "All of our supplies come in through those dock doors over there." He pointed down the main aisle to the open garage door more than a football field's length away.

Beep-beep-beep. Dr. Gallaway stopped their golf cart. A forklift trundled across the intersection. "The dock foreman records the date and time and description of the items received as they unload the trucks. He assigns each box or pallet a number and a letter. The man on the forklift takes the boxes to the row with that number and the shelf with that letter." He turned and followed the forklift.

Annabelle leaned forward. "I read you get between six to ten semitrucks full of supplies each day. Is that true?"

Dr. Gallaway shot Annabelle an approving glance. "It's closer to twelve trucks a day right now while we merge the two labs." He turned again.

Take as many turns as you like, Dr. Gallaway. You won't get me lost. Irene took pride in her God-given sense of direction.

"Do all supplies get stored here?" Annabelle asked. "Even the food for the residents?"

"All food and dining supplies go to the Mess." He pointed his chin to his right. The aisle stretched into an unlit distance. He glanced both directions down the intersecting aisle, then pulled forward.

Finally, Dr. Gallaway turned again, and they traveled down an asphalt-paved road. They drove past more tile walls. The few doors they saw were normal but marked only with a number and a letter.

Another turn, and the air changed. Here, it held a hint of an astringent, chemical odor. Large observation windows on each side revealed dozens of scientists seated behind microscopes on long stainless-steel tables. Table-height bottles of gasses sat at the ends of the tables. Commercial-sized stainless-steel cabinets blocked Irene's view of the back of the room.

The scientists and the few men who moved between the tables wore white jumpsuits with hoods pulled tight around their faces, masks over their noses and mouths, and white gloves. They even had white shoe covers.

In front of the scientists, alongside their microscopes, sat small metal boxes and trays of bottles full of colorful liquids. The amber, red, blue, and violet liquids in the bottles were the only colors in the room.

The golf cart's motor noise dropped to an idling hum. None of the men in the lab reacted to the golf cart or its occupants.

"These men maintain the collected ova," Dr. Gallaway said.

"Girls, do you remember what ova are?"

"Eggs that will be babies," Sandra said quickly and shot a triumphant smile at Annabelle.

Irene lifted her chin and pulled in a deep breath. She tried hard not to compare her daughters. Annabelle was scary smart, strong, driven, and—distant. Sandra was smart and clumsy and funny and full of hugs and kisses.

Annabelle's reserve was only natural. Losing one's entire family and village at ten years of age had to scar a child for life. Irene hoped Annabelle and Sandra would learn each other's strengths.

"Can we look in their microscopes?" Sandra asked.

Dr. Gallaway frowned at Sandra. "Not today. Perhaps another time."

Irene couldn't believe it, but she wanted to look inside those microscopes too.

The scientist in front of them opened his metal box and removed a stack of glass slides. He placed one slide under the microscope and peered into the eyepiece. He took a long glass tube, dipped it into a bottle of violet liquid, and transferred the liquid to the slide. Another glass tube went into a bottle of amber liquid, which he added to the slide. He reached for the next slide and slid it under the microscope.

"Is this where they make the eggs into babies?" Sandra asked.

Dr. Gallaway's face lit. "Not quite. They are preparing the media —where the activation—um. They are fixing food for the eggs to grow into babies."

Annabelle pointed. "Then those big metal cabinets behind them are the incubators that stimulate parthenogenesis?"

"Why, yes, yes, they are." Dr. Gallaway gave Irene a wide smile. "Your daughters read the materials?"

"I did," Annabelle said. "But Mother's book didn't explain how you make the parthenogenesis work for human ova."

Dr. Gallaway gaped at Annabelle, shot a glance at Irene. "Mother's book?"

"A college-level biology book." His concern amused Irene. *Did he think I'd written a book about his research?*

"I see." The doctor cleared his throat. "Well, young lady, it is a very involved. Simply put, the scientists transfer ova that began cell division into a growth medium and then into incubator that controls light and temperature."

"The book said you apply the correct electrical current with a micro-sized device," Annabelle said. "Can we see that?"

He turned and squinted at her. "Not this trip."

"For parthenogenesis to occur in vertebrates," Annabelle continued, oblivious to Dr. Gallaway's reticence, "the females are without male contact, and the temperature and humidity have to be just so. Is that true of human ova as well?"

"Yes. But the specifics are proprietary, young lady. Nothing for you to worry your little head about." He faced forward. Drove away.

The hateful expression Annabelle turned on the doctor made Irene shiver. The moment passed. Annabelle's face relaxed into her usual neutral half-smile. But that wasn't the first time Irene worried about Annabelle. Initially, she'd excused Annabelle's behavior as a stage her adopted daughter would outgrow. Irene's gut squirmed. *Felix thinks I'm overreacting. But I'm certain these episodes are occurring more frequently.* Irene glanced at her adopted daughter, whose expression had changed to avid interest. *Felix is probably right. It's nothing more than teenager hormones.*

The doctor turned again, and the astringent odor of alcohol grew stronger. Ahead of them, the roadway glowed. Nearer, the light obviously came from another large observation window.

The window framed an occupied operating room. Irene gasped. *They are operating on someone now?* She glanced at her daughters. *They're too young to see this.*

But both of them peered into the room with great interest.

On the operating table, a young lady lay under blue drapes. Fortunately, they had a view from the top of her head. Her splayed legs faced the doctors and nurses in green scrubs on the opposite side of the room.

An anesthesiologist sat next to her head and fiddled with knobs on an oven-sized machine that held three different colored tanks.

"Are they taking her ova now?" Sandra asked.

"We call it harvesting," Dr. Gallaway said, "but yes. That's what they're doing." He kept the cart moving, though slower than Irene would have wished.

"Is she one of the unfit?" Annabelle's strange smile made Irene's uneasiness return.

"She is a volunteer from a home for the unfortunate."

"How do you take out all the unfit stuff from her eggs? Or is that proprietary information too?"

He smiled. "Not at all. I learned how to do that when I studied at the Lankenau Hospital Research Institute, where Robert Briggs and Thomas King discovered how to clone frogs."

Irene gulped. *I do not want to know the details.*

"I collected and cared for the frogs...."

———

FORTUNATELY THE DOCTOR didn't indulge in the gory details about his frogs. Shortly after he finished, they turned again.

A mechanical *whoosh-swish* warned Irene. She hoped she had prepared the girls for this. The next window revealed a seemingly endless room. It held row upon row of red, semitransparent teardrop-shaped sacs hung from the ceiling. Tubes snaked from the bags to pipes overhead.

Rows to the far right held blood-red, opaque bags the size of an orange. On the far left, fetuses grew inside light rose-colored, watermelon-sized bags, recognizably human fetuses.

Irene swallowed the lump in her throat. Ignored the tightening of her stomach. Not merely human fetuses. *They are God's soldiers. My soldiers. Mine and God's.*

"Oh, Mommy, it's the babies!" Sandra exclaimed.

"They aren't babies yet, Sandra," Dr. Gallaway said.

"Look at them. This is killer-diller!"

Irene forced herself to frown at Sandra. "What have I told you about using slang?"

Sandra made a face. "This is super awesome science." She over-enunciated each word.

"They are the unborn," Annabelle said. The reflection of the red light made her olive-colored skin sallower.

Irene had read about the nursery, but to stand here in front of all those babies without mothers... Her heart twisted.

She studied the nearest watermelon-sized bag. Only about a foot long, the fetus inside had translucent skin with an intricate web of visible blue veins and arteries running through.

The science behind this project flew way over her head, but Dr. Gallaway was growing God's army—here—on Earth. God wouldn't let them do this if it were wrong. Still, she had difficulty understanding how they could be the army that would make her the Prophet's wife who ended the war with the rebels.

"That one moved." Annabelle pointed to a bag in the next row.

The bag swayed gently. The fetus's elbow stretched the bag. Irene remembered when her skin burned, overstretched by baby Sandra's movements.

The fetus brought her fists to her mouth. She kicked her legs and the bag swung harder. Bumped the pole. The fetus startled, made a crying face, then curled into a tight ball.

"Did she hurt herself?" Sandra asked, her voice soft and concerned.

Annabelle hopped out of the cart.

"Annabelle!" Irene leaped after her daughter. Grabbed her arm.

"It's all right," Dr. Gallaway said. "We can stop for a minute." He turned off the engine.

Irene released Annabelle, who went to the window, pressed her hands and face against the glass. "How old is she?"

Dr. Gallaway drew up beside her. "I'd guess it's about two weeks old. Developmental age is about..."

"Twenty-two weeks." Annabelle didn't take her eyes off the fetus. "She's developing ten times faster than normal."

"Why, yes." Dr. Gallaway shot Irene an expression of pride.

At my daughter's, at Annabelle's, comprehension?

"How do you make them grow so fast?"

"I'm sorry—"

"I know—proprietary."

Dr. Gallaway turned to Irene. "Did she read my entire presentation?"

Irene nodded. "She wants to learn every detail about things that interest her."

"Of course she does." He cocked his head one way, then the other, studying Annabelle. "I think it's time you met some—people—who live here."

"We can meet them?" Irene asked. She hadn't expected that. Dr. Green had been very protective of his first batch. He had said he didn't want anyone to see them until they'd "come into their calling."

"They are ready. Are you?"

"Of course."

He herded them back into the cart and drove down the halls faster.

They passed a room that looked like a living room. Two dozen or more listless women milled about or sat on worn upholstered furniture.

"The mothers," Annabelle said.

Dr. Gallaway agreed.

They passed through a long, windowless hall and emerged into a football-arena-sized area of painted rock dotted by massive pillars.

Bright light flooded the space. Scattered potted plants, bushes and trees, even areas of grass, gave the space a park-like feel. Sweet scents filled the air too. Thick plantings of tiger lilies surrounded the base of each pillar.

On the far side of the arena, twenty girls stood in formation, faced the opposite side of the room. One adult called out echo-distorted words.

In a coordinated precision move, the girls dropped to a push-up position. The adults counted a cadence, and the girls did military-style push-ups.

Dr. Gallaway stopped the golf cart less than a meter from the last row of girls.

Not one girl turned or flinched or reacted to the golf cart.

He turned off the engine and stood on the driver's seat. "Attention, everyone." His voice carried, and two dozen girls with dark hair stood and turned to face them.

Irene went cold. Then hot. Her heart pounded. She sucked in one breath, then another, unable to believe her eyes. *Impossible.* Except for Annabelle's skin color, they were identical. She whirled to Annabelle. Reached for her daughter's hand. "Darling—"

Chapter Twenty-Six

Annabelle stood in the room Dr. Gallaway called the clinic. She peered between the aluminum blinds that covered the window and watched the Annas in the park below.

All the Annas wore a black vest with a red X that extended from shoulders to waistband. Annabelle remembered that vest—was it a crossing-guard vest?

The teacher gave one Anna a wand and tied a blindfold over her eyes. The others ran and hid in doorways and bushes and behind potted plants.

I know this game.

Most of the overhead lights went out. The blindfold came off, and the girl scanned the park. Then she took off across the grass. She poked the wand into a bush. An X on a vest lit up, and the player wearing it staggered onto the grass and crawled back to the starting point where she lay on the ground, glowing and writhing.

Annabelle's ears and neck grew hot. That wasn't the way she and Sandra played tag. *But I know that hurts.*

"Annabelle, please be brave. Do as Dr. Gallaway asked."

She faced her mother.

Mother sat in a chair near a beat-up old desk, folding and unfolding her handkerchief in her lap. She did that whenever something upset her.

Sandra sat behind the desk drawing pictures with a pen and

paper the doctor had given her. Against the wall behind the desk, thick books filled a tall bookshelf. On the top shelf, a dozen five-gallon jars held dead babies in liquid.

Dr. Gallaway stood at the other end of the desk, near the door. Beside him stood a young woman in a gray business suit.

The doctor held a long skinny swab and a tube. "Come close, Annabelle. This won't hurt a bit."

Right. Whenever doctors said it wouldn't hurt, it usually hurt a lot. Still, she *was* brave. She crossed the room, stood in front of him.

"Open your mouth."

She did.

He rubbed the cotton swab all around the inside of her mouth.

It didn't hurt. But the stick tasted like wood. Nasty.

The doctor put the swab into the test tube. *Snap.* He broke off the end of the stick and put a stopper in the test tube. "Take this to Dr. Smith in cytology."

"Yes, sir." The young woman took the tube and left, closed the door behind her.

Dr. Gallaway turned to Mother. "Dr. Smith is very good. We'll get the results in a week."

"A week?" Mother said as if that were such a very long time.

"An outside lab would take eight weeks."

Mother twisted her handkerchief fast, tighter.

Finally, Annabelle understood. "You think I am one of them?" She pointed out the window.

Mother rushed over, put a hand on each shoulder, and squatted to face-level with Annabelle. "It doesn't matter if you are. You're my daughter. Papa and I love you. That's what's important."

Annabelle cocked her head. "If I am one of them, do I have to come here to live?"

"No, darling. You will always live with Papa and me."

"But you're upset. Why does them looking like me upset you?"

"It surprised me." She looked up at Dr. Gallaway. "It surprised all of us."

Annabelle knew she was lying. But it was a white lie. *Mother doesn't want me to feel bad. Why does she think I'd feel bad?* "Is being unnaturally born a bad thing?"

Mother swallowed as if it hurt to do so. "It doesn't matter how or where you were born. You are our Miracle. Our daughter. You will always be our daughter."

Returning to the window, Annabelle looked down at the Annas. "Don't worry, Mother," she said without looking at her mother. "Anna 2378 told me the truth. We are the same. I am one of them. But I am different too."

Dr. Gallaway smiled down at her as if he'd taught her that himself.

Mother made a catch-her-breath sound. "Why do you say that?"

"I am resurrected, like Jesus."

"Oh." Mother's soft voice sounded funny.

A thrill ran through Annabelle. "It will be all right, Mother. You are like Jesus's mother."

This time no sound came out of Mother's mouth, though it had the shape of an *O*.

"Jesus loved his mother like I love you."

Dr. Gallaway cleared his throat. "Perhaps you'd like to see the Annas' school and living quarters?"

A school. In a mine. Will it remind me of who I am? "I would like that very much, thank you."

The golf cart ride took ten minutes. Dr. Gallaway stopped outside an unpainted building. "This is the school."

Annabelle rushed inside and stopped cold. Her insides shrank. The classrooms had a chalkboard and a teacher's desk and student desks. It even smelled of pine and chalk dust, like her above-ground school.

Dr. Gallaway explained they didn't have an auditorium or gym because they could use the courtyard for those things. He showed them the library and the cafeteria. They were ordinary too. *School down here isn't special. Not at all.*

They walked out of the cafeteria into a courtyard. Created by four unpainted buildings in a square, the courtyard gave Annabelle prickles up and down her back.

Somehow she knew the wide yellow lines painted on the concrete were walkways. They outlined and crisscrossed the court-yard and met in the center. A tall pole stood in the center. *The shaming pole.*

She twirled, stared at the buildings. *I've never been here before. So how do I know about the pole?*

Dr. Gallaway passed the pole as if it were unimportant.

She followed him.

"This is one of the bunk rooms." Dr. Gallaway opened the door to a long room lined with neatly made bunk beds on each side. Taut gray blankets covered each bed. Each blanket had red identifying numbers embroidered down the center.

Another not special— Her chest tightened. A floppy rag doll lay on top of a bed. Her vision dimmed as if the doll lay at the end of a long, lightless tunnel. *That's mine!* She closed her hands into tight fists. *Rage steals thought. Thought before action.*

She blinked and blinked again. *Where have I heard that before?* Ghostly images swirled through her memory. *Images like this, but different. Not underground. In the sun. My life before?*

She glared at the doll. *Different. Not mine.* Brown curly yarn for hair and an embroidered face with big, brown, stitched eyelashes arched over smooth brown eyes. Tiny pink stitches outlined lips that curved upward. Soft knit socks made the doll's arms and legs. Like hers. But this one had a yellow knit top with small white buttons and a green brocade skirt—the same but different. She glanced around the barracks. *Everything is the same—but different.*

A fierce tingling swelled in Annabelle's chest. She'd always known she was special. That she was born, or made, for something special. Now, without a doubt, she knew. More than any of the girls here—she was an angel of death.

The swelling of her chest bothered Annabelle. *Was it the thing Mother called pride?*

No. Pride is a sin. This feeling is righteous. This is my destiny. I am an Azrael—but different. Twice born. Better than the best angel of death.

Chapter Twenty-Seven

Irene sat at her triple-mirrored maple vanity in her bedroom. She opened the message her driver had passed to her as she exited the car. The single piece of paper looked like something a child had done. Letters cut from magazines and pasted on the paper formed a message. "Target searching mines for lab." Her stomach twisted. *Miranda's looking for a lab? Dr. Gallaway's lab?*

She stood, paced the floor. *I've only known about the lab for two days. How does Miranda know? Wait. Wrong questions. How can I warn the doctor?*

This isn't something to discuss on an open telephone line. She called for her driver.

En route to an appointment she didn't have, Irene tapped the intercom to the driver. "Paul, I have sensitive information for Dr. Gallaway. What is the fastest, most secure way to get that information to him?"

"The satellite phone."

"You have one?"

"Of course."

He pulled into an off-street parking lot. Opened the trunk, handed her the satellite phone through the passenger window. "When you've finished your call, roll down your window."

She told Dr. Gallaway about Miranda and the rebels searching for the lab, but he brushed off her concerns. "There are hundreds of mines and caves they'd have to search. Besides, our security is impenetrable."

"I'm glad to hear that." Ending the call, she figured the doctor knew best. "Take me home, Paul."

The aroma of roast beef greeted her at the door, and the housekeeper's soft footsteps pattered around in the kitchen.

I must be silent and supportive to be a good wife of the Prophet. But it's unseemly for me to cook for the family. Obeying the rules in public was one thing. Irene glanced up the stairs. *Not being an involved mother in private? Intolerable.* Worry about Annabelle made her chest ache. Four days since the trip to Kansas City, and Annabelle still acted gloomy and preoccupied.

Irene marched up the three flights of stairs, determined she'd help Annabelle.

A curtain of quiet hung over the too-neat playroom. In a rocker in the corner, the nanny silently read scriptures.

Sandra sat with her forearms on the game table, her head on her arms. "Eight, nine, ten. Ready or not, here I come." The legs of her chair screeched. She stood. "Oh. Hi, Mommy. We're playing hide-and-seek. I gotta go find Betsy Wetsy." She dashed out the door. Disappeared from sight.

Irene swiveled, cocked her head at the nanny. "The doll is playing hide-and-seek?"

"Annabelle's idea," the nanny said. "Makes the game last longer. I told her it was acceptable. Was I incorrect?"

"No, you were right, of course," Irene said. But her stomach squirmed. "I think I'll peek in on them. Maybe I'll play too." She went into the hallway.

"But Betsy Wetsy is a good Fellowship member." Sandra's voice held an edge of distress.

"And so we spare her," Annabelle said, but in a much lower register than normal.

Irene's stomach dropped. She tiptoed down the hall, stood outside Sandra's room.

"Toni Doll is an apostate, right?" Annabelle asked.

"Yes, she's a bad doll," Sandra said."

"Thy will be done."

Irene stepped through the door. Her hand flew to her chest. She gasped aloud.

Annabelle pulled on a black shoestring wrapped around the neck of the Toni Doll as if she strangled the doll.

"Annabelle! Stop that this instant."

Sandra leaped to her feet, clutched her Betsy Wetsy doll in its pink, frilly dress.

Annabelle locked eyes with Irene. Her eyes held a coldness that weakened Irene's knees. Irene clutched the doorframe. Her throat clogged with a scream she wouldn't loosen. She wanted to turn away but didn't dare. *What do I say? What do I do?* She swallowed a hot, jagged-edged lump. "Give me the shoestring," she said, surprised by the calm in her voice.

"Are you mad at us?" Sandra's eyes shimmered bright and watery.

Who's she afraid of? Me or…? "I'm not mad," Irene said. "But this game must stop. Now." Her voice cracked. She gulped again.

"We're playing a game called capture the unbeliever," Sandra said. A worry line creased her brow.

Irene held out her hand, palm up. "Annabelle." Focused on keeping her hand steady.

Annabelle took the shoestring from the doll's neck and placed it in Irene's hand. "Of course, Mother. Did we do something wrong?"

Irene balled the shoestring into her fist. A darkness filled her, chilled her through and through. "Not wrong exactly," she said. Crossed the room. Sat on a chair at Sandra's tea table. "Come, sit with me."

The girls complied. Each looked at her for an answer.

She drew a deep breath. *Dear Lord, help me find the right words.* "Does the Fellowship Council have young girls on it?"

"No, Mommy."

"No."

"Of course not," Irene said. "Do you know why they don't have young girls on the Council?"

"'Cause we're little?" Sandra said.

Irene tried to smile. "Partly."

"Because children lack the experience of the adults," Annabelle said.

Irene gently cupped Annabelle's chin. "Exactly, Annabelle. See, adults have enough experience with prayers and studying the Lord's Word that they can be just in their decisions."

"You think I was being unjust?" Annabelle drew back, freed her chin from Irene's touch.

Always direct, Annabelle's question pained Irene. "I think you're too young to understand all that one must know before making those kinds of decisions. This is a game no one—especially girls—should ever play. It's a very serious decision." Unendurable pain pierced her chest.

"Oh." Annabelle cocked her head. "Is this another one of those 'you'll understand when you're older' things?"

"Yes, I'm afraid it is." Irene couldn't take her eyes off Annabelle.

Annabelle weighed Irene's words with a puckered frown.

"Can we play something else now, Mommy?"

Irene smothered the startle that shot through her. She'd almost forgotten Sandra was here too. She put on a good mother smile and faced Sandra. "Of course, darling."

"Let's play musical chairs."

"Okay."

A change washed over Annabelle's face, from a calculating near-adult to smiling child.

Stunned, Irene gulped air. Gripped the edge of the tea table. Held the good mother pose.

The girls left the room and skipped down the hall to the playroom.

Irene closed her eyes. *Thank you, Lord, for the words, for a crisis averted.* She opened her eyes and her fist. Stared at the shoestring. Her hand shook. A scan of the floor found the saddle shoe missing its shoestring. She picked up the shoe and threaded the shoestring. It took longer than normal.

Chapter Twenty-Eight

Eight days of peanut butter sandwiches, and this endless night is too much. Miranda scowled at the artificially lit subterranean road she walked. Wrinkled her nose at the ever-present tang of minerals in her nose. Adjusted the strap of the Kodak Rangefinder camera that irritated her neck for the thousandth time. After so many days of eating, sleeping, and searching in the mine, she needed fresh sea air. But she'd destroyed her boat. The ache in her center made her want to curl into a ball.

"What was your life like before all this?" Karl kept his voice low and shifted the weight of the box of copy paper he carried.

Huh? How did he know what I'm thinking? "Life on a boat is routine chores for days on end, followed by short bursts of fast decisions and making the boat do impossible things."

He gave a gentle laugh. "I meant what was it like being the daughter of the First Apostle."

Miranda's stomach clenched. *How does he know who I am?*

"I understand you removed yourself from that life, but the new Prophet's Lady is your sister. That's some powerful stuff."

Right. He heard me tell Ethan about Irene's letter. The perpetual night of this stupid mine is messing with my head. "I'd already left home before all that happened." Talking or thinking about her life before was a waste of time. Fatigue and the weight of the camera made her neck hurt. She rubbed the tender spot under the camera's strap.

"My turn." She nodded toward the next dock. A single fluorescent light above the block wall revealed a sign: G35-27.

Karl pointed to a nearby closet-sized alcove in the rock wall.

Low-to-the-ground security lights lit the five steps up to the dock level. The painted concrete block bore no sign of occupancy, like all the others. She pressed her lips together. *Eight days, and we're no closer to finding a way into the lab. At this rate, we'll never find one.*

Miranda played the flashlight across the floor. The undisturbed, heavy dust confirmed her impression. She marked an X through the spot on the map and returned to the road.

Caught up with Karl in the recess where he waited. He raised his eyebrows in a query. She shook her head. *Not a darn thing worth all this time.* They headed toward the next dock.

"Why do you think your sister wants peace?" he asked in a low voice. "Have you two talked?"

"No. She sent a message, asked to meet." *A message I still haven't answered.*

"And you believe she would meet with Monkshood and talk peace without killing us all?"

"I wouldn't have said anything if I didn't." Miranda's stomach pitched. "But unless Ethan, Beryl, and SABR want peace—it won't happen."

"I doubt all of SABR wants peace," Karl said. "But I've heard Monkshood wish for peace."

"Then why did he act like I was a lame brain for suggesting it?"

"You surprised him. And—"

"And what?"

"And you have to approach Monkshood in the right way."

The dim lighting meant he couldn't see her. She glared at him anyway. "So I did it wrong?" She gave a hushed snort. "I suppose you could do better?"

"Well, yeah."

"Why didn't you help me convince him last week?"

"It's all in the timing, Miranda. Gotta have the right timing." He grunted and shifted the weight of the box of copy paper he carried.

She reached for the box. "I can carry it for a while."

"No, madam," he said. "It's too big for you. You'd have to grow six inches taller and have much stronger arms."

She screwed her mouth sideways. He exaggerated her lack of

stature and had no idea how strong she was thanks to life on the *Lady*. She studied the map. "The next one is also gray." Picked up her pace.

Safety lights at the dock G35-28 revealed closed, green garage and man-doors that had no business signage or logos. Miranda scanned the area.

Humming a barely audible version of "Stormy Weather," Karl walked toward the dock.

"Freeze," Miranda called in a forced whisper.

He froze, one foot in mid-air.

She motioned for Karl to back up and take cover.

He scurried to the wall, hugged the shadows.

She waited for a response from inside the dock. None came. Shielded her flashlight and stole across to the object she'd glimpsed.

In the pale circle of light sat a freckled-orange, star-shaped blossom with a stubby stem. *A tiger lily.* She picked it up. Inhaled its sweet scent. *Where did you come from?* The firm petals meant it hadn't been here long.

She swept her flashlight back and forth across the concrete drive to the raised dock. No more blossoms. No dust or debris of any kind. But imbedded in the wall at dock level was a small, round lens. She sucked in a breath. Searched the opposite wall. Found the matching lens. *A burglar alarm system?* No pilot light or reflection showed in or near the lens. *So no power? But why no dust?*

She joined Karl in the deeper shadows against the wall opposite the next pillar.

"Whew. That was close," he whispered. "I could have triggered that alarm. Thanks. I owe you one."

"Sorry. False alarm," she said. "No power."

"And another one gets an X."

"It's unused, but with no dust on the dock and the flower…"

"A flower?" He set the box of paper on the ground. Held out his hand.

The orange blossom took on a brownish hue in the dim safety lights of the unoccupied dock. She placed it in his palm.

He glanced at it, grunted. "Must have fallen off some lucky young lady's bouquet."

The stem is unwrapped. So not from a florist? Miranda held her palm out.

Karl hesitated. Then placed the blossom in her hand.

His cold fingertips lingered on her palm.

That's odd. The poor lighting and cast shadows hid his expression. She tucked the tiger lily behind her ear. *Why would a young lady with a bouquet be here in the unoccupied bowels of the mine?* The sweet scent haloed her. *Someone told me about tiger lilies once.* She couldn't remember anything more. Except a buzz inside her said this flower was important.

"No power," Karl repeated. "It's unused. Mark it with an X." He used his flashlight, peered at his wristwatch. "Time to head back to the parking lot."

Miranda trapped her flash between her chin and her neck. Shined it on the map. Her pen paused above the gray irregular square numbered G35-28. *Beryl wouldn't mark an X through this one. She'd want to investigate it.* "I'll mark this spot with a question mark," Miranda said.

"That makes it one more empty warehouse to search."

"The flower and lack of dust make it suspect."

He shrugged. "Hope your sister's willing to wait until you're ready." He left the box behind.

Miranda sucked in a long breath, held it. *What if Irene didn't want to wait?*

Chapter Twenty-Nine

Beryl leaned against the cold metal of the pickup in an unlit nose-in parking area. Sipped lukewarm water with a strong mineral flavor. It didn't refresh. Checked the time again. *Miranda and Karl, are you in trouble? Do I send half the team to search for them? Search the next section, let them catch up?* She'd give them five more minutes, then decide.

Behind her, Wanda and Leslie sat on the tailgate beside the orange five-gallon water cooler they'd bought in town. David stood nearby. None of them had found anything but concrete block walls where docks and warehouses should have been.

Damn it. Eight days. We should have found something by now. Beryl couldn't decide whether to call Ethan and beg for more time or give this hunt another twenty-four hours.

A two-tone whistle echoed from the road. A flashlight flashed. A pair of backlit shadows approached. The taller shadow, Karl, and the shorter one, Miranda.

"Clear." She hoped Miranda and Karl were late because they'd found something, snapped her flashlight on. Gasped.

Couldn't believe her eyes. Strode forward and snatched the tiger lily from behind Miranda's ear. "Where did you find this?"

"On dock G35-28's driveway," Miranda told her. "I know they were Anna's favorite, but that doesn't mean these have anything to do with Anna or the Azrael."

The orange petals with brown spots tore into Beryl. She couldn't catch her breath. Couldn't stop the mind-pictures of the tiger lilies. Couldn't stop remembering five-year-old Anna's shining eyes and gap-toothed smile for her first homegrown tiger lily. Or the barracks lined with tiger lilies. Bloody tiger lilies. She forced those images back into her memory fortress. Hardened her ribs and stomach.

"You were at the hospital when we found the barracks," she said. "And too young to remember how Anna loved tiger lilies." Blinked away a ghostly memory. Fixed her eyes on Miranda. "They filled the flowerbeds around the Azrael barracks with them. Where did you say you found it?"

"Warehouse G35-28."

"That's it, that's got to be the lab." Beryl stormed down the road.

"No one's there," Miranda said, running after her. "There's no power."

Beryl didn't care. *Have to find proof.* She pounded the concrete road for the mile to reach the suspected lab. The others followed.

She rounded the corner. The first dock had two green doors, a garage door and man-door, each numbered G35-30. Breathing hard, she stopped. Wanted a quiet approach to the lab. Waited for the others to catch up.

Miranda appeared first. The rest came in close behind her. Shadows cloaked their faces, their emotions. Harsh catch-up breathing filled the space.

"Did you take a picture before you picked it up?" she asked Miranda.

"No. We thought it fell out of a bouquet."

No picture. Damn. No. Doesn't matter. "The only picture that'll convince Ethan is one of an Azrael." *Damn him. Stop it.* Cleared her mind. Focused. "Sit rep?"

"One light above the doors. No light from inside. No power to the security cameras set at floor level."

Security, all right. Infrared? Her heart knocked against her ribs. *Pretty significant security for a warehouse. What you'd expect for a secret lab.* "You all wait behind the next pillar. I'll enter the lab first. Do a perimeter check. Watch for my signal. Run like hell if an alarm sounds."

She crept up dock G35-28's steps. The main door held an observation window. A one-way window. She inspected the door, didn't find any wires for an alarm. She tried the doorknob. It turned. She sucked in a breath. *Damn. Another false lead? But it was a tiger lily.*

Determined to check it out anyway, she drew her pistol. Entered. Swept the empty warehouse with her gun barrel. Infrequent security lights provided dim, yellow light. Enough to avoid running into walls. Enough to identify six sections. Enough to crush her hope of finding the evidence Ethan required.

Three flashes from her flashlight brought the others. In a quick whisper, she assigned one area to each of the others. Took two for herself.

The first section she searched held a vacant corridor full of rooms stripped down to bare walls. No furniture. No light fixtures. No frigging sign of what had been in the room. She hurried to the next section.

The empty corridor of offices-in-a-cave stretched eerily and infinitely beyond the dim security lights. She gritted her teeth against the scream that bubbled inside. *This has to be the right place.*

She crushed the wilted tiger lily. Its sweet floral scent exploded, overloaded her senses. *Damn. I'll never get that washed off.* Tossed the ruined flower aside. Went to the next office.

Sweeping her flashlight around the room, light bounced back at her. Deep inside the room, a stainless-steel counter ran across the top of a long line of cabinets. In the center of the counter sat a single basin, stainless-steel sink.

She searched the cabinets. All empty. Turned the faucet. Not a drop of water.

Bracing her hands on the cold counter, she closed her burning eyes. Tried to clear the fatigue that fogged her thoughts.

A two-tone whistle pierced the air. Three times.

She checked her watch. Seven o'clock in the morning. She'd promised the others four hours of rest. *Dammit, searching warehouses one at a time is taking too long.*

She joined Karl by the dock doors. He had found nothing.

The echo of footsteps rang around them.

A beam of light came out of the east-west corridor, advanced toward her and Karl. *Leslie or Miranda? Is one of them missing?* Her stomach clenched.

Miranda and Leslie stepped into the dim light cast by the security lights.

They should have been searching separate areas. "What are you two doing together?"

"There was literally nothing in the section you assigned me," Leslie said. "So I searched for the room where I watched Alex."

Beryl knotted her fists. Resisted punching Leslie's soft belly. "Just say it. You were mistaken. This isn't the lab."

"It is," Leslie said. "I found the red door. Retraced the route. Found the nursery. And Miranda."

"Did it still have furniture? Baby things in it?"

"No," she said. "But it's the room."

"How do you know?"

"Dents on the carpet from a crib and a rocker. And when I pounded on the carpet—it smelled of baby powder."

Beryl raised her fists, pressed them to her pounding forehead. "That's not proof."

Miranda stiffened. "It is proof. I saw it too."

"Proof Ethan will accept?"

Miranda's shoulders slumped. "No. He won't."

Karl took a step forward, closer to Miranda. "Maybe they abandoned this place a long time ago?"

"No." Beryl glanced around at the rock walls. "The flower—the baby powder—the lack of thick dust all mean they moved out recently."

Karl grimaced. "Then, even if this was the lab, it's a dead-end."

"We'll search the dock and warehouse that David and Wanda are watching next," Beryl said. *Our time is running out.* "It might be the real lab."

Miranda's mouth dropped open. "What do you mean, 'the real lab?' Leslie said this is where she came. You believe her about the doll, but not about this?"

Beryl gestured at their surroundings. "Look at this place. Everything looks the same. She could be mistaken. There could be a duplicate. We don't know—"

"Of course we don't know. She does!"

"Whether this was the place she babysat that kid isn't important. All that matters is that we find proof they are creating Azrael. That we destroy the Azrael." *Maybe I should just blow any underground space we suspect they're in...*

Miranda drew back. Stared suspiciously at Beryl. "Don't you mean that what matters is saving lives?"

What's her problem? Beryl squinted at her. "No, I mean we kill the Azrael."

"A peace treaty will save lives."

Beryl rolled her eyes. "We don't have time for this."

"Then we make time." Miranda faced Karl and Leslie. "Another assault will cause hundreds, maybe thousands, of deaths, and if it's like the first time, more will die in retaliation." She glanced at Beryl, then addressed them again. "My sister is ready to talk to us."

Leslie frowned. "Monkshood said he'd tried that once. I don't know what happened, but it didn't sound good. And David didn't think that was a good idea either."

"We can't stop the Azrael," Miranda said. "We tried and failed. Peace talks give us a chance."

Karl bounced a glance between Miranda and Beryl. "She's got a point."

"Then maybe you two should go see just how peaceful a talk with Fellowship leaders is." Beryl laced her tone with a mocking note.

Miranda's expression hardened. "Your stubbornness will get you killed."

"Not before your Pollyanna optimism gets you dead."

Miranda looked up at Karl. "I'm leaving. Are you coming?"

He studied his shoes a moment, then met Beryl's eyes. "Seems like our best shot."

Wait. He thinks she means it. A second look at Miranda sent a cold kick to Beryl's gut. *She can't just walk out of here.* "You aren't taking the truck."

Miranda's eyes flashed, and her chin lifted. She wrenched the strap off her neck and thrust the camera at Beryl. "We'll walk."

Her reflexes kept the camera from hitting her in the gut. "Don't be ridiculous. You can't walk out of here."

"Watch me." Miranda whirled and marched away.

The soldier inside made sure Beryl didn't move.

Quick footsteps pounded across the concrete and faded away.

How did I misjudge Miranda? She did the drills every day. She's fast and strong and... pig-headed. I didn't abandon her. She abandoned me. Beryl controlled her breathing, but her blood seethed.

"Aren't you going to stop her?" Leslie asked.

"Miranda's an adult."

"But—"

"We have another warehouse to search." She strode out the same door Miranda did.

Chapter Thirty

Bored with her sister's games, Annabelle plopped onto her bed and glared at the pink walls. She didn't understand why Mother had been so upset. *About the Annas. And my game. They were dolls, not real people.*

Of course, she doesn't understand. She's not my real mother. My real mother would understand. Wouldn't she? Do I have a real mother?

So many sisters… No, not sisters. Anna said, "We are the same."

How can I be the same? I was born in Buenos Aires. Wasn't I? Why can't I remember? The ache burned in her chest again. She hugged Dollie, and the burning faded. *Somehow, I am the same.*

Yes. And we hunger, an unfamiliar voice whispered.

Without moving a muscle, Annabelle slid her eyes back and forth, scanned for the person who spoke. No one else was in her room.

She leaned over the edge of her bed, lifted the bed skirt. Nothing and no one. Got on her hands and knees and tilted her ear to the heat register. The familiar whir and rumble of warm air forced through metal vents came from the vent. Annabelle scanned the room again. Javier lay motionless on a rock under his heat lamp. She giggled at the idea that Javier could talk.

She searched her closet—nothing but clothes and toys. Arms folded over her chest, she peered at the walls and ceiling. Maybe she'd heard a spirit.

"Are you a ghost?" She used her library voice, afraid she'd frighten the other voice.

No answer.

"Are you my guardian angel?"

Not a guardian.

"An angel?"

Almost.

"An angel of death?"

We are so much more.

Annabelle concentrated. "I am the same as the Annas. And you are an angel." *An angel who talks to me. My angel.*

Warmth spread through her. Her chin jutted. *The angel Gabriel visited the first Prophet.* "Can I see you?" *Maybe I'm a Prophet too.*

She stood before her dresser. Peered into the mirror, focused on the reflections of her bed, bookcase, and beanbag chair. "I can't see you." She frowned at herself for a long minute.

She leaned forward, stared into her own eyes. "You're inside me, aren't you?"

See how smart we are? We'll figure out what we need, won't we?

Annabelle blinked and cocked her head at her reflection. "Why don't you tell me?"

Wrong question.

She frowned. *What's the right one?* "What's your name?"

You can do better.

What else? "What do we want?"

Now you're being silly.

This is like being in school. You want me to figure it out?

Her chest filled with that proud-of-myself tingle.

She sat at her desk, rested her arms on it, and stared out the window at the almost leafless tree outside. *What I want to know is who the angel is. Who I am. The Annas know where they came from. Why can't I? Dr. Gallaway thinks I am the same as the Annas. He said they have a special school to teach them.*

The tingle in her chest spread to her entire body. *That's it, isn't it? I need to return to the Annas. Go to the Annas' school.*

The angel inside her hummed a beautiful song. It lightened and lifted her. Made her long for wings. *Mother must take me back.*

She pushed her chair back. Remembered how upset Mother had been when she saw the Annas. *Mother said she wasn't worried.*

She said she and Papa would always love me. But she'd been quiet all the way home.

She's afraid of the Annas.

A smile grew inside Annabelle. *She's afraid of me too.*

With Dollie under her arm, she trotted downstairs in search of Mother.

Chapter Thirty-One

Miranda leaped off the four-foot-tall dock. Strode down the middle of the road in the artificial cave. Her shoes slapped the pavement as fast as her pulse thumped.

"Hey, Miranda. Slow down." Karl's whisper came from behind her. "You're making too much noise."

Biting back a "there's no one here to notice," she slowed to a brisk walk. But her heartbeat plunged ahead.

"I'm with you, no matter what. But I can't help if you don't tell me where we are going." He matched her pace, drew alongside her.

"We're going to set up a peace talk between Irene and Monkshood. And save lives."

"Yeah, I figured that. But—where?"

Wherever they went, it would be without Beryl. The enormity of what she'd done hollowed Miranda. Her steps faltered. *Where* am *I going?*

The rock walls broken only by the bricked-over docks with violet-colored doors were familiar. Her feet had carried her to the section where the truck was. "First, we go to the truck."

"But Beryl said…"

"Not for the truck—for our rucksacks."

"Oh. We should hurry in case Beryl hides it…or something."

Invisible in the unlit parking spot, they missed the green pickup on their first pass. Turned around. Using their flashlights, they found the truck and their rucksacks. Added food and water to their supplies. And extra ammo.

Leaving the truck tied Miranda's stomach in knots. For the past three years, she and Beryl had been inseparable.

"Now where?" Karl asked.

Can't tell him I don't know where or how to begin. Answer Irene's letter? Can't wait for the mail—if Beryl has her way, there will be no hope of peace. Call Ethan? Not before Irene agrees to meet me.

An overhead fluorescent flickered, created eerie moving shadows. Increased the tightness in Miranda's chest. *One step at a time. Next—call Irene.*

"Next, we find a telephone," she said. "Do you remember seeing one somewhere inside here?"

Karl skewed his mouth sideways, and his gaze grew distant. "Nope. Not in the cave… I think we'll have to find a filling station."

An ocean of white noise drowned out their conversation. Set in a concrete wall, a pair of industrial fans pushed gale-force wind further back into the cave. Miranda's thoughts cleared. *I need a plan —a location, rules, contingency plans—before I call Irene.*

The roar faded to a drone. "I won't ask where Monkshood is," she said. "Can you give me a hint—a nearby city? One with a large population?" She shifted the weight of her rucksack. The straps sliced a burning trough into her shoulders.

"Large like New York or L.A.?" Wary and puzzled tones colored Karl's voice.

She caught her breath, chilled by the possibilities. "Not necessarily." *Don't let him be that far away.* "A place Ethan could reach within a day or two. A city bigger than Springfield. Big enough we can disappear if needed."

Another light high above their heads lit an empty cathedral of rock the size of which made them less than specks of dust.

"You know that we're in the middle of no-man's-land, don't you?" Karl said in a maddeningly reasonable tone.

"I get that," she said. "Just give me a clue—is he closer to Kansas City or Chicago or…where?"

Karl hooked his thumbs under the straps of his rucksack. "He's closest to Kansas City."

"Does he plan to leave soon?"

"Should I guess?"

Miranda balled her fists, reined in the "you are not helping" shout that wanted to burst from her. Stopped herself from shining her flashlight in his face. *Of course he doesn't know. He's been with us.* "Wonder how much bus tickets to Kansas City cost?" She stubbed her toe on something. Pinched her lips tight against a false cry of ouch. Her shoe had protected her. She pointed her flash at her feet. *Oh. It's the train tracks.*

"I'm a rebel," Karl said. "I never carry that much cash on me. Can you hot-wire a car?"

"No. That was—" *Beryl's thing.* "I never learned how to do that."

"What are we going to do? Hobo it?"

"Aren't freight trains too slow?"

"Bet we'd get there as fast as a car. Few stops between the ware-houses and delivery locations. No roadblocks."

"Don't the police arrest people who try to hop the train?"

"We can avoid them."

"You've hopped a train before?"

"A few times."

Hobo Miranda? There's always a first time. "The train tracks are back there." A brief glance at the map oriented her. She led the way toward the perimeter and the train tracks.

They strode past more sealed-up warehouse docks, passed large, stone-colored power boxes hung on the rock wall, and odd little black storage sheds.

She passed the familiar shape before it registered. *A telephone.* Backed up. Stared at the black wall phone mounted on a yellow board secured to the rock wall. Above the phone, instructions in bold black letters on the yellow board read, "Dial: O for Security, 1 for Maintenance, 2 for the Rental Office, and 9 for an outside line." She drew in a shaky breath, blew it out. Swallowed. *I can do this.* But she couldn't take a step.

Karl kept walking for a few seconds, then stopped and turned toward her. "What did you see?" he asked and rejoined her. "Ah." His head swung toward her, his expression expectant.

"I don't want to put Beryl and the others in danger."

"Keep your call short."

"Right."

She squared her shoulders and headed for the telephone.

Chapter Thirty-Two

Irene hung up the wall phone in the kitchen, closed her eyes, and prayed that she was doing the right thing. Dr. Gallaway had sounded delighted she would bring Annabelle back. Nausea burned her throat.

It'll be okay. Annabelle thinks she's like the others. Her good, kind nature will shine and show that she doesn't belong there. Irene pasted on her good-mother smile and faced her daughter. "There, it's done. Dr. Gallaway is pleased to welcome you to the school tomorrow."

Annabelle's anxious expression smoothed, and she raised her chin. "Thank you, Mother." Without another word, she turned and went upstairs.

Intolerable pain ripped through Irene's chest. Her legs quivered. She sat heavily on the hard, wooden chair of the telephone desk, unable to move, to think.

Ring. Ring.

She jumped. Answered with a shaky, "Hello?"

"Irene. Please don't hang up. I got your letter. We need to talk."

Irene stiffened. *It can't be. Miranda wouldn't dare call.* "Who is this?" she asked, cold and hard.

"You know who. Don't use my name. Please. Listen. It's time the two sides talk—"

"How did you get this number? Friends can't get this number."

"It doesn't matter. You still want to talk peace?"

The heaviness inside Irene lifted a bit. She chewed her lower lip. "You and the SABR leader are interested in a peace talk?"

"Yes. Will you come?" Hope and eagerness suffused her voice.

If there is no war, we don't need to grow or teach more Azrael. There'd be no school. Annabelle would stay home. "Are you the leader of the apostates now?"

"No, but if you agree to meet with us, he'll come."

What if this isn't Miranda? "How do I know this isn't a trap?"

"We'll choose the city. You can choose the date and time. We both have to agree on the place within the city."

I shouldn't even be talking to her. "Any day or time?"

"Within reason."

"What city?"

"Kansas City, Missouri."

Irene stifled a gasp. "Why Kansas City?"

"We will not walk into a Fellowship stronghold like D.C." Her tone held a scolding edge.

Irene couldn't make herself hang up. *If this saves Annabelle... If I could truly bring about peace... I would make a difference.* "How about five p.m. tomorrow evening?"

"In less than twenty-four hours?" Her voice sounded strident. "We need more time to get everyone there."

"Everyone? No. Only you and Monkshood—that's the leader's code name, right? You, him, and me. No one else."

"And we what? Trust that you won't bring Second Sphere agents?"

"We have to trust each other," Irene said.

"The Fellowship doesn't make trust easy."

Heat flamed through Irene. "You exiled me—our parents. If anyone has trouble trusting, it should be me." She tightened her grip on the receiver until her knuckles ached. Forced herself to loosen her fingers. "If you want peace, trust me. I'll meet you on Sunday. Not one day later." She bit her lower lip to keep it from trembling. *I planned to stay anyway, so I can bring Annabelle home when she gets homesick....*

"All right. Five p.m. On Sunday. In Kansas City. I'll speak to Monkshood, and we'll contact you with the location we prefer."

Irene lifted her chin. "I have a suggestion."

"Go ahead."

"The train station. It's public. Busy. Accessible from many directions."

"Sounds like you know the city well. Have you been to the Kansas City train station before?"

"Don't be silly. I haven't. But I read about it. It's the third largest train station in the country."

"All right. If that day and place will work for him, I'll send you a message tomorrow."

"Why not another telephone call?"

The dial tone buzzed.

Irene lowered the receiver into her lap. Lost in a storming sea of emotions she couldn't see, couldn't move, until the phone's off-the hook howl snapped her out of it. She hung up. *It's time Mrs. Wynter's team shows me what they can do.*

She lifted her chin. *This trip may not be as bad as I feared. Whether we agree to a peace treaty or my men capture them, I'll be the Prophet's wife who saved the country.*

Chapter Thirty-Three

The rough, charcoal-gray walls and dim light suited Beryl's mood. She strode through the dark. *Don't care if Leslie followed. Don't care that Miranda had gone off in search of peace. Don't. Care. The tiger lily and the doll prove Azrael were here.*

She paused at the intersection, whistled high-low-low-high notes. The rock ceilings bounced noise like a rubber ball and carried the warning to Wanda and David.

Beryl ducked into the recess in the wall that concealed them. Hunkered down beside David. "Anything?"

Panting, Leslie crowded into the niche, closer to Wanda than Beryl.

"Nothing." He glanced from Beryl to Leslie and back. "Where's Miranda?"

"Gone." Beryl's eyes stung. She blinked, cleared her eyes and mind.

He glared. "What do you mean, gone?"

"She's going to set up peace talks," Leslie whispered.

"Are you serious? You let her go on a suicide mission?" David rose.

Beryl grabbed his arm, controlled her tone. "You want to waste your time following her will-o'-the-wisp dream? Or do you want to stop the Azrael?"

He pressed his back against the rock. Tapped his heel in a soft, rapid rhythm against the roadway. "She's gonna get herself captured."

"Or kill—oof!" Leslie rubbed her shoulder and scowled at Wanda.

"She can take care of herself," Wanda said.

David ran a hand through his hair. "She's my sister. I gotta help her."

"If she'd wanted your help," Beryl said, "she would have asked." She focused on the fenced-off area across the road.

The chain-link with green vinyl strips woven through the links blocked access to the four-foot-high concrete dock. A simple lift latch secured the gate. *No visible padlock. Might be an alarm.*

"See anyone?" Beryl asked.

"Not a soul," Wanda said. "No traffic. Nothing."

The fence stood at least nine feet tall. *Bet I could get up it, climb down the other side.* She sat back on her heels. *Should wait, be smart.*

Do it, do it, do it pounded in her blood. Her muscles tensed. *Aw, hell.*

She trotted across the road.

"What are you doing?" David's harsh whisper reached her. "Wait!"

The fence came so close to the dock's edge it forced her to stop one step below the top edge. She glowered at the camera box. *Want me? Come and get me.* She reached up and shook the fence.

The chain-link rattled and rang, echoed through the space. She counted to fifteen. *Nobody home?*

She climbed to the top. Wriggled over the fence. Glanced toward the others.

David, Leslie, and Wanda gawked at her from the edge of the road.

She waggled her fingers at them, climbed down to the dock.

A single, caged lightbulb above the door cast a yellow light. She darted to the hinge side of the man-door. Still no alarm.

The hairs on the back of her neck stood, and the thrum of *do it, do it, do it* urged her to rush inside.

She gripped the doorknob. It turned. She jerked her hand away. *This can't be good.* She needed backup—even amateurs.

No latch on this side of the fence either. The twenty-four feet long gate was on wheels. She rolled it open a few feet. No traffic in either direction. She waved the others to come.

David hoisted himself up, stood beside her. "This one looks abandoned too."

Leslie and Wanda scrambled up the steps.

Wanda rolled the gate back into place.

"Something's hinky," Beryl said. "Door's unlocked. Watch for traps."

"Traps?" Wanda said in a breathy tone. "You figure this is the lab?"

Beryl cocked her head in a follow-me and led them inside.

Security lights made a dim puddle of light near the door. Beyond the light lay pitch black, the depths of the earth black, endless, light-absorbing black. She fought to ignore the rising twinges of *I can't see, I can't see, I can't see*. Fought the urge to swing her gun barrel all over the place. Fought to control her breathing and forced those thoughts back. Turned on her flashlight.

One by one, the other three turned on their lights.

"One long whistle—everyone out," she whispered. "Three short —means help. Two shorts, one long—gather here. Got it?"

The soft chorus of yeses echoed as a prolonged hiss.

"David." She pointed her flashlight left. "Leslie." Right. "Wanda, guard the door." She pointed her flashlight five feet in front of her and followed it.

Cool, dry air moved around her. *The ventilation system still works.* The mineral-scented air held a hint of something else, something familiar. Her internal alarms pinged.

Swishing her light right and left, she pressed forward. The stink grew stronger, distinctive. Memory snapped into place. Her stomach dropped. Her chest hollowed. *Rotting human flesh.*

She trailed one hand along a man-made wall, found a corner.

The air changed.

An oily residue slicked her skin.

A metallic, coppery taste fouled her tongue.

The further she walked, the thicker and oilier the air grew.

Her fingers found a doorframe. A doorknob. She opened the door.

The putrid stench of rotting flesh robbed her of breath. Nausea twisted her stomach. Her eyes watered. The lumps stacked on warehouse shelves were bodies. She backed out, closed the door, and retreated to the corner.

She gasped for air. Tried to clear her sinuses. Tried to clear her head. Tried to weigh her choices. *Who? How many? Based on the stench, they've been dead a week or more. Too many. Need help.* She whistled three short blasts and waited.

An orb of light bounced toward her. David halted beside her. "What's up?"

The pitter-pat of running footsteps echoed, then a light bobbed across the floor. Leslie appeared. "I'm here—ugh. What stinks?"

The last light swept side to side, closer and closer. Wanda stepped into their light, wrinkled her nose.

"I found—bodies," Beryl said. "A lot of them. The cool temps down here slowed decomposition but—"

"That's the stench." David rubbed the back of a hand across his mouth.

"Azrael, I hope?" Wanda said.

"Doubt it." Copper filled Beryl's mouth, soured her stomach again. "We have to find out what happened. Document it. For Ethan."

Leslie paled. Wanda and David nodded.

"This is worse than Tucker's. Cover your nose and mouth." Beryl pulled her handkerchief out of her back pocket. "Breathe through your mouth. Not too fast, or you'll pass out."

She led them around the corner. Opened the door, and the full stench hit them.

David choked, coughed, then muffled his next cough.

Wanda gave a nasal groan.

Leslie gagged.

Then, nothing but ragged mouth breathing.

Beryl snapped a picture. The flash illuminated the horror of six units of sixteen-foot-tall warehouse shelving crammed with bodies. She crossed to the first shelving unit, waved the others to the rest.

Bloated beyond recognition, the bodies lay on rough wooden shelves. Four shelves per unit. Four or more bodies lay on each shelf. A blanket covered some. A few had pillows.

Beryl climbed an attached ladder to the topmost shelf. Four bodies lay in the width of a full-sized bed. All wore faded housedresses. One had her head nearly severed from her body. *A garrote.*

Proof. Beryl held her flashlight under her chin. Stuffed her handkerchief in her waistband. Fetid fumes burned her nose.

She pointed the camera at the victim. The play of light and shadow made the misshapen face and swollen, protruding tongue a grotesque mask. She willed the flash and the fast-speed film to pick up the nightmarish images.

Tears streamed from her eyes. She peered through them. Studied the other bodies. No visible bullet or knife wounds. No foam at the mouths or vomit.

The next level down, all the women still had their heads attached. Beryl snapped another picture. Down another level. A blanket near her had something printed on it.

She used finger and thumb and gingerly straightened the soggy, blue blanket. Printed in yellow lettering, it read Missouri School for the Feeble-Minded. *How dare the Fellowship hold itself above others when it...* Killing the feeble-minded innocents who couldn't protect themselves placed whoever killed these women lower than cockroaches. She tried not to breathe hard, but hot electricity zipped through her veins. *Focus. Get the damn pictures.* She snapped several of the blanket then the bodies. Held it together long enough to photograph and check each of the bodies on the bottom shelf.

She hustled out of the room and around the corner. The need to kill surged and surged and demanded action. She bent and braced her hands on her knees. Sucked in air. Again and again. The nausea hit. She pressed a fist to her mouth, mashed her lips into her teeth. The need to kill became the need not to vomit. The last spark of electricity fired, and she got control of her breathing. Eased the nausea.

Wanda came around the corner. Squatted, elbows on knees, and head in hands. Her shoulders heaved up and down.

Leslie appeared next. Braced an arm on the wall. Buried her face in her elbow.

The door banged shut. David lurched around the corner. "I heard stories..." His voice cracked, raw.

"Every story you've heard is softer than reality." Beryl couldn't keep the harsh edge from her words.

She led them away to cleaner air—air tainted only by minerals—snorted, and blew her nose. The stench remained burned into her nose and memory.

Raspy breaths and trembling and clutched stomachs filled two long minutes.

"Did anyone else notice something peculiar?" Wanda asked, breaking the silence.

David sniffed his hands. Made a face. "You mean besides the dead bodies?"

"All them—were white. No black or brown skin anywhere."

"All Azrael are white," Beryl said, flat and hard.

"And all from a home for the unfit, weren't they?" Leslie pressed her lips tight.

Beryl stared into the dark, not seeing anything but the flashes of memories she thought she'd buried. "They ripped them open. Stole and altered their eggs. To grow monsters in mechanical devices."

"Mechanical?" Leslie's strained whisper rose.

"Like steel drums." Beryl's muscles tightened, resisted the relentless memory of rows and rows of steel uteri. "When the women ran out of eggs…"

Someone must have survived the island blast. Or was off the island. Someone who knew how— Three pairs of eyes watched and waited for her next words. "Find any bullet holes, garrote marks, signs of poison?"

The three of them shook no.

"You examined every body and found nothing?"

Shoulder shrugs and head shakes by all three again. Their eyes avoided hers.

Then how the hell… Shit. It would take close examination to see an injection sight. And she wouldn't make any of them go back into that room. "There's got to be a control room nearby. We need a clue where they've gone. We'll stick together this time."

No one argued, and no one strayed.

Two corridors over, a metal ladder led up three steps to a room set into the rock.

Inside, a one-way observation window looked out over a black void. Dozens of built-in cabinets filled the opposite wall. The cut ends of dozens of power cables and phone lines littered the beige carpet. Aside from the sharp scent of ozone, the air held no hint of human occupation.

"Search every inch," Beryl said. "They missed something. Show me anything you find. Everything you find."

Beryl crawled beneath the one-way window that stretched the length of the room. The smooth, thick, beige carpet kept its secrets.

"Well," Wanda drawled. "Would you look at that?" She stood in the middle of the row of cabinets, peered at a board she'd pulled out like a drawer.

Beryl scrambled to her feet. Ignored the flutter in her stomach. Hid how her hands trembled. Joined Wanda.

Wanda's flashlight revealed a map glued to the board—or part of one. Someone had scraped off parts of it.

"Where'd that come from?" Leslie asked.

"Just pulled on this front piece, like this." She pulled on the next cabinet. "Well, I'll be. There's another one."

Beryl found a board-drawer on this side of the first one. Scraps of a map in shades of green, dotted by blue lakes and crisscrossed with blue rivers and yellow highways. A scrap near the outside edge held a city name—Topeka.

The maps spanned an area from eastern Kansas to part of Illinois. The missing pieces must have included Chicago, St. Louis, Springfield, and Kansas City.

Wanda tapped the middle board. It gave a hollow thud. "This is where we are." She eyed the other two boards. "How many of these hellish caves exist?"

Beryl walked from the Illinois board to the Missouri, then to the Kansas one. She rubbed her tight neck muscles. "Did the experiment fail? Was it too expensive? Or did they lose their lease?"

"Trust me, the landlord might want to, but he would never ever tell the Fellowship they lost their lease," Wanda said. "What if this place failed—and one of these others succeeded? They'd move to the successful place, wouldn't they?"

That made sense. "More workers means they need more space." Beryl studied the end map. "One of these places is larger than the other. Which one?" She searched the scarred wood for a hint. "Do we split up and check all of them or take a gamble with one?"

"Split up and search a mine larger than this one?" Wanda said. "Without help? The four of us can't cover this place. A larger one?" She snorted.

David dug in his right pocket.

"What are you doing?"

"I have a quarter we can flip."

"No." Beryl leaned forward, her nose inches away from the scarred wood. The Kansas board had deep gouges. Especially around where Kansas City would be. The western Missouri board, not as gouged. The Illinois board had almost no gouges. Did the glue give out? Her inner alarms pinged. Her blood hummed. Or did they want to hide the Kansas location most? She strode to the door. "Come. It's a long way to Kansas City. We'll contact Ethan on the way."

Chapter Thirty-Four

U nlike the gentle motion of Miranda's boat, the train rocked in a herky-jerky motion. She and Karl sat on a metal balcony just above the coupling of a refrigerator car. Unprotected, easily seen. Karl had insisted that it was better than being inside a boxcar and unable to watch for trouble.

Frosty air froze her fingers and toes. And the diamond shapes of the balcony's metal grid flooring dug into her butt.

With each clack and clatter of the refrigerator car, she considered and tossed ideas on how she'd convince Ethan to meet with Irene.

The train rumbled over a well-lit cross street. Made the bright yellow streetlight appear to blink on and off when they left it behind.

Less than three feet to her right, Karl huddled with his unzipped sleeping bag drawn tight around him.

Asleep? Maybe. Too dark to tell. She shifted her weight to the other hip. Heaved a sigh.

"Penny for your thoughts," Karl said above the train noise.

"Will we reach Kansas City soon?"

"In about an hour."

"How long before I can talk to Ethan?"

"Depends. He could be at the safe house. Or he could still be en route." His head swiveled toward her. "But it'll be past midnight. I expect he'll be asleep."

"Right. So it'll be morning before we can talk. That won't allow enough time to plan." She hugged her knees and rested her chin on them. "He's going to refuse."

"No, he won't. I told you, he wants peace as badly as you do."

"How long have you been with Ethan?"

"Almost two years."

That would have been shortly after Ethan had recovered from his injuries. A lifetime in the rebel underground. Obviously, he'd earned Ethan's trust. He knew where to hitch a ride on a train. Irene's phone number at the residence. Where Ethan would be and how to contact him. Without Karl, she'd have never gotten this far. "Thank you for helping me."

"Why wouldn't I help? Everyone wants peace, even Beryl."

His words struck deep inside Miranda and re-inflamed the raw wound there. *Maybe he's right, maybe if I hadn't lost my temper—no, he doesn't know her like I do. Everyone else might want peace, but not Beryl.*

An approaching train whistled and blasted its horn. It roared past in the opposite direction, stirred the frigid air into a frenzy. Miranda shivered, wished she'd insisted on being inside a boxcar, and drew her sleeping bag tighter around her shoulders.

Individual arcs of light appeared here and there, then melded into a generalized glow. Enough light to see homes with bicycles leaning against the porch and urban homes transition into edge-of-the-city businesses.

Karl stood, rolled his sleeping bag and stuffed it into his rucksack, slipped his rucksack's strap over one shoulder.

Muscles tense, Miranda stowed her sleeping bag too.

With a firm grip on the metal handrail, he leaned out, peered ahead and behind them.

Their train slowed. The light grew around them, enveloped them. More tracks and more trains appeared. Their train moved slower and slower.

Karl touched her arm. "Remember," he shouted. "Jump and run, or tuck and roll. Get ready."

The train lumbered into a switching yard full of dozens of tracks and trains.

"Now!"

Miranda hit the ground with a jolt. Took several jarring and off-balance steps. Skidded in the gravel. Arms spread, she wobbled, then gained her balance. Caught her breath and assessed the damage. Nothing broken.

The caboose swayed down the tracks, slowing for the train's next stop.

Karl jogged up to her. "You all right?"

"I'm good. Which way?"

"Follow me."

She trotted after him through moonlight-dappled uphill streets, around houses, and through trees.

Their serpentine path passed quaint bungalows with terraced yards in various stages of repair. A historic neighborhood Karl called Westport.

"In a moment, I'll start moving faster. Stay with me," Karl said in a low voice. "Once we start, we can't stop." He widened his strides.

Miranda dashed after him, up the front walk of a bungalow with a stone porch. Followed him through the unlocked door, through the house, out the back, and across the unkept backyard, surrounded by a peeling white picket fence.

He jumped the fence into a neatly tended backyard.

Miranda launched herself over the fence and ran to catch up.

He stopped at a low, angled cellar entrance on the side of the house. Scanned the area. Threw open one of the double wooden doors.

She followed down four creaky wooden steps, reached the bottom.

Above them, the door shut, and the moonlight vanished.

Someone wrenched Miranda's hands behind her back. "No. Wait —" Miranda squirmed against her assailant. Her shoulders and wrists burned. He was much stronger than she was. Her shoulders slumped.

"Mushrooms need damp ground," Karl said in a loud and confident tone.

"Karl? What are you doing here?"

A lightbulb flicked on. Lit half the basement.

A man beside Karl uncocked his pistol, slid it into his shoulder holster.

Daring to hope, Miranda searched for Ethan. On her right, against an unpainted cement block wall, stood neat rows of mason jars that held green beans and corn and red beets on wooden shelves. Against the wall she faced stood a workbench littered with hand tools.

"Miranda?"

She gasped. Peered into the shadows. "Nick? Is that you?"

"Yeah." *Click.* Another lightbulb came on. Nick stood on the bottom step of wooden stairs leading up. He had bed-head, jeans, an untucked shirt, and bare feet.

Her heart lightened. "I didn't think I'd see you again so soon."

"Let her go," he said to the man behind her.

Freed, she staggered toward Nick.

He folded her in a warm embrace, then gripped each of her shoulders. Peered at her. "How are you here? Are you all right? We heard *Lady* had wrecked. I thought—"

"I'm fine. The Second Sphere was onto us. The wreck was a ruse."

He drew her close again.

She drank in his warmth, his presence.

Someone in a dark corner of the room coughed and cleared his throat.

Grinning, Nick released her. Still looking at Miranda, he stepped back. "We weren't expecting you. Did you change your mind?"

She clamped her lips shut tight. Wanted to say yes. *But not until there's peace. Then nothing will force us apart or take you from me.* She forced her tight lips into a smile. Shook her head. "That's not why we're here."

Nick glanced at Karl. "Why are you here?"

"Did you find them?" Ethan stepped out of the shadows, focused his intense stare on Miranda. "Did you actually see an Azrael?"

"No," Miranda said. "They had abandoned the cave, cleaned out. No sign of them or anyone."

Ethan nodded. "I knew it. That girl's resemblance is a coincidence." He turned away. "I'm going back to bed—"

"Wait," Miranda insisted. "I have other news. Hear me out. Please."

He studied her face. "What?" Wariness filled his eyes, and his face darkened with doubt.

She stood a little taller. "Irene has agreed to meet. Here, in Kansas City. This Sunday."

"You told her I was here?" An over-the-shoulder head-jerk signaled others Miranda hadn't seen.

Two men sprang from the shadows, pistols drawn. One ran to the door, the other checked the windows and peered outside.

"You would rather I pick a city she could get to first?" Miranda asked. "She picked the place—the train station and the date—tomorrow. You choose the time."

"No visible enemy, sir," one of Ethan's men said, "but we should leave before first light. The presence of the Prophet's Lady in town will undoubtedly double, maybe triple, the Second Sphere agents here."

Ethan turned away from her, put his hand on the stair rail.

With two quick steps forward, Miranda seized Ethan's arm. The muscles in his arm hardened as if he would tear free from her. "How many people have already died because of the fighting?" she said. "Not the Second Sphere. Not the rebels. The innocents. The women and children and elderly. How many more will die if you continue fighting in the streets?"

Ethan's look of disappointment in her ripped through Miranda. "You think this fight has been about anything but saving the innocents? What makes you think I haven't been working toward ending the fighting?"

Open-mouthed, she released him. Couldn't believe— *Wait, he said ending the fighting. He didn't say peace talks.* "How? With a bigger bomb?"

"The Azrael don't exist. We don't need to make peace with your sister."

"Have you recruited hundreds of new rebels?" Miranda asked. "Bought or stolen more guns?"

Ethan cocked his head. His look said you-know-I-haven't.

Miranda propped her fists on her hips. "Then you know it's only a matter of time before the Fellowship, the Second Sphere, will defeat SABR."

"So we should give up? Allow the Fellowship to kill folks whose only crime is that they have a different color of skin or worship a different way?"

"Part of working out a peace treaty is protecting those people. Protecting everyone."

"And what's making the Fellowship keep their word?"

"Irene and Felix won't—"

"Really? You trust your sister more than I do."

She threw a desperate look at Karl.

"Sir, if I may?" Karl stepped forward.

Ethan cocked his head, gave a brief nod.

"What if the Azrael are being reborn? What if the Fellowship doubles or triples their army of Second Sphere agents? How do we keep fighting when the borders are closed and we've no more weapons or ammo?"

"Miranda's Safe Harbor—not *Lady*, obviously. The other boats will bring in shipments." Ethan faced Miranda. "We need the ammo. The refugees won't have to hide—no one will have to hide if we get enough—"

"They won't have to hide because they'll be dead," Miranda said forcefully. "Including you. The Fellowship will still rule the country, and they'll do whatever they want. And it'll all have been for nothing."

"Miranda, we have to fight for the chance."

"We make peace," Karl said. "for the chance to win from within. You've always said that was our most effective weapon."

"Then tell me, how do we keep the Fellowship from attacking us in the meantime?"

"We tell them we'll blow up their churches and schools," Karl said. "We'll say we've got planes in Mexico loaded with explosives that will hit the Fellowship Center and the homes of prominent Fellowship members."

Ethan gave Karl a startled look. "Our stockpiles are too low. We can't do that."

"They don't know that," Karl said. "A small demonstration would convince them we have what we need."

Nick nodded. "We were just talking about something like that." He and Ethan stared at one another for a short eternity.

Ethan hooked his thumbs in his belt and turned. "I guess I'll take my nap after we figure out where we want this meeting to take place."

Mouth agape, Miranda tried to tamp down the hope that swirled inside. *Irene and Ethan will meet. For a peace talk.* She bit her lip to keep from tearing up. Her chest swelled. And her inside smile was worldwide. *It's not peace, not yet. But it's a chance.*

Chapter Thirty-Five

White knuckled, Beryl stopped the truck, signaled a left turn. A billboard sign stood in front of the exposed limestone and in large blue letters declared SubTropolis the world's largest underground business complex. Already on edge after the repeated truck breakdowns during the last twelve hours, her jaw muscles clenched.

"Oh, my," Leslie said in a breathy way that could have been awe or fear.

"It's a slogan," Beryl said, her tone hot and tired. "Nothing more than a sales gimmick."

The gas station attendant had mentioned the mine's size to David when David had asked for directions for an imaginary job interview. *Exaggeration. Had to be.*

The short, street-level drive led to the twenty-feet-wide tunnel entrance to the former mine.

She drove into the tunnel, down a gentle slope to a stop sign. The walls opened up. Both the intersecting road and the one straight ahead ran as far as Beryl could see. Massive, rectangular rock pillars reaching from floor to ceiling, lined the roads. The roads, pillars, and air were dry, but the air smelled like wet rock.

Instead of the multi-arrowed sign in Springfield, a green street sign labeled the road. Below the street sign, a fat, black "Visitors Welcome" arrow pointed left to the leasing office.

Sticking to the main road, Beryl drove through the intersection. Nodded to Leslie.

The ceilings and walls and the top two-thirds of the pillars were painted a brilliant white. Fluorescent tubes in a continuous string overhead bathed the area with light.

Over her shoulder, Leslie called, "You can come out."

Visible in the rearview mirror, David and Wanda emerged from under the tarp.

Between the next two rock pillars stood dozens of identical white panel delivery trucks. Above the trucks hung a glowing a neon sign, the Ford logo.

The same sign hung above the dock to her right. Its garage doors opened to a well-lit parts warehouse that stretched farther than Beryl could see.

Across bumpy railroad tracks, the lighting overhead changed. One fluorescent tube every forty feet. Between lights, thick gray shadows fell on the road. In the recesses between pillars, shadows turned charcoal gray and faded to black. The truck's headlights only reached so far.

"Is Ford the only business down here?" Leslie asked in a subdued tone.

"Does it matter?" Beryl said, gruff because Leslie's priorities were wrong.

The road curved, then straightened. Open spaces lay between many of the pillars. Between some pillars, the road ramped up or down to a different level of the cave. Other spaces were closed off with brick or concrete block walls. These spaces had signs saying, "This Space Available" and "Coming Soon."

Another curve, and this stretch of road had half as many lights, with no end in sight. The heaviness inside Beryl grew to boulder size. *This place is worse than a rabbit's warren.*

"Wow." Leslie slumped in her seat. "This place is a lot bigger than the one in Springfield. I stopped counting doors when I reached one hundred sixty. It must *really* be the world's largest underground complex."

Eight miles later, Beryl drove out of a different garage door onto same road they came in on. She squinted against the still bright-gray sky. Only half a block from the main entrance.

"Call Ethan," David said from the truck bed. "There is no way we can effectively search that place. Make him give us more time."

"And more men," Wanda said.

Beryl knew better than to ask. Her gut ached. The boulder was now a mountain.

"Being underground distorted our sense of space," Beryl said and turned left onto the road. "I'll drive the perimeter. Give us a better idea of what we're facing here."

Even if each space had only three doors, that still meant fifty spaces —large warehouse spaces—to investigate. Even if they could determine what each space was once every two hours, that meant a minimum of four solid days of work. Based on the previous cave, it would take a lot more than two hours for most of the places. Who knew how many spaces they'd passed unknown in the dark? Only four days and thirteen hours remained before Ethan's damned deadline.

"It doesn't matter how big this place is or how long it takes," Beryl said. "I'm going to find the proof, and when he sees it—he'll help us destroy every lab and Azrael in existence."

She reached a grassy dead-end. The grass divided the road from a gravel parking area. Off to the right, a one-lane, deeply rutted dirt road continued to follow the river. The main road had turned, became part of a large circle drive in front of yet another pair of garage doors in the limestone.

"Guess we can't circle this place. I'll turn around." Beryl checked over her shoulder.

A liquid-oxygen tanker truck disappeared into the garage door nearest the corner.

She threw the truck into reverse, made a hand-brake turn, and raced to the spot.

The garage door lowered behind the tanker.

She jammed on the brakes.

From the truck bed came "What the heck?"

Leslie braced both hands against the dash. Gulped air.

In the rearview mirror, David rubbed the back of his head.

"That's the place," Beryl muttered. "Has to be."

"Really? Why?" David peered at the unmarked door.

"LOX. Liquid oxygen. There was a giant tank of it on the island. They used it for the…the fetuses." The horror of finding her daughter's dead, mutilated body pierced her again. Her heart thumped at breakneck speed. Pumped her blood with the fire-hardened steel needed for the blade of ruthless reprisals.

"There's a keypad on a post back there," Leslie said. "I'll bet there's a security code you have to enter to get in."

Beryl blinked. Tempered her blood and considered the keypad.

"It's so close," Wanda said. "They have to be connected."

"You have a point," Beryl said.

The Fellowship must have chosen the former limestone mine because they thought it made the lab secure from any threat. But every installation had a weakness. And she sure as hell planned to exploit every one.

Chapter Thirty-Six

T he limestone cliffs didn't glitter under the chilly, gray Kansas City sky, but when the garage doors clanged shut, the light still changed. The harsh fluorescent reflection off rocks painted white meant Irene was one step closer to losing her daughter. Her heart shook her entire body.

She stole a side-eyed glance at her daughter. The young girl sat next to her with no outward emotion at all. Irene couldn't decide if that was a good sign or not.

The limo trundled through the cave to the Center for the Advancement of Inborn Character, Dr. Gallaway's lab.

Too soon, the limo stopped in front of the building where Annabelle and Dr. Gallaway had first met. Dr. Gallaway stood at the entrance, hands clasped behind his back.

The driver opened Irene's door. She stood. Chill bumps raced down her arms, followed by a flush of nausea. *I will not cry.*

Annabelle exited the vehicle. Stood on her tippy-toes in front of Irene and offered her puckered lips.

Irene ignored her alternating chills and flushes and accepted the peck on her cheek. Blinked away tears that threatened.

Annabelle followed their driver to the trunk and took her little brown suitcase from him. Dr. Gallaway had told Irene to pack only underclothing and one personal item. The school provided everything else.

Her brave daughter walked toward Dr. Gallaway. Halfway there, she stopped, twisted to face her mother, and waved.

Irene forced a smile and waved goodbye. *I will not cry.* Annabelle joined Dr. Gallaway and preceded him through the office doors. The doors clicked shut.

Sharp pain robbed Irene of breath. *I will not cry.* Her vision blurred. *I will not cry.* She squashed the urge to drag her daughter back home. *I. Will. Not. Cry.* She practiced deep breathing until the tears behind her eyelids subsided. Then squared her shoulders and climbed back into the limo.

During the drive back out of the caves, she knotted and unknotted the corner of her handkerchief. A light rain plinked against the car. Made it hard for her to focus on the peace meeting tomorrow.

Her driver stopped at the covered entrance to Union Station, Kansas City's train depot.

"Give me ten minutes," she told him. "I'll buy my ticket and find out where to wait for the train, then I'll be ready to go back to my hotel."

She climbed the stone steps and entered the building through its brass and glass doors into an immense space. Rose-brown marble walls stretched up a hundred feet to colorfully painted plaster ceilings.

A grid of light and shadow cast on the geometric terra-cotta floor made her whirl and gaze at the arched windows that rose to incredible heights above the entry doors.

Three glittering chandeliers hung from the ceiling in this main or Grand Hall. And there, at the entry to the Grand Plaza, hung the black clock that had to be as tall as a man.

A cacophony of clanking carts, clamoring voices, and clattering wheels bounced around the space, brought her back to her purpose.

She strode to the half-round ticket office that stood in the center front of the Grand Hall. She purchased a one-way ticket to Columbus, Ohio, which she had no intention of using. Standing under the clock, she scanned the Grand Plaza, where hundreds of people sat on wooden benches or paced the floor and awaited their train.

A tall, colorful hat is what I need to stand out in this crowd.

A quick walk around the perimeter of the Grand Plaza made her appreciate Paul's plan. Besides the four men who would linger in each corner of the waiting area, there would be one at each of the front doors. He and one other would cover the platforms. Dwarfed by the space, concern that she didn't have enough men rippled through Irene.

"Southern Belle Number Three Forty is now loading passengers on platform one-A," a male voice announced over the PA system.

A flurry of noise and movement erupted. People stood, gathered belongings, and hurried to a door on the west side of the hall. *Paul had said the chaos of arrivals and departures was perfect.*

The parade of people leaving dwindled and disappeared. Silence fell. Irene stared about the hall, astonished. Far fewer people remained in the hall. *That might be problematic.*

On her way back out of the building, she stopped at the ticket office and picked up a train schedule.

————

THE NEXT MORNING, Irene didn't even get out of bed before she dialed the front desk. "I told you to put through any calls for me, regardless of the hour."

"I'm sorry, madam. No calls came for you."

Her heart twisted. *Annabelle didn't call?* "Are you absolutely certain?" She sat on the edge of the bed, held her breath until he triple-checked. *Annabelle didn't call.*

She hung up the phone and clapped her hands to her aching heart. *Maybe Annabelle's too frightened. I should call Dr. Gallaway.*

The open telephone line buzzed in her ear. *He said if there were any problems, he'd call.* Reluctantly, she replaced the receiver.

After breakfast, she went shopping for a tall, extravagant hat. Forgot her worries at a charming shopping area called the Country Club Plaza. According to a historical marker outside one shop, the Plaza was an outdoor shopping area designed in pseudo-Moorish Revival architecture echoing the style in Seville, Spain. To Irene's delight, she discovered a millinery shop where she bought a jaunty turquoise pill box hat with two dyed pheasant feathers. She left the shopping area with a newfound confidence.

She spent the rest of the afternoon preparing for her big day.

At five minutes until five, dressed in her gray wool suit and coral blouse and her new turquoise hat, she climbed the steps to Union

Station. Paused at the door. *Steady, Irene. You will show the world what you can do.* She lifted her chin and strode inside.

Out of the corner of her eye, Irene spotted the first of her men. Leaning against the wall opposite the information booth, he sported a green fedora with a green velvet band and a valise with a large Eiffel Tower travel sticker on it. Knowing he was here, and the others were close by, settled her. She controlled her irregular and fast breathing. Strode forward to the spot directly beneath the giant black clock hanging from the ceiling. Gripped her turquoise handbag with both hands. Fortunately, she'd waited in enough reception lines and such that she knew how to stand still for a long, long time.

Chapter Thirty-Seven

The second hand ticked forward on the immense black clock that hung above the intersection between Union Station's Grand Plaza waiting room and the Grand Hall. Seated in the waiting room, Miranda's chest buzzed and her fingers tingled. She fingered the sweetheart collar of the white button-up blouse she wore. Fidgeted with the folds of the pink flare skirt. Clothes delivered to the safe house once she'd told Ethan her sizes. She couldn't help it—glanced up at the clock again.

Two minutes until five. Two minutes until Irene arrives and the peace talks start.

Dozens of train passengers scurried from the ticket booth to the waiting area. The click and shuffle of shoes, murmurs, and shouts of passengers, and the clangor of vendor cart wheels on the terra-cotta floors surrounded her.

Throat tight, she scanned the crowd. *So many innocents.* It was highly likely that some were Second Sphere. And some, like Nick, were SABR—rebels.

Stagnant aromas of popcorn and hotdogs and spicy aftershave lotions made her queasy.

"What will you do if your sister doesn't show?" Ethan spoke in an even tone, only slightly louder than the chatter and clatter around them. He sat on the same mahogany double bench she did, faced the opposite direction.

"Irene will show," Miranda said. "She wants peace as badly as we do." *Peace is worth the chance. Even if...* She refused to follow that thought any further.

She shifted her weight, crossed her ankles. Dull light from the gray, rainy day lit the tall, multi-paned windows high on the entry wall and added somberness to the thoughts Ethan had stirred.

"We can leave now, and she'll never know."

Part of Miranda wanted to say yes. "If we don't stay, we'll always wonder if peace would have been possible." She swiped her damp palms on her skirt.

The black minute hand of the clock ticked forward. *One minute to go.* Below the clock, people flowed in and out of the Grand Plaza. So many people, Miranda couldn't spot Nick. Miranda gripped the edges of her seat, willed herself to stay still. To wait.

Seconds ticked past.

She worked hard to keep her breathing regular.

The giant black minute hand jerked forward. Five o'clock.

Movement in the Grand Hall, and a turquoise-green pillbox hat with two pheasant feathers dyed to match caught Miranda's eye. Wavy red hair brushed the woman's shoulders. *Turn around.*

As if under Miranda's silent direction, the woman made a slow turn toward the Grand Plaza. Turned her face up toward the clock.

The newspaper clippings hadn't done Irene justice. She'd slimmed down since Miranda last saw her. Well dressed, though matronly.

Pulse thumping in her throat, Miranda scanned the people around Irene. Several men tipped their hats or said a word in passing. *People already recognize her.*

A man in a brown tweed suit brushed against Irene's right shoulder. He didn't hesitate. Didn't tip his hat. Didn't look at Irene. The hairs on Miranda's neck raised. *He ignored bumping into the Prophet's wife?*

Miranda clicked her tongue. *Pretty shoddy undercover work. Shoddy? Irene's security team, Second Sphere agents, professionals. What's going on?*

"Missouri River passengers now disembarking," a male voice announced over the PA system.

The doors on the east side of the hall banged open. Passengers from those trains flooded the waiting room. Just as Ethan had planned.

A steadying breath, and Miranda stood. Paused. No one paid attention to her. She squared her shoulders and walked toward her sister.

"Hello, Irene."

Irene did a half-turn to face her. "Hello."

Miranda swallowed to clear the thickness in her throat. "Let's take a walk." She turned to the west.

Low thunder rumbled, rattled the chandeliers.

Irene lifted her chin. "I didn't come because of you."

"And I didn't come because of you. We came because we want peace. So does Monkshood."

"I'm here to talk to Monkshood." Irene glanced around. "Where is he?"

"He's here. We'll talk to him in a minute. I thought we should talk first."

"This walk and talk is so your people can see if I'm alone." She spun. "See, it's just me."

"You have fooled no one, Irene. We know you have protectors here. We have them too. What we need to know is how badly you want peace."

"No offense—I am trying to be a good Fellowship member, but I didn't come here to talk to you."

Miranda stopped opposite the barber shop's striped poles. Faced Irene. "If you want peace, you and I talk first. Otherwise, go home."

Irene pressed her lips together and locked eyes with Miranda.

"Do you want peace, Irene?"

Irene's eyes flashed, and her cheeks twitched. "My daughters and I narrowly missed being killed in a car bomb incident." She cleared her throat. "I never ever want them to be at risk like that again."

"The car bombing in Arlington?"

"Yes."

"I understand. And I'm sorry," Miranda said in a strained tone. "I've lost friends in this fight. I don't want anyone else hurt either."

"This fight isn't the Fellowship's fault." Irene's cheek twitched again. "Sorry. That's irrelevant. We both want peace. So what do we do now?"

"Keep walking." Miranda turned and walked back the way they'd come. Irene walked beside her.

Miranda stopped directly below the clock at the entrance to the Grand Plaza and scanned the people seated on the benches. Ethan had moved, part of their plan to keep Irene's people guessing. She scanned the rows twice before she spotted the black Homburg hat with two yellow pencils stuck in the green band. Continued to glance over the occupied benches and led Irene to the bench behind Ethan. Miranda sat and patted the seat beside her.

Irene gave an exasperated sigh, but sat and folded her gloved hands in her lap.

A faint fragrance reached Miranda. *White Shoulders, Irene's favorite perfume. Mama's favorite too.* The hairs on the back of Miranda's neck raised again. She scanned the crowd. *Nothing out of place. Is the danger I sense real?*

Irene huffed impatiently. "Now what?"

"Now you sit and you face the clock at all times, and we talk." Miranda scanned the crowd again.

"We've been talking. Where is he?"

"Don't turn," Ethan said. "I'm behind you, Mrs. Earnshaw."

Irene stiffened but didn't turn. "Call me Lady Earnshaw."

"We have conditions for these talks. Are you going to listen or not?"

She gripped the edge of the bench, pressed her lips together until they whitened.

Electric energy zipped through Miranda. *Is she about to betray us?*

Irene blew out a breath. "I'm listening."

Miranda pressed against the cool back of the bench.

"We will agree to a four-week cease-fire if you meet our conditions," Ethan said. "Break any of these conditions, and Washington, D.C. will feel the impact."

"What does that mean? More bombings? More needless deaths?" Irene's voice went up a half-octave.

Miranda pitched her voice low and quiet. "It means that if you break your promises, we will obliterate the Fellowship Center in D.C. and every Fellowship building across the country."

Irene swallowed and did a slow blink, then pinned Miranda with her gaze. "I will promise to listen. I can't promise more until I hear your conditions."

"Then listen carefully," Ethan said in a conversational tone. "You will release all SABR prisoners within two weeks of the agreement. The Prophet and the Fellowship Council will retire their advisory positions to the government."

A ball of cold fury gathered in Miranda's gut. *He's demanding that the Prophet retire? That'll never happen. What are you doing, Ethan? Purposefully sabotaging the peace talk?*

"I cannot—" Irene gripped the edge of the bench seat on each side of her.

"These are our conditions for peace."

"What if we have conditions?" Irene's voice held an imperious tone Miranda had never heard before.

"When it's our turn to listen, we'll listen."

A sort of sixth sense shot an alarm through Miranda. Without moving, she scanned as much of the crowd as she could.

Brown Tweed Man leaned against the wall nearby. No briefcase. No ticket sticking out of his pocket. He held a train schedule as if he were reading, but his eyes shifted in a scan-the-crowd motion.

Irene glowered at the clock or the person beneath the clock. "It's hot and stinks in here. Get on with it." She patted her face with a white lace handkerchief.

Brown Tweed Man reached into his suit coat.

Adrenaline surged through Miranda. Without changing her expression, she murmured the Latin code word *"Curre."* Run.

"Southwest Chief Number One Ten is now loading passengers on platform four-A," a male voice announced over the PA system. People on the benches stood. Others moved toward the door.

The bench she sat on shifted. She prayed it was because Ethan now crouched in the aisle.

"Wait. What did you say?" Irene asked. "Ethan?"

"You heard him. It's your turn to talk." *Gotta keep Irene distracted. Give Ethan time to disappear into a stairwell, change, get to the train platform, and escape.*

"Well, I can't really say anything," Irene stammered.

Miranda stood.

Irene put a hand on Miranda's wrist. "What's going on?"

"You betrayed us." Miranda jerked her hand loose. Ran. Yanked open the nearest door. Ran down the escalator onto the midway. Down that hall to the train platform.

Glanced right. Left. *Oh, no.*

Ethan struggled with a man over a gun.

Her head screamed run, but her heart screamed *Ethan needs help.*

A door between her and Ethan banged open.

Nick glanced toward her. Toward Ethan, then back at her. Mouthed, "Run." He whirled. Dove toward the fight.

The door banged again, another agent appeared, and turned on Nick.

Miranda yelled, "No!"

The agent spun. Pointed his weapon at her.

Miranda whirled and pelted down the platform. Zigzagged to throw off the agent's aim.

On the far end of the platform, a black man straightened from behind his vending cart full of books, magazines, and candy. Curiosity, confusion, then alarm flickered across his face.

"Run." She waved toward the doors. "Hide."

Boom.

The bullet zinged past her.

The vendor's expression went slack. He crumpled. Hit the cart and slumped to the ground.

A couple of books fell from the cart, which rumbled a few feet away.

Miranda raced toward him.

Another shot zinged—closer this time.

She ducked behind the cart. Pushed the cart toward the fallen man, firing her pistol blindly above the cart.

Thwack. A book took a bullet.

She drew even with the man. Pressed her fingers to his neck. No pulse.

A growing pool of blood puddled beneath him.

No one was supposed to die. The vise around her chest tightened.

Ping-ping-ping. The L-shaped shelves repelled bullets. She peered between the cart's shelves.

The agent wore that damned brown tweed and a smug smile.

Sound receded. Her vision tunneled between the top and second shelf.

She steadied her gun barrel on the top of the second shelf. Lined up her sights.

The agent darted out from behind the pillar, dashed to the next pillar.

You guys don't know the meaning of peace, do you? She aimed at the pillar.

He peeked around the pillar, then slid around it.

Crosshairs on the center of his chest. She squeezed the trigger.

He fell facedown. Didn't move.

Don't leave it to chance, said the Beryl in Miranda's head.

Miranda strode forward. Towered over him. Delivered a kill shot.

Whirled. *Nick? Ethan?*

Out of sight.

So was the agent they had fought.

"There's one," a man shouted behind her.

She vaulted off the platform. Leaped over rails.

Heavy feet thumped after her. Floodlights ended the shadows.

Shoulders tensed, she dove between train cars. Headed for the fence.

Chapter Thirty-Eight

Annabelle sat at a student desk in the front row of the classroom full of ten-year-old Annas. Ignored the ugly teacher who prowled the back of the room. Only her second day and already she was bored. Bored by *normal* classes. Bored by the simplicity of this arithmetic assignment.

A ruler smacked across Annabelle's knuckles. Raised another stinging, angry-red welt. Inside, something roared that this should not go unpunished.

Annabelle kept her expression bland, bored, and without moving her hand or releasing her yellow pencil, glanced up from her seat. Stared into the teacher's brown eyes. "Yes, ma'am?"

"Are you too stupid to know your own name?" Teacher towered over Annabelle. With her graying bun on top of her head, long, narrow face, and pouty lips, Teacher reminded Annabelle of a spitting llama.

The need to punch Teacher was like a volcano about to erupt. *Twelve hours isn't long enough to always respond to my new name.* "I am Anna 3000."

"Dr. Gallaway said I must grant you leniency as you are new. You have it, but only for today. Tomorrow, inattention shall be punished."

I solved your stupid math problem five minutes ago. Aloud, she said, "May I solve the problem on the board?"

Teacher stood too close. Reeked of lavender water. "Go ahead. Try."

Annabelle wrote each step of the solution on the chalkboard. Brushed chalk dust off her hands and faced Teacher, who had followed her to the front of the room.

"Well done," Teacher said.

Other classmates solved the next four chalkboard problems.

The bell rang. Annabelle hesitated. No student moved until Teacher said, "Dismissed."

The other Annas stood and prepared to leave.

Annabelle stuffed her books into her carry bag. Her black carry bag had a large red Fellowship shield on it, just like the thirty other Annas. One of the not-sisters now, she wore the same dove-gray sheath dress the others did.

She fell into line, the last in line, and followed the others with the same precise rhythm of steps.

After a quick stop at the dorm to put away their books and don their bright blue, one-piece, active-wear bloomers, they formed another line and waited at the door.

The first-level and second-level classes marched past. Her class fell in behind the last second-level classmate.

Annabelle and eighty-nine of her not-sisters quick-stepped out to the courtyard, then walked to a chalk line in the too-green plastic grass to the front of the yard.

Annabelle suppressed a smile. This courtyard was where she'd first seen her not-sisters. She still didn't have a better word for their relationships. *They aren't kin. They aren't friends. They are all exactly the same. Except for me. I am different. And one day soon, I'll figure out my special destiny.*

A whistle blew, followed by a shout. "One hundred jumping jacks."

Annabelle raised her arms in unison with the other girls.

After jumping jacks, they did chin-ups, push-ups, squats, and knee raises.

Her heartbeat strong and steady. Her chest swelled, and her muscles sang with the glory of use.

Five laps around the courtyard, and then a teacher shouted, "Challenge!"

The other girls paired off.

"Go."

Without gloves or training mats, the girls sparred with one another. *Full contact sparring?*

Grunts and oofs surrounded Annabelle. Flesh smacked flesh. Bodies thudded against the turf.

Annabelle didn't have a partner. She stood at ease and waited for Teacher's instructions. A hazy memory floated through her head. *Knees loose. Feet shoulder-width apart. Use your opponent's energy.*

The math teacher, accompanied by an Anna, came to Annabelle. Teacher studied Annabelle for a long moment. She shook her head as if Annabelle had fallen short of her expectations. "We will assess your skill. Then I'll assign you a partner."

The numbers printed across the chest of the girl's bloomers said she was Anna 2009. She was half a head taller than Annabelle and had small breasts. Her dark hair hung down her back in a long braid. She pushed two fingers into Annabelle's left shoulder, hard.

Annabelle rotated and dipped her shoulder under Anna 2009's hand. She straightened, and her shoulder pushed the other's hand up.

Anna 2009 drew her fist back and let it fly toward Annabelle's stomach.

Annabelle deflected the blow with her forearm.

"Interesting," said Teacher. "Spar for ten."

Anna 2009's undercut glanced across Annabelle's ribs.

Annabelle dodged the next fist.

She took a few blows. Measured her opponent. Parried the other's punches. Finally, she threw a right cross.

Her fist landed squarely on Anna 2009's left ear. The impact stung and reopened the minor cuts from the ruler.

Anna 2009 screamed. Her hands flew to her ear. She fell to her knees. Sobbing, she collapsed into a fetal position.

Teacher scowled at Anna 2009. "Crybaby. How could you lose to the newcomer?" She faced Annabelle. "You realize you probably deafened her—washed her out of the program?"

Annabelle met Teacher's glare. "She should have kept her guard up."

Her look re-measured Annabelle from head to toe. Then she scanned the other girls. "Anna 1990, on deck."

Anna 1990 stopped in front of Teacher and stood at attention. A whole head taller than Annabelle, Anna 1990 exuded the confidence of a tiger about to spring.

"Spar with Anna 3000. Watch out for her right cross."

Teacher bent, lifted the sobbing Anna 2009 by the arm, and dragged her out of the courtyard.

For the next ninety minutes, Annabelle sparred with Anna 1990. Annabelle lost the first three of their matches and won the next five.

A shrill whistle blew a long note.

Annabelle bowed to her partner. Couldn't help a smug grin. *God is good. My body remembers what I do not.*

She erased her grin and straightened up. Stood at attention with the rest of the Annas.

The end-of-class bell rang.

Anna 1990 and the other Annas fell into line again. Annabelle joined them.

A male voice called, "Anna 3000. On deck!"

She trotted up to the teacher. Stood at attention. "I am Anna 3000, sir."

"Come with me. Dr. Gallaway would like to see you."

He took her to a room that looked and smelled of alcohol and medicine, like her doctor's clinic back home. Except it had a machine that filled the wall behind the exam table. She crossed the room to investigate.

Dr. Gallaway breezed into the room. "Hello, Anna 3000. How are you today?"

"I am fine, thank you. Why did you want to see me?"

His teeth showed in his big smile. "Since you are new, there are some tests I need to run."

She rolled her eyes. "More tests?"

Dr. Gallaway tried to cover his laugh with a cough. "Yes, more tests."

His pretended jolliness did not fool her. Her bruises from the fighting already ached. She hoped these tests wouldn't hurt. Got on the exam table.

"Don't move." He rubbed a spot in her hair with a wad of soft cotton soaked in alcohol. Then dabbed a gooey substance there and attached a wire. And he did it twelve more times. Then attached wires with little suction cups different places on her arms and legs and chest.

"All you have to do is look at the ceiling. Never look away." He strolled out of the room, clicked the lights off, and closed the door behind him.

A picture of a field of blue flowers appeared on the ceiling.

A black-and-white cow replaced the flowers, followed by a golden puppy. The pictures flashed faster. She focused on them for the five seconds they were there.

More pictures flashed past. She almost didn't notice the dead, rotting bird.

She wished she were with her not-sisters.

Ten more images of farm animals and flowers flashed past. The next image showed a pig cut open. Its bloody heart and entrails spilled on the floor beside it.

What kind of test is this? Is it supposed to make me remember something? She remembered nothing.

The kittens and puppies in the picture above her romped in the grass.

A sharp tingle stung her right arm. She bit her lip. Didn't shout.

A dead black man floated in clear water overhead.

A crystal vase held red roses.

Sharp, needle-like pain pricked her left hip. She sucked in a breath. *Let no man injure us.*

An Asian woman with a gaping wound in her throat stared blankly.

Pink flamingos posed in a pond covered with lilies.

A dozen long, sharp needles jabbed between her ribs. Her vision narrowed. Her pulse beat with such intensity it was almost impossible to lie still, to keep her eyes on the ceiling.

A man lay face down in a pool of blood. They had burned the Fellowship symbol through his clothes into his back.

We hunger.

A herd of llamas trotted toward the camera on a paved street cut through the mountains. The picture reminded Annabelle of Buenos Aires.

A burning knife stabbed each of her arms. She gasped and arched her back. Tears streamed from her eyes.

Any who dare to lift a hand against us must die. Kill.

Not now. Wait. She breathed through the pain.

Waiting is for the weak, said the voice inside.

The rotting corpse of a beached whale.

I am not weak.

Why do we wait?

God will show us when and where.

A giraffe reached for leaves at the top of a scraggly tree.

Annabelle tensed, but kept her eyes open and did not flinch. Focused on the ceiling square behind the pictures. It had exactly twenty-four holes.

A weird buzzy sensation came from her right leg. She was glad it didn't hurt.

Overhead, an image of rumpled, silky bedsheets glowed. A fat man in a shiny suit sat on the floor with his back to the bed and a garrote tied around his neck. The knot looked wrong. *How do I know that?*

A black kitten stared down at her. But there was no stabbing or tingle or buzz. Not for it or the next dozen pictures.

A door opened and closed. "Thank you," Dr. Gallaway said. The ceiling darkened. "Close your eyes. I'm going to turn on the lights."

She pulled the suction cups off her chest and arms and legs. He pulled all the wires from her hair with one tug. She sat up and considered scrawny, anemic-looking Dr. Gallaway. He would have screamed during that test.

He smiled. "If you hurry to your dorm, you've just enough time to get a shower before mealtime. Do you need someone to show you the way?"

"No, thank you," she said in the dulcet tone Mother had taught her. "I remember." *And I'll remember what you've done.* She closed the office door behind her.

Chapter Thirty-Nine

Miranda pelted out of the rail yard. Pounded past downtown shops and closed warehouses. Zigzagged through alleys darkened by the setting sun. Sprinted from alleys to streets to alleys until every breath drew razor blades through her chest.

Darting from shadow to shadow out of the reach of streetlights, she spotted a building. It had unlit windows and an awning that stretched the length of the building. The awning hid the sidewalk in an extra layer of murk.

She slipped into the murk. Darted down the alley behind the building. Wedged herself between two reeking commercial dumpsters. Tried to gasp silently. The boom of her heart was trying to be quiet. Tried to disappear.

Running footsteps came closer, very close. Stopped.

She held her breath.

Slow footsteps padded past, returned, then faded away.

Overhead, thick, dark clouds moved in and hid the stars. The shadows deepened. The wind stirred her sweat-soaked shirt. Sent a shiver through her. But the sounds of pursuit had vanished.

Winding around the darkest streets, she headed south. Looped back on her own route to be certain no one followed.

At last, she glimpsed the glow of the giant flame at the top of the Great War Memorial, their meet point. West of her. A quarter mile away. *Be there by midnight, or you're on your own.* A short walk, out in the open, up a street that bridged over the rail yards and up the hill to the flagpole at memorial's entrance gate. *Maybe a lifetime away.*

Against the dark, cloudy sky, the two-hundred-seventeen-foot tall tower of limestone glowed as if lit with divine light. The lofty flame atop the tower flickered in the gusty wind. Pale gray plumes of smoke drifted away.

She stole uphill through the park that surrounded the Liberty Memorial. Clusters of three or four winter-bare trees dotted the slope below the tower.

Skirting the brightly lit memorial and museum building, she avoided the walkways. Stayed in the trees. Scanned the area over and over for enemies.

A one-way, U-shaped road between two tree-lined walkways offered vehicles access to the tower's front terrace from a cross street. Though iron gates closed off the road after hours.

Dividing the road for its length was a wide, grassy median. In the median at the far end, spotlights lit a pair of high-flying flags. The stars and stripes and the Fellowship's shield flapped in the wind.

Dry leaves swirled around her feet. The wind dried her sweat-soaked clothes. Made her shiver and her teeth chatter. *I should have listened to David—and Beryl.*

She darted across the road to the grassy median surrounding the flag. Four spotlights pointed skyward, focused on the flags that snapped audibly in the night's turbulent breeze. She stole a peek at her watch. *Ten thirty.*

Like the walk on the east side, leafless trees lined the western walkway. Didn't provide shelter from dying traffic on the road behind them. Didn't reveal any human-shaped shadows. Didn't make her feel safe. Still, she waited. And no one appeared.

She returned to the relative shelter of the barren trees on the east side. Hunkered down, back against rough bark. Kept vigilant. Waited for midnight.

Her nose and fingers and feet burned with cold. She descended the hill, climbed back up. The activity warmed her enough to wait again.

On the west walkway, the dark form of a man appeared. Darted from one tree to the next toward the cross street.

She didn't move. Avoided drawing attention to herself.

He reached the end of the walkway and stopped.

She pressed her back against the tree, tried to be one with it.

The man darted across the road to the central median and the flag.

Her heart lifted, urged her to join him. *Not yet. Not going to make another mistake.*

A soft sound reached her. The man hummed "Stormy Weather." *Karl.*

She hummed softly at first, then louder.

He ducked and glanced around.

She stood.

Still humming, he crossed the street and joined her. Stopped less than an arm's length from her. Grabbed her by the upper arms and drew her close.

She stiffened.

"I'm not assaulting you," he whispered. "I'm giving us a believable cover."

"What did you see?" She moved only her eyes, scanned for the threat he saw.

"No one. Just a precaution."

She relaxed a little.

"That's not very convincing."

She gritted her teeth and forced tension out of her muscles. "Have you seen—any of the others?"

"Not since you were in the Grand Plaza. You?"

She suppressed a worried sigh. "No."

"Did you have any trouble getting here?"

Something in his tone made her give him a sharp glance.

He focused on something over her shoulder.

"No trouble to speak of. Did you?"

He looked left and right. "We should go to a safe house."

"I want to wait for"—she almost said Nick—"the others. We said we'd wait until midnight."

"If we could," he said, reminding her. "I think I shook off the agent who tailed me, but—"

Movement in the corner of her eye. She focused on it. Too far away to be distinct, the lumpy shadow could be a couple coming up the walk. Bent, they lurched like landlubbers struggling to gain their sea legs.

An aging couple? Moonshine drunks? Or a ruse to lower her suspicions? No one ever appeared drunk in public. Though eleven thirty at night in a closed park wasn't exactly public.

"Company's coming," she whispered.

Karl stiffened. "We should leave."

"Wait." She watched the pair stop and start several times.

The closer they came, the more obvious they were two men and one of them was drunk—or hurt? Miranda's heart thumped harder.

They stopped again at the end of the road, under a tree. One man lowered the other to the ground. He straightened and crossed to the flagpole. He stepped into the light and immediately backed out.

Miranda caught her breath. *Nick.* She took a half step.

Karl tightened his grip on her arms.

"Let me go." She wriggled free. "It's Nick." She ran to the flagpole, to Nick. Threw her arms around him. "Oh, thank God."

"Are you all right?"

"Yeah. You?"

Nick gave her a tight hug. "Ethan's been shot."

Miranda's stomach recoiled. *My fault.* She swallowed and croaked, "Where?"

Nick glanced toward Ethan, a still-as-a-corpse shadow that lay under the trees on the far side of the road. "In his bad leg. I wrapped it but can't stop the bleeding. I need to get him to the safe house." Nick gave Miranda a wan grin. "He insisted we come here for you first."

"We'll get him to the safe house," she said, her voice strained. She motioned for Karl to join them. "Karl and I will help."

She kneeled beside Ethan. Refused to cry. "You are one tough rebel."

Ethan's grin barely made it past grimace.

Nick bent, put an arm around Ethan, and with Karl's help, lifted him to his feet. The four of them headed into the night.

Chapter Forty

Irene stayed on the brown, yellow, and orange-striped sofa in her hotel suite long after the doctor left. The ice-cap bag he'd given her, now melted, lay on the square coffee table.

He had stitched the cut above her left eye and given her some pain pills. Hours later, her left eye ached and her entire head throbbed. She squeezed the lilac-colored throw pillow and closed her good eye.

The awful scene at the train station played out in her mind's eye over and over. Miranda bolting for the door. Her grabbing Miranda's arm, almost stopping her until someone rammed into her. Knocked her face-down onto the bench and then the floor. Guns. Shouts. Screams. Blood everywhere. Her blood.

She opened her eyes. The injured one only opened halfway.

The aroma of her fish and roasted vegetables dinner made her stomach growl. It waited on the table under room-service, silver-dome covers. She stood. A wave of dizziness made her wobble. She sat back down. Hard. Tympani drums boomed in her head. Squeezing the pillow didn't help. Gingerly, she cupped her hand over her wound and eye. The drums didn't stop.

She tossed the pillow aside. Groped for the medicine bottle on the end table. Took out two more pain pills. *The doctor had said only two every six hours. The doctor didn't have this devil-spawned headache.*

She popped the pills into her mouth and chased it with watery ginger ale.

————

A LOUD BANG startled her awake.

"Irene!"

"Isth that you, Felixth?"

The lights came on—glared painfully.

"Irene, what were you doing at the train station? Oh, dear. You were injured. Are you all right?" Felix sat on the edge of the sofa.

The movement awakened a dull ache. "No. Not a'right." She couldn't open her eyes. "Light—hurts."

Someone, not Felix, turned on the table lamps but turned off the overheads.

Felix touched her forehead.

"Ow."

"What happened?"

"She lied. It wath a shet-up." So groggy. "Gotta sheep…"

"Irene, Irene." Insistent hands shook her shoulders.

"Ahh! Stop. Hurts."

Hands pulled her to a sitting position.

"Where am I?" Neck stiff, she peered blearily around. *I'm still in the hotel, on the sofa.* A dull ache above her left eye bloomed. "Must've fallen asleep." Focused on Felix. "What're you doing here? Thought you had a—a—something to do."

"I came as soon as I heard you got hurt." He sounded annoyed.

She one-eyed him, tried to figure out why he was upset.

An armed Second Sphere agent stood by the door. *Is he supposed to be here? Tired…need to go to bed.* The bed and its lilac-colored blankets sat all the way in the next room.

"Why were you at the train station?" Felix spoke loud and slow, enunciating each word as if she were deaf.

"I—" *Wait. How did he find out?* "Don't remember."

"I received word that you were with the rebels. With Miranda. And they opened fire on you."

"Received word?" She stiffened. "From who? My driver?"

"Of course not. Remember the car bomb?"

"You have someone watching me?"

"He's your bodyguard. He's supposed to protect you. When you tried to evade him, he followed you."

Her chest recoiled as if he'd struck her. "He followed me here?" A blaze raged inside. Burned away the fogginess in her brain. "He's not a bodyguard. You're having me watched." She stood up, carefully. *Can't fall over now. Not in front of Felix and my guard.* Crossed the room to the coffee service on the table. *Empty?* She put her hands on the table and leaned heavily onto it. "What time is it?"

"One in the morning."

Felix came here in the middle of the night? The pain in her chest twisted. She faced her husband. "What has happened to us? To you? Do you think I'm untrustworthy?"

He stood and gave her a cool look. "You seem to have forgotten. I'm not just your husband anymore. I'm the Prophet."

She could scarcely breathe. "What—what are you saying?"

"As the Prophet, I need to know before you decide to meet with the rebels."

"They'd agreed to a truce. Miranda wanted to talk to me. She's my sister."

"I wouldn't say that too loud."

Irene's mouth dropped open. She'd never imagined he would say anything so— *Have to control this before it gets worse.* She closed her mouth, put on her I-was-wronged face. "If anyone could talk to her, I thought I could. But I was wrong. She didn't honor the truce. And she did this to me." Irene pointed to her stitches. She stood, placed her hands on Felix's chest and gave him her best hurt-and-pleading look. "Tell me we'll hunt her down. We'll stop the apostates."

Felix raised his chin, studied her. "We will." His arms wrapped around her, but his embrace didn't smother the flames of his betrayal.

Chapter Forty-One

Beryl peered around the corner and down a dimly lit driveway to what should have been another vacant underground warehouse. But there was no dock. The only opening in the wall was the extra-large, floor-level air-return vent. Energy surged through her, warmed her ears. "That's the door?"

"Affirmative," Wanda whispered. "It opens outward."

Beryl had to admit she wouldn't have given it a second glance. "David, you're with me," she said, her voice no louder than a sigh. "Wanda—getaway driver. Leslie—guard this end. You two remember the phone number?"

"Yeah." Wanda's flat tone held an undercurrent of resentment.

Don't have time for whatever her problem is. "If we aren't back in an hour, or things go bad, get out. Find a pay phone. Call, ask whoever answers for the Silver Special. They don't know what that means, hang up and get out of town."

"Got it." Now Wanda's tone was a soldier acknowledging orders.

Beryl made eye contact with David. "Backup and guard duty. I'm recon."

He gave her a grim nod.

She pulled the vent door open. It opened without a sound. She ducked and darted inside. David followed.

To avoid the cave's mineral smell, mixed with some unidentifiable odor, she breathed through her mouth. *Shit! Could the air be bad? Sniff. Still breathing. Must be safe enough.*

She straightened to her full height. The light from the road made skinny rectangles on the smooth rock floor.

David, a few inches too tall, stood with his neck bent and head forward.

Six strides from the door, the light dimmed. Six more, and the light vanished.

She touched the flashlight on her hip, then whispered, "No lights. Touch."

A grunt answered.

She walked blindly into the never-ending obsidian filled with mineral-scented air. Rough rock sandpapered her fingertips.

Behind her, David's soft breath sighed in and out. In front of her, a silent, endless void.

Her eyes strained to see something, anything. The small of her back and between her breasts grew damp.

She pressed onward.

A distant hum came from ahead of them.

She slowed, and David's hand bumped against her back. His breath warmed her neck.

The buzz ahead morphed into a distinct, if faint, *whoosh-swish, whoosh-swish.* Her mouth went dry, and she slowed her steps but didn't stop.

The deeper into the tunnel they went, the louder the rhythmic *whoosh-swish* grew. Her chest tightened. *A heart? Not a heart. Can't be a heart.*

Her inner alarms screamed warnings. She eased one of her pistols out of its holster.

The same whisper of movement came from David.

"Electrical equipment?" he whispered.

"Must be." She inched forward.

The obsidian gradually lightened to a dark charcoal, then to slate.

The *whoosh-swish* grew louder and louder. Notched her alarm higher and higher. She stopped.

Ahead, the light divided into soft pinkish-gray horizontal beams.

She crept up to the opening of another vent. Peered through the nearly closed, up-angled slats. The heartbeat sound came from inside.

Dull red light illuminated rows of inert, pear-shaped shadows that didn't touch the floor. *No movement.*

She ducked and stepped out of the vent door into the dimly lit room and froze.

The *whoosh-swish* surrounded her. In front of her, rows and rows of blood-red sacs hung from overhead scaffolding. Her heart tattooed the inside of her ribs. She blinked and refocused. *This is it. The lab.*

From each sac, three tubes rose to a rack of pipes overhead. Detailed electronic readouts showed green lights above each sac. All much more sophisticated than the system on the island.

Down each row, the sacs were the same size, but each new row had larger and larger sacs. The larger the sac, the more transparent it was. Transparent enough to see the fetus growing inside.

The sight filled her with a nightmarish sense of a déjà vu. Nausea burned her throat. She swallowed, controlled her breathing. Tightened her grip on her gun. *Ethan wants proof? Wait till he sees this. She lifted the camera, snapped a picture from the vent doorway. A few feet to the left, she snapped another. Further inside, she shot several angles.*

Dim pinkish light came from a long observation window on the outside wall. Behind her stood stainless-steel cabinets with a stainless-steel countertop.

She holstered her gun and searched the cabinets. Gallon jugs of fluids and tubing and connectors and syringes filled the drawers and cabinets. The skin of her back twitched as if someone watched her. A slow pivot revealed no humans, no fully formed Azrael, and no visible cameras. She got back to work.

At the end of the cabinets, six clipboards hung from hooks on a pipe attached to the wall. She fanned the pages. Dates and numbers on each of them. Snapped a photo of each of the first pages.

The last clipboard displayed drawings—layouts—of this space or the entire facility. An X marked what she presumed was this location. A series of tiny arrows pointed—*the way out?*

She unclipped those pages and tucked them inside her shirt. Replaced them with several pages off the previous clipboard.

Finally she faced the sacs, the artificial wombs, again. Her breathing and heart rate raced each other. She fumbled for the camera. Peered through the viewfinder. Saw ghostly metal pseudo-uteri mixed with the red sacs. Her vision blurred.

She blinked and cleared her vision and her head. Prayed the fast film would pick up the sacs and their contents in the dim light.

Snap, click, snap, click. She advanced the film and moved to the next larger row of sacs again and again. Moved as quickly as she dared through gradually dimming light and rows of larger and larger sacs.

Curled in a ball, the larger fetuses looked more and more like a little girl. A girl with dark hair, all her fingers and toes.

In the last row, the bag was the size of a large rucksack. *The being inside was large enough to be…what? Born? Decanted? Large enough to look like Anna. Like my Anna.* Like the ten-year-old Azraels she'd killed. But here, there were more than a dozen. More than she'd ever seen.

The camera shook. *Not my Anna.* The shaking continued. *Not my Anna. Murderers. Monsters.* Three slow deep breaths, and her hands steadied. She raised the camera again. A red light glowed in the lower right corner of the viewfinder.

No. It's too dark. Without a flash, the camera won't capture the unborn. I need this picture. Ethan needs to see this. Maybe the flashlight pointed away—

With a flick of the switch, light flooded the sac. The childlike being inside opened her eyes—locked a laser gaze on Beryl then, screwed up her face, and opened her mouth in a silent scream.

Beryl fell back a step. Bumped the next sac.

Beep. Beep. Beep. Alarms screeched. Red lights flashed.

Shouts echoed. Footsteps pounded—an army of footsteps. Closer and closer.

Beryl ducked and ran for the tunnel.

David threw open the vent door.

She kept running.

He followed.

"They went this way," a male voice echoed down the tunnel, Beryl couldn't tell if he was near or far. But the only place his words made sense was at the vent doorway.

The tunnel reverberated with pounding feet closing in.

The camera battered Beryl's chest. Her elbows banged against the rough wall.

She hoped their pursuers had sense enough not to shoot. Hoped they had sent no one to the other end of the tunnel. Hoped Wanda was ready.

Sweat poured down her face, burned her eyes. She swiped a gritty hand across her eyes. Stumbled. The camera swayed—bounced crazily against the rock wall. She stayed upright. Charged forward to stay in front of David.

Ahead, light grew. A surge of energy sped her heart, her breath, her legs.

"Start the truck," she yelled. Crashed through the tunnel door. Staggered several steps and squinted against the light.

David stumbled into her, fell to his knees.

In the center of the intersection, Wanda revved the truck's engine.

"Hurry!" Leslie kneeled inside the truck bed, her gun aimed at the tunnel.

Beryl grabbed David's arm, pulled him to his feet, and they sprinted to the truck. She glanced over her shoulder.

Two men banged out of the tunnel, raced toward them.

She shoved David toward the open passenger door.

Leslie opened fire on the men.

Beryl drew her pistols, whirled and fired.

The truck door slammed. David's gun banged three times.

One man ducked back inside the tunnel. The other dashed for cover behind a pillar.

Beryl holstered her guns. Grabbed the edge of the pickup, hoisted herself up—

Something hard slammed into her side, burned across her lowest rib.

She toppled into the truck bed. "Go!"

Chapter Forty-Two

Under the porch light, the bungalow's coat of paint took on a warm khaki color. The door was painted a tiger-orange. Miranda hurried up the porch steps.

Behind her, Nick and Karl dragged a semi-conscious Ethan. They brought him up the steps and into the deepest shadows of the porch.

She gave three urgent raps on the door.

The door opened. Warm air, the aroma of strong coffee, and yellow light spilled out. A man with neatly trimmed white hair and a short beard cocked his head at Miranda. He followed her glance at Ethan and the others. "Georgia, clear the table. We've got an injured man here." He glanced over his shoulder. "They need help."

A younger man came out, scooped Ethan up in his arms as if the injured man weighed nothing, and hurried down the hall.

"Ben." Nick hurried after him. "Glad to see you made it."

Miranda and Karl trotted after them.

Ben placed Ethan on a sturdy, dark oak table in the dining room.

Ethan moaned and opened his eyes, sought Nick. His voice was soft and strained. "Everyone here?"

"We've got Miranda, Karl, Ben, you, and me."

"The others."

"It's early yet, sir."

Ethan gave a half-sigh, half-groan, and closed his eyes.

"I'm Doc Owen," said the white-haired man. He nodded at a handsome, big-boned woman with long silver hair. "My wife and chief nurse, Georgia. Give us some room, please."

"He has a gunshot wound in the right thigh," Nick said. "Same leg he injured two years ago."

"Any other injuries I should know about?"

"He and the shooter struggled over the gun," Nick told the doctor. "I didn't see the fight. I—"

"All right, thank you." Georgia advanced toward them, arms spread in a gathering-shooing motion. "The kitchen's to your left. Help yourself. There's fresh coffee."

"We need to set up security—" Nick began.

"Their sons have the front and back covered," Ben said.

"Give us room to work." Georgia's tone was soft but firm. "We'll let you know what we find."

———

OVER THE NEXT HOUR, Doc and Georgia's two sons introduced themselves. The twenty-something young men, an older and a younger brother, instructed them on the house rules. "Smoke" was the code word meaning emergency escape. The escape route was in the coal room in the basement. They set up watch and sleep locations and shifts for Miranda, Nick, and Karl.

Free for a couple of hours, Miranda paced around the front room, circled behind the gold-colored sofa in front of the midnight-blue tiled fireplace, and back to the sofa.

The scent of an astringent grew, overpowered the aroma of coffee. A reminder, as if Miranda needed it, of Ethan's condition.

One of the matching armchairs had been pulled away from where it flanked the fireplace. Ben, a SABR operative who'd been at the train station, sat in close to the window. Leaning forward, he peered between the closed drapes and watched the front walk. On her fifth or sixth pass, he aimed an irritated "sit and be still" over his shoulder at her.

She plopped into the other chair. Its cool walnut arms chilled her. She clasped her hands together to still them. Bounced her knee. Blew out quick breaths. Couldn't sit any longer. Crossed the room and peered down the hallway.

Nick stood in the arched doorway to the dining room, arms folded over his chest, focused on the doctor and his patient inside. "Well?" Nick asked, then stepped aside. The doctor came out into the hall, his bloody gloves held out as if he carried a small invisible box.

"Come." Doc Owen led them into the narrow, U-shaped kitchen, where the aroma of percolating coffee overcame the antiseptic smell.

Nick stopped in front of the white enamel refrigerator.

At the side of the fridge, barely inside the kitchen, Miranda stood and raked her teeth over her lower lip over and over.

Doc Owen removed his gloves and tossed them into an under-the-sink waste can. Turned on the water. "He is a very lucky man. The bullet missed the femoral artery and went straight through." He lathered his hands, wrists, and forearms with soap.

His tone held a "but" that made Miranda's throat go dry.

"What aren't you saying?" Nick asked.

The doctor rinsed his hands, grabbed a red-and-white checked towel from the countertop. Dried his hands. Turned off the rushing water.

The hum of the refrigerator and an expectant hush filled the room.

Doc Owen rubbed the back of his neck, then faced Nick. "The bullet ripped through scar-damaged muscle and nerves. Healing will be slow. To regain his best function, he will need daily physical therapy."

Hand over her mouth, Miranda repeated his words in a shaky whisper, "To regain his best..." She swallowed, steadied herself with a hand on the refrigerator. "Will he be able to walk?"

The doctor locked eyes with her. "If the bullet didn't damage the nerve this time. If he takes the time to recuperate. If he completes his physical therapy."

Pain knifed through Miranda, drove the air from her lungs. *My fault! Beryl and David knew Irene would betray us. I should have...* A fire started in her gut.

Nick rubbed his mouth and jaw. "When can we move him?"

"He needs time to recover—several weeks, maybe more."

"If we want to live, we can't stay here for a day, much less a week."

Doc Owen folded his arms over his chest. "He's not going

anywhere unless you're going to carry him. The pain meds I gave him will keep him out for at least six hours."

The fire in her gut burned hotter. "It'll be daylight by then," Miranda said. "You, Karl, and Ben should leave while it's still dark. I'll stay here with Ethan."

Nick whirled and gaped at her. "I am not leaving you and Ethan here. I'll reach out for some extra men. We'll set up a perimeter and stay here."

"No." Miranda put a hand on Nick's arm, willed him to feel the fire that burned in her. "I'll keep Ethan safe. You and the others have to make Irene pay for this."

The fight in his glare morphed into grim determination. "Who says we can't do both?"

Chapter Forty-Three

The truck shot out of the cave. Beryl raised up on an elbow and peered over the tailgate. Its wheels squealed through the hard right turn. It rattled and bounced over the poorly maintained road they'd come in on. Wind rumbled, tossed her hair. The sting of her flesh wound was as irritating as a mosquito buzzing around the room.

Visible against the pinking horizon, two dark sedans pursued. Closing the distance. Fast.

She beat on the cab window.

"I see them," Wanda shouted. "Hang on."

Another sharp right. Beryl slid across the truck bed into the side-wall. The smarting in her right side exploded into a fiery burn. She drew in a stoic breath through her nose.

"Try to hold still," Leslie said. She clung to the truck's rail with one hand and pressed a cloth to Beryl's side with the other. "You're losing a lot of blood."

"It's a flesh wound," Beryl said through teeth gritted against the burn. Stupid.

Leslie raised Beryl's shirt. "Let me see."

Keeping a tight grip on the side rail, Beryl rolled to her left. Gentle fingers pressed around her wound.

"It's bleeding a lot," Leslie said, "but yes, it's a flesh wound."

"That's what I said, isn't it?" Beryl forced her scowl into a simmering smile.

Leslie ignored her, reapplied the cloth with more pressure this time.

A deep ache accompanied the burning. A groan escaped before Beryl clenched her jaw.

The bump and swerve of the truck at its top speed bounced and slid her across the wood slats and channels of the truck bed and renewed the fire in her side. *So stupid. I blew our one-way inside. And lost most of our supplies.*

The cars that followed kept up.

"Grab something," Wanda shouted.

Beryl two-handed her grip on the rail. Brakes squealed. Body slammed her into the bulkhead. She grunted against the pain.

The truck swung around in a tight U-turn. Fishtailed. Beryl fought the momentum that pulled her legs right. The flames of a blast furnace erupted from her wound.

Wanda straightened the truck, and it picked up speed. They left the stench behind.

Ignoring the bone-deep, hit-by-a-bat ache and the stench of hot rubber, Beryl peeked over the tailgate. The pursuit cars attempted to do a U-turn, and one momentarily blocked by the other.

They wove in and out of the early-to-work vehicles trickling onto the four-lane highway. A braking turn crashed Beryl into the bulkhead again. The gasp that escaped her was loud and long.

The truck slowed to a crawl. Artificial light flooded the area. Wanda had pulled in some place.

Beryl propped herself on an elbow. Peered over the rail. Parked eighteen wheelers stood in front and on both sides of them. Trucks blocked every view of the street. Behind them, a row of tall Ponderosa pines blocked the view. "Where are we?"

"A Stop-and-Go," Leslie said.

Beryl grunted with approval. *Where did Wanda learn to drive?*

Wanda spoke through the open window between the cab and bed. "Figured we should lie low for a while. How bad is it?"

"I'm fine. Bullet barely touched me."

"It's bleeding like crazy," Leslie said. "Stay still. I can wrap it now."

Leslie bandaged it well. Tight, but not too tight.

"This place will have a payphone," Beryl said. "Stay here. I'll be back in a minute."

"You're covered in blood," Leslie said. "I'll go." She stood.

"No, you'll stay put," Beryl said. *I won't be babied for a scratch.* She scrambled to her feet, to prove the stinging was nothing. "I'm not incapable." *But damn, it hurts worse than a direct hit.* She finger-combed her hair, straightened her wet-with-blood blouse. *I need something to hide my bloody shirt.* "Give me your jacket." After a quick inspection revealed bloodstains on Leslie's jacket, Beryl demanded David's charcoal-gray overcoat. Shrugged it on.

"You need to stay still," Leslie said. "Let the bandage and pressure stop your bleeding."

"I won't bleed to death from a flesh wound." Beryl hopped out of the truck. Ignored the fresh burn in her side until she'd moved out of sight of the truck, then put a hand to her waist. *Damn. Stings like a son-of-a-bitch. Double damn those SS agents or cave security, whatever the hell they are.*

Inside, the store was warm and humid and smelled of bacon and biscuits. A customer stood at the counter. The register dinged, and the clerk asked for five dollars.

Beryl pretended to look at the salty snacks hanging on the display and scanned for the place for pay phones.

A clerk mopping the floor came down the aisle toward her. He glanced up. His eyes widened. "Wow! What happened to you?"

"Who me?" Beryl looked down. *Damn it.* The coat hung crooked, revealed the large bloodstain on her shirt. "Oh." She put on her rich tourist, the Widow Wilkens fake Fellowship member smile. "Not mine. Accident down the road. I need to call for help."

"Oh. Glad you're not hurt. Phone's over there." He pointed to a hallway in the back corner with a lift of his chin. A sign that read Restrooms hung above the opening.

At the end of the hall, a bank of three pay phones lined the wall opposite the restrooms. A man with a scraggly beard, a potbelly, and a worn leather jacket muttered into the center telephone.

A glass exit door stood at the end of the hall.

She strode to the last telephone. Dug in her jeans for change. *Shit.* She'd forgotten she wore dusty, grimy jeans. *So much for the rich lady act.* She picked up the receiver. Dropped a dime and dialed a long-distance number collect.

"You've reached Vito's Pizza Shoppe, Chicago's best pizza," a cheerful voice of indeterminate sex said. "How may we help you?"

"I'd like to get the number for one of your Special Silver deals in Kansas City, Missouri."

"One moment, please."

The man at the center phone hung up and walked away.

"What did you want on that Special Silver?" a deep, graveled voice asked.

"Lots of oregano."

"Got it. That number is 816-555-3216."

"Thank you." She hung up, repeated the number to herself. Fished her dime out of the change box and used it again.

"Thank you for calling the Prairie View Road Pizza Shoppe. Order by the pie or the slice. What can we make fresh for you?" The nasal voice seemed impossibly young.

"I need a Special Silver deal for four with lots of oregano."

"Yes, miss. We'll deliver that to 2930 Holly Street in Kansas City, Missouri. Thank you for calling."

The disconnected line buzzed in her ear. *2930 Holly Street*. She hung up and went out the door.

Chapter Forty-Four

Irene woke, opened one eye. Her left one wouldn't open. She touched it. Puffy. Tender. Above her eyebrow—stitches. *Right. Union Station. Felix.*

She sat up. The left side of her face exploded. Nasty-tasting, acidic bile burned the back of her throat. After few deep breaths, the nausea receded, but her headache was about to take the side of her head off.

Bright sunshine glowed around navy blue drapes. Navy-blue floral bedspread. Butter-cream walls with white trim. *I'm home? Felix brought me home? He sent an agent to spy on me!*

She sprang out of bed. Grabbed her pounding head with both hands. Plopped back down on the edge of the bed. It took several long moments before she could think clearly.

He has never acted this way before. Do I confront him? Or do I show him I am not someone he can push around without a cost?

She replayed the mental tape of last night's horror at the train station. *D.C. will feel the impact.* Her chest tightened.

Felix said he'd take care of the rebels who hurt me, but he doesn't know everything. Shall I call him? Her jaw tightened, and she drew her brows together, which pulled the stitches on her forehead. "Ouch." *No. He's spying on me. On me! I don't think I can trust him anymore. Besides, his Second Sphere agents have bungled it every time. Dr. Gallaway's new-improved Azrael will stop the rebels. My Azrael.*

The hands of her yellow Bakelite alarm clock pointed to ten after ten. *Felix has been at the Fellowship Center—or wherever—for at least two hours. He won't be home for hours. After I make myself presentable, I'll call Dr. Gallaway. Inform him of what his Azrael need to do.*

Slippers on, she padded down the hall to the bathroom. The woody scent of Felix's aftershave hung in the air. Nausea burned the back of her throat.

Under the bright light above the mirror, her reflection revealed a swollen-shut left eye surrounded by a reddish-purple bruise that reached from her hairline to her cheekbone. Above her left, an L-shaped cut held together with five black, wiry stitches looked like a third eyebrow.

A bottle of prescription pain pills and a glass of water sat on the back of the sink. She gulped down two more pills.

She dressed, placed her black pillbox hat on her head, and hid her injuries with its dark half-veil. Grabbed her address book out of her shiny patent-leather purse and hurried downstairs. Nodded at the housekeeper vacuuming the living room and kept going.

A cloud of sweet floral scent from a spray of fresh orange and bronze mums on the entry table greeted her.

She hurried to the kitchen, grabbed the kitchen telephone's handset, and dialed Dr. Gallaway. The distant *brrr-ring* on the other end sounded once, twice, three times—

"Hello, Dr. Gallaway speaking."

"This is Irene—"

"Lady Earnshaw. Annabelle is fine."

Every muscle in Irene's body tensed. *Were they attacked too?*

"None of the girls were anywhere near the breach. My agents are on top of it."

"The breach? Of the lab? How could they—" *His agents are on top of it?* Irene's heart took off. Her ears heated. She smacked her hand over the mouthpiece of the receiver. *How on top of it can they be if they allowed the rebels to breach their* hidden *underground lab?* Her heart drove a blindingly hard tympani drum beat above her left eyebrow. *Are there no competent men? Men who actually do their jobs?* She strangled the receiver's mouthpiece. Expelled four forceful breaths. Fought to regain use of her Ladyship voice. "Is Annabelle really okay?"

"Oh. You weren't calling about the breach?"

"No, I wasn't calling *about the breach*. But I am now. What happened?" *Too strident? No, not strident enough.* Unable to stand any longer, she dropped into the chair without grace. Set off booming bass drums in her head.

"Well, er, it wasn't as bad as it sounds—" He breathed a long, audible sigh.

"Don't tell me what it wasn't. Tell me what happened."

"Two intruders got inside the incubator lab—"

"How? Did they hurt the babies?"

"They came through an escape tunnel. Tripped the alarm before they could do anything to the unborn. Security shot one and chased the getaway vehicle."

She could breathe again. "Did your agents catch them?"

"Their driver was *very* skillful."

"They got away." She balled her free hand into a fist. *I was a fool to think Miranda and the rebels really wanted peace.* Her jaw ached, and her forehead pulsed. "Were you going to tell me about this?" *Lord above, please spare me from men who think they know better.*

"I, er, didn't want to bother you—"

"Then I'm glad I called."

"Right. Er, why *did* you call?"

"They have to pay for what they did—"

"Oh, yes! I saw the late news. How are you?"

Her stomach bubbled and rose to her throat. "The news?"

"Yes. All the stations carried it. It's big news when the Prophet's wife gets injured during a rebel attack. Your injuries, are they bad?"

"Oh." *Have to contain this. Will this new Felix even care? Of course he will. He'll be upset that I've damaged his public image— Can't think about that now.* "I've got a—" *Minor? No. Nothing they do is minor.* "They tried to blind me. Gave me a terrible concussion and an ugly cut above my left eye."

"That's awful. If there's anything I can do—"

She smiled and winced. Her forehead throbbed. "There *is* something you can do. We cannot allow the rebels to hurt anyone else. You can stop them."

"Me?" Dr. Gallaway said. "Oh. You mean the—"

"Yes, the secret project." *Was he actually going to say Azrael on the telephone?*

"We have a dozen—recruits—ready for an exercise like this."

"A dozen?" *Including Annabelle?* Her stomach lurched.

"My dear lady, these recruits can handle this."

"That dozen, does it include Annabelle?"

"Do you want her included?"

"You think she's ready for this so soon?" Held her breath.

"I would need a full assessment from her instructors. I will ask if you'd like."

Her head spun. Waves of nausea rolled. "No," she answered in her Prophet's Lady persona. "No, not now. Annabelle is destined— for greater things."

"Oh-kay. I doubt she's completed enough training to be part of a team, anyway. So, no problem. We won't include her."

She relaxed her shoulders, her grip on the receiver. "Good. Only a dozen recruits, you say?"

"A dozen extremely capable recruits."

"This—exercise—will show me what they can do."

"To do their best, they'll need information. Everything you know."

"Well, I—" *Can't say yet. Need to find out what cover story they gave me.*

"Not over a public telephone. Perhaps you could send a courier?"

"Excellent idea, Doctor. I shall do that."

"While I have you on the phone—"

Irene sat straighter. Glared at the telephone. "You said Annabelle was okay."

"She's such a quick study. We've moved her up three levels already."

Irene's chest hollowed. "Already?"

"Yes. In fact, I think she's done this sort of thing before."

My miracle child? No, not Annabelle. She can't be an Azrael. She has a dark side, but—she would never hurt— Memories of Annabelle strangling Sandra's doll returned so abruptly, Irene gasped. The weight that encased Irene's heart ripped it away. It fell into a deep chasm. "Um, does she know about the train station incident?" *If Annabelle knows, she might want to come home—to be my daughter, Sandra's sister. Be normal. The image of her strangling the doll taunted her. No. God wouldn't help Felix raise... A miracle child wouldn't... But what if she was? What if she would strangle a person instead of a doll? Sandra?* Irene twisted the handset's green, curly cord around her index finger so tight the tip of her finger whitened.

"You needn't worry about that," Dr. Gallaway said. "None of our girls watch television."

"Oh." It took her a moment to recall she'd asked if Annabelle knew about the incident at the train station. "Good." But Irene didn't know if she was relieved or upset.

"You've no need to worry. Annabelle is in her element."

She unwound the cord around her finger, one loop at a time.

"Are you still there?"

"Yes, um—" She cleared her throat. "My concussion—"

"I've kept you on the phone too long. Send the courier as soon as possible."

"I will." She replaced the telephone receiver on the hook. Wrapped her arms around herself as if that could hold her broken heart together.

Focus. Who do I trust with this information? A courier service—no. A stranger won't do. One of the bodyguards? Felix's bodyguards? I'm not that stupid. Paul? Her driver had proven himself, got her out of the train station. Didn't rat her out to Fe—to *the Prophet.*

She called and instructed him to come to the house.

The rumble of the vacuum cleaner upstairs stopped.

The housekeeper's footsteps thudded down the staircase. Irene grabbed juice and a Danish, passed the housekeeper at the foot of the stairs.

When she was certain the housekeeper was out of earshot, she turned on the television. A black bar across the top of the screen read Special Report. Black and white images showed panicked people running out of the Kansas City train station. Showed her, blood streaming down her face, being rushed out between her driver and a Second Sphere agent. The NBC and the CBS channels ran the same story. Elephants stampeded inside her forehead.

She took her breakfast dishes down to the kitchen sink. A wave of dizziness hit. She staggered to the kitchen table, sat. When the spinning stopped, she noticed a piece of the Prophet's stationary held in place by the vase of orange asters. Felix's familiar scrawl read: "Rest well. I won't be home for dinner. I'll be ensuring that the rebels feel the Prophet's wrath."

He depends too much on his precious Second Sphere agents…. Hmm, how would he feel if he knew the Prophet's wife had a way to stop the rebels? Maybe I should take his favorite lunch to him. Make him understand exactly what I can do.

She hurried into his office to look at his schedule for today.

Stacks of unopened envelopes lay on his desk brought in by the housekeeper, no doubt. Irene sorted the stack suspiciously. But found no pink, handwritten, or perfumed letters. *My cease-and-desist letter worked.*

That minor victory was nothing compared to the situation she faced now. She renewed her search for Felix's calendar. It wasn't on the desktop or the top center drawer or the top right drawer.

The bottom left drawer stuck. She yanked it open. Flipped through the hanging file folders.

The last file folder held a pair of silky, lavender ladies underdrawers with tiny sprigs of lilacs printed on them. She gasped. Couldn't take her eyes off of them. *Not mine. Not mine.*

She dropped the underdrawers into the folder, slammed the drawer shut. Sank back into Felix's chair. *One of those harlots must have mailed it to him.* Her blood ran molten. An evil suspicion crept into her head. *Was she here? A harlot? In my home. In this office.* She leaped out of the chair and whirled. No telltale evidence.

She scanned the room. *Another woman's unmentionables are in my husband's desk drawer. In the Prophet's desk. Intolerable. And he thought I acted with disregard for* his *position.* A frenzy of must-act-now erupted inside her.

I have to stop them. She had the means to do that now. She glanced at her watch. Her driver would be here any minute.

She grabbed the list of harlots from upstairs and returned to the first level.

The housekeeper carried a basket of wet laundry toward the back door.

Ding-dong.

"I'll get it," Irene yelled to the housekeeper and opened the door.

Flash bulbs popped. Journalists shouted, "Lady Earnshaw. Lady Earnshaw."

Her driver, Paul, stood on the stoop, respectfully holding his chauffeur's cap. She grabbed his arm, pulled him into the vestibule, and slammed the door.

Chapter Forty-Five

Annabelle moved lightly on her toes, stayed inside the red lines painted on the artificial grass and out of her opponent's reach. Every muscle, every nerve hummed with the power of the angel within. She darted in and drove an upward punch under her opponent's breastbone.

The older girl gasped for breath, collapsed to her knees.

Annabelle swung an uppercut to the girl's jaw.

The girl's head snapped back, and her eyes unfocused. Her eyes fluttered. After a couple of shuddering breaths, she reached out, tapped the artificial grass three times.

Teacher blew a shrill note on her whistle.

Head high, Annabelle stepped out of the red fight box. She shot a look up at the rocky ceiling and silently thanked her inner angel. *We haven't lost a fight yet. And we've advanced through the classes faster than anyone in the school's history.* Teacher had already promoted Annabelle to the next to oldest class, the Cherubim. This fight ought to get her into the Seraphim class.

But I hunger.

What do you hunger for?

Silence.

Annabelle knotted her fists. She'd tried eating a bunch of food. Ended up with an upset stomach and an angel who still hungered.

Fighting the other girls quieted the angel—for a day. The more violent fights worked longer, but never satisfied.

"Anna 3000. Come forward."

"Yes, ma'am." Annabelle's chest swelled. *Teacher noticed how well I fought.* She marched up to the front of the class. Stood at attention in front of Teacher.

"Anna 3000, you will serve thirty-two hours in isolation for delaying victory."

Teacher's words hit Annabelle like a one-punch knockout. She didn't move, not even a muscle on her face. She couldn't breathe. Her heart sledgehammered. She couldn't process. *I'm being sent to isolation? But I won.*

Two junior teachers stepped forward and stood on each side of her. The one on her left put a hand on Annabelle's elbow.

Breathing hard, Annabelle jerked her arm free and marched between them.

Teacher is wrong. You won. Show them! Take the junior teachers.

And get expelled? Sent home to Mother? No.

Gray padded walls, floor, and ceiling. The only openings were the door and a hinged pass-through at the bottom of the door.

Her breathing and the thump of her heart filled the room. She executed an about-face. Only the door's outline broke the monotony. Her stomach growled and twisted and hurt.

"I didn't get lunch," she said in a quiet, humble tone.

No response.

"I am hungry. I need my lunch."

No matter how loud she yelled or pleaded, no one answered her. And she got no lunch.

So that's the way it's going to be. She pressed her lips together. *Teacher is trying to teach me by delaying my lunch. So what if I played a little before I ended the fight? I won. And I can take your stupid delay lesson. I'll stand here the whole time.*

Waiting wasn't hard for Annabelle. She stood, without moving, and waited. Waited for Teacher to realize she'd made a mistake. Waited for the door to open. Waited for an apology.

You can delay as long as you want, Teacher. She dropped and sat cross-legged on the floor in the center of the room. Closed her eyes and silently ran through the multiplication tables.

Chills swept through her. Her lips grew dry, chapped. Fatigue pulled at her. She curled up on her side, facing the door.

Hinges creaked. The pass-through opened. A cinnamon-colored plastic tray slid toward her. It held a paper cup and a paper bowl.

Annabelle scrabbled toward the pass-through. It snapped closed before she reached it.

The cup held warm water. She stirred the cloudy liquid in the bowl. It tasted like cold potato water. *Another lesson?*

The flames inside returned. *I won my fight. I will win this one too.* The angel within roared.

Annabelle soothed her angel, "We must bide our time."

We must make them pay.

We will.

Chapter Forty-Six

Miranda came down the stairs achy, gritty, and unrefreshed by her brief nap. She slipped past Ben in the living room and tiptoed down the hall to peek in on Ethan.

Karl greeted her outside the dining room. "Morning." He jerked his head toward the room. "Ethan's still asleep."

"When will he wake up?"

"No telling, according to the doctor."

Someone had cleaned up all traces of Ethan's blood and put a pillow beneath his head. A green chenille blanket tucked around him transformed the table to a bed, an illusion belied by the sturdy wooden table legs that showed beneath the blanket. Ethan wasn't as pale as he'd been. Or was that her imagination? At least he slept. More than she could do.

Karl put a firm hand on her elbow, steered her to the kitchen. "There's coffee on the stove. I'll pour you a cup."

She accepted the coffee. Sipped. Hot and sweet, it sat uneasily on her stomach.

"Guess we're staying put for a while…" Karl's voice faded.

She froze, cup poised at her lips. Eyed Karl. "We, who?"

"All of us. Did you expect something else?"

"Guess not." She thumped her cup down on the counter. *Where's Nick?*

"My break's over. If you need me, I'm lookout out on the porch." He nodded toward the back door.

A stiff smile was all she could give him.

The screen door banged shut.

Deep in shadows, the living room drapes covered the big picture window. Karl sat on watch. Peered out between the edge of the drapes and the window frame.

Nick rose from the sofa when she entered the room. His smile didn't hide the circles under his eyes. "Did you get any sleep?"

"A little. Did you?" She quirked an eyebrow at him.

"Not yet." He hadn't changed either. Blotches of dried blood stained the legs of his jeans. "Doc Owen and I just got back." He gestured for her to sit.

She settled onto the sofa, one leg drawn up so she could face him. "Where did you go?"

He draped his arm across the back of the sofa, his hand not quite touching her shoulder. "Turns out Doc's house holds more secrets than I knew. It's connected to an old underground streetcar route."

"It's abandoned?" *Why does everything have to be underground in this part of the country?*

"According to Doc, it's been closed for about ten years. He thinks few people even remember it exists."

"Well, that's handy, I guess."

"More than that. It's a way to get Ethan to safety."

She swallowed the retort she wanted to make. "Doc Owen said we shouldn't move Ethan for a week or more."

Nick gave her a self-satisfied smile. "Doc said Ethan shouldn't walk. This tunnel is plenty wide enough. We can find something, so Ethan doesn't have to walk."

"Something like?"

"A wheelchair or a wagon. Heck, even a wheelbarrow would work." His grin widened. "It won't matter if it's day or night, warm or cold. And we can go as slowly as Ethan needs."

"Go where? Are you telling me there's another safe house connected to this tunnel?"

"No, it's not that easy. It's about an hour's walk in the tunnel to an industrial area. Then we'll have to get a car and drive about forty-five minutes to an abandoned building where no one will find us."

The tension in Miranda grew. "And what about Irene? And the goons who attacked us?"

Nick blinked at her. "What do you mean?"

"What do I mean? You said we'd make her pay."

"I said that we could do both—and I found a way we can do both."

"How does getting Ethan to an abandoned building make Irene pay for her lies and for killing that poor man?"

Nick drew his arm back, sat straighter. "You mean Joe? We'll avenge his death, but Joe would understand that protecting Ethan, protecting SABR, comes first."

She almost couldn't get enough air to ask, "Joe? Joe died at the train station too?"

Nick gave a slow nod. "I thought you knew about Joe." His brows drew together. "Who else died?"

She turned, put both feet on the ground, and stared at her hands knotted together. "A vendor… He was just doing his job…" Her throat tightened, choked off her words. *Two men died because Irene lied to me. Because I let her set us up.* She locked on Nick. "What is your plan to make Irene pay?"

"She's the Prophet's wife. It's going to take some time to—"

"No, the time is now. She's here now. Now is when we need to strike—while she's here—before she goes back to her Fellowship fortress, Washington, D.C." The pity and concern on Nick's face sent her to her feet. "If you won't do anything, then I guess I'll have to."

"Miranda? Nick? What are you shouting about?" Ethan called from the dining room. "Come in here. Let's talk."

She pressed her lips together. Sent daggers at Nick and marched down the hall to the dining room.

Pale but alert, Ethan faced the doorway, propped on his elbow, his legs immobile and flat on the table.

Miranda sucked in a breath at the sight of him so weak. "You shouldn't worry about anything. You need to rest."

"I'll be fine. I've healed from a lot worse, if you'll remember."

She'd never forget dragging him, semi-conscious, onto a stolen boat three years ago. She'd sent a barely breathing Beryl on an auto-gyro to the nearest sympathetic hospital. The autogyro was a two-seater with no room for her or Ethan, whose severe concussion and broken leg needed less immediate care. She didn't know how she did it, but she got him onto the boat and, in time, to the hospital. But the guilt of all the thumps and bumps he'd endured as she dragged him still haunted her.

Nick breezed into the room. "Lie down, Ethan. You need to rest."

"I can't rest when the two of you are shouting at each other. What is the argument?"

"We need to punish Irene for her breaking the peace talk truce," Miranda said. "Make her pay for betraying us in a way that sends a message to the Fellowship that we won't be disrespected."

"Please, lie down." Nick went to one of the spare dining room chairs, grabbed two pillows kept there, and put them under Ethan's head. "I told her we will get the message across, but we have to take time to plan."

"We need to act now," Miranda said. "If SABR can't handle it, I will."

Ethan settled back against the pillows. "Do you honestly think that's the best use of your abilities?" His smile softened his words. "That you can do better than SABR against the Fellowship's second most important person?"

"I—" She pressed her lips closed against saying something even more stupid. Irene had security before. It would be even tighter now.

Nick rubbed the back of his neck. "You have a better way with words. She gets it now. Thank you. We should leave. Let you recuperate."

Miranda couldn't help gazing at Nick. With his compassion for others, he shouldn't be a soldier. "He's right," she told her uncle, who also shouldn't have to be a soldier. Be injured—again. "I am so sorry." She gestured at Ethan's injured leg. "This was my fault. I—I had to try." Her stomach rolled. "I am such a fool." She ignored her stomach and the tingling in her chest.

Ethan gave her a paternal smile. "You can't take all the blame."

She bowed her head and wrapped her arms around herself, elbows tucked in close. "It was my idea."

"I agreed to it—we all agreed. We knew it was unlikely to work, but we had to take the chance too. So many lives lost—" Ethan's voice held a sorrowful note.

The weariness and pain etched on his face sent another pang through her.

"We can't give up." Nick cast a worried glance at Miranda, then Ethan. "Not now. We have to stick to the plan—"

Ethan stiffened. "We're not giving up. Not even close. This little skirmish confirmed what we suspected."

"What plan?" Miranda asked Nick. Turned and asked Ethan, "Suspected what?" Each of them avoided meeting her eyes.

Ethan made eye contact with Nick, who gave a slight shake of his head.

She tossed a back-and-forth glance, then realized, *whatever they're planning is a strike against the Fellowship.* She faced Ethan. "I was wrong. I'll do whatever is necessary until we stop Irene and Felix and end the Fellowship forever."

The doctor breezed into the living room. "Sorry to interrupt, folks." He bent and spoke into Ethan's ear.

Ethan drew back. "Really?" He whispered a response. The doctor hurried out of the room. "Seems like we weren't the only ones who got ourselves into a scrape. Beryl's team is coming in hot, with at least one injured."

Miranda stifled the need to wipe the dampness on her upper lip.

"Who is on watch?" Ethan cast an inquiring look at Nick.

"Ben's in front. Karl and one of Doc Owen's boys, Freddie, are on the back porch. David's watching the south from one bedroom. Junior, Doc Owen's other boy, is watching from the north bedroom."

"Good." Ethan struggled to sit up. Swung his legs off the edge of the table. Gasped.

"Where do you think you're going?" Nick asked.

"To the living room."

"You need to rest," Miranda said like a parrot who repeated the only phrase she knew.

"I will not greet our guests laying out like a dying man."

Nick put a restraining hand on Ethan's shoulder. "Doc Owen said you shouldn't put any weight on that leg if you ever want to walk again." His voice was low and taut. His smile was fake.

"Then help me. We have to hurry. Tell Ben so he can pass the word. We've got incoming friendlies. They've shaken off Fellowship agents pursuing them and need shelter."

Nick lifted Ethan off the table, carried him to the living room, and placed him in the chair.

In the living room, Ethan barked at Ben, who hurried to carry out his orders.

Nick positioned Ethan's injured leg on the ottoman, then took over Ben's position at the window.

"What should I do?" Miranda asked.

"Stay with me." Ethan gave a wry grin. "Protect me from Beryl."

Beryl? Miranda's insides twisted, certain she could not face her aunt again. *Not after walking out. Not after I left Beryl two searchers short. Especially not after my brilliant plan, my peace talk ended in absolute failure. She will never forgive me.* Miranda rubbed the hollow of her neck. *I'm the one who'll need protection.*

Chapter Forty-Seven

T he burning in her side sapped Beryl's energy, but she forced herself up the narrow concrete steps that cut through terraces of flowers and evergreens. Followed a walkway up wooden steps into the dusk-enhanced shadows of the covered porch and to an orange front door.

She held herself upright and knocked.

A handsome, if horse-faced, woman with long, silver hair answered the door. "May I help you?"

"Delivery," Beryl said. "A Special Silver deal from the Pizza Shoppe."

"That's our order." The woman stepped back. "Come on in."

Beryl entered a small, overly warm foyer filled with the mouth-watering aromas of garlic and tomato. Straight ahead, the hall ended at a windowed door. A staircase rose on her left and a wide, arched doorway on her right opened onto a living room with a golden-yellow sofa. She took a step forward. Stopped cold.

Seated in a yellow armchair to one side of a tiled fireplace, Ethan had his legs up on a stool. One leg of his slacks, slit to the hip, hung open, revealed a large white bandage wrapped around his thigh.

"Ethan?" Her steady voice hid the memories of love, marriage, and differences that made her insides jelly. That made her want to be sappy, to run to his side and make certain he was okay. "Are you—"

Opposite Ethan, in an identical chair, sat Miranda.

"You're here too?" The shakes vanished, and Beryl's chest tightened. Her memories shifted to Miranda walking out on her, not believing in her, in the Azrael, in the fight that must happen. "You're—together?" *How long has Miranda been here? Long enough to further convince Ethan the Azrael don't exist?*

Leslie, Wanda, and David crowded into the doorway behind her. She took a couple of steps into the room, tried to read Ethan and Miranda.

"You're hurt!" Miranda rose and moved toward her.

Now she wants to care about what I feel? Beryl jerked her hand up in a stop gesture. "It's nothing."

Miranda hesitated for a moment, then clasped her hands together in front of her and stood still.

"For nothing, that's an impressive amount of fresh blood on your shirt." Ethan didn't stand. "Let Georgia take care of the nothing that's still bleeding."

"*You're* hurt." She nodded at the bandage on his thigh.

His crooked smile teased her. "It's nothing."

Georgia, the silver-haired woman, stood in the hallway. "This way."

Beryl locked an intense gaze on her husband. "We need to talk."

He shook his head. "After Georgia fixes you up."

A glance at her shirt confirmed what he said about still bleeding. She followed Georgia into the dining room.

Georgia's tender but thorough cleaning turned every breath into a searing stab in Beryl's side. A coat of antibiotic ointment and a fresh gauze dressing didn't cool the pain.

Georgia rummaged through linens in the sideboard's bottom drawer.

Beryl accepted the clean, light-blue button-down shirt she offered and followed the woman to a tiny half-bathroom off the kitchen.

She washed a lot of grime down the sink and hurried back to the living room. *A buffet? Is this a safe house or a party house?*

Stacked on a folding card table in the center of the room were plates and silverware and pale blue napkins. At one end of the table a serving bowl held steaming tomato and meat sauce, a larger bowl held pasta, another bowl held salad, and crumbs covered the bottom of a bread tray. The aromas twisted her too-empty stomach.

David ladled sauce over his hungry-man serving of pasta. "Hey, Beryl. Come help yourself." He settled on a folding chair in front of the curtains and dug in.

Wanda and Leslie sat on the sofa and held their plates while they ate. Miranda returned to the matching chair across the fireplace from Ethan. Nick sat astride a folding chair, stared out between the window frame and drapes. Beryl didn't know where Karl was, didn't care.

"Eat," Ethan said. "You'll need the energy. We leave here soon."

She hesitated, hated that he was right. Scooped up a small serving of pasta and sauce. "We found it—the lab." She sat between Leslie and Wanda.

"You did? After Miranda left?" He glanced at the rest of her team. "Did you all see it?"

The others spoke at once, each telling their version of events.

She gulped a bite of pasta covered in sweet marinara with a hint of garlic and olive oil. "Doesn't matter." The others quieted. "We have pictures." She eyed Leslie. "Where's the camera?"

"She gave it to me while Georgia bandaged your wound," Ethan said. "Karl took the film to a SABR-sympathizer's photo lab to be processed."

"I have a map." She took the schematic out of her pocket, handed it to Ethan.

He studied it. Raised his gaze to her. "Is this supposed to prove something?"

She swallowed the last of her spaghetti. "It's a plan of the lab."

"It's a fire-escape plan. Could be for a lab, an office, or even a school."

The bolt of murderous adrenaline that shot through her overpowered her pain, tensed her muscles. She snatched the paper from his hands. "You should believe me." The need for blood curled her fists. The map crinkled.

Ethan cocked his head and searched her face as if he didn't recognize her.

She eased her fists open and tamped down the bloodthirsty beat of her heart. "You would have believed me once."

He'd already turned his attention away from her to exchange looks with Miranda.

Beryl glanced from him to Miranda. *How much of his disbelief did you reinforce?* She locked onto Ethan again. *How many times have you betrayed me? Betrayed our Anna?* She cursed herself for thinking she could have persuaded him about anything. For believing he held onto any love from their marriage.

He gazed at her again. "Tell me what you saw." His tone was that of a commander looking for a report. That, she could work with.

She placed her sauce-stained plate on the card table. Leaned forward. "They have better, much more sophisticated equipment. There were hundreds of extrauterine devices. Not metal cannisters like on the island but soft"—a wave of lightheadedness hit her. She blew it off—"red sacs that hung from the ceiling. Rows and rows of larger and larger sacs. At least as many as were on the island. Maybe more."

Ethan scoffed. "That's impossible."

He used to know me better. "Are you calling me a liar?" She used a quiet tone that silenced everyone.

Scritch-scritch. He scratched his chin through his untidy beard. "No, I'm not." He shook himself, focused his gaze on her. "But—more unborn than on the island? As hard as that is to believe, I'm listening. Go on."

"I couldn't tell if any have been…born. But it's clear the Fellowship is raising an army. Again."

Ethan propped his elbows on the arms of the chair, his hands folded in his lap. Stared at his right thumb rubbing his left one. "We don't have enough ammo or men to do two large operations," he muttered.

"That's fine," Beryl said. "You keep the male SABR fighters. I'll take the female ones."

He gave her a look that said he didn't appreciate her sarcasm. "You know I meant I don't have enough SABR soldiers, male *and* female." He folded his arms across his chest. "I'm sorry, I can't spare anyone."

Can't means won't. He doesn't believe me. Won't help me destroy the Azrael. Even though she'd half expected it, his response drained her. She sagged against the sofa.

David stood. "Sir, they know we found the lab. They'll move it. We have to strike now."

"Even if everything you say is true, this lab cannot be my priority."

"Those abominations Took my family," Wanda said. "My cousins and grandmother—my *father*." Her heated tone was low and tight. "Are you saying they don't deserve justice?"

Beryl straightened, watched the others' pleas, and Ethan's reactions. *They can plead my case better than I can.* She propped her elbows on her legs, leaned on them. Pressed her prayer hands against her lips to keep from ruining things by speaking.

"Of course, they do. Their lives are important, but you're asking me to—"

"We have to destroy that lab," Miranda said.

Burying her surprise, Beryl sent a distrustful glare at Miranda. *After your little stunt denying the new Azrael exist, quitting the search, quitting me, you think you'll make everything right by* saying *you believe now? How many times have I told you, actions speak volumes louder than words?*

Evidently, Miranda had surprised Ethan too. After a moment of staring at her, he said, "I thought you wanted peace."

"We both know how well that went."

"No matter. It has to wait." Ethan struggled to his feet.

"It *can't* wait." Miranda stood. "Beryl and I will do it with or without SABR."

Wait. Did she say we? She'll fight the Azrael?

"I'm with them," Wanda said.

Leslie piped up at the same time. "I'll help too."

"Count me in." David leveled a look at Ethan. "SABR—hell, the U.S. of A. won't survive if we don't stop the Azrael."

"All right, all right, all of you, calm down." Ethan leveled an intense glare at Beryl. "When the pictures are developed, I'll consider changing our timeline. But those pictures are going to have to be pretty damn convincing."

Chapter Forty-Eight

Making certain she stayed out of sight, Irene peeked between the drapes she'd pulled shut. Squinted through bright sunshine at the mob of reporters on her front lawn. The throbbing behind her eye made it hard to think.

She'd hoped the reporters would have left by lunchtime, but it was almost time for Sandra to come home from school and they still trampled her grass. They'd harassed her housekeeper to tears, and Irene had sent her home.

Trapped in my own home. She picked up the ice pack from the side table. Water sloshed. *Need more ice.*

She refilled the bag in the kitchen.

Ding-dong.

If that's the reporters again, I'm going to call the police. She paused at the round mirror in the entry hall, adjusted her hat's veil to conceal the bruising. Cracked open the front door.

A familiar Second Sphere agent stood on the stoop. Bulbs flashed behind him.

"Jason, it's about time," she said. "Get rid of these reporters, would you?"

"I am sorry, Lady Earnshaw. May I come in?" Without waiting for an answer, he came inside and shut the door behind him.

Her breath caught, then she drew herself up and demanded, "What's the meaning of this?"

He pressed his lips together like a schoolboy caught being naughty and held out an envelope. "I have a summons for you."

"A summons?" Her heart slammed in her chest. *An official request for an appearance in front of the Fellowship Council?* She gave a weak laugh. "There must be some mistake."

"No, madam. Please. It's my duty to have you read it in front of me."

She took the envelope with two fingers. Neatly typed on the front of the envelope was a name and address. Her address. But it read Irene Clarke Earnshaw. *Not* Lady *Earnshaw? And they used my maiden name?* Her mouth went dry.

She tried to read Jason's face. "Someone's made a mistake—"

"Madam, please—read the summons."

She tried to smile. "Can you tell me what this is about?"

Jason stood with his hands behind his back.

She went to the hall console, picked up the brass letter opener.

Irene Clarke Earnshaw shall appear before the Fellowship Council at one o'clock p.m. The Council's emissary shall remain at her side from the delivery of this summons until her appearance before the Council at the First Fellowship Church on this twenty-sixth day of October in the year 1963 of our Lord.

She shrank inside. The paper rattled in her shaking hands. She mustered up all the indignation she could. "This doesn't explain the reason for this summons." She locked on Jason. "Why are they summoning me?"

He took a deep breath. Wouldn't meet her eyes. "Your marriage is to be annulled."

"My what?" The air in the room vanished. Wave after wave of dizziness hit her. The walls tilted. Her knees buckled. The summons fluttered to the floor.

Jason took her arm, helped her the few steps to the seating area. Brought her a glass of water.

She took a sip, then held the cold glass for a long moment. *I don't understand.* She put the glass on a coaster on the side table. *How can this be? Felix wouldn't abandon me...our daughters. What will happen to us? Where will we live?* "Is this—" Her voice cracked. She cleared her throat. "Is this what Felix wants?"

Jason unbuttoned his black trench coat, pulled an envelope from the inside pocket of his suit coat. "It's from the Prophet."

She took it, stared, unable to open it.

Mercifully, Jason took three steps away, then stood still and silent.

The official dove-gray stationary with the gold Prophet's seal embossed in the lower right corner also held Felix's familiar, cramped, nearly illegible scrawl.

I must obey my higher calling.
I know you'll understand.
F~

She folded the note, stuck it back in the envelope. Placed it in her lap, folded her hands over it, and stared at the opposite wall. *Higher calling? Is this the Lord's will?*

After a while, Jason asked if she wished to freshen up before they left.

"Sandra will be home soon."

"Miss Linda waits outside. She will stay and see to Sandra."

At the mention of their daughter, Irene's thoughts cleared. *Thank God Sandra won't have to take part in this travesty.*

An annulment? The Lord knows that if anyone has a reason to file for the dissolution of our marriage, it's me, not that…that adulterer. She lifted her chin and squared her shoulders. "Yes," she said in her best Lady of the Prophet voice. "I will freshen up."

She marched up the stairs. *I will not let the Council think I am defeated. I will look my best.* She huffed out a breath. *I kept insisting Felix wouldn't…but he did. He sinned, and now he's punishing me to hide his sin. They can hold this sham of a ceremony. Felix, not even the Council, knows who I am. Nothing they do or say will change who I am, what I do. I am the Lady Earnshaw, destined to save our country with my army of Azrael. We'll see who the people follow when I do that. Felix, no. The entire council will beg for my forgiveness. And they will pay dearly for it.*

Jason followed her to the bedroom door. He granted it was improper for him to watch her change clothes. Agreed to wait in the hall.

As if I would ever crawl out a third-floor window.

She closed the bedroom door. Changed into her nicest royal-blue suit. Styled her hair and placed her favorite blue and white tilt hat on her head, the one without a veil, so everyone could see *she* was the wounded party.

Forty minutes later, Irene clenched her jaw and stood along with at least a thousand pastors and deacons and other Fellowship church officiates in the cavernous First Fellowship Church. Not in the first row. *They don't have the decency to put me in the family row? And not in the second row, but in the middle of the congregation?* At least she was on an aisle and could get out faster after this was over.

The Fellowship Council sat behind Felix in the pulpit. Each with smug, self-righteous expressions.

Unlit candles stood in the candlesticks. No flowers adorned the dais. The Council's banner with its blood-red Fellowship shield on black silk hung across the railing.

Lucas Matthews rose from his seat. Crossed to the pulpit. Made a show of opening a fancy, black leather presentation portfolio. "On this day—"

His plummy tone made Irene's stomach pitch.

"We, the Fellowship Council, decree that since the Prophet is a man of God for the people—all the people—the Prophet is married to God and his service. Therefore, the marriage between Fellowship member Felix Earnshaw and Fellowship member Irene Earnshaw nee Clarke is annulled and dissolute. This is the will of God."

"Thy will be done," the voices of the officiates and deacons and pastors responded.

Lucas Matthews continued, "Hereinafter, Irene Earnshaw nee Clark will no longer be addressed as the Lady of the Prophet. All rights and responsibilities of the Lady of the Prophet once assigned to this woman are dissolved. Irene Earnshaw nee Clark will cease all official duties immediately. The Prophet and Council have graced her with one week to remove herself and all her possessions from the Prophet's residence..."

A thousand pair of eyes bore into her back as he spoke. Chin high, pulse roaring in her ears, Irene sat through the blessedly short details on how they divided the property. *According to them, I own very little of what is in* my *home.* Back straight, chin high, she stared ahead.

Finally, the Council Steward called a close to the meeting and dismissed everyone. Without ever having met her desperate looks, Felix left the pulpit, followed by the Council.

She kept a serious and kindly Lady Earnshaw look on her face, but a wildfire raged inside her. *Of course, they didn't allow me to respond. The men have closed their ranks to protect the Prophet because they have sin in their hearts too.*

On her way out of the church, it was as if she didn't exist. No longer part of the handshake at the door ritual. No warm greetings for Lady Earnshaw. Not even any eye contact from a single person. No place for her. Not here anyway. She hurried to her waiting car.

"Get me home," she told her driver in a high, tight voice that didn't sound like hers. She kept her back straight and chin up, though her jaw muscles twitched like she'd had too much caffeine.

Even more reporters, photographers, and television cameras choked the front yard. Her driver took her around to the back. He had to push through a crowd of trespassers with flashbulbs, but got her inside with most of her dignity intact.

She locked the kitchen door behind her. *Never needed to lock my doors before.* Useless arguments raged inside her. She tamped them down. *Sandra and I will pack. We'll get Annabelle, and the three of us will go* on *a retreat—somewhere no reporters can find us.* Halfway up the stairs to the fourth floor, she called, "Sandra, darling, pack your things. We're going on a fun trip together."

No answer.

Everything inside Irene twisted into a breath-robbing knot. She hurried to the common room. "Sandra? Linda?" No answer. No sound. Nothing. "Hello?" Her heart lodged in her throat. "Sandra?" She rushed into her daughter's room.

Sandra's mountain of stuffed animals, her music box, her toy box, even her bedspread and sheets—gone. Unable to believe her eyes, Irene ran her hand over the smooth, bare mattress. No ruffles, no squishy bear, no dolls. She yanked the closet doors open. *Empty.*

She couldn't breathe. The room spun. She staggered across the room. Fell to her knees at the foot of Sandra's bed. Screamed, "You can't do this." Beat the bare mattress.

Exhausted, she pulled herself up and sat on the corner of Sandra's bed. *Did the Council think* my *girls are possessions?* Owned *by the Prophet? By Felix?*

She ran downstairs.

Felix's office door stood open. The books on the shelves, the photographs on the walls, even his desk—gone. *No, no, no.* She clenched her teeth against her body's quaking. *They did all this while I was at that sham of a ceremony dissolving my marriage?*

She stumbled out into the living room. Stood, trembling, in the center of the room. *How can he do this? Why? How do they explain his daughters if he has no wife?* She straightened her spine and set her jaw. *They won't get away with this. No matter what they say, Felix is still my husband.* Glared at the empty room. *I'm not staying here for another second. I will find Sandra. And I will show Felix, the Council, the rebels—the entire world—I am a good wife, an exemplary mother, and a great Prophet's Lady.*

She marched upstairs, packed, and called her driver.

By the time she walked out the door, the only sign of the reporters who had hounded her was the trampled grass. She stared at the ruined lawn. "It will cost a fortune to replace all that grass..." *Not my problem.* She allowed herself a spiteful smile and climbed into the car.

The limousine took her straight to the airport, where she bought a one-way ticket to Kansas City.

Chapter Forty-Nine

Night clouds and urban lights hid the stars and dappled the purple horizon. Miranda sat on a wrought-iron bench in the backyard of the safe house. She pulled the sweater she'd borrowed tight against the chill wind that knifed through her. After more than forty hours cooped up inside the stifling bungalow and enduring endless arguments, she needed fresh air.

A trace of wood smoke from a nearby fireplace flavored the crisp air. Miranda's longing for the simplicity of life on *Lady* intensified.

Behind her, the screen door squeaked opened and clicked shut.

"Mind if I join you?" Nick asked.

"It's cold."

"I don't care if you don't."

They sat side by side, not touching, not talking.

Muted sounds came from the neighboring houses—a mother calling her children, canned laughter from a television or radio show, and nearby a slow, poignant piano solo of "Georgia on My Mind." Normal sounds. Peaceful sounds.

The ache in Miranda's chest tightened. She had forgotten what normal life sounded like.

"This is nice," Nick said. "You can almost imagine what life could be."

The strings introduction of "Guide Us, O Thou Great Jehovah," the theme song for the Fellowship-required Hour of Prayer, grew louder as one house after another tuned in, until the chorus drowned all other sounds.

Miranda shivered, but not because of the late fall weather. "Have I been on the boat so long I've lost touch with"—words failed her—"how many people live in fear?"

"Of course not." Nick wrapped a warm arm around her shoulders. "Fear filled your boat. It's why you created Safe Harbor. Why we fight. Why SABR must win—*will* win."

A flush rushed through her. A yearning for the cottage, Nick's arms around her, a life… A life she couldn't have, not now. A life, lives, that could end before… She broke free of Nick's embrace, glared at him, fists knotted tight. "We can't—*I*—can't plan that someday life."

He cocked his head, and his eyes searched her face.

"What we've had…it's not normal. How can we talk about the future or normal when we haven't even had a proper date?"

Even though Nick's eyes never left her face, he pulled back a little and the ache inside grew sharper. "I'm not saying no…" She groped for the right words. "We should let this thing between us grow and not try to make it something it might not be after a few months of peace."

"I understand," he said, soft and sympathetic and steady. An adoring smile lit his face. "You didn't say no. I'll take that. I can wait —as long as you need."

What if I need longer than you can wait?

The screen door behind them banged open.

"Karl's back with the photographs," Leslie shouted. "Oh, I'm sorry. I didn't mean to interrupt."

Nick stood. "You didn't interrupt." He tilted his head toward the house. "Let's go see those photos."

Miranda hurried into the screened-in porch. "Did someone tell Beryl?"

"Yes. She was coming downstairs when I came for you. Bet she's already looking at the pictures."

———

ARMS FOLDED ACROSS HER CHEST, Miranda leaned against a pale green wall at the foot of the room. Trapped her lower lip between her teeth.

The over-warm dining room featured an arched niche papered with white stars on mint green. Within the niche sat a walnut buffet topped with pair of silver candlesticks on a white lace runner. Nine people crowded around the matching rectangular table for six. Nick and Ben stood near the head of the table, near Ethan.

Ethan tossed four grainy photographs, a study of indistinct blobs in shades of gray, onto the table. They slid and fanned helter-skelter across the glossy surface.

What the heck? Miranda gaped at the ruined photographs. *Even the ones I took didn't come out, right?* Her gut tightened. *Something isn't right.*

"It wasn't *that* dark." Beryl shuffled the over-exposed photos as if images would appear.

"However it happened," Ethan said. "They are what they are, and what you have isn't proof."

"Did the camera bump open during our escape?" David said, but his tone said he didn't believe that.

Leslie shook her head. "It wasn't open when she handed it to me."

"If it opened in the tunnel, no light could get to the film." Beryl snorted. "No. It had to happen after we got here." She glared at Nick, then Karl.

Nick sighed. "I opened the camera in a closet and sealed the cannister. No way the film got exposed to light. Old film could do this."

"I just carried it." Karl held his hands up. "Nick gave the cannister to me sealed tight."

Wanda studied one photograph from every angle. "Maybe the developer fogged the film on purpose?"

"I told you, the owner-operator is one of us," Ethan said dryly. "He would never do anything against us."

Miranda had had enough. "What did you expect, Ethan? That Beryl would ask an Azrael to say cheese for the camera?"

"I expected photographs of something more than vague shadows. We can't afford to divert supplies, much less people, to a questionable target." He stood, winced, and shifted his weight to his good leg. "I must consider the big picture, no matter what my personal feelings are."

Ben hurried forward to help Ethan.

Karl moved out of their way.

With Ben's help, Ethan hop-limped out of the room. Nick and Karl followed.

Beryl rested her chin on her hands, eyes on the useless photographs.

Miranda scanned the glum faces around the table. "Okay, so we can't count on Ethan or SABR soldiers to help us." She pulled out a vacated chair and sat. "How do we destroy the lab by ourselves?"

Beryl's eyes measured Miranda, then the others. "Without SABR's help, this could be a suicide mission."

"Let me rephrase." *It's not suicide if you destroy the enemy first.* "How do we do it and not kill ourselves?"

"We need to plan how to survive first" Wanda said. "Find the safest way to get out. And that will be our way in."

"Yeah." David leaned back and his chair creaked. "But we need to destroy the place. And not bring the mountain down on top of us."

"This is just one lab," Leslie said. "What about the other ones? If we don't do them all at once, the others will know we're coming."

Destroying the labs won't stop them from starting over. It's like an octopus—but it regrows more tentacles than we cut off.

David screwed his mouth sideways. "We don't even know how many more there are."

"Focus" Beryl said. "First, we destroy this one."

"No…" Miranda sat straighter. "Ethan's right. So is Leslie. Look at the big picture." Four puzzled faces turned toward her. She gave them a grim smile. "We have to cut off the head of the octopus."

"What the hell does that mean?" Beryl's voice and facial expression shouted her skepticism.

Chapter Fifty

Miranda braced her hands on the dining room table, scanned the faces of David, Wanda, and Leslie. Locked eyes with Beryl. "Remove—the Prophet, the Counselors, Patriarchs, Shepherds, and all the Second Sphere generals."

"What does that have to do with destroying the lab?" Ethan's voice came from very close behind her. "And the Azrael?"

Startled, Miranda's hand grazed her empty coffee cup. It wobbled and clattered. She stilled it. Steadied herself.

Ethan stared at her from the doorway, leaned on a crutch. Nick stood behind him.

She licked her lips. "We destroy one lab, they build four more. To stop them, we have to stop the Fellowship leaders—especially the ones who know how to grow the Azrael."

"Do you know how many people that is?" Ethan's smirk didn't match his gentle tone.

"Of course she does." David's heated tone held a warning.

"One hundred seven men," she said, "plus the Second Sphere Commandant and fifty generals is one hundred fifty-eight men, plus the lab people." *Ethan knows that.*

"Located all over the country," Ethan said. "How the heck do we kill them all at once?"

She quirked her mouth. "I don't know, but if we don't—we *will* fail. They *will* kill us, one by one, until we are all dead."

"Come. We should talk." Ethan limped away, toward the living room.

Miranda glanced at Beryl, whose jaw twitched.

"What about us?" Wanda gestured at David and Leslie.

Miranda cocked her head at Nick and, moving only her eyes, glanced at Beryl.

"Beryl, you're with us." Nick's amused smile and wink got no response from Miranda, or Beryl. "The rest of you relax for a bit. We'll fill you in soon."

In the dimly lit living room, Ethan eased himself onto the fireside chair farthest from the window. He lifted his injured leg, grunted, settled it onto the brown hassock.

Karl straddled a folding chair facing the window. He spared them a glance, then continued keeping watch out the window.

Beryl stalked across the room, peered out of the drapes on the opposite side of the window.

Feigning total confidence, Miranda settled onto the sofa and barely acknowledged Nick when he sat at the other end.

Eyes on Miranda, Ethan rested his elbows on the chair arms and templed his fingers. "Where and when did you get the idea to kill so many?"

"Just now. I don't like it, but how else—"

A human-sized shadow with an insect-like head rose behind Ethan.

Miranda's blood pounded. Her vision tunneled. Mouth went dry. *Azrael.*

The dark angel raised her arms over Ethan's head.

Not again! Miranda leaped to her feet. Drew her pistol. Fired three shots—

Azrael's arms dropped, and her torso toppled, trapping Ethan.

Unintelligible shouts rang out in every voice.

Karl stood, his folding chair collapsed, clanged to the floor.

Beryl whirled. Pointed her pistols at Miranda, then the Azrael draped over Ethan.

Miranda's breath rushed. Her pulse thumped. And her ears rang. She lowered her weapon with steady hands.

"What the hell?" Ethan struggled against dead weight.

"Ethan?" Nick pushed the body off Ethan. It thudded to the floor. "Are you all right?"

"Yes, thanks to—Miranda? Who is—was—that?" He twisted in the chair, saw at the dead body. His mouth slowly dropped open. "An Azrael?"

"How'd she get in here?" Beryl glared at Karl.

"Not important right now." He cupped his hands around his mouth, shouted, "Fire!"

Beryl took a position beside the arched doorway.

Miranda took the opposite side.

Bang-bang!

Her heart battered her ribs. She aimed at the top of the stairs, where the gunshot came from. *Azrael work alone. Must be Second Sphere.*

A volley of gunshots came from the back of the house. *They've surrounded us.*

The lights blinked out. All of them. *They cut the power.*

In the dark, the noise of a scuffle scraped and thumped overhead. Three more gunshots rang out. A chill raced down Miranda's spine.

"Follow the plan." Beryl's whisper moved away from them. Her shadowy form crept silently up the stairs.

Miranda glanced toward Ethan.

Nick scooped Ethan up in his arms, staggered toward the hall.

They'll never make it. "I'll cover you." Miranda aimed down the hallway. Stepped into the hallway. Swung her aim to the front door. "Go."

Nick carried Ethan across the hall and entry to the basement door. His footsteps thump-thumped down the steps.

Shadows moved in the hallway. Miranda pointed her pistol at it. "Who's there?"

"It's me, Wanda. Leslie's here too. David's covering the back."

Why? "Where's Freddie?"

"Basement."

Oh. Did he turn off the power? "I've got you," Miranda said. "Go."

Wanda, then Leslie, rushed to the basement.

A third shadow moved.

"David?" Miranda's finger tightened on the trigger.

"Miranda?" David's taut voice held relief and concern. "You should be—never mind. Get downstairs."

She eased the pressure off the trigger. "What about you?"

"I'll be down in a second."

Unable to see inside the basement doorway, Miranda slid a foot forward, groped for one step after the other. Groped for a railing that wasn't there.

A flashlight lit the bottom steps. "Go to Freddie," Doc Owen whispered.

Freddie stood in a poorly lit doorway. He motioned her to come.

She stepped past him, and the yellow-orange light flickered like a fire, revealed a menacing mechanical man shape. Her already rapid heartbeat bulleted.

The mechanical man was a boiler furnace, its pipes, reaching arms. The flames behind its open grate door were like a flame-breathing gap-toothed mouth. It radiated hot, dry air and a faint chemical scent.

Nick and Ethan stood in the glow from the furnace. In front of the coal room doorway, Leslie and Wanda were shadows against the light-absorbing black coal behind them.

"Excuse me." Freddie eased past Miranda to a wheelbarrow full of ashes between the furnace and the coal room wall. He moved the wheelbarrow and opened a section of the rock wall, half as tall as a normal person. "One at a time. Don't touch the furnace."

Good knee first, Ethan crawled in, dragged his injured leg. His shoe scraped against the floor.

Nick followed. Leslie and Wanda crawled in after them.

Miranda listened and watched the door for the others.

"Go," Freddie whispered. "I'll wait for them."

She ducked into the tunnel.

Chapter Fifty-One

"My flight was uneventful," Irene told a stunned Dr. Gallaway, "but exhausting. I'd like to go to my room now. We'll discuss details in the morning." She stood by the frosted glass wall of his subterranean office building. Ignored the question that made her insides quiver worse than Jell-O on a plate. *What if he rejects me too? Where will I go? What will I do?*

"I—we—weren't expecting you." His finger-combed hair and pajama top over jeans emphasized his confusion. "You needn't have come. Two teams of Azrael are tracking the intruders. In addition, we've set a pair of guards at every escape tunnel. There will be no more intrusions."

"I'm glad you've taken precautions," Irene said. "But that's not why I'm here." *The allowance the Council granted me is a pittance, not at all adequate for the Prophet's wife.*

"Oh?" He eyed the six-piece, pink luggage set piled in the back of a nearby green golf cart.

Chin high, deep breath. "You'll hear about it, eventually. The Fellowship Council illegally annulled my marriage to Felix." She folded her arms in front of her, an excuse to warm her chilly hands. *Do they turn the heat off at night?*

"Oh. I, er, I'm sorry to hear that." He shifted his weight. His cheek twitched. "What does it have to do with me?"

"This project is under my purview. I'm here to ensure its absolute success."

"Well." Dr. Gallaway scratched an eyebrow. "This is unusual."

"Unusual or not, I am determined." *You must let me stay.*

"Lady—er—Mrs., er. What should I call you now?"

His words twisted the knife Felix and the Council had driven into her chest, drove the air out of her. *The Council will punish me or anyone who uses Lady to address me.* She sucked in a big breath of mineral-tainted air. "You may call me Irene."

"Okay, Irene. Why here? Surely you should stay in D.C. while you…reverse the annulment."

"My attorneys will take care of that," she said and wished she'd thought to retain one before she'd left. "When the apostates, the rebels, dishonored the Fellowship and its flag of truce—when they attacked me—this project became my number one priority. The Council did not change that. They agree"—*technically, not a lie*—"we must crush the rebels." *And in crushing them, I prove I am the true Prophet's wife. The Council will fall over themselves to reverse the annulment.*

"I see." Dr. Gallaway brought his hands together, prayer-like in front of his mouth. Tapped his fingers together in a rapid, nervous tempo. *Tap-tap-tap, tap-tap-tap-tap.*

The relentless tapping set Irene's teeth on edge. She wanted to grab his hands and stop that noise. Instead, she said, "My family built a considerable estate in Buenos Aires. I inherited it all. Your funding won't suffer."

Dr. Gallaway rubbed his nose and peered out over the parking area. The diesel odor from her hired limousine still hung in the air.

"If you'll have someone deliver my bags to my room…"

Dr. Gallaway faced her. "I'm afraid we have no accommodations of the quality you're used to."

"Creature comforts are unimportant. What's important is the project. We must eliminate every single rebel in the country."

He folded his arms over his chest. "There are uncomfortable truths you must understand."

Irene didn't blink, but shrank inside. *Haven't I had enough for one day?*

"Our angels are fighting angels."

Relieved, Irene smiled. "I know that."

His expression didn't change. "You will see a big change in Annabelle."

"After forty-eight hours?" Irene laughed nervously. "How big a change can that be?" *Has she changed so much I can't take her out of this place?*

"We breed the Azrael to be aggressive and violent." He held up a hand, stopping her from commenting again. "Here, at the school, we encourage that aggression and violence in every way we can. You must understand. Your adopted daughter *is* one of them, an Azrael. We've barely started, and she's already revealed her aggression and violence."

A sour taste bubbled in the back of Irene's throat. She fought to sound calm, curious. "Violence?"

"She's already seriously injured several students during sparring exercises. Those injuries caused two deaths."

Lightheaded, weak-kneed, Irene's throat constricted, didn't allow her cry of pain to pass. *Annabelle's killed—twice?* Somehow, Irene remained standing.

Dr. Gallaway seemed unaware of her reaction. "Will you be able to live here and allow us to do what we must so she will continue to grow into her role as an Azrael?"

Heart shattering like crystal on concrete, her thoughts flew a thousand directions. It took long moments for her to focus, think coherent thoughts. *My daughter, an Azrael who works at the whim of—wait. Felix doesn't know. The Council doesn't know. It's a secret project. My project.* Her heart lifted. *If we don't tell them, it really will be* me, *leading the Azrael. My Azrael will make Miranda and the rebels pay for what they did to Daddy and Mama—to me.* The pain in her chest eased. She breathed more normally for the first time since facing the Council. I *will save the Fellowship—the entire country—from the rebels. Felix and the Fellowship Council will know they have wronged me.* A sense of destiny filled Irene.

The doctor cleared his throat, gazed at her worriedly, expectantly, impatiently.

She locked eyes with him. "I am honored the Lord led me to Annabelle. Honored that she will protect and serve the Fellowship." Irene curved the corners of her mouth. "Honored and proud." A new energy built inside her.

Dr. Gallaway's smile erased the worry from his face. "Well then, we can put you in Teachers' Housing"—he gestured for her to get into the golf cart holding her luggage—"temporary accommodation. Until a better one is available."

———

TEACHERS' Housing was an unassuming building full of one- and two-bedroom apartments. Irene was grateful that regular, man-made ceiling and walls surrounded her instead of rock.

Her new living room held a desk, a settee, and a tiny table for two. A kitchenette stood on one side of it. Her bedroom and a private bathroom sat on the other side. It was nicer than the first apartment she and Felix had had in Argentina.

"It's not what you're used to." Dr. Gallaway's tone hinted he expected complaints.

She gave him her warmest smile. "This is more than I expected."

"I'll have the men build something more suitable. It will take a week or two."

"Small matter, Doctor." She took her hat pin out and removed her hat. "We've important work to accomplish—and little time to do it."

Chapter Fifty-Two

Exasperated, Beryl glared at Freddie, then his father, Doc Owen. They stood in the main part of the basement. Doc ignored her and continued tending to Junior, who lay on a table beside the stairs.

"Go," Freddie whispered. "Dad will finish soon, and we'll catch up."

"Fools," Beryl said. "Get him into the tunnel, now."

"I must stop the bleeding," Doc said without lifting his head.

She couldn't hear movement upstairs yet, but Beryl figured the Second Sphere agents would begin a second-wave assault soon. "They're too stubborn to listen, Ben. We have to leave now." The wall of heat from the coal furnace shortened her breath.

Ben shook his head. "It'll take both of them to get Junior into the tunnel. I'll stay. Take the rear guard."

Not going to waste any more time arguing. She ducked into the tunnel, and the oppressive heat cooled quickly. She ignored the tremors that made her weak and crawled. Battles, particularly kills, always gave her the shakes. But this was more than that.

More than one Azrael on a job was something she'd never heard of in all her years of fighting. *Miranda killed one. I killed two. How many did they send? How did they know where we were?*

A metal-on-metal scraping sound behind her tightened her

throat. *Freddie closed the access? Trouble?* She stopped. Couldn't hear the furnace anymore. *This passage is so tight, turning around will leave me defenseless.* Her back twitched. She crawled faster.

Her forward hand flailed in space. She jerked it back. Grabbed her flashlight, turned the light on. The access tunnel ended in mid-air, in a larger tunnel.

A two-foot drop landed her in the main tunnel. Red brick all around, the main tunnel was about twenty feet wide. Its arched ceiling stood about eighteen feet high. The cool, musty air didn't move.

North of her, the yellow lights of Ethan and the others swept back and forth, moved away.

She shined her light up the tunnel to the house. No sounds of the others coming. No gunshots either. Leaving four men behind, especially men like Ben and Doc Owen and his sons, a part of war that she hated. *They knew the risk. And I know what I have to do.*

Lips pressed tight, light pointed at the rough brick floor, she trotted north, toward the lights. Closed the distance.

The patter of footsteps that had grown louder, that had filled the tunnel—stopped. The lights ahead went out. Belatedly, Beryl switched her light off too.

Unforgiving dark blinded her. Her inner alarms shrieked, the back of her neck warmed, and her body readied itself for a fight.

Plink. Plink. Plink. Water dripped somewhere close by.

"Who's there?" The disembodied voice belonged to Miranda.

"Me. Beryl."

Light swept over her face. "Anyone else?"

"Nope. Not yet." *Miranda, the peace lover, killed an Azrael.*

"Keep moving." Miranda's soft voice echoed down the tunnel.

A dozen flashlights clicked back on. Georgia led the way. The rest of the flashlights came on, revealed Nick and Karl carried Ethan in a fireman's hold between them. Leslie and Wanda followed. Without another word, Miranda turned and joined them.

David dipped his head. "Glad you made it. Miranda worried about you."

Sure she did. So worried she left us short-handed in the cave. Damn it. Now's not the time. More important, who the hell betrayed us? The Doctor? Is that why he insisted on staying behind?

They walked slower, louder than Beryl liked. Every five minutes, she looped back five hundred feet, but caught no sight or sound of Doc and crew. Or of pursuit.

She glared at Ethan's back. *You had to have proof. Hope you're happy.*

A flashlight swept the ceiling. The group came to a halt. Only heavy breathing and a smothered cough punctured the silence.

Beryl worked her way up front. "What's the holdup?"

Squatted on her heels, Georgia pointed her flashlight at Nick and Karl. They lowered Ethan. Ethan kept his injured leg off the ground, balanced on one foot by waving his arms in the air.

Sweaty and breathing hard, Nick braced his hands on his knees. Karl arched his back, shook out his arms.

David and Wanda linked hands in a square, scooped Ethan up.

"I can walk," Ethan protested.

They ignored him.

Wriggling his arms and shoulders, Nick moved to the back of the group.

Georgia swished her flashlight across the ceiling and headed north again.

Beryl held back, took up the rear. Didn't look at Miranda. Tried to figure out what was going on with her niece. *Left me to find peace, then you propose killing more than a hundred men? Then the woman who wouldn't touch a gun except during practice drills, quick draws and kills an Azrael? Something is off.*

The tunnel stretched downward on a gentle slope toward the river. Beryl looped back behind the others over and over. *Doc and the others should have joined us by now.* She figured they were captured or dead.

Miranda and the others trudged ahead. Their silent, shoulder-slumped shadows revealed their fatigue.

On and on, they walked through the dark, echoing tunnel. The longer they walked, the more time Beryl had to think and the jumpier she got. *The Second Sphere had to know where we were and know to send more than one Azrael. And the only way that makes sense that is if someone among us is a traitor.*

Whispers of footsteps and ragged breathing came from all around her. A pebble clattered. The sound bounced around the brick walls like an errant ping-pong ball.

The hairs on the back of Beryl's neck stiffened. *Those echoes aren't the pebble.* She swept her flashlight across the ceiling in front of the group and turned it off.

"To the walls," a strained, unrecognizable voice whispered. Footsteps scurried, then fell silent. Flashlights clicked. Darkness swallowed them.

Beryl strained to see the shape of the tunnel behind them, to see whoever followed them. A light winked.

She drew her pistols, dropped to a one-knee-on-the-ground firing position, aiming uphill and at the center mass of the Azrael she assumed followed them.

Footsteps, clearly more than one person, echoed, grew closer.

"Family is the brightest light," Doc Owen's voice rang.

"Brighter together." Relief colored Georgia's tone.

A half-dozen flashlights flicked on.

Doc Owen hovered near Freddie and Ben, who carried a bloodied, semi-conscious Junior between them.

"Junior." Georgia's soft cry held anguish. "Is he—?"

"He'll live," Doc Owen said.

Beryl peered behind them. "Were you followed?" *Doesn't make sense that Doc or his family put themselves in danger by betraying us.*

"I think we shook them off," Ben said, "but let's not wait and find out."

Georgia led the way again. The two injured men came next. Then Nick and Miranda.

In the rear, Beryl walked backward, pistols in hand. *Who's the traitor? Ben? Nick? David or Leslie? Karl? Miranda?* Beryl's gut squirmed. *Miranda shot the first Azrael like she knew it would appear.*

Fifteen minutes later, they reached a vine-covered, floor-to-ceiling chain-link fence. Light glimmered through the leaves. The light was too white for sunlight.

After a whispered exchange, David and Karl put Ethan down. Each of them held one of Ethan's arms, supporting him as he balanced on one foot.

Ethan shook them off, limped forward, and faced the group. "Before we split up, we need to share intel."

He didn't say, in case someone doesn't make it to the next safe house.

"Where you were when the attack happened? Did you see who attacked us? How many did you see?" He cleared his throat.

"Miranda shot the Azrael who would have killed me. We were in the living room."

"Azrael were upstairs too, sir," Ben answered. "I saw two of them climb onto the roof of the back porch. I shot at them, kept them back, but there was a third one I didn't see. The third one came through the other window. If Junior hadn't killed her, she would have killed me." He rubbed his neck. "Junior took a bullet meant for me..."

"Three? They're attacking *in groups?*" Ethan's doubt echoed.

"I took out an Azrael on the front porch," Karl said.

"Wanda and I took over for Junior," David said, "so he could help upstairs. We dropped three Azrael. Came through the screens on the back porch."

"They were small, were they—" Wanda hesitated. "Children?"

Beryl's inner alarms went off. She hadn't noticed, but her mental replay agreed. The Azrael were small. She curled her fists, whirled on Ethan. "Have enough proof now? Are we going to destroy that damn lab?"

"We'll discuss that once we're safe."

"Safe? Where is that?" Beryl couldn't keep the heat from her voice.

"An abandoned building Doc Owen knows about twenty miles away," he said. "Pete and the others will meet us there."

Beryl's skin tingled. *Pete, SABR's strategist?* She fought off hope. "Pete's helping with your big plan?"

Ethan made eye contact. "*Our* plan... I was about to tell you when the Azrael tried—" He shifted his weight off his wounded leg. "Details when we're safe."

Safe? Someone betrayed us, and Azrael are attacking in teams. We won't be safe until every single Azrael is dead.

Doc Owen gave them the address. "No one will look for us there."

"We hid a van." Freddie worked the chain-link, revealed a pre-cut, vertical opening. "It's close, but I don't think everyone will fit in it."

"Don't worry," Miranda said. "You and Doc take the injured in the van. The rest of us will split up into twos and threes. Find our own transportation."

What the hell? Miranda's taking charge? Beryl suppressed a snort. *Not of me. She has too much to explain.* "Less talk. Move out. Now." She slipped out into a moonlit parking lot behind a factory building. Sprinted toward the closest shadows.

Chapter Fifty-Three

Cold, achy, and filled with the echo of nightmares, Miranda tiptoed around David's sleeping form huddled under newspapers. *Am I really ready for the oh-so-not-romantic life of a rebel?*

She'd arrived at the abandoned Odd Fellows Orphanage and School building shortly after Ethan and Doc Owen and his family. Doc Owen had taken the injured down the hall to a room he claimed was the school's clinic.

The others arrived in twos and threes during the moonlit early morning hours. She saw Wanda briefly. But even among the rebels, blacks and whites didn't sleep in the same room.

Beryl had arrived in the early morning too. Of course she'd gone off to another room.

Miranda tucked her chilled hands under her arms and stepped out into the hall. Metal lockers lined the hallway. Here and there, locker doors stood ajar as if waiting for a student.

Broken tiles crunched and wood creaked. Ethan hobbled toward her, using a T-shaped length of pipe as a crutch.

They met in the entry.

"Good morning," Miranda said. "I see someone's been scavenging." She tried to sound amused, but the remnants of nightmare-fueled adrenaline kept her muscles tense and hardened her tone.

Large cobwebs heavy with dust draped the crumbling remains

of a grand, split staircase with a half-landing. Centered on the first floor, below the landing, a marquee read "Welcome to the Odd Fellows School and Orphanage. Meet the faculty." Following the welcome, a pyramid of fading black and white portrait photographs revealed the ghosts of stern-faced teachers.

"Freddie is amazing," Ethan said. "Even found a little padding." He tilted his crutch to show her. Cloth, possibly an old towel, tied with twine, padded the arm rest.

"I'm glad you're up. We need to finish our conversation."

Wood creaked.

Miranda whirled and drew her pistol. Aimed toward the sound.

Beryl cautiously picked her way down the left staircase. "Yes. Tell us *our plans*."

Miranda's adrenaline-drunk heart careened out of control. She released the breath she held and eased the tension in her shoulders. Her heart took longer to calm.

"I came out here to find you," Ethan said. "Pete and Conrad are waiting for us in room one fifteen." He pointed back the way he came. "Past the infirmary." He didn't seem the least bit startled by Beryl's appearance.

"They're here?" Beryl eyed Ethan suspiciously. "How? When?"

"I was going to tell you last night before I got—"

Beryl charged past him and down the hall.

He gave a wry grin. "She will make and execute the plan before we catch up."

"Should I wake the others?"

"Not yet." He graced Miranda with an admiring smile. "I need to— Things happened so quickly last night. I owe you my life. Thank you."

"I couldn't let them take another life, especially not yours." She squared her shoulders. *I am ready.* "Let's make sure they take no more lives."

Morning light filtered through cracked windowpanes clouded with years of grime. Room 115, a former classroom, was devoid of furniture. Peeling paint dappled the walls, and wires drooped from irregular holes in the ceiling.

Beryl stood at the end of the room and glared at the back of a man at the wall-to-wall greenboard. Miranda recognized him by his slight frame and his jug-handle ears.

Pete Foster, SABR's tactician, freehand-sketched a map in white chalk on the greenboard.

"Good to see that some people never change," Miranda said.

Screech! Pete hunched and wriggled his shoulders, then turned to face them. Waved. "Hey, Miranda. Good to see you."

"And you, Pete." He *had* changed. Always pale, his skin had grayed, and his eyes held a depth, a hauntedness, that aged him.

"Isn't this a how-do-you-do?" Conrad Arthur's booming Texas drawl announced him. He stood in the doorway, peered upward and laughed at his hair brushing the doorframe. His once copper-red hair had paled since she'd last seen him. "Just stepped out for a minute and y'all showed up." He flashed a wide smile. "We ready to start this rodeo?" He joined her and Ethan at the center of the room.

Beryl gave an audible snort. "Yes, tell us what to do."

Pete gestured at his drawing. "The target's size is one of several problems."

"We don't have to attack the whole cave." Beryl's sarcasm sliced across the room.

"Of course not," Pete said. "But its size limits our options. Also, we don't want to allow anyone from the lab, or even any that work there, to escape. If even one person alerts the Second Sphere—we're done." He held up a hand to stop Beryl's next protest. "Explosives are too risky. And its size and powerful circulation system means smoke bombs aren't an option either."

"And we don't have enough men to use overwhelming force," Ethan said.

"We have no time to waste." Beryl folded her arms over her chest. "They are already sending out Azrael to kill."

Pete locked eyes with her. "An old limestone mine has hundreds of fissures. Stable until an explosion buries everyone under tons of rock and earth."

"Beryl's right," Miranda said. "We have to use the fastest and most destructive method possible to destroy the Azrael-growing lab." *And as many Azrael as possible.*

Beryl stepped forward, and tiles crunched. "I don't care if you think we can only use stink bombs—I'm destroying that place in twenty-four hours, plan or no plan."

Pete's jaw dropped. "Why didn't I think of that?" He turned, cocked his head, and studied the drawing. "A gas—something—"

"Poisonous?" Ethan's controlled tone held heat.

"Not lethal—smelly."

Miranda couldn't help it, blurted, "Skunks?"

Conrad guffawed. "You can wrangle those critters by yourself!"

"Too unpredictable," Pete said thoughtfully. "A gas—something that will irritate the throat and nose—set off the alarms."

"Alarms?" Beryl stiffened, then relaxed. "Of course, they monitor air quality."

Pete consulted the map on the trifold SubTropolis brochure. Added small white circles to his drawing.

"You'd need a hell of a lot of gas." Ethan waved his hand at the sketch. "That's millions of cubic feet of space."

Pete grinned. "Nothing like a hint of something foul in the air to make people skedaddle fast. You said we could drive through without a problem?"

"Yes," Miranda said.

"No, we can't," Beryl said. "They'll recognize our truck."

"Of course," Pete said to Beryl. "Conrad can procure a vehicle or two. We'll send in a couple of teams to plant the bombs throughout."

"If we place stink bombs in or near the ventilation shafts"—his finger *tap-tap-tapped* the circles he'd drawn—"the fans will give everyone a whiff, fast." Pete pointed at Conrad. "Our people will need breathing apparatuses like divers use."

Conrad rubbed his chin. "Not many scuba places here in the Midwest, but firefighters have similar equipment."

"Even better," Pete said. "The air quality alarms will trigger a call to the Fire Department. If our people look like firemen..."

"We'll need forty firefighting suits and air tanks." Conrad gave them a Texas-wide smile. "*Those* I can get but—"

"Not in twenty-four hours," Miranda finished for him. "We can't wait. They're already on alert, maybe ready to move the lab."

"I was going to say you'll have to train on the apparatuses." He eyed Ethan. "The team will be here in the next twelve hours?"

Ethan nodded. "Train them tomorrow afternoon. The assault begins tomorrow night." He looked at Beryl and Miranda. "Thirty-six hours will have to do."

Chapter Fifty-Four

Irene had spent the morning with Dr. Gallaway, touring the Center for the Advancement of Inborn Character, learning how it worked. Now he was taking her to some sort of demonstration.

The doctor drove past the last white building with red doors. The change from light to dark came in an eye blink. As if the natural, rough rock walls gobbled light, the pavement markers and reflector strips on pillars winked on and off, and the cart's headlights grew shorter the deeper they drove into darkness.

After what seemed forever, he pulled off the road, stopped. Off to the right, pairs of green reflectors defined a path that disappeared in the dark.

"Remember, not a sound." His disembodied voice sent a flutter through her.

The vinyl seat squeaked, and the cart wiggled. A dim red light clicked on behind her. Dr. Gallaway rummaged in the baggage area.

He grabbed a couple of lightweight jackets and a couple of camera-like things with telescopic lenses and a chin strap. Handed her a jacket.

She exited the cart, slipped on the jacket.

"You'll need this." He held out one of the camera-like things.

Unlike any camera she'd ever seen, it had a strange web of straps.

"Put it on like this." He pulled the device over his head, the camera in front of his eyes. In the dim red light, he looked like a bug-eyed creature.

A giggle bubbled up. She clamped her lips shut. The camera-thing was heavier than she'd expected. "Oh." Blinding light made her turn away from the cart.

"Sorry." Dr Gallaway climbed across the passenger seat. Turned the headlights off.

The underground world glowed green, the nearest pillars a lighter shade than the farther ones.

Green letters glimmered, spelled OBSERVER across the doctor's chest. "Dr. Gallaway?"

"Shh." He touched her arm, startled her again. "Come."

Even the red reflectors they walked between looked green through the strange camera. The path ended in a series of short, horizontal lines—steps up. Metal creaked under her feet.

Two adult shapes loomed ahead of her. The word TEACHER glimmered across their backs. A table in front of them held four UNIVAC computers with blank screens.

Dr. Gallaway pointed as if tracing something on the floor below.

Green lines on the floor marked a rectangular perimeter. This area was as large as the recreational park area except it had no plants or furniture or… A figure darted across an open space, arms groping in front of her. One hand touched a pillar, and she disappeared behind it.

A second, shorter figure furtively followed the first, hid on the opposite side of the same pillar. A Fellowship cross and shield glowed on its jacket. *An Azrael? Annabelle? Playing hide-and-seek?* Irene leaned forward, grabbed the ice-cold railing in front of her.

The taller figure crept around the pillar. *Dress, long hair…a woman.* The woman walked backwards, an upside-down cross glowed on her jacket. *Blasphemous!*

Crouched, the Azrael turned toward the approaching woman.

The woman backed closer and closer to the Azrael.

Irene put a hand over her mouth.

Chapter Fifty-Five

Annabelle took off her night vision goggles and stared into the inky black. Her natural eyes picked up nothing. She stood six feet away from a pillar that was twenty-five feet in circumference, yet she couldn't see it.

She clicked her tongue. The sound came back to her, muted by the pillar. She took three steps to her right. Clicked again. No bounce back. She moved forward with cat-like steps. Stretched her left arm out. Her fingertips brushed cold rock.

A soft, irregular *whoosh-whoosh* caught her attention. *Footsteps?*

She considered putting her goggles back on. *Where's the fun in that?*

Annabelle's angel charged Annabelle's senses with adrenaline. *She comes. Listen.*

The *wisp-wisp* of clothing accompanied the footsteps. The target's ragged breathing, like a directional beacon, told Annabelle the woman stood at four o'clock, about ten feet away.

Faintly, a dry sliding sound, like the sound of a bare foot sliding across the concrete, came. And again. Slow. Uncertain. A soft whimper.

Terror spread like an oil slick around the target. Her whimpers and movements became the sonar that allowed Annabelle to target her.

And the angel within Annabelle roared with delight. *Let's play!*

The target gasped. Slid forward and stopped.

Annabelle guessed she'd found a pillar and thought herself safe.

Twenty quick steps across the smooth concrete brought Annabelle close. She extended her arm, and her fingertips caressed the rock pillar. She stepped closer. Turned and let her back skim the pillar. Side-stepped around so she'd come up behind the woman.

Oblivious to her danger, the target took deep breaths, as if preparing to dash away.

The woman's energy, her body heat, sent a thrill through Annabelle.

The hairs on Annabelle's arms raised.

The woman slid one foot across the asphalt.

Annabelle took a step. Stood close enough to be the woman's shadow if there were light.

The woman froze. "Who's there?" Her whisper was barely audible.

Annabelle leaned forward. Lowered her garotte in front of the woman. Whispered, "I am the Angel of Death."

The woman screamed and tried to run.

Gack.

Annabelle smiled a rapturous smile and twisted the ends of the garrote.

No more loud breathing. The woman's bare feet thumped against the floor fast, insistent. Then slower and slower. Her weight sagged against Annabelle.

Annabelle's blood lifted her to a bright, exalted place where God smiled upon her.

The light went out. Gravity pulled. She sank to her knees. Eyes closed. Head bowed. "Thy will be done," she whispered reverently and vowed she'd stay in that bright place.

Chapter Fifty-Six

With a death grip on the freezing metal railing of the observation platform, Irene blinked and blinked and swallowed a painfully dry lump. She started at the harsh terrified scream of the unfit woman. Sucked in a breath when the scream was cut short. Watched the unfit woman struggle against the Azrael's garotte. Irene put her free hand to her own throat. Her pulse and her breath were so fast she couldn't tell the difference.

Slowly, slower than watching water boil, the woman's struggles weakened and stopped. The Azrael let the body drop to the floor, then swept her arms back, and looked heavenward. Exposed the lettering on the front of her jacket.

Anna 3000. *My Annabelle?* Irene's chest hollowed. Her vision grayed. If not for her grip on the railing, she would have fallen.

A tap on her shoulder made her jump and gulp back a squeal.

The doctor gestured toward the stairs.

Numb, she followed him.

They returned to the golf cart, removed their headgear, and rode back toward the lights.

She sat stiff and still and shaken. She'd expected violence and even death, but *Annabelle?* Irene shivered. Couldn't reconcile her little girl with what she'd seen.

The doctor drove into a lighter, brighter area. Her heartbeat and breathing and thinking barely slowed. The sight of the Azrael, of

Annabelle, staring upward returned to her over and over. She studied Dr. Gallaway's profile.

His glance toward her held no discernible emotion.

"What did I just witness?"

"The target was unfit and sentenced to death."

"I know that. What was she—the Azrael—doing afterward?"

"Oh. That's part of the psychology of the Angels."

Something sinister and spidery slithered down Irene's spine. She kept her tone cool, controlled. "Psychology?"

"You don't believe the myth we created, do you?" Dr. Gallaway's glance pierced her. "That God sent them to Earth?"

She bristled. "Do not assume that my faith is blind, Doctor. And do not assume that your science explains everything." *First Felix and the Council, now the doctor? Men.* She tired of being forced into a corner of helplessness. "You said I shouldn't interfere when the teachers *helped* the girls." She leveled a penetrating look at him. "Are you telling me you drive these girls insane?"

Dr. Gallaway huffed. "Insanity is extreme irrationality. Why would we wish that on these girls? What we do only wakens and intensifies what already lies within them."

What already lies within them? Inside Annabelle. Memory sliced through Irene. She'd had many glimpses of darkness in Annabelle.

They zipped past the nursery with its rows and rows of red sacs, the infirmary, and the Azrael barracks. Drove through the large, park-like exercise area where sweet flowery scents lessened the mineral taint in the air.

What if everything the doctor said is the truth? If Annabelle—if all these—girls are born with darkness inside, God put it there. They are God's handiwork, His angels.

But Annabelle was different too. *She was dead. And through Felix, God brought her back… for a reason. Brought her to me… for a reason. An Azrael. To fulfill my—our—destiny.*

Chapter Fifty-Seven

Squeezed with thirty other combat-ready adults like sardines into a classroom built for a dozen children, Beryl's inner alarms buzzed. The gray light muddied by filthy windows, and the heavy storm-is-coming air didn't help.

Everyone around her had the battle-hardened look of the survivors, but she knew no one other than her own team. Saw no one who sent her alarms into high alert. And yet, her internal alarms buzzed low and continuous.

The rebels in the classroom struggled with Conrad's instructions on how to put on the ill-fitting firefighter bunker gear. Filled the room with nervous laughter, grunts, muttered curses, and a muted shuffling, rustling noise.

She bent to pick up the dark beige pants with brilliant lime-green safety strips down each leg. Her butt bumped into the guy behind her, who chose the same moment to bend over. She gritted her teeth. *Damn it.*

Her feet slid easily into boots she could walk out of after she closed the fastenings. She stuffed the cuffs and extra of the over-long pants inside the boots and refastened them. Now they were snug enough to stay on. She adjusted the suspenders and closed the underarm holster that held her spare .45 over the suspenders. Shrugged on the beige and lime-green bunker coat.

In his lecture, Conrad had said firefighters called it a bunker gear because they used to keep it next to the firefighter's station bunk bed. Beryl didn't care. It was a uniform—boots, pants, and jacket accented with that bright lime-green stripe. It went against the grain to wear something that shouted *see me*.

Pulling the pants up to her waist, she buckled on a utility belt heavy with a fire ax, flashlight, and door chocks. Zipped then snapped her jacket closed. Slapped the helmet on, left the chin strap looser than recommended. Shrugged on the air tank. Settled it on her back. Then she jumped up and down to test the weight of it all. *Heavy*. Heavier than anything she'd worn for the past two years.

She waited, standing at ease, but curled and uncurled her toes inside the rubber boots. Adrenaline-fueled foreboding raced through her heart and lungs and crackled along her skin.

Conrad and two other men worked their way around the room, checking off the fit and function of the equipment.

Three people away, Conrad told a rebel, "Mask on." Checked the fit. "Good job." Moved to the next person in the row.

Two people to go.

Sweat trickled down her back.

Finally, he stood before Beryl. "Have you seen Karl?"

Not the greeting she'd expected. "He's got to be in here somewhere. Why? Is there a problem?"

"No problem. He'd asked me a question earlier. I didn't know the answer then, I do now. Don't worry about it. I'll catch up with him." He gave her one of his big Texas smiles. "Mask on."

She pulled on the mask of the self-contained breathing apparatus. The face-wrapping shield of clear plastic with its elephant-trunk hose delivered air and muted the sounds around her. The smell changed…canned air. Already pumped up, her heart and lungs worked harder. *Yeah, a big nope*. When the fighting started, the tank and mask would have to go.

Conrad double-checked the seal of her mask against her face.

He snugged the straps a little tighter. "Breathe."

She inhaled through her nose for a count of four, held her breath for four beats, then exhaled for four.

"That's it," he said. "The stink bombs we're using will release ammonia. If you breathe enough of it, if the fans are off long enough…breathing *will* get dicey."

"Good," Beryl muttered. "Oxygen-deprived Azrael will be easier to kill."

"What did you say?"

"Never mind," she said louder.

He gave her a curt nod. "Breath control will save your life. Running out of air is the fourth most likely problem to occur."

"The first one is getting lost." She mocked his lecture tone. "For firefighters, two and three are falling through a roof or floor. In our situation, rockfall and cave-ins are more likely."

He patted her shoulder harder than necessary. "You'll have the disorientation of the sameness of the mine and the dark. Stay on your knees, one hand on a wall at all times."

"Yes, Papa." Sarcasm aside, he was right. But on her knees and touching a wall all the time would be slow. And slow would mean death by Azrael.

"Foxglove, I'm serious." His concerned expression pulled her back. "We can't afford to lose you again."

"Whether or not I survive, isn't important. SABR will go on —*must* go on. Must destroy the Fellowship and all it upholds."

His glare drilled through her. "We *will* fight on, but there are some who won't survive without you."

She didn't want to think about what he meant. Forced a smile. "Don't worry, I still have some tricks up my sleeve."

"I sure as hell hope so."

She clipped the holsters for her Colt 1911 pistols onto each side of her equipment belt.

He frowned at the guns. "Those are supposed to be hidden—a last resort."

She opened her jacket, revealed her 45s.

"The noise and ricochets—"

"Deafness and minor flesh wounds will mean I survived."

"Conrad?" Wanda's radio voice called.

He glanced around. "Warren will get to you."

Beryl glared at Conrad. *Warren, a black man, was the only one checking non-white rebels' equipment.* "You afraid you'll get cooties from her?"

Conrad held his hands up in a hands-off gesture. "It's not a good idea for a white man to help a black woman. Too easy for someone to misinterpret what's going on."

She twisted her mouth into a shaming frown. "Who's going to judge you here? Besides, there's nothing to misinterpret about helping her put on bunker gear." Beryl unclipped her radio mike from her shoulder. "Wave your hand, Zinnia. He's not on the radio and can't tell who called."

A gloved hand waved in the air above a dozen heads.

Conrad sighed and locked eyes with Beryl. "I'll help her on one condition."

Beryl didn't bother to keep her smile off her face. "What condition?"

"That you promise me I'll see you afterward."

"I promise," she lied.

Chapter Fifty-Eight

nnabelle counted her curl-ups under her breath, "Sixty-two, sixty-three, sixty—" Her voice was a minor murmur among the other Annas counting their reps.

Artificial, bright-green turf of the school's well-lit exercise yard stretched between pillars. The pillars marked off spaces. In one space, Annas sparred in pairs. In the next, ten more worked on the pull-up bars, and beyond them, another ten did push-ups. Together, they formed a five-by-two grid. Six Teachers wandered the grid lines. Commenting, teaching, correcting.

Ignoring five of them, Annabelle focused on one Teacher. The one who had unjustly sent her to isolation. The one Annabelle planned to school…soon.

"Five minutes." Under a tight, tawny topknot, Teacher had a hard face with small squinty eyes. She walked past. Made no comment, no correction, no teaching.

The angel within chortled. *We've fooled her. She thinks we're obedient.*

Annabelle's powerful heart beat fierce and ready.

At a quarter after, Teacher blew a long, shrill note on her whistle.

Annabelle rotated to her next station. Pulled her chin above the bar twenty-two times. "Twenty-three, twenty-four, twenty-five…" *Only twenty-five more to go.*

Three long blasts of a whistle called everyone to Assembly.

Heart quivering, Annabelle dropped to the ground. *Three blasts. Someone's getting punished.* She toweled off and hurried to stand at attention in her assigned place on the assembly yard.

"Anna 3642, come forward."

Annabelle exhaled quietly.

Anna 3642 strode to the front, stood straight and tall. She was one of the youngest not-sisters. Her head didn't even reach Teacher's shoulders.

"This is Anna 3642's third transgression."

Two Seraphim, the highest ranking of the Azrael, grabbed Anna 3642 and dragged her to the Shaming Pole. Forced her to face the pole. Stretched her arms around the pole, tied them with leather strips to a large metal ring. Then stepped clear of the Anna and the pole.

The Teacher cracked the scourge whip.

The little Anna's body arched, but she didn't make a sound.

Careful not to change her expression, Annabelle's jaw tightened.

Red welts crisscrossed the young Anna's back. Still, she did not cry out.

Annabelle's muscles ached to react. The angel within roared. *Disrespect.*

Crack-Crack-Crack!

The little Anna fell limp against her restraints.

Teacher struck the Anna two more times, each more vicious than the first.

Annabelle could barely restrain herself. Didn't understand why they did not stop Teacher. *Anna 3642 is our not-sister, one of God's Azrael.* The scripture says no man may harm us, but didn't that apply to Teachers? To all who might intend harm?

"We will not tolerate laziness." Teacher handed her whip to one of the other teachers.

An attendant crossed to the Shaming Pole, untied the Anna, and carried her away.

Annabelle watched the other Annas out of the corner of her eye. *Why do they do nothing? The Word tells us, "Let no man or beast harm you." Why do they tolerate this abuse?*

This is what they know.

They've never walked among the Elite and the unwashed—never had a little sister or a kind mother—never learned they are miracles.

Her chest filled. Her heart lifted. She'd risen from the dead for this.

"Dismissed," Teacher said. "Change for lunch."

Annabelle walked back to the barracks with the others.

Her chest thrummed. Her blood burned. Her angel hungered. *I will lead them out of tyranny. It is my destiny.*

Fully dressed, Annabelle walked through the steamy, yellow and green-tiled shower room to the older Anna's vacant bunk room. They were out on a maneuver. She walked out of the other end of the barracks. Made a sharp right.

A teacher strode across the roadway from the assembly area to the Teachers' Housing.

Like an invisible angel, Annabelle concealed herself in the shadows.

From one pillar to the next, she crossed campus.

The angel within writhed with hunger.

Soon. First, we learn.

She took a shortcut, leaped through a golf cart that sat in the unlit, unpaved parking area, ran along the short wall of the infirmary, then down the road, avoiding medical and research staff heading to the mess hall.

Finally, she reached the nursery. Hunched down and peeked through a corner of the observation window.

Three pairs of attendants in hooded white coveralls walked down the aisle between red pseudo-uteri. They stopped at each fetal sac. One jotted notes onto a clipboard. The other pushed buttons on that sac's control board. Turned knobs testing each of the three tubes that entered the top of the sac. Then moved on to the next sac.

She waited until they returned to the next room to do whatever it was they did there. Then raced to the unlocked door and entered the nursery.

Tiptoeing between the sacs that held the unborn, she gazed at the tubes, dials, and knobs that kept each of the unborn alive. The hairs on her arms raised. She straightened her spine, lifted her chin. These were her unborn not-sisters. Their yearning to be born stirred inside her.

Only the scientists and Dr. Gallaway know how to care for the unborn. We will spare them. But they must work for us. Obey us.

Lunch hour over, she returned to class, where she performed like an average Azrael. And watched Teacher like an avenging angel.

Between lunch and lights out, seconds took minutes and minutes took hours.

The lights dimmed, a poor replica of sundown. Students and teachers returned to their quarters.

Annabelle waited for the "nighttime" lights to enter the dim hallway of the Teachers' barracks. Though she'd only followed Teacher home once, she recalled the exact door. Stopped outside it. Palmed her wire garrote and knocked.

"Come in."

Annabelle entered, closed the door behind her.

The Teacher looked up. "Hello, Anna 3000. You're up late." Teacher returned her attention to the papers on her desk. "What can I do for you tonight?"

Annabelle crossed the room and stood next to Teacher.

Teacher looked up again. Puzzled. "Yes? What is it you want?"

"You are evil in the sight of God," Annabelle said.

"Excuse me?"

"His will be done." Swift and sure, Annabelle dropped the garrote around Teacher's neck and snapped it tight.

Teacher's eyes widened, her veins bulged, her fingers clawed at her neck.

Annabelle held tight while Teacher struggled, weakened, ended.

The light lifted Annabelle higher than she'd been before.

It was a sign.

Returning to normal was painful. But filled with a new purpose, Annabelle didn't mind.

She cleaned her garrotte on Teacher's blouse and left.

Her angel within sang a joyful hymn all the way back to her bunk.

Chapter Fifty-Nine

The four steps carved into the rock led to an unassuming unmarked metal door. Irene stopped. The door had a number pad where the key lock would be. A number Dr. Gallaway wasn't offering. *I'll see he gives it to me soon.*

Dr. Gallaway entered the numbers, opened the door, and ushered Irene inside.

"This is Command and Control," he said.

A muscular man in a white button-down shirt, no tie, and no coat charged up the center stairs toward them.

"This is our chief of security, Victor. This is Lady Earnshaw, er, Irene."

Victor didn't crack a smile. "I know who she is."

"Of course you do," she said, dismissing him. She ignored the gooseflesh that riddled her skin. Scanned the colder-than-necessary room.

The room had a pitched floor like a college lecture hall. Much smaller than a lecture hall, it had only three tiers with six desks on each side of a wide middle aisle. At each desk sat a man staring at a UNIVAC computer. The men flicked switches, typed commands, or studied their screens.

Every desk faced the floor-to-ceiling, wall-to-wall screen across the back wall. The screen showed black and white images of semi-trucks entering the cave.

"Display all," the doctor said.

Buttons clicked.

The wall of images brightened and divided into twenty images of different locations within and outside the facility. She recognized the main drive into SubTropolis and the drive into CAIC. There were also views of two dock entrances and three hallways that ended in man-doors. Six cameras focused on numbered doors. Two views were of extra-large, wall-mounted air vents. "Is one of those the tunnel that the intruders found?"

Victor bounced a glance between her and the doctor. "You know about that?"

"Did you or did you not install a camera after the incident?"

Dr. Gallaway gave a sharp nod. "Show the tunnels on number eighteen through twenty."

She fixed her gaze on that image. "Those are all the escape routes?"

"Yes," Dr. Gallaway said. "In case of fire or—other emergencies. The tunnels are tall enough you and I can walk through without a problem. However, Victor must duck his head."

Irene studied the views. Turned and found the extra-large vent cover on the wall to her left. Lifted her chin. "Where does that one go?"

Dr. Gallaway's glance held a new appreciation. "To the runway at the top of the quarry."

"An airplane waits there?"

"That would expose our exit strategy," Victor said coolly.

The pain of her fingernails digging into her palms helped her stay calm. "And?"

"An autogyro will be there in minutes."

"I assume you placed armed guards at each of these?" She pointed at eighteen and nineteen.

Almost imperceptibly, he stiffened, and his eyes flicked away from her gaze. "Yes."

He might be a problem. "How many cameras do you have?"

"Enough." Victor's tone was sharp.

Dr. Gallaway gave him a look.

"Four hundred."

She scanned the walls. "Where is your map?"

"Excuse me?"

She drew herself up and glared at him. "You have a map of the campus, don't you?"

The lines in the corners of his eyes tightened. "Give the lady the static map with labels. Full screen."

A dotted schematic came up. The rows and rows of gray dots were pillars. Labels identified various parts of the campus, a park, an administration building, a chapel, and more. Receiving, laundry, and maintenance were clumped together on one side. Research and development, including the housing for the unfit, were close to the "killing field." Everything she'd seen in this morning's tour of the campus stood on the opposite side of the map.

Ring-Ring.

She started at the unexpected sound. Turned to Dr. Gallaway. "Wouldn't the radio be more secure?"

"Radios only work line-of-sight down here."

"Interesting."

A man in the front row stood, faced them, and held his hand cupped over the mouthpiece of a telephone receiver. "Dr. Gallaway?"

"For me?" He started down the steps.

"No, sir. For her."

Irene marched down the terraces. Took the receiver from the man. "This is Lady—ahem—this is Irene Earnshaw."

"This is K."

"How did you? Did Paul tell you where to find—"

"Listen closely. No time. Attack on SubTropolis tonight. Midnight. Key players involved." *Click.* The line buzzed.

Irene's grip on the receiver tightened. Her thoughts spun. *Oh, no, I'm in danger* twisted into *how dare they,* followed quickly by *I will make them regret this* which hardened into *I've got them!* Her pulse soared. She whirled, skewered the doctor and his head of security with a glare she'd learned from her mother. "Gentlemen, we have less than nine hours to prepare."

Chapter Sixty

N o moonlight or starlight escaped the storm clouds
overhead, and the crisp air smelled like snow. Miranda
snugged the collar of the firefighter jacket she wore
tighter. The movement shifted the backpack-like straps of the
oxygen tank she wore on her back. She adjusted the straps, double-
checked her mask still hung from a snap closure on the strap. Soon
they would enter the mine, and she would need it.

She led her team up the gravel road around the quarry behind
SubTropolis and the lab. Far below, spillover from the quarry's security light allowed them to see, but the light grew more distant the
closer they came to the top of the bluff.

At the end of the road, she glanced back at the members of Team
Sierra, gave them a thumbs-up. Wanda and two of Conrad's men,
Carlos and Gary, responded with their thumbs-up.

She left the road and the distant glow of the security light. Crept
into the black clutches of barren bushes and trees on the bluff top.
Tried not to think about the people, the Azrael, one hundred sixty
feet below the earth she walked on.

Conrad had taken an autogyro over the top of the bluff. Mapped
out the quarry and the bluff top and the probable locations of security cameras. Based on Beryl's report, he'd identified two ventilation
shafts that should lead to the lab. One was Miranda's target.

She glanced at the timepiece on her bunker sleeve—they had less than ten minutes to get to their assigned ventilation shaft and drop the stink bomb Carlos carried. Her muscles tightened. Her already dry throat turned bone dry.

Another glance behind her confirmed her team still followed. Her forward foot landed on the edge of a downward slope. She pitched forward. *Can't be the cliff...*

Oof! She windmilled, hit the ground sooner than she expected. Landed hard. Twisted an ankle and collapsed to the ground. Sent up a cloud of something that made her cough.

Gasping and shaking, Miranda did a quick check. Her ankle ached, but nothing else hurt. *No, she didn't fall off the cliff. But the hole was deep enough.*

She put her hand down, determined to stand. Touched something soft and kind of squishy. Recoiled. Took a breath. Shook off the creepy-crawlies. Forced herself to place her hand on the shifting surface and pushed herself up to a stand. The thing beneath her feet squished and rolled, like she was trying to stand on a water balloon. A foul stench puffed up from the ground. The pain in her ankle sent her into a crazy hop-step balancing act until she found firm footing and froze.

She pulled her flashlight. The hole was deeper than she was tall. *Six? Eight feet?* She pointed her light at her feet. *White dirt? No.* Freshly exposed earth covered in a white powder. *A waste disposal hole?* She swung her flashlight in an arc wider than her arm-span.

"Miranda?" Wanda whispered.

"Down here."

Three flashlights focused on her, effectively blinded her.

"I'm all right." Shielded her eyes from the light.

"Oh my God." Not a whisper.

"Wanda?"

"Turn around. Slowly." Whispering again.

The creepy-crawlies returned full force. Miranda turned, her flashlight aimed mid-chest. *Not a hole.* She stood in a trench longer than her flashlight could reach. White powder covered irregular mounds of— Miranda emptied her lungs. Bodies. *Lots of bodies— women's bodies.*

Shaking, Miranda sucked in air and blew it out, steadied herself. She bent and gently wiped the powder away from the nearest body. Naked, a young woman, no older than Miranda, lay with arms and legs at odd angles as if she'd been thrown away. Beneath her were at least two other bodies. Miranda aimed her flashlight down the length of the trench. As far as her light reached, bodies filled the bottom of the trench. *So many bodies.*

A wave of nausea and dizziness hit. *Why—?* She focused on breathing. On remembering. *The Fellowship doesn't need a reason. If you are not Fellowship elite, you're…disposable.*

Her blood heated. Her breathing steadied. Her resolve grew. The grave proved two things: the lab's existence and the depravity of the Fellowship.

She dusted her gloves together. Stepped closer to the side of the trench. Accepted Gary's extended hand. Climbed out.

"There's a grave like this near my daddy's house." Wanda's barely audible whisper compelled Miranda to grab Wanda's hand, squeeze tight.

The radio clicked. Static buzzed for five seconds. Followed by five seconds of silence. Clicked and buzzed twice more.

Miranda set her jaw and raised her chin. Strapped her mask on. Double-checked the fit of her team members' masks. Submitted to Wanda's inspection.

Now they had to wait. First for the sirens of real firetrucks carrying real firemen, then for Ethan's signal.

Ethan and Pete's team hid in a semitruck trailer across the railroad tracks. They watched the front drive of SubTropolis. Watched for people to exit the cave. They'd radio the go signal as soon as firefighters entered.

Minutes dragged by. The memory of the trench full of dead women kept Miranda focused. *I'm doing this for Manny, and Hector, and*—her heart twisted painfully—*for Sarah.*

Wheee-oh. Wheee-oh. Wheee-oh.

Miranda stiffened. Her pulse barreled faster.

The sirens grew louder and louder. Stopped below them.

The fire department response time was as predicted.

Click Buzz. Click. Click. Buzz. Buzz.

She led them out into the night-shrouded meadow to their assigned ventilation shaft. Twelve feet in diameter, the ventilation pipe's faint yellow glow came from indirect light sources far below.

About six inches below the surface of the ground, a metal grate covered the hole. A four-by-four hinged gate gave access to a metal ladder.

The ladder, inside a half-circle safety cage, plunged down one side of the vent. Miranda and Carlos knelt beside the ladder.

She reached down, laced her fingers through the grate. Carlos did the same. Together they opened the gate, carefully laid it back against the metal grid enough that it caused only a faint clink of metal against metal.

Wanda and Carlos and Gary drew their pistols, ready to cover her descent.

She swung a leg over the edge. Her shoe hit a rung, slipped, and flailed. Her heart hurtled toward her throat. Her stranglehold on the smooth metal edge of the vent tightened. She glanced down. Focused on the ladder. Placed her foot on the first rung, then swung her other leg over and began her descent.

Chapter Sixty-One

I rene clapped her hands over her ears.

The shrill alarm screamed *wah-wah, wah-wah*. White lights strobed.

Every man in Command and Control typed furiously on their machines and shouted over one another, the siren scrambling their words into meaningless sound.

"Report," Victor shouted. "Where's the gas leak?"

Her heart slammed against her chest. *It is not God's plan for me to die in a hole in the ground.* She tried to sound calm. "What kind of gas leak?"

"It's the air quality alarm," Dr. Gallaway shouted back. "Don't worry. It's finicky. Gives a false alarm about once a month."

Oh, thank God. A false alarm. But her heart battered her ribs with the same rhythm of the ear-shattering alarm. "Someone turn that thing off."

"Give them a minute," Doctor Gallaway answered, hoarse from shouting. "They're trying—"

The sudden silence wasn't totally silent.

Alarms still pulsed outside the room.

Men shouted about sectors.

Irene's ears rang, and her pulse thrashed in her ears.

The camera views on the wall flickered from one location to the next. In each, lights strobed, created elongated, moving shadows.

"Come on, people," Victor shouted. "Is it a gas leak or isn't it? Find it."

"Sir, the alarm originated from the main sensors in SubTropolis. Still trying to determine what triggered it and where the leak is."

Camera one showed a half-dozen Azrael staggering out from their hiding places near the entrance. Red-faced, hands covering their mouths and noses.

"What's happening to them?" Irene asked, transfixed by the sight.

Cough-cough-cough. On the lowest row of desks, one man couldn't stop coughing. A second and third man started coughing too.

This can't be happening. I haven't been here for a full day yet. She leveled her most forceful glare at the doctor and his security man. "Seriously? You have all these men and all this equipment, and you can't figure this out?" She raised her voice. "First man who identified what and where gets a five-hundred-dollar bonus."

"Sir—" The young man darted a look at Victor, then focused on her. "I mean, madam. Primary SubTropolis Control Center reports rising ammonia levels in sections Forty-four and Seventy-four."

"Confirmed. Ammonia levels rising in Sector Eighteen to Twenty-two."

"Spreading to Sectors Nineteen through Twenty-one."

"Sir, levels are rising in all sectors."

"All?" She ignored her ready-to-collapse shakiness, remained standing by sheer willpower. She turned to Dr. Gallaway. "Is ammonia lethal?"

Dr. Gallaway swallowed. "It would take a massive amount of ammonia to reach toxic levels in this—"

"But it's possible?"

He nodded.

"Set all fans to high."

"Sir?" One young man at the top row of multi-monitors turned to Victor.

Victor's jaw twitched. He shot Irene a look full of malice. "Do as she says."

"Yes, sir. Setting all fans to high, sir." *Cough-cough.*

She couldn't tell if the air was clearing. *How long will it take?*

Dr. Gallaway opened his mouth as if to say something, but coughed and choked and coughed.

A loud bang echoed throughout the room. Every light and every monitor went dark, immersing them all in an impenetrable, featureless black.

"Don't move—" *Cough-cough.* "Auxiliary power will be up—" *Cough-cough-cough.*

"Oh, dear." Irene pinched her nose shut and covered her mouth against the harsh, burning odor—ammonia. Tears filled her eyes, trickled down her cheeks. "It's the attack," she sputtered and coughed. The air set fire to her nose and throat.

A trio of yellow emergency lights glared. Sent more tears cascading down her cheeks. Blinking rapidly, she couldn't clear her vision enough to move safely. "Where are the Azrael?"

"They know what to do," someone, maybe Dr. Gallaway, answered.

"Maintenance to"—*cough-cough*—"power plant." *Cough-cough-cough.* Victor gasped for breath. "Now, fools"—*cough*—"now." He staggered to the end of the row, opened a closet. Slid a gas mask over his face. By gesture, he ordered the man at the nearest desk to distribute the masks that filled the closet. Brought back masks for Dr. Gallaway and Irene.

Even with the mask on, it took a couple of minutes for the cough and tears to stop. "Where are the attackers?" Irene asked.

None of the camera views showed on the wall.

"Rebooting, sir—madam," answered the man sitting at the nearest UNIVAC computer.

Her breath rasped through her throat. She couldn't unclench her fists. If she weren't the Prophet's Lady, she'd scream. "Get those cameras back online."

Four images splashed onto the wall. Camera one's yellow emergency lights revealed a steady stream of firefighters entering the campus by the main drive. Camera eighteen showed a dimly lit open space—*part of the park or the fighting arena?* The yellow lights that illuminated camera twenty-one displayed the nursery.

"Yes," Dr. Gallaway exclaimed. "The extra generator worked. I must go there at once. There may be some fetuses that need extra oxygen or—"

On screen, a shadow appeared and disappeared. Irene frowned, uncertain if she'd seen anything. Another shadow darted from left to right. "Who is that?"

"Where? Oh. Looks like more firefighters," Dr. Gallaway said.

"They just entered. How'd they get back there so fast?"

"They're your attackers," Victor said.

"Where are your Azrael?"

"Right where they're supposed to be."

Camera twenty-one's view took on the green tint of night vision. Small, lithe forms passed in front of the nursery, followed by the thick and clumsy firefighters.

Warmth spread through Irene. "And you're certain they'll follow instructions?"

"Absolutely." Dr. Gallaway's voice rang with conviction.

She couldn't wait to show Felix what she'd done.

Chapter Sixty-Two

Miranda landed on ground level— *It's not ground level if you're below ground, is it?* She stood in a vacant area between pillars filled with eerie echoes of hooting alarms and dimly lit by distant safety lights. A quick check of the perimeter confirmed no personnel or Azrael awaited.

Within minutes of tapping the code on her radio, the others joined her. The helmet lights, masks, and firemen's bunker gear they all wore made them unrecognizable. Their only distinguishing features were the real firefighters' names fastened to the suits.

Wanda and Gary watched the roadway, and Miranda took a position twenty feet from where Carlos worked.

In no time, he tapped her shoulder, gave her a thumbs-up, then flashed all his fingers. The stink bomb would detonate in ten minutes.

Miranda's pulse ticked up another notch. She nodded, made her way across the dirt to the roadway. Light and dark played tricks, made her misjudge the roadway as smooth. She stumbled across lumps and depressions, made it to the far wall without falling.

Dual emergency lights mounted near the normal-looking ceiling lit the quiet lobby area Miranda and her team entered. Lush hanging plants obscured the frosted glass of the front wall and three group-ings of chrome and green-blue armchairs across the room. A hallway split the back wall in half.

She signaled Wanda and Gary to take the right side of the hall. Carlos followed her. Their assignment was to find documentation of the Fellowship's involvement in and use of the Azrael.

The first office held a standard beige metal desk, four chairs, and metal file cabinets filled with general correspondence and funding requests. Miranda snatched a couple of invoices for liquid oxygen and unusual amounts of other liquids, stuck them in her rucksack. Moved on through the next two offices.

Thumbing through the folders of the file cabinet in the fourth office, she found one labeled Dr. Gunter Huerkamp. Inside, whoever Dr. Huerkamp was, he'd written the letters in German. She waved Carlos close enough they could talk without using their radios.

She touched her faceplate to Carlos's and shouted, "Do you read German?" She held the letter up in front of him.

"German? No. But Gary does." His helmet muffled his voice. "We should take those. He can translate them later."

She removed the other ten letters from the folder, put them into her rucksack. Replaced the empty folder in the file cabinet. Opened the top drawer of the next cabinet.

Curious. Numbers, not names, labeled the folders. She pulled out a file. Stamped on the front cover was the word "terminated."

The student had no name, only a number. The report detailed manipulations, lies, and aggressive behavior as if they were desirable traits. But this student failed because when she witnessed the torture of an unfit person, she exhibited sympathy.

Killed because she had sympathy? Sickened, Miranda slipped the folder inside her rucksack. *How can Irene…? She's the Prophet's wife— willing to sacrifice peace. Me.* Miranda's jaw twitched. She pulled the string closed, slung the bag over her shoulder, and strode out of the room.

She led Carlos down the hall, finished searching the rest of the offices. Met Wanda and Gary at the end of the hall.

Miranda gestured her question.

Wanda waved her hands over one another. *Nothing found.*

Outside of the building, Miranda led them into a park-like area between massive stone pillars. The intermittent flashes of light from emergency lights were so far apart, they needed their helmet lights.

Even dulled by her helmet, the *wah-wah* of the siren drove her pulse faster.

According to the map, another enormous building stood about one hundred yards to her ten o'clock. Bathed in light one moment and ebony ink the next, she didn't trust her vision. The siren made her doubt her hearing too. She and her team moved forward, ready for an ambush. They took turns pivoting and covering their backs.

Sweat trickled down her face. Stung her eyes and tickled her nose. Taut nerves and muscles ached with readiness for action. *This is too easy.* She'd expected resistance from a security team or the Azrael by now.

A large, dark rectangular shape came into view. No wonder she couldn't see the building earlier. *No lights. No lights? Crap. It's a trap.* She whirled.

Her helmet light revealed one of her team struggling with an almost invisible foe.

A tiny flash of light in the corner of Miranda's eye sent her pulse soaring. She drew her gun, stepped to the side, and spun.

An Azrael lunged toward her. Fast.

With her left arm, Miranda blocked the Azrael's blow inches from her chest. A blow struck her right wrist. She lost her gun. *Where is it?*

Something tugged down her right sleeve. She blocked the Azrael's next blow. Drew her own knife. Drove the blade toward the Azrael. The Azrael blocked her.

Miranda feigned collapse. Swept her left hand across the concrete for her gun.

The Azrael took a half-step forward, bent to slash at Miranda.

Miranda slashed the Azrael's mask.

The Azrael coughed and dipped one knee. Slashed and ripped Miranda's pants. Leaped up.

Miranda grabbed the Azrael's knife hand by the wrist.

The Azrael gripped Miranda's right wrist.

They fell to the floor. Rolled.

The Azrael coughed and coughed. Loosened her grip on Miranda.

Miranda drove her knife through muscle and deep into the dark angel's side.

The Azrael worked her mouth soundlessly. Fell to the ground. Blood bubbled between her lips.

Miranda yanked her knife out and rose to one knee. Looked for her gun. Found it. Scanned for her teammates.

At her twelve o'clock, about fifteen feet away, a firefighter exchanged parries with an Azrael. *Wanda?*

Two more firefighters grappled with an Azrael each. One at two o'clock. One at six.

Bang! The gun's retort echoed, made it impossible to tell who shot it.

The firefighter tackled the Azrael. Forced her gun hand over her head. They struggled. The gun waved over their heads.

Miranda sprinted toward them. Plowed into the side of the Azrael. Drove her to the ground.

The Azrael's head bounced on the concrete drive. She convulsed once and was still.

Don't leave an enemy until you know he won't get up. Miranda fired. The bullet entered through the Azrael's eye.

Miranda leaped off the dying girl and spun back to help the others.

One firefighter turtled. The Azrael leaped on top of the firefighter. They rolled across the road. The Azrael rolled over. *No.* The firefighter pushed her over, then lay still.

Miranda cast a glance up and down the road. *Clear.*

She dashed to the Azrael. Shot her in the chest. Kneeled at the fallen firefighter's side. Peered through the face shield at Wanda's sweat-streaked face.

"Are you hurt?"

Wanda sucked in a big breath. Shook her head. "Only—winded."

Miranda turned in time to see her fourth teammate take down the Azrael he fought. Ragged breathing filled her helmet. Thunder rolled in her temples.

Finger on the trigger, she scanned for more enemies. Ready to shoot—to kill more enemies.

Her muscles quivered. She stiffened. *Oh, dear God.* She closed her eyes. *I went blood simple. Beryl said that can happen during a battle.* She pushed her breath out in short bursts. *Gotta get control…* She set her jaw, opened her eyes.

Gary reached them, offered Wanda a hand, brought her to her feet.

Carlos joined them. Blood seeped between his gloved fingers, pressed to his shoulder.

"How bad?"

"Might need a stitch or two later," he said in a pain-strained tone.

Her entire team was blood-spattered and heaving for breath. But they all had survived.

Four bodies lay strewn about. Four dead Azrael.

Nausea burned the back of Miranda's throat. *Not going to lose it. Not now.* She clenched her teeth. *This is being a soldier. The way of real —of lasting peace.* She steadied her breathing. *We're not done. There will be more.* She raised her arm, motioned forward. "They know we're here now," she whispered into her radio. "Stay sharp."

Chapter Sixty-Three

Beryl followed the real firefighter further into the underground warehouse. Inside, a deafening siren whooped. Amber safety lights in the ceiling created islands of light that flashed on and off as the light rotated.

The firefighters had arrived to search for "innocent" victims of a "mysterious gas leak." *As if anyone could be innocent.* Only the top-ranking firefighters knew the gas leak was a ruse and that there were SABR soldiers dressed as firemen in their ranks.

Her official job was to save innocents by destroying the Azrael. All she wanted to do was destroy every damn Azrael on the planet. And the quacks who grew them.

She forced herself to slow down, keep the fireman's pace, and fought the illusion that her eyes had adjusted to the dark.

They reached another dock.

Two firemen raced up the stairs, grabbed the chains on each side of the closed garage door and pulled. The chains rattled, the metal door groaned and opened onto an empty warehouse.

Her inner warning system screamed louder than the *whoop-whoop* of the gas detector alarm. With one hand on her pistol grip, she crouched, ready for an ambush. But no shadow moved. No guns blasted. Sweat dampened her undershirt.

The radio crackled. "Team India entering building G seven seventy-six. That's Golf seven-seven-six."

A handful of firefighters tromped up the steps and into the space.

Beryl watched them disappear into the dark. Other than the sound of her own breathing, she heard nothing. No attack. No screams. Nothing.

Ahead of her, the line of remaining firefighters split. Half trooped west. Half marched north.

Beryl continued north, toward the nursery. Walked the long raven-black subterranean roadway. Between pillars, the amber safety light muddied until the shadows swallowed it.

The space between safety lights stretched, forced them to use helmet lights.

They came to a T in the roadway—*the dead end*. She radioed the captain, "Unit six-four-one and team will take this one."

"Unit six-four-one taking Main C-fifteen," the voice on the radio repeated. Static scrambled the next voice, repeating the information. They'd repeat that from line-of-sight radio to line-of-sight radio over and over, all the way back to the entry drive. Eventually, it would reach Ethan.

She turned off her headlamp and changed the radio to her team frequency. And, much against her preferences, fulfilled her team-player role and waited.

A helmet light approached. "Unit four-seven-three accounted for."

Of course Karl is the first. She answered with a quick on and off of her flashlight.

Something about Karl made her want to punch him. She would have thought him the traitor, but Ethan trusted him. And so far Karl had pulled his weight. She still didn't trust him one hundred percent. Didn't like him. *But no one ever said you had to like your fellow soldier.*

Ed came next, then Trey.

She led them toward the vent-covered tunnel opening.

On either side of them, the spaces between pillars were unfinished and dark.

Without the fan noise, the cave was utterly quiet. The sound of her own breathing filled her helmet and her ears.

Her headlamp pierced the light-eating blackness. Anything, anyone could be beyond her headlamp's reach and she wouldn't know. She hand-signaled her team to fan out across the road. She walked the road's centerline.

The radio squawked. *Shh-shh.* Brought her up short. *What's that supposed to mean?* She reached for her mike.

The radio erupted with static. "This is Team India. We're under attack."

She drew her pistols and eyed the shadows.

"India needs our help," Ed radioed.

"Too far," Karl said.

"Cut the chatter," Beryl said in her harshest tone.

The safety lights overhead flickered once, twice, blinked out. The fire alarms stopped shrieking.

Her ears rang, and her heart sped into overdrive. *They're onto us.* She pressed her mike button on and off in the pattern that meant *keep your eyes open.*

There. The light from her helmet caught the vent cover that opened onto the tunnel. She pointed.

Ten feet ahead of her, shadows rose from the roadway. Stood, arms and legs spread. Seven Azrael road-blocked the forty feet between pillars, blocked the tunnel entrance.

A wave of déjà vu washed over Beryl. Her breath caught, trapped by a ribcage rigid with the pain of killing her own daughter over and over.

A scream came from her far left. A man charged the line of Azrael, firing wildly.

The rock walls amplified the bang of his pistol to deafening.

The line of Azrael charged toward them.

Beryl raised her guns. *I won't let them stop us.* She pulled both triggers, watched two Azrael fall and two more spring up in replacement.

Out of bullets too soon, Beryl fell back behind the main line of defense. Echoing guns blasting from both sides deafened her. She slammed her second quick-load device into her gun's cylinder.

Someone slammed into Beryl.

An Azrael.

Beryl blocked the Azrael's wicked combat knife inches from her neck.

The Azrael grabbed Beryl's right wrist.

Beryl allowed the girl to push her wrist down but swung her pistol back up toward the Azrael's stomach and fired twice.

The Azrael took a step back, then slumped to the ground.

Beryl put a bullet in the center of the girl's chest and one in her head. Whirled.

In the center of the road, one of her men grappled with an Azrael.

Beryl aimed, but at this distance she couldn't tell her man and the Azrael apart.

Another Azrael materialized, rammed Beryl into the pillar. Her hip bounced off the concrete skirt of the pillar. Her right elbow slammed against rough rock. Her hand went numb. She lost her pistol.

The Azrael latched onto her left wrist. Tried to make Beryl drop her second gun.

Beryl brought her numb, right fist down on her attacker's head.

The Azrael stumbled to her knees, scrambled in loose dirt.

Beryl placed three shots in the Azrael's chest, twisted to face the roadway.

It was vacant.

She tried to quiet her ragged breathing. Listened.

Karl? Ed? Trey? Her ears rang. She couldn't hear anything else, not even radio static.

The ringing in her ears faded. Her breathing steadied. She didn't dare use her headlamp or flashlight, but without light she couldn't tell bodies from bumps in the road.

Across the road, a black form stumbled onto the roadway. A flashlight flicked on and off, on and off, spelled his name.

Karl. Bet he still can't hear. On the move, she clicked her flashlight on and off, signaled him her identity. Zigzagged toward him.

They met in the middle of the road.

She touched her helmet to his, yelled, "Ed? Trey?"

"They didn't make it."

Damn. "We've a job to finish."

Chapter Sixty-Four

Annabelle ignored the wail of sirens that echoed across the underground campus. She whirled, faced the next fire-fighter. Looped her garrote around his head, twisted it, and kicked his axe out of reach. It skittered across the asphalt road toward the school and into the utter dark between security lights. This firefighter hardly resisted. She choked the life out of him and let him drop to the ground.

The siren wails and dark of the underground campus receded, replaced by the light that lifted her. She raised her face, threw her arms back, and basked in that exalted place. Her angel within crowed.

The light didn't last, but a surge of renewed energy filled her. She marveled at the Lord's gifts. She had just made it back into her bunk, and a call to Assembly had wakened her. Hasty assignments and a vague threat she'd suspected were an exercise turned out to feed her angel within.

She bent and removed her garotte from the neck of her attacker. Wiped the sinner's blood from it, coiled it, returned it to her pocket. Rubbed tears from her burning eyes, grateful that the stench had lessened enough that she could breathe easier.

Whisk-whisk, whisk-whisk. Footsteps. *Another intruder?* Her ears warmed, and she left the roadway. Climbed to the rough ground behind the nearest pillar.

The captains of the Seraphim came out of the dark, surrounded her. They held no weapons. But their circle closed around her.

A trick—a hazing? Now? Annabelle stood, knees slightly flexed, combat knife in hand.

"We ask you, why has the Lord allowed sinners to best our sisters?"

Annabelle tried to read their unreadable faces. "Why ask me?"

"You are the Resurrected," Anna 2001 stated.

They are up to something, but it is not a fight. Annabelle relaxed her stance, sheathed her knife. "Our Prophet brought me back from death. So yes, I was resurrected."

"I ask again, why do sinners best our sisters?"

She heaved an impatient sigh. "Because we take orders from sinners who say they speak for Him." Her throat tightened. She spoke truth, but feared her not-sisters weren't ready for it.

One after the other, the captains took a knee. "You are the Chosen," they chorused.

Annabelle eyed them warily. "What do you mean?"

Anna 2001 gazed up at her. "Our earthly father, Dr. Gallaway, and his servants are—of earth. We obey them. But you are the Resurrected, the Chosen. Our Father above sent you. We pledge ourselves to you and through you renew our pledge to our Father in heaven."

Nonplussed, Annabelle's remaining tension vanished. *They see me. My purpose.* She gave them a brief benevolent smile, then hardened her face. Stood tall, taller than a teacher. "Rise. Never kneel before anyone but our Prophet and our Lord."

The Annas rose. Waited for her next words.

Her heart lifted and her angel within sang exultations.

"I am the Resurrected," she said. "The Chosen. Hear me. Dr. Gallaway is many things, but he cannot lead us in this war. Report your troop's current status so I may lead us to victory for our Lord."

Anna 2001 said, "I have four squads. All have suffered casualties. They cover A Sector."

The main entrance. Annabelle favored her with a nod. "Next?"

Each captain reported at least one casualty and told of orders Annabelle considered ill-conceived. They were drill decisions, not combat decisions.

"We need more information," Annabelle said. "Where is Dr. Gallaway?"

"In Command and Control."

"Take us there."

Chapter Sixty-Five

Pistol drawn, Miranda stopped inside the doorway of the subterranean building. A total absence of noise from equipment or people or even birds and bugs turned the sweat that had gathered under her fireman's bunker cold. Only one safety light at this end of the building.

She signaled her team. Wanda entered, stopped at the hallway entrance, and waited. Gary leapfrogged ahead of her and Carlos behind him.

Miranda rotated to the front, opened the first door. Neat rows of student desks faced a teacher's desk and a wall-to-wall greenboard. She couldn't take her eyes off the greenboard.

On it, a chalk map of the underground complex was full of arrows and circles. Arrows and circles that duplicated what Peter had drawn this morning. SABR's plan of attack. She sucked in a breath. The hairs on the back of her neck lifted. *There's a traitor amongst us.*

Wanda, Gary, and Carlos stood beside her, as transfixed as she was.

Gary's gloved fists clenched and unclenched.

Who betrayed us?

"They know where we came in," Wanda whispered. "Where we were going. Why didn't they try to stop us?"

Miranda managed not to stare at her teammates. *Not Wanda. Carlos? Gary? Someone else?* "We have to assume they will," she said.

"We should warn Monkshood." Wanda's whisper held tightly controlled anger.

"We need find out *who* betrayed us…what their plan is." Miranda couldn't tell if either man acted guilty or afraid. No longer trusting them, she kept everyone together.

She took the lead and searched every classroom and closet. Found an assembly hall and a music room, but no people and nothing about attacking SABR.

Past the music room, a fire door opened onto the long hall of another wing of the building. There were fewer doors in this wing, and they were unlabeled and staggered.

This is taking too long. Maybe Gary or Carlos will betray the other if I split them up. She trusted Wanda would understand why, then split them into two teams. Wanda and Gary would search the west side. She and Carlos would be on the east side.

Miranda burst through the first door and into an unoccupied, one-room apartment. With helmet light only, she searched the space while trying to monitor Carlos. Among the functional furniture and clothing, the only personal item was a pair of blue knitting needles and four inches of a pink unfinished project.

All the apartments had the same impersonal decor. She opened the door to the sixth and final apartment on her side of the hall. Caught a faint scent of perfume, White Shoulders. She stiffened. *Is Irene here?* Miranda scoffed. Shook her head at her paranoia. *Millions of women like that perfume.*

An unpacked suitcase lay open on the twin bed. It held women's clothing, expensive women's clothing.

Carlos picked up something that glinted silver.

Miranda moved in for a closer look. Set in a plain silver frame was a photograph of Irene and Felix standing behind two young girls. A sinking sensation swept over Miranda. *Irene* is *here. Why?*

Sandra had grown, had to be seven or eight by now. The dark-haired girl must be a friend. Felix hadn't changed. Irene… Blood pounded in Miranda's temples. *I believed you wanted peace.* She ground her teeth. *Did you move here before or after causing the deaths of those men?*

She noticed Carlos watching her. Signaled him to search the

kitchen area. Once he'd moved away, she yanked the top desk drawer open. A tray held pens, a pair of scissors, a letter opener. Topping a stack of the Prophet's official stationery was a single sheet with Irene's familiar handwriting.

Miranda picked up the paper titled Things I Must Do.

The first item, Convert Miranda, had a line through it.

Miranda dropped the paper onto the desk. Clenched and unclenched her fists. *I was such a fool. She never wanted peace.*

Movement caught her eye. Carlos approached her. She tilted her head toward the bathroom. He hesitated then followed her direction.

Miranda picked the paper up again, continued reading.

K report only to me.

Take control of the Azrael.

Present captured rebel leaders to Council.

Make those who judge me for Annabelle's skin color beg forgiveness.

I will be in the history books as the Prophet's Lady who defeated the rebels. It is my God-given destiny.

Miranda's chest hollowed. The paper rattled in her trembling hands. *Wanda's right, we have to tell Ethan. K—report about—? Is K one of us? K for Keith? Katherine? Karl?*

But Karl is one of Ethan's lieutenants. Ethan trusts him. And Karl sided with me when I wanted to stop looking for the lab. Her stomach dropped. *He knew how to contact Irene.*

Ice balled up deep inside. Her vision clouded. She gripped the edge of the desk. *I confided in him.* She tried to remember exactly what she'd said. Icy tendrils reached from the inside out. *He's on Beryl's team. I've got to warn her. Warn her backup team—* She caught her breath. *Nick. Dear God, Nick and his team are her backup.*

How? Karl will hear a radio relay. What if there is more than one traitor? Gotta think. I can warn Beryl and Nick or Ethan. Can't do both. Only one other person I can trust right now.

She signaled the team to meet at the exit.

Huddled them together so they could hear her without using the radio. "Pairing up is too slow. We need to split up. Each of us take a building. Meet at pillar eighty-one-ninety in ten minutes." She assigned the two men buildings on one side of the roadway. Assigned herself and Wanda the buildings on this side.

Carlos and Greg trotted down the road toward their assignments. She waited until the darkness swallowed them.

Miranda caught up with Wanda. Tapped her on the shoulder.

Wanda jumped. "What?"

Miranda told her about Irene's list and her plan. "We can't trust anyone else." She chewed her lower lip. It would be much longer and more dangerous to warn Ethan. "I'll warn Monkshood. You go warn Beryl."

"No." Wanda put a hand on her shoulder. "You need to be the one to warn Beryl. I'll go to Monkshood."

Throat tight, Miranda shook her head. "It's too dangerous. They'll be guarding the entrance."

Wanda smirked. "And no one's guarding the nursery? Go. Warn Beryl."

"All right." Miranda gripped Wanda's forearm. "Be safe."

Chapter Sixty-Six

Miranda's helmet light reflected off white rock and brick walls ten feet away. It didn't reach the next pillar. *Why aren't there any safety lights?*

Her ears tried to fill the silence with an inside-a-deep-well hum, and her skin twitched under phantom caresses. She swallowed and moved forward as quickly as she could.

To her left, her headlamp couldn't penetrate the undeveloped space any more than a candle would. Something moved. She sucked in a breath and stared at the formless, motionless black. *A trick of my eyes.* She breathed easier.

Her light revealed a hunched yellow shape. She drew her gun. Advanced. It was a push blade for clearing roads. *What is it doing here all by itself?*

Got to move faster. Quit giving in to the brain, trying to see something that isn't there.

A rumbling sound came from all around her. Triggered her pulse to bullet speed.

She hurried to the next pillar, pressed into its shadows, and scanned for the source of the sound. *A train? A car?* Ten seconds. Twenty. Thirty.

The sound stopped. She waited another fifteen seconds. A tinny ringing filled her ears. But the rumble had gone.

Can't keep stopping. I've got to get to Beryl. She walked faster.

Scritch-scritch. Scritch-scritch.

The back of her neck prickled. She wished she believed that a mouse made that noise. Breathing hard, she combed the area with her helmet light. Only found the monotonous rock walls and darkness between pillars.

Sweaty and shaky and still breathing too hard, she stopped with her back to the next pillar. Tried to steady herself. Held her breath.

Crunch, crunch, crunch. The soft, rhythmic sound stopped.

Someone is following me. She took four loud steps, paused, and listened.

The *crunch-crunch* stopped one step after she did.

Her chest tingled. She turned her helmet light off. Everything went black.

She tried to slow her breathing. Couldn't. Put her right hand on the rock of the pillar and kept walking. Reached the end of the pillar.

Where's a security light when you need one?

She waved her hand in the void. Took a dozen steps.

Bang!

Miranda ducked and ran, arms outstretched.

The gunfire continued. It was close but not near her. She couldn't tell the exact direction because of the echo. But she knew. *Beryl and Nick are in trouble.*

Her radio hissed and clicked. *Team November?* Her chest hollowed. *They ambushed Nick.* She flicked on her helmet light. The pillar in front of her was number ninety-nine, seventy-one. *Almost there.* She moved faster.

A hundred feet or more down the road, a security light spotlighted a human figure dashing across the road. She pointed her gun downfield, but realized he wore a fireman's bunker.

Another firefighter followed. Then a third figure darted out, leaped onto the firefighter.

They rolled on the ground in a strenuous, silent struggle. Miranda ran toward them.

She aimed her pistol at one, then the other, uncertain which was foe or friend.

One figure stood with his back to Miranda.

The other figure writhed on the ground.

The one standing blocked Miranda's view of the fallen one.

The standing figure whirled, advanced toward the shadows as if following the first man.

Security or Azrael didn't matter. Miranda fired. More to drive the assailant away than to kill.

Instead of focusing on her, firing on her, the figure kept going. Vanished in the dark.

Miranda crouched beside the fallen firefighter in the middle of the road. Scanned for enemies. The silence was unnerving. Trembling, she turned the body over. Peered into the mask.

Dead brown eyes stared up at her. She puffed out three rapid breaths. *Not Nick. Or Beryl.* One of Nick's team, if she remembered right. The shakes made her weak.

"Nightshade? Where are you?" she called in a loud whisper. "Anyone?" Nick didn't answer. No one did.

She aimed her helmet light at the wall. Someone sprawled on the asphalt.

It took her two tries to stand. Stiff-legged, she trudged to the body. It lay face down. A red blossom center mass.

Ragged breathing filled her ears.

Please don't be Nick.

Or Beryl.

She kneeled. Rolled the man over.

Oh. Oh. The pain in her chest robbed her of breath. Her eyes filled. "Nick," she whispered. "Open your eyes, Nick. It's me."

His eyes were closed. His expression blank. No fear. No pain. No awareness.

It hurt to breathe. She shook him gently. "Nick, please."

His head rolled loosely.

She lay her head on his chest. His still, deathly quiet chest.

No. No. No. Her heart dropped to somewhere she'd never find it again. She gasped huge, ragged breaths. Shook as if she lay naked in a snowbank. *I'm sorry. I'm so so sorry. You were right, and I was wrong. I should have told you. I want to live in that cottage with you—to grow old with you. I want—I...*

She couldn't move. Couldn't see or hear. An emptiness entered. Emptiness and pain.

Pain deeper and darker than anything she'd ever experienced.

Someone grabbed her arm and yanked.

She couldn't let go of Nick.

Bang-bang-bang.

"Miranda. We have to get out of here." Wanda's grip tightened.

Miranda tilted her head. Her mouth dropped open. *I must be hallucinating. I sent Wanda in the other direction.*

Bullets zinged overhead. Shards of rock showered them.

"Damn it." Wanda lost her grip. "That hurts."

"Where did you come from?"

Pistol still in her right hand, Wanda clutched her left thigh. Her mouth moved, but a barrage of bullets drowned her out.

"No." Miranda rose and fired at the shadows. "You can't have her. Run, Wanda, run."

Chapter Sixty-Seven

Annabelle threw the door open with a bang and strode into Command and Control, scanned the room. The room, shaped like half a bowl, reeked with the sour stink of men. Rows of men at desks worked on UNIVAC computers. Three rows on separate tiers, each one lower than the next, divided by a central aisle. The computer men were not threats. Neither was—*Mother?* She stood in the center of the bottom of the bowl between Dr. Gallaway and a man with a soldier's bearing.

"What are you doing here?" the soldier man asked in an imperious tone. "Why aren't you at your stations?"

"I, the Chosen, am taking command." A simple statement.

"Anna 3000?" Dr. Gallaway's voice was tight.

"Annabelle—" Mother didn't move.

The soldier-man scowled, strode up to the second tier. "You will return to your stations at once or suffer the consequences."

Annabelle moved to the center of the top tier. Looked down at the soldier-man. "No man may command us. We are Azrael, the instruments of God."

The soldier-man charged up toward her.

She shot him.

His lifeless body thumped to the floor, slid down one step, and stilled.

Shouts of startlement chorused. The men at the desks leaped to their feet, pressed their backs to the nearest wall or cowered beneath their desks.

Dr. Gallaway bent at the soldier-man's side a moment, then stood, took a step toward her. "Anna 3000, Annabelle, it is God's will that we help you."

Annabelle waved her hand, and one of her Seraphim appeared at Dr. Gallaway's side, her weapon trained on him.

A second one took an identical position at Mother's side.

"Annabelle?" Mother sounded uncertain.

"We are the Resurrected, the Chosen One. We are God's will."

Mother put a hand to her chest, and her eyes glowed like she was proud of Annabelle.

She wasn't proud of the game I played with Sandra less than a week ago.

Dr. Gallaway opened and closed his mouth, then dipped his head.

Realization lifted her, left her breathless. *God has opened her eyes. The Doctor's too. They see me, the Chosen.*

Annabelle swept the room with a benevolent smile. "He who can educate me will be blessed."

They all avoided eye contact with her.

Her blood blazed. *Cowards. Which one do I kill?*

"Ahem. Annabelle? May your mother have a word with you?"

Annabelle smiled. "You may."

Mother's pink tongue licked her lips, but she did not speak. Her posture and face conveyed confidence, but fear glinted deep in her eyes.

"You are my earthly mother. No harm will come to you. Speak."

Wariness replaced the fear. "What I have to say is for you and you alone."

Annabelle swept down, past the dead man, to the bottom of the bowl and took Mother's icy hand. Led her to the corner of the room. Light from the images played across Mother's face, turned it into a monstrous mask like a child shining a flashlight from under her chin. "What is it, Mother?"

"These men fear for their lives. You are Azrael." She gestured at the Seraphim. "You don't need weapons. Set them aside. Get rid of the body. Show these men they are safe. That they can trust you." Mother's lips curved upward. "Then ask about the tracking systems." Mother's eyes glittered. "With the right information and the right strategy, we—you—can stop these rebels forever."

Annabelle scanned the men. Pale, sweaty, and wide-eyed. *Mother is right.* She raised her voice. "Put away your weapons." She pointed at two of the Seraphim. "Take the body away."

One grabbed the man's shoulders and the other his feet. They carried him out of the room.

Annabelle smiled, turned her palms up and raised her arms in front of her, spread her arms to embrace all within the room. "Please, sit down, gentlemen. You have nothing to fear. Continue your good work." *Mother says thank you is a powerful word.* "Thank you."

Slowly, the men moved away from the walls and returned to their desks. Chairs clanked and scraped the floor. They quieted and settled into place.

Still smiling, Annabelle tilted her head and asked the men, "Who will show me what these machines do?"

"I—I w-will," stammered a young man who came out from under a desk next to the center aisle of the first row. He brushed his blond hair out of his eyes.

She crossed over to him, sat in his chair.

He took a chair from the next workstation.

The two Seraphim returned.

"See that we are not interrupted," Annabelle said. Then she watched the young man work the machine.

The cameras recorded real-time action, but the machines also could identify authorized personnel. A map of the campus speckled with a rainbow of dots appeared on the wall. Sprinkles of purple Azrael dots appeared across the map. Administration's orange dots clustered here in the control room. Yellow worker dots filled the cantina. And the green scientists and blue teachers clumped inside the research building at the end of campus.

"The red dots, they are the intruders attacking my Azrael?"

"Yes."

Red dots came up the main road and through the docks. More clustered in the school building, near the killing field, and in the nursery's escape tunnel.

"Camera views." Her finger touched the school building, the killing field, and the escape tunnel on the screen in front of her.

"You heard her," the young man next to her said to the room. "Let's show her what we can do."

Keyboards clacked. Images flickered across the wall.

Here and there, the cameras revealed small groups of firefighters.

"That's her. That's Miranda." Mother's voice shook. "Camera eighteen."

In the school building? Did she find our plan? "Shall I order her death, Mother?"

"No." Mother swallowed. "I mean, I'm sure you will use leaders like Miranda for the Lord's purpose."

His will be done. She addressed her Seraphim. "You know the faces of the rebel leaders. Take them alive."

"And the others, my Chosen One?"

"Send the sinners to hell."

Chapter Sixty-Eight

Filled with the pulse of machines, Beryl figured the tunnel was either a cocoon of safety or the claustrophobic closet of hell. She wanted to burst through the vent into the lab, but the ambush at the tunnel's entrance called for caution. She peered through the vent slats.

The red amorphous bags hanging in the semi-dark room made her blood run so hot, so intense, it chilled her. No human shapes appeared. She drew both her pistols, pushed the vent door open, and stepped out and to the side.

Still no one? They expected their little ambush to stop me. Now they'll learn the error of their thinking.

"We'll split up," she whispered. "Search for the control center." But Karl hadn't followed her out. "Karl?"

Bent over, Karl backed out of the tunnel, pulled a body behind him. "Sorry I'm late."

He dragged the dead Azrael out onto the floor. Her head thudded against the floor. "She came out of that last alcove right after you passed."

Beryl grunted her thanks. *Did I underestimate him?* "I'll look for the control center. You secure this room." She took three strides, realized Karl followed her. Her internal alarms raised the hairs on her neck. "It'll be faster if we split up."

"When our team is down to two, it's only faster if there are no more Azrael lying in wait."

She opened her mouth to insist, then pressed her lips closed. The facility was two pillars deep by six long. Sixty feet between each pillar. *It's a lot of ground to cover. And he doesn't want to split up? What's he up to? Maybe it's best to keep him where I can watch him. If he poses a problem I can't handle, I'll call my backup team. Nick should have his team covering the entrances to this place.* "Okay," she said. "Keep up." She trotted down the aisle.

———

BERYL HAD EXPECTED to find the control room in the center of the facility. It wasn't.

They searched the north wall, then started down the long west wall.

In the southwest corner, they found a door standing open.

She dashed inside, ready to shoot. Stopped short inside the vacant control room.

Loaded with computers and a wall of gauges and switches, the room hummed. The lights were dim, the computer screens dark, and the door on the opposite wall was closed. The scientists or controllers hadn't left in an obvious hurry. Hypercautious, she crossed the room, checked under and behind each vacant desk.

The smell sent them all running? Scientists *didn't recognize the odor of ammonia? They left their precious Azrael farm?* She couldn't believe they trusted their machines that much. Didn't see signs of a trap. But her inner alarms shrieked and her back prickled as if she were watched.

Red, yellow, and green dials on the wall of gauges showed levels of liquid oxygen, ammonia, and amino acids. All necessary to keep those abominations in the red sacs alive. "Destroy it," she told Karl. "Everything." It was the only way to be certain.

A thick conduit pipe ran down the corner of the room. The primary power line. She gave a determined grimace. *My bunker will protect me.* She swung her axe in a powerful arc. It bit through the conduit and into the wall. Sparks flew. The lights went out.

The axe stuck in the wall. She released it and stumbled backward into a desk. Grinned at Karl except… Her chest tightened. He wasn't there. He wasn't anywhere in the room. *Where did he go? Why? Did he go investigate something? Why didn't he say something? Warn me?*

Rows of intact gauges showed green lights on Karl's half of the wall. *He didn't even try to smash—*

Wait, Green lights? The prickles on her back multiplied. *How can they be green? I cut the power.* She wrapped her hands around the grips of her pistols, but didn't draw them. Turned a slow three-sixty. Nothing looked out of place.

Her gaze came back to her axe, still stuck in the wall. *No matter what Karl's up to, no matter why, the scientists all left. I will finish this. And if he has betrayed me and shoots me in the back, at least I destroyed this batch.*

She yanked her axe out of the wall. Smashed it against the rest of the gauges over and over until every damn light was out.

Sweating and huffing for breath, she stepped back, surveyed the damage. Gave a satisfied snort. *No one can put those back together.*

She dropped the axe on the floor. Her exertion-sped heart rate kicked up another notch. *No one tried to stop me.*

She drew her pistols and crept to the door. Opened it a crack. Peered out. "What the hell?" Her mouth dropped open. She strode into the aisle. Stared at the red sacs that seemed unaffected by loss of the control room gauges and power.

She considered ripping each sac open. But that would only stop this batch from growing. *What I would give for a bag of explosives… Gotta be a backup generator. Where? Next door?*

Bang-bang-bang!

The glass cabinet doors shattered behind her.

She dove to the ground. Drew her pistols and pointed them toward the front of the lab. Didn't shoot. Didn't know where to point them. Didn't know how many shooters there were. *Gotta draw them out.* She crawled under the red pseudo-uteri. Under the fifth row of red sac, she punched upward into the bottom of the sac.

Three more shots rang out. *Only one shooter. Karl?* Whoever it was, they avoided hitting a sac, even if it meant missing her. She crept away from the shooter, away from the front door, under red sacs when she could. Took shelter behind a cabinet. Listened. *The lub-dub of the pumps will cover any noises I make if I'm careful.*

The shooter was careful—and patient.

Beryl peered over the top of the cabinet.

Another three shots forced her back down to the floor.

She crept back to the control room and exited through the back door. Stepped into darkness. Sidled along the building, around pillars, to the dimly lit roadway. Turned the corner and froze.

To her right, a shadow—a memory—a here-and-now nightmare strode toward her. *Anna? No. Not my Anna.*

A young girl dressed in black with a long braid across her shoulder aimed a pistol at Beryl's center mass. Deadly joy glittered in her eyes.

I should be dead. Why isn't she shooting? A glance to the left, and Beryl's helmet light illuminated more of her look-alikes. Three of them. *No. Not three. Seven.* Seven little Azrael, shoulder to shoulder, blocking the road.

Hesitation is death. Beryl pulled the triggers of both guns.

Chapter Sixty-Nine

Helmet light off, Miranda emptied her gun, covering their retreat, then ran after Wanda into a forest of pillars, uneven ground, and perpetual midnight.

Bullets sped past them. Pinged on the rock walls. Sharp flecks of limestone pelted her thick firefighter's bunker.

She glanced over her shoulder. Muzzle flashes strobed. Bright, spasming dots filled her already restricted vision. Still, she ran.

Uneven ground pitched her forward. She windmilled her arms. Elbow banged against the rock wall. A hot and cold bolt of electricity blazed from her elbow, zapped her fingers. She clapped her free hand around the numb one and her pistol.

The spots that plagued her vision coalesced into an oval. An oval with familiar features—Nick's. Her chest and throat tightened. A sob escaped her.

She sagged against the rock. The emptiness inside deadened the echoes of gunshots around her, deadened her skin, deadened her.

She sank to the ground. Hugged her knees. *I should have known… should have stayed on the Lady…*

"Miranda? Where are you?" The harsh, nearby whisper penetrated the paralyzing shroud around her.

She flicked her flashlight on and off.

Wanda limped to her. "You…okay?" she asked, gasping.

"Yeah," she lied.

"We have to get out of this cave. Warn the others."

Her paralysis returned. "It's too late. They've been two steps ahead of us this whole time."

Wanda leaned over, touched her helmet to Miranda's. "Are you the same captain who taught me that there are some things that are worth fighting for?"

I didn't know then. I didn't know what it did to a person. "I'm not a soldier like Nick or Beryl." *Leave me alone.*

"You've saved countless refugees because you believed they deserved a better life."

"I'm tired of running. Of fighting and losing. Of…" *Death. Didn't know this pain.* She wanted to curl into a ball.

"Of course you're tired." Wanda took a breath. "No one said this would be easy." Another breath. "The cost is high. Sometimes it's personal. But the cost of not fighting is higher, isn't it?"

The cost of not fighting… Sharp as a blade, Wanda's words twisted inside Miranda. She'd lived unaware of the fight while people like Nick and Wanda and Leslie lost homes, careers, and loved ones. *All those losses… Nick….*

"We can't"—gasp—"give up." Wanda stopped, winded.

Oh, God. Don't die, Wanda. Not you too. "You're right," Miranda said aloud. "Let's go." She put Wanda's left arm over her shoulder. Supported as much of Wanda's weight as she could and moved as fast as possible. But with every step, Miranda bore more and more of her friend's weight. *I have to find a safe place for Wanda to rest.*

She carried Wanda and her loss the same way she'd carried old nuggets of regret, resentment, and rage. Her stomach hardened against the pressure. Wanda's ragged breathing, harsh through the radio, lit a smoldering fire that burned the back of Miranda's throat.

Hanging onto Wanda's belt, Miranda dragged her past two pillars and turned right. At the end of the second pillar, she found the road. Across the road was a wall of concrete blocks. *Shelter?*

She followed the wall, turned right at the corner pillar, found a door. *Unlocked, thank God.*

Inside, she helped Wanda to the floor, then flipped on her flashlight. Bunk beds lined the walls to the right and left as far as she could see.

Across the room, a pistol appeared above a stack of mattresses. "Freeze."

Miranda raised her hands. "Don't shoot."

"Miranda?"

The voice, distorted by Miranda's helmet, sounded familiar. "Who are you?"

A figure rose from behind the mattresses. A firefighter. She removed her helmet, switched its light on, and aimed it at her own face. "It's Leslie." She waved them forward. "Quick. Get behind here."

Miranda half lifted Wanda to a stand. Carried more of her weight than before and moved her to a position behind the mattresses.

"Wanda's shot." Helmet light on, Miranda took the pocketknife from her belt. Slit Wanda's pants open. Blood flowed out. Puddled on the floor.

Leslie crawled to Wanda's side. Examined her leg. "Through and through." She pulled a small box out of her utility belt. Padded and wrapped Wanda's wound with gauze.

Wanda continued to gasp for breath. Barely reacted to Leslie's ministrations. Or the faint whining that grew louder and set Miranda's teeth on edge.

Wanda's low air alarm. Miranda jerked Wanda's mask off.

Wanda gasped. Coughed. Hard.

Miranda checked the time. *Uh-oh.* She checked her air own tank's gauge. *I'm out too.* She took off her mask and tank. Her eyes stung. Ammonia burned her nose and the back of her throat. She coughed and couldn't stop.

"Breathe through your mouth," Leslie said. "You'll get used to it in a few minutes."

"Where's David?" Miranda choked out.

"We got separated."

"How long ago?" Mouth breathing helped.

"Forty-five minutes." She cocked her head at Miranda and Wanda. "What are you doing in section D?"

Miranda exchanged a glance with Wanda. "The Azrael have an exact copy of our attack plan."

Leslie gave her a wide-eyed look of alarm. "But that would mean—"

"Yes. Someone on the inside," Miranda said. "I was on my way to warn Nick"—she swallowed, ignored the mental images of his pale still face—"and Beryl. Wanda was going to warn Monkshood." *Ethan.* "Did you?" she asked Wanda. "Warn him? Why were you at the nursery?"

"Security kept forcing me to turn back," Wanda said, almost sounding like herself again. "I couldn't see them, so it could have been Azrael or Second Sphere—or maybe it was all of them. They were at every intersection."

Miranda leaned forward. "They shot at you but didn't hit you until—you got to me at the nursery?"

"Well, yeah," Wanda said. "I was running, sticking to the shadows."

"But they killed Nick."

Wanda gave Miranda a startled look. "They *should* have killed me." She stared miles past Miranda. "Should've killed *us.*"

"It was like they were herding you somewhere, wasn't it?" Leslie asked.

Wanda sat back. "Exactly."

"Why? Why keep the three of us alive and bring us here?"

"I don't know, but we've been following their lead." Miranda set her jaw, knotted her fists. "Not anymore. We're getting out of here."

"The only way out of here is through that door. And they shoot every time I open it."

"Haven't heard gunfire since we came inside." Miranda crept around the mattresses and across the room. Eased the door open.

Nothing happened.

She nudged the door with her toe.

A barrage of gunfire erupted. Sprayed into the concrete block walls and the door. Chips of concrete flew.

Miranda slammed the door shut and flattened against the wall. The heat of run-or-fight energy fired through her. "We will *not* die here. We will find a way out."

"You don't think I've been trying to find one?" Leslie said. Three rapid, forceful sighs burst from her lips.

Miranda swept her flashlight across the ceiling and down the row of beds. She spotlighted the black metal lockers between bunks. The black lockers with the red-numbered Fellowship Shield on them.

"This is an Azrael dormitory," Wanda murmured.

Staring at the lockers, Miranda had a crazy idea. *They can't all be little kids, can they?* She darted to the first locker. Opened it. "What if we didn't look like firefighters?" Miranda held out the black even-too-small-for-Leslie jumpsuit. "We disguise ourselves and walk right past them."

"Two problems with that plan," Leslie said. "One—the Azrael outside know we aren't Azrael. And two—our people will shoot at us. And they won't miss."

Miranda gave her a grim smile. "Then we'll have to be careful, won't we?"

Chapter Seventy

Irene worried her thumbnail with her teeth and watched the control room screens. "There! Camera three-ten. That's her. Where is she going?" *She saw our plans. Why is she going deeper into the cave? Why isn't she running to tell Ethan? Unless...* "Show me the view across from the entrance."

The images on the screen went fuzzy for a second, then a full-wall image of the railroad tracks across from the entrance to SubTropolis appeared. A gas station sat on the other side of the tracks. An unmarked semitruck sat in the station's parking lot. The truck where Ethan thought he hid.

"Show me who went into or came out of that truck."

The images on the wall sped through a rewind to the point the truck arrived late yesterday evening. The all-night gas station provided ample light.

Only two people left the truck, never to return. Neither of them was Ethan. *He* must *be inside still. I have to stop Miranda. Her surrender is critical to restoring my station.*

Irene turned to her daughter with a sweeter-than-chocolate-mousse smile. "Annabelle, darling. I know your sisters are working hard, but do you think you could spare one or two to nudge Miranda back toward the entrance?"

Her daughter faced her but didn't seem to notice her.

Irene overpowered her shiver by crossing her arms over her

chest. "I wouldn't ask except that we need to show the world that the Fellowship, that God's calling, can make even the worst among us into one of the faithful."

Annabelle regarded her for a long moment, then eyed one of her lieutenants who trotted down the steps. Annabelle whispered an order in her lieutenant's ear.

The lieutenant hurried up the stairs and out the door.

"Put camera three-ten in the lower left corner," Annabelle said. "Follow the target wherever she goes."

Irene smiled to herself. *Miranda and the rebels, and Felix and his precious Council, will learn what happens when you cross me.*

Chapter Seventy-One

Beryl's chest hollowed, and her inner alarms went ominously silent. The hairs on the back of her neck stood. She stopped firing and scanned the road in front of her over and over. Vacant as far as she could see—which wasn't far, but it shouldn't be empty. She'd gotten the first two Azrael—she was sure of it. But the instant she'd started shooting, they'd all melted into the deep shadows between pillars. Even the bodies vanished.

She swallowed. *If they were going to kill me, I'd be dead.* She did a slow three-sixty. Her helmet light made pitiful pools of light between a darkness deep enough for death.

A soft scrabbling sound, a crunch of gravel, came from her left.

They're trying to surround me. She turned off her helmet, blinded herself. *And anyone who's watching.*

They'll expect me to move to the walls. She stepped back three steps and stayed in the center of the road.

If they weren't Azrael, she'd think they were trying to capture her. *But Azrael don't capture. They kill. Every time.* Beryl eased her weight into another step back.

"It is God's will. You will put down your weapons and come with me."

The whisper of breath on her neck and the familiar voice sent Beryl's insides plummeting like a landslide of rock and dirt.

She brought her pistols across her body. *I'll take down the one behind me and the ones on the side if I have time.*

Someone grabbed her right hand. A second person seized her left hand.

"That is not God's will."

Beryl struggled to point the barrels at the target—any target.

The Azrael on each side pulled her hands and arms until both of her shoulders screamed.

A garrote dropped around Beryl's neck and snugged up under her jaw as if in warning.

Not going down without a fight. Beryl put all her power into a mule kick, but the Azrael behind her avoided contact.

The pressure around her neck increased. She gasped. Tried to reach for the wire garrote.

Couldn't move.

And still they didn't kill her.

She quit fighting. "What do you want?"

The Azrael took her pistols but didn't answer and didn't remove the garrote.

Beryl forced herself to relax. *Don't wear yourself out. Watch for an opportunity.*

Chapter Seventy-Two

Miranda eased the barracks door open just enough that someone would see the smoke. She scurried around the mattresses that Leslie had set on fire. Thin tendrils of steel-gray smoke curled toward the ceiling.

She crouched beside Wanda, who crouched next to Leslie, and tugged at the waist of the not-stretchy-enough black Azrael uniform she wore. She ignored the stuck-in-a-seashell noise that filled her ears. They choose to keep the helmet radios off. Didn't want the wrong people to hear anything.

The smoke thickened. Irritated her throat and made her eyes water. Still, no one came. The smoke was thick enough it should alarm the shooters outside. *Why aren't they storming in?* A wave of dizziness hit her. *They are going to let the fire do their dirty work.*

Clouds of smoke rolled across the floor. Flames crackled and licked the ceiling. Sweat trickled down Miranda's back.

The hand on Miranda's shoulder shook with Wanda's attempts to suppress her cough.

If they don't come soon…I'll open the door more. She stood.

The door sprang open.

She shrank down and hid behind the mattresses again.

Two Azrael stormed inside. They shouted, and two men armed with fire extinguishers came in. The extinguishers and fire hissed. Thick smoke blanketed the room.

Miranda and Leslie stood. In their black-trimmed-with-red Azrael suits that had a red Fellowship Shield emblazoned on the shoulder, they were indistinguishable from the others. Unable to find a suit that fit, Wanda walked between them as their prisoner. They hurried out the door and onto the vacant road.

Pulse battering her ears, Miranda kept expecting someone to question them, stop them, even shoot them. But no one did. She led her friends deep into the shadows beyond the barracks.

She checked behind them, couldn't see the barracks any longer. Paused long enough to put Wanda's arm over her shoulder to ease the strain on Wanda's wounded leg.

"Pillar numbers are decreasing," Leslie whispered. "We're headed in the right direction."

Miranda grunted. Surprised at their luck. Surprised the disguises worked. No one demanded they stop. No one shot at them. No one even followed them.

The uneven, loose soil beneath them made them lurch like drunken sailors for what felt like hours but was only minutes. Faint yellow light showed between the pillars two or three rows ahead. The road.

Wanda stumbled and gasped in pain. Miranda struggled to stay upright. She hoped Wanda had the strength to get back to the main entrance. Feared they moved too slowly.

Once they left this undeveloped area, they'd be moving down roads dotted with safety lights. Lights that would expose them. Expose two unusually tall Azrael, helping a wounded prisoner instead of killing her.

She left Wanda with Leslie at the edge of the road. Scouted both directions. The dark, vacant, and silent road worried her. But Wanda needed a doctor. And Ethan needed to know about Karl.

She trotted back to her friends, whispered, "All clear. Let's get out of here." She slipped Wanda's arm over her neck and shoulders again, and the three of them set out as one.

Even the road had dips and bumps, but it was much easier walking. And with Leslie helping Wanda too, they walked faster.

"Sisters?" a voice called. "Where are you going?"

Every muscle in Miranda's body tensed. "This prisoner's needed by Command."

"Halt," a male voice, David's voice, called from in front of them. "Stop, or we *will* shoot."

"David?" Miranda called, but gunfire erupted from behind them, drowned her out. Guns in front of them answered.

Miranda pulled Leslie and Wanda into a run, down an unused drive to a dock. She hoped to find a door, an escape. But concrete blocks walled off the dock.

She herded her friends into the shadows below the dock. Crouched in the dock's shadow, shielding Leslie and Wanda. Miranda gasped for air. For a way out of this mess.

The bang and boom of the guns bounced off the rock walls, multiplied, and vibrated through Miranda.

"David needs our help," Leslie said.

"He thinks we're the enemy." Miranda's desert-dry mouth made her words indistinct.

What are the odds we'd end up in the middle of a battle between Azrael and rebels? She scrubbed her face with her hands. *I have to make David hear me. See me.* She had an idea. Didn't like it. But nothing else would work.

She stepped back, deeper into the shadows, forced Wanda into the corner. Removed her helmet and hood. Fumbled with the flap over the zipper that ran down her back.

"What are you doing?" Wanda's whisper held a note of are-you-crazy.

"I'm going to make David see me," she whispered.

"Stop." Leslie put her hand over Miranda's. "You think going out there nearly naked will help him?"

"I made the choice to dress as Azrael. I will not put you or Wanda at any more risk. What other choice do I have? David and his team can't see us as anything but Azrael right now."

"You don't have to undress," Wanda said. "I'm not in one of those costumes. He knows me. I can reach him."

Miranda's jaw set. She pushed "no" through her teeth. "You can't move fast enough. And I can't let you take the chance."

"And we won't let you get hypothermia or a bullet." Leslie glared at her.

"This is ridiculous," she began. A sliding noise behind her made her whirl around.

Someone, impossible to say who, scrambled to their feet. Flattened against the rock pillar.

"We surrender," Wanda said, pushing her way in front of Miranda.

Crap. Miranda drew her gun.

"I won't fall for another of your Azrael tricks." David's voice held a hard edge.

"It's me, Miranda." She turned her flashlight on her own face.

"Miranda? What the hell are you— Lights out. Now."

She flipped the switch. Plunged herself into a darkness she couldn't blink away. A gun fired once, twice. *David?*

Scuffling and grunts sent flames of *fight now* through her. She raised her pistol, but her eyes were too slow to adjust. She couldn't get a clean shot.

All went silent. Nothing moved on the vacant driveway. She took two steps. Remembered Leslie and Wanda. "Stay."

She hurried to the drive's opening. Peered around the pillar and down the road. Two bodies down on the rebel side. Her throat tightened.

The rest of the road stood vacant. *They took him.* Her chest deflated. She collapsed to her knees. *I turned on the damn light, and they got him.* She trapped the scream that bubbled up with both her hands.

Chapter Seventy-Three

Blindfolded and hobbled, Beryl counted steps and turns.

Her captors pushed her forward.

She shuffled, constrained by the ropes around her ankles. A shove on her shoulders threw her backward. She locked her jaw against her startled yelp. Pinched between her own body and the surface of a cold, metal chair, her bound and numb wrists shot hot arrows up her arms.

Wait. This place, this room, is cold. There's a slight breeze. And there's no hint of ammonia in the air. Do they have power in this place? Am I still in the cave?

Strange clicks and snaps came from a few feet in front of her.

Someone yanked off her blindfold.

Damn. So bright it's like a blizzard's whiteout.

She ducked her head to the side and blinked and blinked until her eyes adjusted.

The rock walls painted white means I'm still in the cave. She squinted against the bright lights aimed at her, made out the shape of a movie camera on a tripod across from her.

At least two people stood behind the camera and lights. No amount of squinting allowed her to identify them. She couldn't say for certain they were female.

I should be dead. Why didn't they kill me when they had the chance? Beryl couldn't figure it out. She tried to touch the knot around her wrist. *They must think they can use me—for what? Could they still want Kara's accounting book?* The rough rope burned and chafed her wrists. *No. Kara's dead. They don't care about her anymore.*

They can't believe I'll let them send me back to Redemption.

Doesn't matter what they think, I won't be tortured again. I won't go back to Redemption. I'll make them kill me first.

Chapter Seventy-Four

Miranda stopped in the middle of the road. A whiff of a coppery scent mingled with the fading aroma of ammonia made her tremble, terrified for David. *First Nick, now—David?* A surge of powerful *no more* set her into motion. "Wanda, Leslie. They took David. We have to go." They took too long to join her. "Now." She rushed to them, grabbed Wanda's arm, and forced them to march to the beat of her heated pulse. *Got to find that bitch. Save David.*

"Where did they take David?" Leslie's voice had a hitch in it.

"How do I know?"

"We're following them, aren't we? We're going to rescue him, right?"

Miranda stopped in the middle of an intersection under the glow of the yellow security light. *Did they go straight? Right? Left? No blood trail. No breadcrumbs. Which way?*

"I'm slowing you down." Wanda sucked in a big breath, bent over, hands on her uninjured leg. "You two go ahead." Another big gulp of air. "Find David. I'll warn Ethan." Wanda's face, slick with sweat, had a yellow cast to it.

"You can't do that." *It's the security light that makes her look so close to death.*

"Yes, I can." She straightened. "Slow is quieter. And it'll be easier for one person to slip through and outside than three."

"You're sure?"

"Go."

Miranda nodded. "Take the right. It'll lead you back to the entrance. Don't take any risks. Go straight to Ethan." She trotted down the main road. Fast.

Leslie trotted beside her, couldn't keep up, and dropped behind.

In the deep shadows beyond the reach of the safety light, Miranda's chest ached as if it were being split in two. She didn't know which way they took David. Or if he still lived. She slowed, then stopped. Stared ahead, desperate to keep going, to find David. But in this maze of midnight, madness, and murder, her chances were less than slim. Her friends still had a chance. She turned around.

Leslie's form, silhouetted against the glow of the light behind her, ran toward her with a limp as if she were injured instead of Wanda. *Crap. Not instead, but as well. She's hurt.*

Leslie can't keep up. And Wanda won't make it back on her own. Miranda sighed. Ignored the pain in her chest. Trotted back to Leslie. "Come on. I'll come back for David, after I get you and Wanda to the entrance." *Hang on, David. Hang on.*

———

MIRANDA WORRIED HER LOWER LIP. Their pace was slow. They'd got out of the laboratory area and back into the main part of the former mine. But still had a mile or more to go. And judging by how much more Leslie limped, she wouldn't be able to help hold Wanda's weight much longer. Wanda hopped between them, unable to put weight on her injured leg.

With every step, Miranda scanned the road ahead and behind them, the walls and driveways recessed between pillars. The air grew fresher and fresher the closer they got to the main entrance. And the tension in Miranda's muscles grew.

The vacant roadway was so quiet she could hear the buzz of the security light long before they entered its twilight. The back of her neck tingled. *Why aren't the Azrael from the barracks stalking us yet?*

Her companions said nothing, but they sensed it too. Leslie's head swiveled back and forth, and Wanda pushed herself to keep going without rest.

In the distance ahead of them, the archway of the tunnel brightened from pitch to heather gray.

Miranda's heart thumped against her throat. "Be ready for an ambush," she whispered.

She slowed their steps and scanned more frequently.

The light at the end of the archway strobed and grew larger and lighter, brighter.

Three hundred feet from the entrance, she let go of Wanda, whirled to watch their backs. *Still no ambush? It makes no sense. Why would they give up? They wouldn't unless they—* Her heart dropped. *Ethan?*

She grabbed Wanda around the waist and ran, heedless of the cries of bewilderment from Leslie and Wanda.

Wind chilled her. Bright lights blinded her. Strobed to red and back to white. Filled her vision with spots.

Hands grabbed her. Tugged her free of Wanda and Leslie.

She struggled to free herself.

Voices murmured soothingly.

"Have you seen Monkshood? I need to talk to him right away."

The hands guided her, forced her to sit on a bumper. The spots cleared. A medic's face came into focus. He wrapped a blood pressure cuff around her arm.

She ripped the cuff off her arm, stood, and shouted, "Where's Monkshood?" She whirled around, tried to focus, to get her bearings. "Monkshood?"

Chapter Seventy-Five

Annabelle studied her from behind the movie camera and lights.

The woman's salt-and-pepper-colored hair stuck to the dried blood on her right cheek. One side of her face had an odd droop.

Doesn't look recent. An old injury?

The woman didn't struggle like the other prisoners.

We'll have to keep a close watch on this one. She's up to something.

Skin riddled with gooseflesh, the woman didn't ask why she wore only her underclothes. She glanced around the room, then sat erect, stared straight ahead, and waited.

With a tight smile on her face, Annabelle nodded. *This is an enemy worthy of me.* "What is your name?"

The only sound the woman made for five long minutes was the click of her chattering teeth.

Annabelle stopped smiling. "There is no need to suffer. We know you are Foxglove. We know your real name. So spare yourself. State your name for the camera."

The woman's eyes shifted to stare at Annabelle.

Correction, she stares in my direction. She cannot see me. Annabelle's hands twitched, tightened into fists. She deliberately loosened her fingers. *This prisoner I will handle myself.* Signaled her lieutenant to leave.

She stepped around the camera and stood to the right front of the prisoner. Faster than Foxglove could blink, Annabelle slipped in close, shot out her fist, and smashed the woman's nose. Followed that with a one-two shot to her ribs and danced out of reach.

Foxglove's chin dropped to her chest. Tears and blood dripped from her nose to the man's undershirt she wore. She took a deep breath, raised her head, and glared at Annabelle.

Annabelle decided not to ask the questions about the "other" rebel assault yet. The assault that Mother's informant claimed to be ignorant about. Foxglove was too important to the rebel organization to be ignorant. But *she won't talk now. She has no despair…yet.*

The blow to the rebel's right cheek made a solid thwack and snapped her chin and head sideways.

Blood and tears flowed. Still, the prisoner made no sound, raised her chin, and glared.

Annabelle allowed the heat to fill her blood and swung again. Landed her punch in the rebel's breast.

"Uh," Foxglove groaned.

Well…she isn't inhuman. I'll find her breaking point.

Chapter Seventy-Six

Miranda hopped across three heavy-duty power cords that snaked across the asphalt from a roaring generator to the semitrailer parked behind the gas station. The power cords held the trailer's swing doors open enough to allow entry. She stepped up on the bumper tube and up into the trailer.

A wall of sour sweat and ozone hit her. Halfway down the trailer, three men crowded around a paper map taped to the steel wall. Behind them, a pair of folding tables crossed the short wall. Two UNIVAC computers and a radio setup sat on the tables. Green steel clamp-on lamps lit up the end of the trailer so much she couldn't identify the three men.

"Monkshood, are you here?" she called. "I have to talk to you. It's urgent."

The men whipped around to face her.

One of them came forward. *Ethan.* His wide smile didn't erase the lines in his forehead. "I'm so glad to see you." He wrapped his arms around her in a brief hug. "Come on in." He drew her to the center of the trailer. "You know Pete and Conrad."

Pete peered owlishly through his glasses at her.

"Glad to see ya," Conrad said, "but from the look of you, I don't think you come bearin' good news."

She hesitated.

Conrad ran a hand through his red hair. "Guess we should get some air, Pete."

"No," Ethan said. "You have jobs to do."

Pete and Conrad turned and took seats at the tables. Pete sat at a UNIVAC, and Conrad sat on the radio.

Ethan turned to Miranda. "You'll have to trust them like I do. Let's sit." He went to a couple of extra folding chairs against the wall. Pulled one out for her. Positioned the other one with its back facing Miranda. He straddled it and folded his arms across its back. "Now. What do you need to tell me?"

Miranda took a deep breath, locked eyes with him. "Someone close to you is a traitor—"

"That's a serious accusation," he said, interrupting her with a tight voice. "I vet my people very carefully. You'd better have some pretty irrefutable proof."

She pulled Irene's list from her T-shirt, unfolded the paper. "That's Irene's handwriting."

He scanned the paper. His jaw tightened.

"I found it on her desk."

"Her desk? Here—in the lab?"

"In the teachers' dormitory. I don't know why she's here, but it looks like she moved in a day or two ago."

"That could be." He rubbed his eyes.

"What do you know I don't?"

"The Fellowship Council annulled her marriage."

"But she and Felix have been married eight years. They have a child—" Miranda sat back in her chair. "Wow."

"Yeah. I imagine she's not happy about that. Unhappy enough to fake anything she thought might bring the Council back to her side."

"Someone told her everything." She told Ethan about finding the copy of the rebel's plans, about Nick's death, the enemies who followed her, trapped her, Wanda, and Leslie, and David's capture.

Miranda finished with "I need a team to help me rescue David, Beryl, and anyone else they've captured. Five or six men and as much ammo as we can carry should be enough."

His pained expression sent chills through her. "I wish I had both to give you."

Her throat tightened. She shook her head. "We can't just leave them there. I won't leave them in there."

The radio squawked. "Monkshood, we need to talk."

Miranda went cold. "That's Irene."

Ethan dashed to the workstation. Conrad handed him the microphone. "Operation Catfish Command here. Come in."

"Operation Catfish Command, is it?" Irene laughed.

Chapter Seventy-Seven

The larger-than-life black-and-white image of the semitrailer flickered on the wall. It took all of Irene's willpower to speak calmly into the radio mike. "Hello, Ethan."

No answer.

"Come, now. I know you are Ethan Matthews." *Not Uncle. Not family. Not anymore. Mama and Father were wrong. If they had killed him instead of faking his death, they'd be alive today.* "You have lost. SABR has been defeated. By me."

Annabelle's cool look made Irene's throat tighten.

"I mean, by my daughter and her sister Azrael." She wished she could see the looks on Ethan's and Miranda's faces. "I have something you want."

"You have nothing I want."

"You think so?"

"If you surrender now…" Even over the radio, Ethan's voice was hard. "I will give you safe passage to the country of your choice."

"If *I* surrender?" *The country of my—* A wave of heat hit Irene. She wadded her handkerchief into a damp ball. *No one will ever banish me again! I should send Annabelle and her Azrael out and Take them.* She whirled, turned her back to the screen. The man at the nearest multi-monitor flinched.

She scanned the room. All eyes were on her. She took a deep breath, walked up two tiers, then turned back to the screen. "Well. If you don't want them, I'll just execute all of them. Of course, we'll pry a few secrets out of them first."

"*If* you had anyone, you'd know—no rebel will tell you anything."

Now to set the hook. "Oh, we have more than a few someones. And if they won't talk—Azrael can glean a few secrets from Hawthorn and Foxglove. You remember them, Miranda's little brother and your wife?"

He laughed. "Those two wouldn't allow you to capture them, not even their dead bodies."

Jaw set, she lowered her chin and glared at the screen. "I can arrange that if that's what you want. I will be certain you and Miranda get a front-row seat."

"Stop playing games, Irene. What do you want?"

"Miranda." Irene smiled a vicious smile and lifted her chin.

"If you wanted Miranda so badly, why didn't you capture her instead of the others?"

"I tire of your yammering, Ethan. Let me talk to Miranda."

"Miranda's not here."

The back of Irene's neck burned. "Don't be foolish, Ethan. We know Miranda's there. Miranda, when America watches you return to the Fellowship, all the weekend rebels will understand the error of their ways and peace will be restored. That's what you want, isn't it? Peace."

"You want her to renounce the revolution? Never. She will never rejoin the Fellowship."

"If you ever want to see Beryl or David again, Miranda, you will join me." She focused on the image of the semitrailer. "I'll tell you what. I'm feeling generous. You have thirty minutes, Miranda. At half past, if you're not standing by my side, we will broadcast the Azrael's *interrogation* of a certain rebel. You'd better hope he answers our questions. The Azrael are swift to deliver judgment."

She gave the signal to cut the connection. Without turning, she said, "Start the clock."

"My sisters report all orders complete."

She's calling them her sisters now.

Irene struggled to control her expression. Part of her wanted to crow. *My daughter is more than one of God's angels. She leads them to victory against the rebels.* Part of her wanted to cry. Wanted her little girl back—both her little girls. Irene's stomach bubbled. *This is Felix's fault.* She knotted her fists. *The world will know my daughter and I defeated the rebels. And when the Council reinstates me as Lady Earnshaw, the world will hear what they did to me. What he did to me. And the world will judge them and find them wanting.* Tremors shook her, and rushing filled her ears. *A Lady never shows her true feelings. Must get control.*

She recited Psalms 65:5-7 to herself, like Mama taught her.

By terrible things in righteousness wilt thou answer us, O God of our salvation; who art the confidence of all the ends of the earth, and of them that are afar off upon the sea:

Which by his strength setteth fast the mountains; being girded with power:

Which stilleth the noise of the seas, the noise of their waves, and the tumult of the people.

The rushing in her ears and her tremors eased. Composed, she turned to face her daughter "Beryl?"

"Give us the live feed," Annabelle said.

The screen flickered, focused. Irene stared at the battered face of her enemy. *Beryl. God forgive me, I'm glad she'll never talk. I can't wait for the Azrael to exact judgment and end her.*

Chapter Seventy-Eight

Miranda retreated to the metal folding chair near the map taped to the semitrailer's wall. Ethan, Pete, and Conrad huddled in front of one of the UNIVAC computers arguing their next move. She pulled out the magazine page Nick had given her. Stared at the cute little cabin with the red tin roof and the garden. Ached for the life they'd never have.

The murmurs grew in volume and intensity. Miranda tore her gaze from the cabin. Outside, the swing doors were wide open now. Rebel soldiers crowded around the entrance to the trailer. Irene had broadcasted her little speech across the firefighters' radio channel and the one the rebels used.

"We should use experienced men in a surgical approach." Conrad's drawl was thick and angry.

Pete shook his head. "It would be suicide. If they took the prisoners outside of the lab, there are fifty-five million square miles of underground nooks and crannies to search *in the dark.*"

"There's got to be a way." Ethan pulled a hand down over his nose and mouth.

Miranda crumpled the damp magazine page with the cabin on it in a tight fist. Stuffed it in her pocket and strode to the men. Feet spread, fists on her hips, she stated the obvious. "There is *a* way."

The three men turned to face her.

"I surrender to Irene."

The veins in Conrad's neck bulged. "No way."

Pete pushed his glasses up on his nose. "You know what she'll do to you?"

"That is most definitely not an option," Ethan said, arms folded across his chest.

"Your men are exhausted and hurt," Miranda said. "We don't know where the prisoners are. We have two choices. Allow our friends to die—or, I play along with Irene."

Ethan stood. "I am not sending you to your death."

"And *I'm not giving up.* Not on David, or Beryl, or on any of the rebels Irene has."

"There has got to be another—"

"Hello, Miranda." Irene's syrupy voice surrounded her. Echoed weirdly.

No, not an echo. The crystal-clear radio signal came from the radios on every rebel outside the trailer.

"This is your fifteen-minute warning, courtesy of our special guest. David, say hello."

Ethan shot Miranda a look. Held a finger to his lips.

"Now, David."

Silence stretched for five seconds.

The smack of a hand on flesh made Miranda gasp and jump. She pinched her lips together and balled her hands into fists.

"He won't talk. Let's try another one. Your code name is Petunia, right?"

"It's a trap, get out!" Petunia shouted.

A gunshot amplified by a hundred radios rang out. Miranda flinched. She took several shaky breaths. *All these deaths are on me. I can't allow anyone else to die.* She squared her shoulders and strode to the steps.

"Where do you think you're going?" Ethan demanded.

"I created this mess. Irene wouldn't even know we're alive except for me." *And my stupid peace talk.* "I have to surrender."

Conrad blocked her. "Do you honestly think she'll release the others if you go back in there?"

"It doesn't matter. I have to take the chance. Give *them* the chance." Her jaw ached.

Ethan's face turned stony, still, like a mask. "It's not your responsibility."

"They knew the risks," Pete said, his voice low and tight.

"And I know mine."

"She'll use you." Ethan's voice was cold, hard. "Make you a public example. I've seen it before. Believe me, you don't want to be part of it."

"This isn't about what I want. What matters is destroying the Fellowship." She locked eyes with him. "If my surrender can give you the time you need for the big push in D.C., then that's what I have to do."

He rubbed his mouth, drew his hand down, pulling on his mouth and chin. "No, I won't have it. I won't have your suicide on my conscience for the rest of my life."

"I'm not committing suicide."

"Sure sounds like it to me," Pete said.

"I plan to get out."

"You have a plan?" Ethan pursed his lips, and cocked his head. "We're listening."

She locked eyes with Ethan. "How much time do your guys in D.C. need?"

Ethan frowned. "What has that got to do—"

"How much time?" Miranda repeated.

Pete's chair scraped against the floor. He stood, glanced at his watch. "Thirty minutes."

"Okay. It's three-thirty now. After I go in, get as many rebels out of the mine as you can. If I'm not out of there by"—she compared her watch to Ethan's—"four-thirty, blow it up."

"What? With you inside?"

"With *them* inside."

"Think about what your death will do to the rebellion," Ethan said.

She gave him a tired look. "I mean nothing to the rebellion."

Ethan's expression softened. "You've never understood how much you mean to me—to the movement. Nick understood. He wouldn't want you to do this either."

She winced inside. "All of it will be for nothing if I don't do what *only* I can."

He broke eye contact with her, scratched the back of his neck. "I have had to do hard things before, but this…"

"You don't get to decide this time," she said. "I do. I can do this

—I will do this no matter what consequences there are. Just promise me one thing."

"Not that I'm agreeing with you, but what do you want?"

"Find David and Beryl, the other prisoners, and anyone else in there. Save everyone you can."

Conrad heaved a Texas-sized sigh. "We'll figure something else out."

"Nothing that we can do in the next ten minutes."

Three pairs of sorrowful eyes regarded her.

Ethan nodded.

"Promise me you'll save them. And that you'll keep fighting, no matter what. Don't let the Fellowship win."

His Adam's apple slid up and down. "We won't stop until we've won."

"Thank you." She turned and left the trailer.

Chapter Seventy-Nine

Beryl blinked and blinked. She still couldn't see. Couldn't rub her eyes. Her hands were numb. Tied behind her back. *What happened? Where the hell am I?* The cold, hard floor beneath her stirred memories of the floor of a cell in redemption. She sucked in a breath. *That cannot be. No,* the mineral-tainted air with a hint of ammonia meant she was—*not in Redemption*—in the mine.

Right, the Azrael put a sack over my head. The left side of her face, even her teeth, hurt like hell. She slid her jaw from side to side. Not broken. *Why haven't they killed me yet?*

A humming motor annoyed her. *They're taking me somewhere. Not in a car.* The floor beneath her was metal. Eddies of air blew across her arms. *Definitely not in a trunk.*

A bump jarred her. Pain lanced through her head, jaw, ribs— everything hurt. *Damn.*

The vehicle stopped. Beryl pretended to be unconscious. Footsteps moved away. She eased one leg's position. *They didn't tie my feet together. It makes no sense. Azrael aren't stupid or lazy.*

The footsteps came back. A yank tore the sack off her head. Bounced her head on the floor. Pain blurred her vision.

"It's so good to see you like this, Aunt Beryl."

An upside-down face came into focus. "Irene?"

"That's Lady Earnshaw to you."

"You're no lady." A punch or kick to her already bruised kidney choked off her laugh, blanked her vision for a moment.

"Make her watch. You won't feel like laughing soon. Not after you watch your party's demise." The level of contempt and certainty in Irene's voice lit a fire inside Beryl.

"Your so-called angels may have won this battle..." Beryl's fat lips and dry mouth made her sound less formidable than she wished. "The war is far from over."

Irene's laugh boomed. "We'll see about that."

Chapter Eighty

The veins in Irene's temples pulsed. Images of the parked semitrailer flickered on the control room wall. No Miranda. No one ventured out of the trailer. She checked her watch again. *They must realize I'm not bluffing. Or since they didn't see it with their own eyes—* "Annabelle, please take—"

"Call me Anna 3000."

Irene whirled to face her daughter.

Standing at the top step of the room's tiers, Annabelle's wintry smile did not soften her aloof facial expression.

Irene's suddenly dry throat hurt. She swallowed. *Annabelle said, I am the holy mother of the Chosen One, and I had nothing to fear.* She lifted her chin. *I am not afraid.* "Anna 3000, of course."

A gasp came from a man on Irene's left. Murmurs rippled across the room. The men stared wide-eyed and open-mouthed at the wall. Irene hoped she knew why. She turned slowly, faced the projection.

Miranda stepped out of the trailer and walk to the cave's main entrance. She took a stance and stood, waiting.

Irene drew in a deep breath. Savored the flush of triumph as long as she dared. Looked over her shoulder at Annabelle. "Anna 3000, please do me the honor of fetching her yourself."

Annabelle, Anna 3000, turned on her heels and left. She would escort Miranda to one of the punishment cells. A soundproof, closet-like room used to test young Azrael.

Now to remind Felix of his wife's—of my—worth. Irene glanced around the room at the dozen men behind their workstations. "Clear the room," she said.

They looked up at her as if she'd spoken a foreign language.

They dare to defy me? "Clear the room. Now."

Chapter Eighty-One

With her weapons secured in holsters hidden within easy reach, Annabelle relaxed in the passenger seat of a golf cart. Her lieutenant drove out of the mine into the brightly lit entrance. Stopped six feet from the woman. Miranda waited without speaking. A line of rebels stood at parade rest on the other side of the street. Hands visible, clasped in front.

Without leaving the cart, Annabelle scanned the area for threats. Both the driver and the lieutenant seated behind the driver also assessed the threat level. They'd keep her safe.

She climbed out of the cart, crossed in front of it, and stood before Miranda. "Mother of the Chosen One asked that we escort you inside without restraints."

Miranda shot her an almost imperceptible glance at the phrase "Mother of the Chosen One." Recovered and stared straight ahead.

"Arms up and out at your sides," Annabelle said.

Miranda complied.

Running her hands down Miranda's body, Annabelle found no weapons. "Please take the second-row passenger seat." She swept an arm toward the cart in invitation.

Miranda strode to the cart and sat without uttering a word.

The rebels watched. Sullen. Silent. Still.

Annabelle returned to her seat, and the driver backed the cart into the cave.

When they'd gone deep enough into the cave that the rebels vanished from sight, Annabelle twisted in her seat and gazed at this enemy who frightened and angered Mother.

From Miranda's sun-bleached hair to her demeanor, and even her well-toned muscles, Mother's fear remained a mystery. It didn't matter that she couldn't see Mother's reasons. Her angel within sparked a chest-tingling rush of destiny-about-to-be-fulfilled in Annabelle.

The cart stopped at an intersection deep inside the darkened cave.

The Azrael seated next to Miranda attempted to place a black hood on the prisoner.

Miranda raised her forearms, blocked the hood. "That's unnecessary."

So the fear-inducing Miranda is afraid of the hood. "You must wear it."

"But I've already been inside the lab. I won't—I can't—cause you any problems."

"You wear the hood, or we knock you out," Annabelle said in a reasonable tone. "You have a choice for the next five seconds."

Miranda swallowed, allowed the hood to be dropped over her head.

Chapter Eighty-Two

Blinded by the hood, Miranda sat in a metal chair, hands handcuffed to the chair legs behind her. She tried to count the seconds and minutes but lost track. Her hands and feet buzzed and tingled, no matter how much she wriggled her fingers and toes.

A click startled her. A heavy door thunked. Soft footsteps approached. Something brushed her hair. She flinched, then steeled herself. A tug at her hair removed the hood.

Cool air brushed her face. First, a fuzzy, matronly shape took form in front of her, then the rock walls of a small bathroom-sized room.

Irene wasn't alone. A man stood to her left, and a trio of armed Azrael stood to her right. The olive-skinned one stood closest to Irene. Behind them was the lone opening in the room. A solid steel door.

"You look awful, like you've lost a war." Irene faked being genuine even better than Mama used to fake it. "You'll feel much better after a bath and some proper clothes."

Miranda's nails bit into her palms. "I've done what you asked. I'm here." She didn't bother to keep the heat from her voice. "Let David, Beryl, and all the rest of your prisoners go."

Irene looked surprised. "I'm pretty sure I said you'd save their lives when you surrendered. I said nothing about freeing them." She smiled as if she were at an afternoon tea party.

The intensity of Miranda's hate was startling and monstrous, piercing and murderous. She wanted to beat Irene to a pulp. *Pretty sure I can knock you out in one punch.* Her arm muscles jerked, rattled the chains of her handcuff. "You don't need any other prisoners. I'm here. Have been here for what? Fifteen minutes?"

A bright light blinded her for a moment. An out-of-focus image appeared on the rock wall. It flickered, distorted on the rocks, focused—on David's battered and bleeding face.

The pain in Miranda's gut doubled her over. She kept her eyes on David, took short, hard breaths in and out. *What did they do to you?*

"David simply won't cooperate," Irene said. "Neither will Beryl —or any of the others. Yet."

"How could you? He's your brother." *Shouldn't have said that.*

"Did you think I'd forget how you banished us? That's not something our Lord demands I forgive."

A series of images flashed on the wall. Beryl's battered face, her eyes swollen shut. A young woman lying unconscious on a dirt floor. A young man gasping and choking, wet hair dripping onto his face. *She wants to break me—to break them.*

"You can save them, Miranda. And only you."

Gotta stall. Make her think I'll go along with her plan. "What do you want?"

"Denounce SABR and return to the Fellowship, to three square meals a day, and to soft beds and beautiful clothes."

You don't have a clue how I've changed, do you? "And if I don't?"

"I'm afraid you and your friends will have a rough time before you die."

The camera view of the young man with wet hair pulled back. He sat in a claw tub full of water. His arms tucked behind him. They'd tied his hands. He braced his tied feet on the end of the tub.

An Azrael appeared, pressed both her hands down on the top of his head, submerged him.

The young man's eyes widened. He bucked, kicked—splashed water everywhere. Bubbles escaped from his mouth. His body convulsed, strong at first, then weaker and weaker until he went limp.

I could have saved him. Her jaw twitched. *As if Irene would keep her word.* Unblinking, Miranda stared straight ahead. *Stick to the plan. Keep her distracted until everything goes boom.*

"Don't get any ideas that your friends outside can help my prisoners. They are safe in another location. Several locations, actually."

We know. Miranda shifted her weight. "They can't be far. It's only been—what, thirty minutes since you caught them?"

"Oh, and don't count on help from your people outside either."

The image flickered again. Azrael herded people out of the firetrucks and the semitrailer at gunpoint. Miranda's stomach dropped. She searched the faces. *Ethan? Irene didn't find him or she'd crow about it. Where are you, Ethan? Rescuing Wanda and Leslie? Setting the explosives?*

Chapter Eighty-Three

I rene entered the security center and swept a glance down the tiers of men working at their multivacs. Her heart thumped triumphant. *I have the rebels and I have Miranda. It's time to show Felix what his* wife *can do for him.* "Everyone take a break," she said. "Five minutes."

Male faces looked up at her. None of them moved.

"Leave, now."

Chairs scraped against the floor and feet tramped up the stairs. Irene stood center bottom of the half-round control center and glared and waited for every man and Dr. Gallaway to climb the three levels. The last to leave, the doctor paused at the door, gave her a measuring glance, and the door banged shut behind him.

She crossed over to the first row of tables. Sat in the right-side aisle seat. Picked up the black Bakelite handset. The handset shook as if she had the palsy. She dialed the familiar number.

Mid-ring someone picked up on the other end.

A loud clatter forced her to pull the handset away from her ear for a moment.

"Uh, hello?"

"You'll want to listen to me, Felix."

"Irene? What time is it? Four o'clock in the morning!"

"I wouldn't bother the great Prophet if it weren't *very* important."

On the wall, the close-up of Miranda showed every twitch of her face, every squirm in the metal folding chair. Handcuffed and with Annabelle and two other Azrael on guard, Miranda wasn't going anywhere.

Mountains of weight lifted from Irene's shoulders. She drew in a deep breath, awed by her own accomplishment.

"Irene," his voice softened. "It wasn't personal. The Prophet—"

"Just listen." She didn't want to hear his excuses. Not now. "I, acting as the Prophet's wife, have done what no one else could do. Miranda and David Clarke and Beryl Mitchell are my prisoners."

"Your sister and—? How? Where?"

She scoffed. "You think it's going to be that easy?"

"What do you want?" The wariness in his tone pricked her heart like a crown of thorns.

"Simple. I want the annulment annulled. You can say it was a false news story, a mistake, or that the devil made you do it. I don't care what excuse you give, but they will reinstate our marriage and my position immediately."

"Irene—look, if you'd stuck around so we could talk—"

Her grip on the handset tightened. The veins in her temples thundered. "The time to talk about it was *before* you had our marriage annulled." *Too strident.* She blew a breath out between clenched teeth. Spoke more softly. "I get to do the talking now. Go to the multi-monitor. You'll receive a code. Click on it and watch. Do it now." She slammed the handset down.

Chapter Eighty-Four

Stomach twisting between rage and despair, hope and no hope, Miranda couldn't look away from the flickering images on the wall of the interrogation room. Several dozen rebels wearing firefighter bunker gear and a few wearing street clothes marched reluctantly into the mine. One man broke free, made a run for it. An Azrael took aim. Shot him.

Miranda bit back a shout. Bit her tongue—hard. The metallic taste of blood and the need to strike out to make Irene pay flooded her senses.

The remaining captives shuffled forward, defeated. The camera didn't follow them inside.

She had to believe Ethan was free. Had to believe he had rescued Wanda and Leslie. Had to believe he'd planted the explosives. She wished she knew what time it was. *How much more time does he need? How can I keep stalling Irene? Convince her I'll do what she says.* She leaned back in the chair. "What do I need to do to save those people?"

"Win hand-to-hand combat."

That was unexpected. Miranda blinked. "You mean a fistfight?"

"I mean a fight to the death."

Everything inside her thickened, hardened, as if Irene's words transformed her into a lump of coal. *Not exactly how I thought this one-way trip would end. Buy Ethan time.* She focused on taking slow, even breaths. Slid her gaze to Irene. "Who am I supposed to fight? You or your daughter, the Azrael?"

Irene gave her a sharp glance. "An Azrael, yes—not my daughter."

"I'll fight her, Mother."

Irene inclined her head and took four paces away. Her daughter joined her. Their whispered conversation was too low to hear.

They faced Miranda again. The girl's cold, reptilian smile nearly cracked Miranda's resolve.

Chapter Eighty-Five

Irene took in the strangled spaghetti of wires lying across the metal deck that overlooked the killing fields. It had taken the technicians hours to set up a generator for lights and communication on the catwalk's deck. *It isn't pretty, but so what?* The humming-grumbling generator on the ground behind them provided the power to the five multi-monitors on the table in front of her. Showed her Felix's skeptical face. A bright desk lamp whited-out half his face, deep shadows hid the other half. She peered at the screen. *He's not at home.* "Where are you?"

"The only place where the monitors allow this kind of communication." His official Prophet's voice held fatigue.

"You went all the way to the Fellowship Center at four o'clock in the morning?" Her stomach burned. *Of course.* "You're recording this conversation?"

"I am the Prophet, Irene. I have a duty to protect myself and my office." He had his Prophet face on, and she couldn't read it.

She blew out a big breath. "Fine. Your view will switch to a well-lit field, so you can watch what is about to happen."

He yawned a big, open-mouthed-yawn. "This had better be...."

At precisely four-twenty, still in her Azrael disguise and weaponless, Miranda stumbled onto the dusty killing field escorted by two Azrael. They removed her hood. She glanced around, then crossed her arms and shouted, "Let's get on with this."

"What?" Felix leaned closer to his screen. "That's your sister Miranda, isn't it? What are you up to, Irene?"

In full Azrael gear and also weaponless, Annabelle strode into view. Stopped and faced Miranda.

"Wait," Felix cried. "Is that Annabelle? Our daughter is going to fight your sister?"

Irene's heartbeat thumped with righteousness. "That is Annabelle, now and forevermore known as Anna 3000, the Chosen One of the Azrael." She beamed down at her daughter, her Angel of Death. "This is only the first," she told Felix. "We will kill the leaders of the rebellion one by one. Once our marriage is reinstated, I'll send you the original tape so you can show the world how the Fellowship metes out judgment."

"What happens if the Council won't put aside the annulment?"

"My Azrael will help them decide."

"*Your* Azrael? Wh—" He gave a rapid shake of his head. "I told you, I didn't ask for our marriage to be annulled. It was the Council's decision."

The veins in Irene's throat and temple throbbed. *The Head of the Council had no say? I think he needs a little more motivation.* She pulled her white lace handkerchief out of her pocket, held it up over the edge of the catwalk. Then raised her voice so Annabelle could hear her. "When I drop this handkerchief, the fight will begin." She glanced at Miranda and puffed her chest out. *You've earned this end, sister dear.* She dropped the handkerchief.

Chapter Eighty-Six

The mineral-dust taste and smell made Miranda's dry mouth drier. She stood in the middle of a large, well-lit, undeveloped area with an uneven, loose-dirt floor. Faced a brightly lit, raised viewing platform.

She'd seen two areas similar to this, though they were both unlit. *I'm either in the one by the nursery or the one close to the middle of the campus. Gotta figure out which one. Each one had escape tunnels nearby, but they were opposites.*

A motor sound to her left drew her attention.

A bruised and bloodied Beryl lay trussed up in the back of a golf cart, stopped between two pillars.

Oh, no. Why did they bring her here? To watch me die? For me to watch her die?

Beryl dipped her head slightly and smiled, a smile warped by the swelling of her face. It was as if she were telling Miranda *you can do this.*

Miranda lifted her chin, gave Beryl a nod, then faced the viewing platform a football field away. It looked like there were two people on the platform. Irene and who else?

Doesn't matter. All I have to do is live long enough for the bombs to go off. After what you did to Nick, to Beryl, and God knows how many others, I can do this. I will *do this.*

She controlled her breathing, cleared her mind, and her heart rate went from wild horses galloping to a do-or-die drum roll that would make Beryl proud.

They'd stripped her of weapons and belts. And other than the loose rock and dirt around the base of each pillar, the fighting arena was clear of debris. Still, she searched for anything she could use to stab, jab, hit, or throw.

Plastic sheeting curtained off a rectangular area of—she counted —twelve pillars. That gave her a lot of room, but the curtains blocked the view beyond. She still didn't know exactly where she was. Where the closest ventilation shaft was.

Miranda tunneled in on Irene. *You said it's a fight to the death. So I have no choice. If I want to live, I have to kill your daughter—then I'll kill you.*

A rustling noise warned her. She whirled. Focused on the Azrael, on Annabelle, standing twenty feet in front of her.

Annabelle stood in a bent-knee stance. She looked relaxed and confident. Under the lights, her olive skin turned a sickly yellow.

The sight reminded Miranda. *How did Irene get the Fellowship Council, or any Fellowship member, to accept you? Or did their rejection cause you to become an Azrael?* She gave the girl a malicious smirk. "All it takes is one look to know you're not an Earnshaw. You're not even Fellowship material."

Annabelle's face darkened. She circled to Miranda's right.

"You're the pity-the-poor-orphan."

Annabelle charged her.

Miranda ran toward Annabelle as if she intended that they collide. Sidestepped at the last minute.

Annabelle rushed past. Whirled and moved back in incredibly quickly.

A gut punch drove the air out of Miranda.

"Oof." Miranda couldn't catch her breath. Her vision darkened. Desperate, she sucked in air. Buried a fist into Annabelle's solar plexus.

Annabelle took a step back but didn't fold, didn't make a sound, and threw a right jab.

Miranda deflected the jab. Missed the uppercut that connected with her chin, snapped her teeth together and her head back. White-hot pain seared her brain. Tears blurred her vision. She grabbed part of Annabelle's clothes, tried to sling her to the ground.

Annabelle wrested free and danced out of reach. Smiled that awful lizard-grin that didn't reach her flat brown eyes.

"I'll bet the kids at school teased you with names like an outsider, or—"

Annabelle barreled into her. Punched right, left, right.

Miranda broke away. Dashed to a pillar near the observation deck. Spun to find Annabelle stalking toward her.

Tasted copper. Spat out a mouthful of blood. Shouted, "They know you're not one of us the moment you open your mouth and speak-English-not-so-good." And she ran.

An over-the-shoulder glance showed Annabelle was closing fast. *She'll catch up in two or three strides. Not good.* Miranda dropped to the ground, tucked like a rock.

Annabelle ran into her. Flipped over her. Pancaked on the ground.

With a fistful of dirt in each hand, Miranda took off again. Skirted out of Annabelle's reach. Made for the observation deck.

Miranda jerked to a halt.

Annabelle's grip on her shirt spun her around, so they faced each other.

Miranda threw the dirt into Annabelle's face. Wheeled and in two strides, slid under the viewers' deck.

The bright lights over the deck defined the perimeter of the eight-foot-wide under-deck area. But little light penetrated the metal grid flooring above her head. She crawled and groped for anything she could use. Overhead, metal creaked and clanged under stomping feet.

"I see you," Annabelle said in a sing-song voice and poked at Miranda with something. *A pole?*

Miranda grabbed for the pole and missed. She snaked to the center of the deck's underside. Hoped it was out of reach.

"Do you really want to die under there?"

She scurried down the length of the deck. *I thought there'd be debris—something—under here. If she gets a gun, I'm a sitting duck.* Metal overhead clanged and rang painfully. She kept crawling.

Her right hand landed on a fist-sized rock. She grabbed it. Kept going. Only a few feet from the end of the overhead deck. She banged the rock against something buried in the dirt. Scrabbled at the dirt with her left hand. Uncovered an ink pen. *Now I'm armed.*

A quick scan of the arena gave no sign of Annabelle. Miranda crawled out from under the decking.

Annabelle landed two feet to the right. Kicked. Caught Miranda in the ribs.

Pain exploded in Miranda's side. Clutching the rock and ink pen to her side, she rolled away. Staggered to her feet a moment before Annabelle kneed Miranda in her side.

Tears blurred Miranda's vision. But she brought the rock up in a roundhouse punch. Caught Annabelle in the ear.

Annabelle groaned and dropped to her knees.

Miranda raised the ink pen. A vibration hit the soles of her shoes, traveled up her legs to her spine. A wall of sound and an invisible blow knocked her to the ground.

She rolled to her hands and knees. *The bombs!* Rumbling and cracking came from everywhere. A rock the size of her head hit the floor in front of her. Cracked into pieces.

Curtains of dust and gravel rained over her. She couldn't see Annabelle.

And she can't see me.

Miranda crawled to the nearest pillar. Got to her feet. Looked for Beryl. Couldn't see anything but a pile of rocks. Her heart lurched. Another large rock thumped to the ground beside her. She flung one arm over her head. Ran unsteadily. *Gotta find that air shaft.*

Chapter Eighty-Seven

The beating her daughter gave Miranda wasn't as exhilarating as Irene had hoped. Especially since Felix kept saying "you have to stop this" from the multi-monitor.

"What punishment would *you* assign to the one who betrayed us so many times?" she blurted out.

He frowned his pious Prophet frown. "That is up to the Council."

"You are the Prophet." *Too much heat.* "You are the voice of our Lord. Be the voice. Stand up for—"

A loud boom came from the multi-monitor. Felix's multi-monitor showed a web of cracks growing across a wall. Pieces of sheet rock fell. *No, not a wall. The ceiling.* Something hit his multi-monitor, knocked it on its side. Irene gasped, leaped to her feet. "Felix? What's happening?" Fuzzy gray static filled the screen. A wave of dizziness hit her. "Felix? Answer me!"

Irene glared at the technician seated beside her. "What happened? Get Felix back immediately."

"I'm trying. But I can't connect to the Fellowship Center. It's like —no one's there."

Irene couldn't catch her breath. "No one but Felix—" She swallowed and pulled herself together. Refocused on Annabelle— *Wait, where's Miranda?*

Miranda ran across the field toward a pillar.

"Stop her," Irene muttered.

The metal of the diamond grid floor beneath her shuddered and swayed. A wall of sound and air buffeted her. She seized the nearest handrail. Hung on and prayed, "Dear Lord, don't let those rocks bury me. Don't let this be my time to die."

Vibrations shook her. Her chest hurt from the pounding of her heart. Her heart didn't slow, but the catwalk stopped moving. A dull rumble like faraway thunder renewed her nightmare of being trapped by tons of soil and rock. Something caught in her throat. Triggered a coughing fit.

The taste of dust filled her mouth. She couldn't breathe without breathing in more dust, triggering coughing. She dug her backup handkerchief out from her bra strap and placed the silken cloth over her mouth. Breathed a little easier. At least the coughing stopped.

An eddy of dust cleared the air, revealed the oddly lumpy catwalk littered with rocks larger than her fists. "What was that?"

Dr. Gallaway's wide-eyed glance did not reassure her. "We have to get out of here!" he exclaimed and rushed past her.

She whirled. "Annabelle?" The killing field was strewn with boulders as big as a golf cart and blanketed with billows of dust. There was no sign of Annabelle. *Please, Lord, let her be okay.* "Annabelle? Where are you?"

A dust-covered form raised an arm and waved.

"We have to leave. Now." Handkerchief clamped to her face, she hurried after the doctor.

Chapter Eighty-Eight

Annabelle gasped for air again and again. She wiped grit from her lips. Her ears rang. *Who knocked me on my back?* Vibrations from the floor rattled through her. A low rumble of thunder—*impossible. Not thunder, but what?* The dim lights flickered. She sprang to her feet and searched for her target.

Across the arena, Miranda struggled to her feet. Ceiling rock fell around her.

Annabelle glanced at the ceiling above her. *Too dark to see.* But no rocks fell near her. *The Lord protects us.* She smiled, lowered her gaze to focus on the target. But the target had moved.

"Annabelle? Where are you?"

Mother? Where? There. Annabelle waved.

A screech from the catwalk tensed Annabelle's muscles, spiked her pulse.

Mother yelled something unintelligible. "—get out—"

Annabelle searched for her target again.

Miranda ran toward the main road.

The earth shuddered. More rocks pelted the ground.

An ear-splitting crack came from Mother's direction. Tons of rock thundered down onto the catwalk. Clouds of dust blanked out the sight.

"Annabelle, help!"

Annabelle glared at the target. *Another day.*

She darted around boulders, through the dust, toward the catwalk.

Chapter Eighty-Nine

Irene winced at the sharp stabbing pain in her right ankle and leaned heavily on Annabelle. They followed the Dr. Gallaway who wove around the fresh obstacles of fallen boulders and rocks littering the underground roadway. Gray dust covered his hair and clothes like a cloak in the dust-choked air.

A bell-like sound accompanied a down-rush of pebbles. Annabelle jerked Irene and Dr. Gallaway back a step. A boulder the size of a coffee table broke from the ceiling and crashed to the ground between Irene and the doctor.

"Ow." Pain lanced through Irene's ankle, forced her to hop on her good foot. *If a falling rock doesn't kill me, my heart will.*

"Only a bit farther, Mother," Annabelle said. "Should I carry you?"

"I'll make it." She lifted her chin. *There's no way God will allow that apostate, Miranda, to cause* my *death—or my daughter's.*

A cascade of rocks released from the wall. Missed Dr. Gallaway by inches.

Irene gave the new obstacles a wide berth. A hundred feet farther down the road, the doctor stopped at a numbered door in the rock wall. Waved her inside.

A light flared. Dr. Gallaway held a flashlight. The light revealed a round, six-foot-wide, steel-lined shaft with a ladder climbing up the far wall.

"We take that up." He pointed at the metal ladder visible through the thick swirling dust. "Pray to God the autogyro's waiting."

Irene's imagination supplied a gruesome image of them caught midway up by the collapse of the steel walls and the crush of tons of rock. She caught her breath, reminded herself that she was the mother of and stood beside the chief Azrael. Irene lifted her chin. *The Lord will protect us.*

Dr. Gallaway started up the ten-story ladder. "Come, quickly."

Irene grabbed a rung. The pain in her ankle forced her to pull and hop one rung at a time.

Annabelle followed close behind. Her warm breath caressed Irene's legs.

The ladder vibrated. Irene squeezed her eyes shut and clung to the ladder. Her heart fluttered. She hoped her death would be quick if it were coming now. Prayed it wasn't.

Finally, the tremors passed, and though her arms and legs shook, she climbed upward. The air grew cleaner, and her breathing came easier.

The sputtering roar of a distant engine grew louder and louder.

"You made it." Dr. Galway grabbed her wrist, hoisted her up onto a concrete roadway that circled a quarry.

She sucked in great gasps of clean air and silently praised the Lord as her spiritual *and* physical savior.

Annabelle sprang out onto the tarmac beside her. Caught her breath, then wrapped an arm around Irene's waist.

They followed Dr. Gallaway. Ducked and climbed into the back of the five-seat autogyro.

The little craft bounced faster and faster down the runway. Its overhead propeller slapped the air, slowly building speed and lift. They rose into the air.

A red-gold ribbon of clouds painted the eastern horizon. Broken trees littered the edges of the forest. Jagged cracks crossed earth pocked with large and small craters.

In the midst of the ruin below, a dark form ran east, dodging craters and leaping over the trunks of fallen trees.

Boom!

The autogyro bucked and twisted and dropped.

Irene gripped the seat and prayed, *I'm not finished, Lord. Don't take us yet.*

The little aircraft steadied, soared higher. Below them, dust clouds obliterated the bluff, the quarry, and even the firetrucks out front.

Stirred by a light breeze, the dust clouds parted, revealed glimpses of ground collapse and landslides all around the bluff. The runner had vanished.

Dark figures gathered around the rebels' trailer in the parking lot of the filling station across the tracks. Irene glared at the rebels until trees and distance erased them from sight. *This battle may have been a draw, but I can't lose with the Azrael and the Lord on my side.*

"Take us to the Fellowship Center in D.C.," she shouted to the pilot. Dead or alive, she would find Felix. Widow or wife, she would find Sandra, and she and her daughters would lead the Fellowship out of these dark times.

Chapter Ninety

Clouds of rock billowed and hid even the viewing deck from sight. Miranda coughed and choked and staggered down the underground road. The clatter and thump of falling rock echoed and sounded as if there was nowhere safe to walk. She covered her mouth with her elbow. It didn't help much.

She wiped gritty rock dust from her face and lips. Tried to spit out the mud in her mouth. Coughed more. Couldn't see landmarks. Didn't know where she was—where the nearest ventilation shaft was.

Another boom rang through the mine. This one sent another shower of dust on her but didn't add falling rock.

A creaking came from behind her. She threw a useless over-shoulder glance into the whitish dust cloud behind her. The creaking grew louder, closer. She sprinted forward.

Running made her draw deep breaths of gritty air. She had to stop. Perched on the squared base of a pillar and gasped for air. Wiped dirt and tears from her eyes. She tried her flashlight again. Across the road, something glowed.

It didn't come into focus until she was close enough to touch the the glow-in-the-dark arrow painted on the pillar. *Thank you for the great idea, Leslie. And bless you, whoever marked this wall.*

She took off in that direction. Coughing racked her body.

Dimmed her vision. She kept going anyway. Another turn, and the cloud of dust turned brighter. *Light from above?*

The shaft of light wavered. The ground trembled. *Is that real?* A ladder scaled the wall.

Miranda stumbled toward the escape she hoped was real.

Reached for it. Grabbed the metal ladder.

Climbed.

The higher she climbed, the clearer the air became. Halfway up, hope of escape gave her renewed energy.

A shock wave body slammed her into the ladder.

Her feet slipped.

Somehow, she hooked an arm over a rung.

Shuddering earth tried to fling her off the ladder.

Her shoulder screamed but held against the force of Mother Earth and gravity.

The rumbling lessened. She found her footing. Her arm and shoulder ached with the slightest effort, but she forced herself to continue the climb.

She pulled herself onto the grass. Knives of pain tore through her shoulder. She rolled onto her back, gasped for air.

The ground trembled beneath her. *Gotta get off the bluff.* She got to her knees, staggered to her feet.

Gaping holes in the trees and trees tilted at steep angles disoriented Miranda. *Which way?* A slow three-sixty turn didn't help until she noticed ribbons of red and gold edging the eastern sky.

She sprinted toward the sun. Reached the edge of the grassy slope to the road below.

Boom!

The concussion knocked her over the edge.

She tumbled down amid brush and trees, rocks, and dirt. Tumbled into a deep, silent dark.

———

INTENSE RINGING in her ears woke her.

"Where am I?" Memory rushed in. *The bluff. Gotta keep moving.*

She couldn't see. Reached for her face. Left arm wouldn't work. Dirt and grit covered her. She wiped her eyes clear with her right hand. Peered about.

She lay on a mound of dirt. A melon-sized rock dug into her right side, made taking a deep breath painful. Gingerly, she moved her right arm, then her left. A firebolt shot from her left shoulder to her fingertips. She blew out through pursed lips, and when the fire lessened, she moved her legs. Battered and bruised, her legs followed her mental commands.

She sat up. Tried to make sense of the changed landscape.

Above her, the bluff had an irregular bite taken out of it. Below it, ochre-colored soil spilled like a skirt at what used to be the base of the bluff. A jumble of trees and rock and earth covered the road, the parking area.

She put her hands down to push herself upright. A more intense bolt of fire made her left arm unusable. She struggled to her knees, then her feet. Her legs held her weight, but with every step, she discovered another ache or stab of pain.

She wove across uneven ground, around the chunks of rock and vegetation that covered the road. Reached the corner and cried out. Part of the former bluff covered a large swath of the road and the railroad tracks and part of the gas station. A handful of dirt-streaked firefighters frantically dug through the dirt and rocks. They had to know not a single truck or person survived that.

She stumbled toward them, the survivors.

"Miranda?"

She whirled toward the voice. "David?"

Across the railroad tracks, a figure streaked with dirt waved and sprinted toward her.

He reached her before she'd crossed the third set of rails. Threw his arms around her. Lifted her in a hug that made her groan. "Sorry." He set her down, feet on the ground.

"They hurt you." She peered at his bruised and battered face through her muddy tears. "Are you all right?"

He laughed. "I will be now. Everything will be all right now."

No, nothing will be all right ever again.

Chapter Ninety-One

Miranda placed her one change of clothes into her rucksack, stuffed a sleeping bag in it, then pulled the strings tight. Scanned the room. It held simple, functional twin beds and a five-drawer dresser typical of this rustic, three-room cabin off Arkansas's Ouachita River. Deep in the forest, it provided quiet isolation. Exactly what they needed to heal after SubTropolis.

Taking the dark green men's sweatshirt off the bed, she pulled over her head and the T-shirt she wore. A bolt of burning electricity raced down her left arm, made her whole arm tremble. Her injuries from the collapse of the cave were minor compared to many of the wounded, but even two months later, certain movements shot pain from her shoulder to her fingertips.

She slipped on a worn, dark-blue peacoat. Picked up her rucksack with her good arm, slung it over that shoulder. Strode into the kitchen half of the front room. Opened the food cabinet. Added some venison jerky to her rucksack. Banged the cabinet closed without worry of waking her cabin mates. She'd heard them leave before dawn.

She glanced at the ancient settee and chairs in the sitting room without seeing them. Memories of the explosions in SubTropolis and seeing David near the train tracks haunted her. She didn't remember the survivors splitting up that night, deciding to take shelter in safe houses scattered across four states. Didn't remember the trip here. Her nails bit into her palms. *Healing was necessary. But took too much time.* She rolled her neck, shook off the memories.

Ethan had kept his word. Rescued David and other rebels. No one had ever found Beryl's body.

Outside, the chill in the air bit Miranda's fingers and nose. Snowflakes sparkled in the early morning sunlight. The tall pines surrounding them, dusted with snow, made a black-and-white patchwork. Matched her mood. Tree limbs heavy with the wet snow bent. She listened to the wet smack of snow falling to the ground and the snap of the tree limbs returning to their original state.

Ethan had insisted they pay their respects to Beryl, Nick, and the others, lost beneath the rubble of SubTropolis. Miranda had agreed to stay in camp long enough to attend, but respects weren't what Beryl—or Nick—would have wanted as long as a single Azrael lived.

She trudged past the yellow water pump. Followed the overgrown path to the slow-moving, muddy river's edge.

Leslie and Wanda looked up from stools made from rough-cut tree trunks. Leslie had recovered, then nursed Miranda through the brain fog of her concussion. Wanda had arrived last night, came for the memorial. With a lift of her chin, Miranda invited them to join her.

"Nice day for a hike." Leslie hoisted her rucksack over her shoulder. She was paler than ever, and her blue eyes were more haunted.

Wanda leaned on her dead-fall walking stick, rose to a stand. She bent, grunted, and shouldered her rucksack.

"You sure you're up for this?" Miranda figured they'd walk at least thirty miles after the memorial. It would take another long day's hike to reach the nearest bus station.

"Walking will help me regain strength and agility."

Her voice held a surly note. Wanda believed Beryl might have escaped somehow. Miranda understood. Wanda needed to shield herself from another loss.

Miranda shut up and strolled toward the site Ethan had chosen for the memorial. She wished she could erase the sight of the mountain of rocks that covered every trace of Beryl. Wished she had the luxury of believing in the fantasy that Beryl had escaped somehow. Wished she'd had the time to repay Beryl for—everything. The debt Miranda hadn't repaid weighed on her. She owed it to Beryl to remain grounded in reality. Owed it to Beryl to find any Azrael who might have escaped SubTropolis, find the other labs, stop every Azrael, even the ones in artificial wombs. She had to restore democracy and their rights by destroying the Fellowship.

Wanda's limp was minimal. "I got word from my father's cousin in Saint Joe. You were right." The huskiness of her voice was deeper, darker than usual. "They moved a lot of the lab before we got there."

More than a fire burned in Miranda. A fierce blast-furnace need to settle the score raced through her veins. "What about Irene? Annabelle?" Leslie's brother had reported those two had fled to D.C. after the rebels destroyed SubTropolis.

"Ian said they took a jet to one of three locations: Philadelphia, Chicago, or—"

Miranda stopped, faced Leslie. "Or where?"

"Overseas somewhere."

Miranda drew in a sharp breath. "And wherever they've gone, the Azrael who escaped will be there too." She curled her fists tight. *Damn. I have no connections overseas. And establishing one in the Federation of Germany would be slow and dangerous.*

She bet Beryl had connections overseas. Her aunt always seemed to know someone, no matter where they went. *I will discover them somehow and use them to defeat Irene, Annabelle, the Azrael, no matter where they go. No matter how long it takes.* But first steps first. "We'll start with Philadelphia." *And figure out how to build a network overseas.*

She stashed her rucksack in a clump of bushes south of the memorial site and near the fallen tree bridge over the Ouachita River. Leslie and Wanda did the same.

Miranda led them east along the river, into the golden sunrise toward the memorial. The falling snow dwindled and stopped. Her pulse throbbed in her temples. Her throat grew tighter and drier, tighter and drier until it hurt to breathe.

A dozen murmuring people had gathered in a clearing around the small rise Ethan had chosen. A single pine tree rose from its crest. By its tall, thick trunk, it had overlooked the river and the pine forest for years and years.

Ethan stood beneath the tree. His shoulders were not as square as they'd once been. Miranda joined him. He put a hand on her shoulder. She didn't react, didn't even look at him, and he withdrew his hand.

David came out of the crowd. Stood beside her. Over the past two months, his cuts and bruises had healed—on the outside. It saddened her that he wasn't ready to come with her.

"We've come here to acknowledge our losses and pay our respects to our fallen friends." Ethan raised his voice over the sound of the murmuring crowd without taking his eyes off the carving on the tree. He had conducted this ceremony thirty times in as many days. Every tree in this copse bore three or four names and dates of fallen SABR members. This tribute to Beryl and Nick would be the last.

The crowd went silent. After a long moment, he cleared his throat and began again. "I know the words I'm supposed to say, but loss is the part of a resistance that I'll never get used to. Especially personal loss." He put a hand on the tree. His shoulders bent more. Beneath his hand, carved out of the bark and the flesh of the tree, were the words:

———

Beryl Clark Matthews
1926-1963
RIP

———

"GOODBYE, MY LOVE." He patted the tree, walked around it, touched each name carved into the bark. When he'd circled the tree, he walked away without looking back.

Her jaw twitched, and her knotted fists wouldn't relax. *How can he be so calm? Why isn't he angry? No, not angry—furious.*

David took Ethan's place at the tree. Touched Beryl's name. "I barely remembered the aunt of my childhood, the person she was before I met the rebel. We had our differences, but I admired the rebel. Rest now."

He looked back at Miranda, then finished a circuit around the tree and followed Ethan.

Miranda hid behind a daughter-of-the-counselor mask, the one for solemn occasions, and moved to the tree. Neither the sharp scent of pine nor cold rough bark comforted her. She dipped her chin to her chest. No tears would come, but plenty of recriminations did. Anger colored her vision, altered the way food tasted, and oozed out of every pore in her skin. She touched the raw scar in the tree that was Beryl's name. *I should have tried harder to save you. I should have… No. Should haves don't do you any good. The only way I can honor your memory is to destroy the Fellowship.*

"Beryl would have hated this," Miranda said aloud. "Too much sentimentality." She drew a breath—razors of cold sliced her from the inside. "But we must remember her. Be like her. Yes, the Fellowship rose again out of the ashes of the Fellowship Center. The Prophet's death didn't defeat them. It wouldn't matter to Beryl. Death is the only thing that stopped her from fighting. She wouldn't stop until ashes were all that remained of the Fellowship. I will follow her example. I will fight them to the death." She didn't turn to see the reactions of her fellow rebels. It didn't matter how they took her words. She wouldn't look at Wanda.

Miranda forced herself to circle the tree to where natural wood glowed in crude letters that spelled Nick's name. Traced each letter and number with her finger.

———

Nicholas Rosenfeld
1934-1963
RIP

———

SHE PULLED the crumpled magazine page from her pocket and smoothed it against the tree's rough bark. Gazed at the charming yellow Cape Cod house with its red tin roof, garden, and picket fence. "You deserved—we deserved that life. They robbed us of that." Empty of pain or sorrow, she stared at Nick's name. The blast-furnace inside ran hotter. She placed the page on the tree below the carving. Took her boot knife, stabbed it through the paper deep into the wood. "I'll be back for this." *When they're all dead.*

THE END

Postscript

If you liked this book, please give it a starred review on its page of the online store where you bought the book or on a book review site like Goodreads). Remember, five stars doesn't mean it's perfect. It means you enjoyed it and look forward to the next book.

Consider writing a comment or two about what you liked or didn't like. Comments in the review section help books get noticed. *I appreciate every reviewer who takes the time to star or comment.*

When I was a kid I thought authors were special kinds of people and had no hope of ever being one. Now I am an author and I love to write about characters whose trials help them discover what they are and the hero they can be. If you'd like to join me on my writing journey sign up for my newsletter, Reading Rebels, and get the latest posts, news, and more from me at lynettemburrows.com.

You can also follow me on social media.
Facebook—https://www.facebook.com/LynetteMBurrowsAuthor/
Twitter—https://twitter.com/LynetteMBurrows

Thank you!

Acknowledgments

The world of the Fellowship Dystopia is not one I want to live in, but it's one I almost lived in. I moved seventeen times before I graduated from high school. No, I was not a military brat. When asked why, my parents said the frequent moves were to find better jobs, better houses, a better life. As a child, I didn't think the moves made my life better. Curious to know more about me? Visit my bio on lynettemburrows.com.

While writing is usually a solitary occupation, it also requires help from many people. I am grateful for the help of these amazing friends, mentors, and beta readers:

Alysen Tellure

Dora Furlong

Jan S. Gephardt

Lisa Norman

Rob Chilson

Terry Matz

William F. Wu

And a special thanks to Arnessie Stroud Laryea.

A shout-out to my amazing editor, Julie Glover, and my wonderful proofreader, Sidekick Jenn.

I wouldn't be writing at all without the unfailing support and love of my husband and number one fan. I miss you.

Finally, thank you, dear reader. I am honored that you've invested time and money to read my book. I hope you'll leave a starred review. And I hope you'll stick around…

And When I Wake, book three in the Fellowship Dystopia series is in progress.

Learn more about about the people, events, and locations that inspire me, my books, progress updates, and sneak peeks at works-in-progress by joining my newsletter group, the Reading Rebels. You can also join the newsletter on my website, www. lynettemburrows.com or you can email me at lynette@lynettemburrows.com.

Also by Lynette M. Burrows

Fellowship

My Soul to Keep, the Fellowship Dystopia Book One